AGAINST A CRESCENT STORM

THE BALKAN LEGENDS

OTHER BOOKS BY A. L. SOWARDS

THE BALKAN LEGENDS SERIES

After the Crescent Strike (ebook and audiobook prequel)
Beneath a Crescent Shadow
Beyond the Crescent Sky
Against a Crescent Storm

DUCHY OF ATHENS SERIES

Of Sword and Shadow
Of Daggers and Deception

FALCON POINT SERIES

Heirs of Falcon Point
Codes of Courage
Roads of Resistance
Bridge of Betrayal (coming March 2026)

STAND-ALONES

A Waltz with Traitors
Before the Fortress Falls

AGAINST A CRESCENT STORM

THE BALKAN LEGENDS

A. L. SOWARDS

SHADOW MOUNTAIN PUBLISHING

This novel is a work of historical fiction and depicts a time and place with widespread violence. Characters and events in this book are products of the author's imagination or are represented fictitiously.

Visit us at shadowmountain.com

Library of Congress Cataloging-in-Publication Data

(CIP data on file)
ISBN 978-1-63993-453-9

Printed in Canada
Marquis, Montreal, Quebec, Canada

10 9 8 7 6 5 4 3 2 1

To my IG Book Besties.

Sharing my books with you brings me joy.

The way you share my books with others brings me gratitude.

I won't try to list you all, but to everyone who has helped with one of my book launches, thank you!

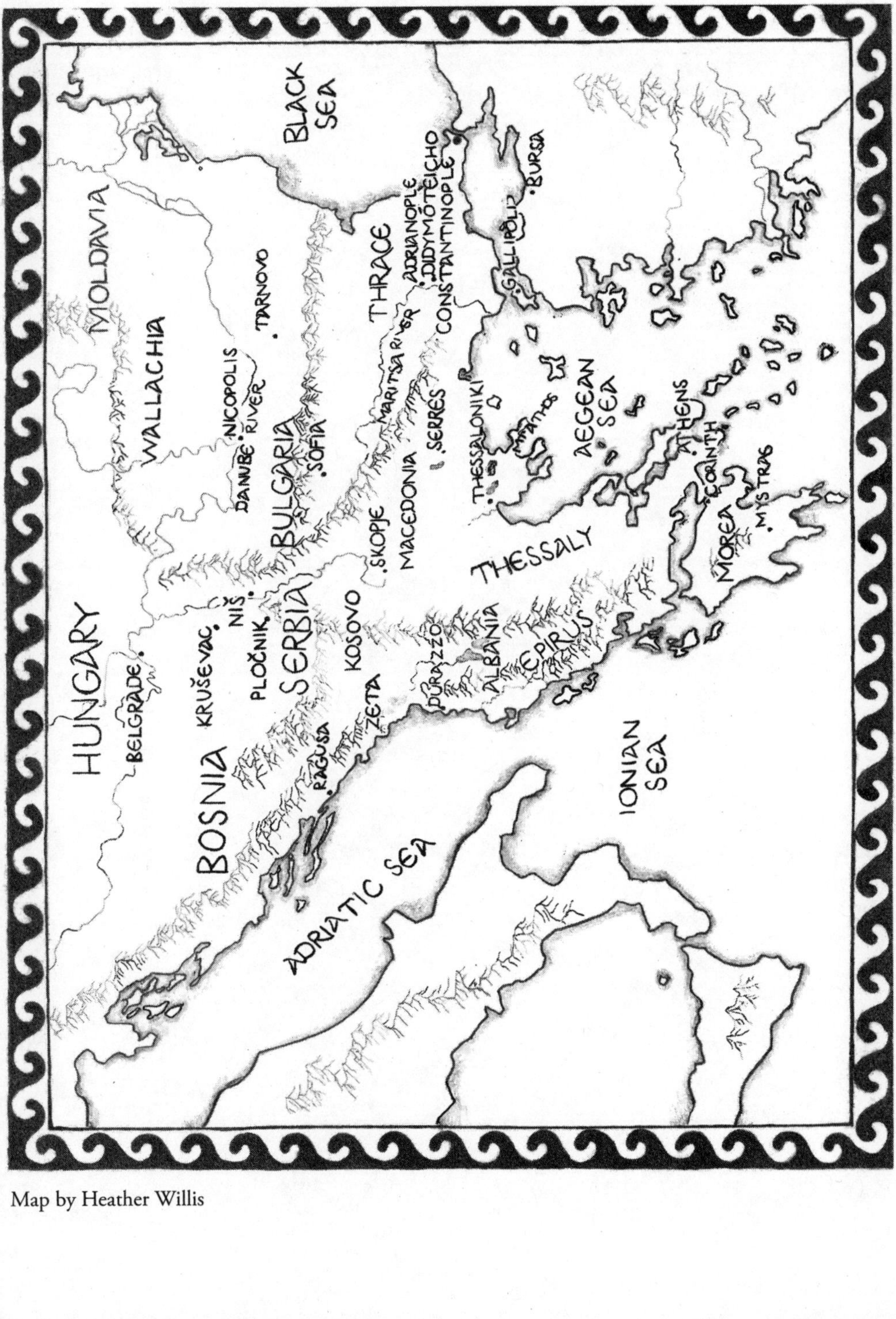

Map by Heather Willis

GLOSSARY AND HISTORICAL BACKGROUND

Acropolis: The heavily fortified portion of a Greek kastron.

Akincis: Ottoman irregular, light cavalry, often serving as scouts or a vanguard to the regular army.

Bogomil: A Christian group considered heretical by both the Catholic and Orthodox churches. They were sometimes punished for their beliefs by branding on the face.

Boukellaton: A dense, ring-shaped loaf of bread baked twice and dried to give it a long shelf life. Normally eaten after being soaked in oil or wine.

Boyar: A high-ranking member of the feudal nobility in Bulgaria and other eastern European societies.

Byzantine Empire: The Byzantine Empire was the eastern half of the Roman Empire, though contemporaries did not use the term. The Byzantines referred to themselves as Romans, and their neighbors often referred to them as Greeks. Their capital was Constantinople and their religion was Orthodox Christian. By the time of this novel, their borders had shrunk significantly, but their cultural influence remained strong.

Chausses: In the context of this novel, leg armor made of mail.

Corselet: A piece of armor meant to protect the torso. It was normally hip length, with or without sleeves. Often made of lamellar in this novel's setting.

Courser: A warhorse, known for strength and speed.

Cupola: Dome-like architectural feature often found on the roof of medieval Serbian churches.

Dalmatica: A garment with wide, three-quarters-length sleeves and a roughly knee-length skirt, generally layered over a tunic. Could be worn by men or women.

Dama: Term of respect for a Serbian noblewoman.

Destrier: The most valuable type of warhorse, trained for battle and tournaments.

Effendi: Turkish title of respect.

Ghazi: For the purposes of this novel, the term refers to an Ottoman raider who depended on plunder for his pay. The word has a more expansive definition outside the setting of the fourteenth-century Balkan Peninsula, but the more limited definition is used for clarity and accuracy in this book's historical setting.

Grad: A fortified Slavic town.

Great Mortality: The term people in this book's setting used to refer to the plague now known as the Black Death, which swept through Europe, peaking in the late 1340s and early 1350s.

Grody: A fortified area of a Slavic town or village.

Gusle: A single-stringed musical instrument held in the lap and played with a bow.

Hauberk: A shirt of mail armor, usually with sleeves, normally mid-thigh in length.

Ispán: Hungarian nobleman who commanded a district and had administrative, judicial, and military duties.

Janissaries: Elite Ottoman infantry. Until the seventeenth century, they were formed largely of Christian children taken from their homes and forcibly converted to Islam.

Kastron: A fortified Byzantine town.

Király: Hungarian term for a king.

Knez: Serbian term for a prince.

Kral: Serbian and Bosnian term for a king.

Lamellar: A type of body armor made from laced plates of leather, horn, or metal.

Meroph: A Serbian serf. Merophs owed labor and/or tribute to their feudal lord and to the church.

Narthex: The entrance area, antechamber, or court of an Orthodox Church.

Nave: The main part of an Orthodox Church between the narthex and the sanctuary.

Ottoman Empire: A Turkish empire established in Asia Minor, then expanded into Europe. Murad I, the founder's grandson, is sultan during most of this story. In the 1380s, many Balkan Christian rulers were vassals to the Ottomans, but Turkish control was not yet complete. The Ottomans were Muslims. They saw Europe as a new frontier—a land of opportunity and destiny.

Palfrey: A horse valued for its smooth gait. Ideal for riding long distances.

Pasha: Ottoman title for a high-ranking military or civic leader.

Scimitar: A sword with a curved blade.

Serbian Empire: The Medieval Serbian Empire reached its zenith in the middle of the fourteenth century and included much of the Balkan Peninsula. It suffered serious setbacks with the death of Emperor Stefan Dušan in 1355 and a devastating loss at the Battle of Maritsa in 1371. The Serb religion was Christian Orthodox, and their culture was heavily affected by both Byzantine and Italian influences.

Signor: A polite term of address in medieval Italian cultures for men of rank.

Sipahi: Ottoman cavalryman, compensated by salary or land grant.

Spathion: Type of sword common in the late Byzantine era, about three feet long with a double-edged blade.

Spaulder: A piece of armor covering the shoulder.

Tessera: A piece of glass, stone, or ceramic that makes up a mosaic (plural: tesserae).

Timar: An Ottoman fief, or land grant, bestowed by the sultan to military or civic supporters. Timar holders drew revenues from their land and owed their allegiance and service to the sultan.

Vlach: An ethnic group in the Balkans, often shepherds during the Middle Ages.

Župa: A geographic area ruled by a župan.

Župan: Serb lord, comparable to a count.

Character List

Characters Living in Sivi Gora

Danilo Darrasević: Serb warrior

Tatjana: Danilo's deceased wife

Župan Ivan Miroslavević: Župan of Sivi Gora, Danilo's cousin

Dama Helena: Ivan's wife

Sofija: Ivan and Helena's daughter

Dama Zorica: Danilo's mother, Ivan and Konstantin's aunt

Philippos: Greek refugee living in Sivi Gora, a groom at the palace

Goran: Member of the Sivi Gora garrison

Cyril: Member of the Sivi Gora garrison

Adamu: Member of the Sivi Gora garrison, Marjan's brother

Slavica: Adamu's wife

Marjan: Member of the Sivi Gora garrison, Adamu's brother

Christophoros: Greek refugee living in Sivi Gora, member of Helena's guard

Niketas: Greek refugee living in Sivi Gora, member of the Sivi Gora garrison

Dalibor: Member of Helena's guard

Zlatan: Member of Helena's guard

Arcadius: A master mosaicist working on the new church in Sivi Gora

Petar: A stonecutter working on the new church in Sivi Gora

Father Dmitar: Priest in Sivi Gora

Župan Đurad Lukarević: Ivan and Konstantin's grandfather, the former župan of Sivi Gora who has retired to a monastery

Serbs from Rivak

Župan Konstantin Miroslavević (Kostya): Župan of Rivak, Danilo's cousin

Dama Suzana: Konstantin's wife

Marko: Konstantin and Suzana's eldest son

Pavle: Konstantin and Suzana's second son

Danica: Konstantin and Suzana's daughter

Miladin: Member of the Rivak garrison

Sveta: Miladin's niece

Bojan: Member of the Rivak garrison

Kuzman: Member of the Rivak garrison

Župan Miroslav: Župan of Rivak until his death in 1371, Zorica's brother, Danilo's uncle, Konstantin and Ivan's father

Darras: Danilo's deceased father

Dama Lidija: Danilo's deceased cousin, Ivan and Konstantin's sister

Knez Lazar's Family and Retainers

Knez Lazar: Serbian prince and leader

Dama Milica: Lazar's wife

Miloš Obilić: Serb noble, Lazar's son-in-law

Dama Jelena: Miloš's wife, Lazar's daughter

Vuk Branković: Serb noble, Lazar's son-in-law

Dama Mara: Vuk's wife, Lazar's daughter

Darko: A warrior serving Knez Lazar, Tatjana's brother

Tihomir: A warrior serving Knez Lazar

Viktor: A warrior serving Knez Lazar

Filip: A warrior serving Knez Lazar

Ivo: A warrior serving Knez Lazar

Other Serbs

Maja Dinić: A mosaic artist

Luka Dinić: Maja's younger brother

Župan Dragomir: Župan in lands near Rivak

Dama Isidora: Dragomir's wife

Decimir: Dragomir's deceased grandson, Lidija's husband

Stojan: Dragomir's grandson

Todor: Dragomir's grandson

Župan Nikola: Župan in lands near Rivak

Ottomans

Iskandar bin Abdullah: Ottoman warrior

Saruca: Iskandar's half sister

Kasim bin Yazid: Saruca's deceased husband and former warrior for the sultan

Hasan: Ghazi raider

Mustafa: Ghazi raider

Sultan Murad: Ottoman sultan from 1362 to 1389

Bayezid: Sultan Murad's son

Yakub: Sultan Murad's son

Çandarlızade Ali Pasha: Sultan Murad's vizier

Lala Şahin Pasha: Ottoman military leader

Evrenos: Ottoman military leader

Eyne Bĕg Subaşi: Ottoman military leader

Arslan: Ottoman envoy and warrior

Sanduk: Ottoman soldier

Osman: Deceased, founder of the Ottoman dynasty, Murad's grandfather

Orhan: Deceased, second sultan of the Ottoman dynasty, Osman's son, Murad's father

Bosnians

Kral Tvrtko: Bosnian king

Vlatko Vuković: Tvrtko's general

Bulgarians

Boyar Kalin: Bulgarian nobleman

Emanuil Asen: Kalin's brother

Ekaterina: Kalin's daughter, Emanuil's niece

Stanimira: Ekaterina's companion

Tsar Stratsimir: Leader of the Bulgarian kingdom centered around Vidin

Tsar Shishman: Leader of the Bulgarian kingdom centered around Târnovo

Hungarians

Király Sigismund: King of Hungary

Ispán Janos Bokori: Hungarian nobleman

Vadas: Bokori's spy

Venetians

Grato: A Venetian ship owner

D'Artusio: Grato's foreman

Contanto: A Venetian merchant

Pascal: Contanto's son

Chapter One
Omens of War

The Balkans, 1389

Danilo had scarcely had a chance to exchange greetings with Konstantin when his cousin swung his fist at a crass Frankish mercenary in the Bosnian tavern. Konstantin's aim, as usual, was right on target.

"Kostya!" Danilo grabbed his cousin's arm before he swung again.

"Did you hear what he said?" Konstantin's expression was controlled, but indignation colored his voice.

Danilo glanced at the mercenary. Blood streamed from the man's nose, and rage showed in his eyes. "Yes. But we're supposed to be making friends, remember?" Konstantin had been sticking up for Danilo since he was a boy, but they weren't children anymore, and the Frankish warrior wasn't the first to cast insults at Danilo because he was only half Serbian. "Let him say what he wants. I stopped caring about things like that a long time ago."

"I care." Konstantin glared at the man, who backed away as he wiped at the blood on his face, smearing it. Two of Konstantin's men, Miladin and Bojan, stood nearby, both with their hands on their sword hilts, ready to defend their župan—and his kinsman—with their lives.

The injured man looked around the drafty tavern that smelled of onion, bread, and dampness as if searching for allies, but the few locals turned away, and everyone else had either traveled with Konstantin from Rivak or with Danilo from Kruševac and Sivi Gora. A few moments more and the injured man retreated to the street outside.

Danilo tugged on the sleeve of his cousin's tunic. "Come on, let's eat before we have to ride again." Danilo hadn't eaten a hot meal in days, and they had more road ahead of them on their journey west to meet with Kral Tvrtko.

They sat on a bench before a rough-hewn table.

"What was that all about?" Miloš Obilić joined them, sitting across from Konstantin. Miloš was middle-aged and muscled, perceptive, and prestigious among the Serb nobility. Danilo had traveled with him for most of the last fortnight, though they'd first met years ago.

"That man insulted my cousin." Konstantin glanced at the doorway as if to make certain the mercenary hadn't returned.

"Rather foolish of him." Miloš accepted a cup of cheap wine and a bowl of stew when the tavern's owner brought food. "But I suppose he hasn't seen either of you in battle. Can't have, or he would have known not to pick a fight with a family as skilled as yours."

Danilo waited for Miloš to remind Konstantin of the importance of their mission and the need for diplomacy, but instead, their companion spoke to Danilo. "Your cousins are protective of you. I'm not sure which one shows it more fiercely." Miloš seemed amused.

Konstantin glanced at Danilo. "Has Ivan had need to protect you lately?"

Danilo accepted his food. "I am perfectly capable of smashing a man's nose, *if needed*."

"Well, what happened? Did Ivan punch someone before you felt it was necessary?"

"It did not involve fists." Danilo would rather leave that particular incident in the past, where it belonged, but Konstantin would give him no peace if he stayed silent. Either Konstantin would pry, or Miloš would give his version of the tale. Danilo had spent enough nights around a fire with Miloš to know any story he told was likely to include a few exaggerations. Better for Konstantin to hear Danilo's account, without any added dramatics. "Ivan hired German mercenaries. Sivi Gora's garrison is strong, but if the Hungarians or the Turks decide to stir up trouble—and especially if they do it at the same time—we can use the extra manpower. One of them claims he saw an ill omen that means I will be the cause of Sivi Gora's destruction. Rumors also circulate that I'm cursed and Tatjana's death was punishment for marrying a Turk."

"That's utter nonsense." A growl shadowed Konstantin's words. "Ivan could search to the ends of the earth and not find anyone as loyal as you. And your father may have been an Ottoman, but you've proven that you have a Serbian soul again and again, as did he, regardless of where he was born."

Danilo tasted the stew. It was warm, but that was the best that could be said for it. "Ivan threatened to cut out the man's tongue when he found him, but I told him it was better to let the matter drop. Punishing whoever started it wouldn't stop the gossip. Besides, I expect we'll need those mercenaries come summer. Mutilating one of them won't exactly encourage devotion."

"Ivan let it drop?" Konstantin didn't seem pleased.

"Not at first. But once I convinced his wife that it was the wisest course, he relented."

Konstantin chuckled. "I don't suppose he would want to argue with both of you at once." He tried the stew and made a face.

Miloš finished his meal and stood. "Now that we've met, as scheduled, and Župan Konstantin has frightened off all the rabble, I'll go check with the others. I want us on the road within an hour." He lowered his voice. "Perhaps Kral Tvrtko's cook can give us something decent to eat if we make it there by sunset."

As Miloš left, Konstantin frowned at the stew.

"It's better than the boukellaton I've been living on for the last week." The hard bread was useful for travel, but Danilo preferred the stew, bland and watery as it was. "Hurry and finish it because I want to show you something."

Konstantin ate, albeit without enthusiasm. Danilo had spent the first nineteen years of his life in the lands his older cousin led as župan before following his younger cousin, Ivan, to his time as a hostage of the Turks, then to his inheritance in Sivi Gora. Danilo was well acquainted with the fine skill of the kitchen staffs in both župas. The tavern fare fell far short, and Konstantin had always had a finicky palate. They'd planned to meet at the tavern for its location along the crossroads, not for the quality of its meals. Konstantin had traveled from the southeast, Danilo and Miloš from the northeast.

"How is Suzana?" Danilo asked.

A smile lit Konstantin's face. "She is recovering well, and we are both pleased that our daughter came before I needed to make this journey."

"How is the baby?"

"Danica is sweet and content, so long as she isn't hungry. When she desires food, she has a robust wail that I take as a sign of good health."

"And the boys?"

"Marko wants to become as good an archer as you." Konstantin finished his stew, and the two men stood. "Spends all his spare time on the archery range. Reminds me of you and Ivan when you were still boys. Pavle doesn't show much interest in weapons yet, but he does well on his pony."

They stepped outside, and Danilo led Konstantin to where his own horse was tied next to Miloš's powerfully built stallion.

"That's a fine animal." Konstantin admired Miloš's horse. "Do you suppose Miloš would sell him to me?"

"Not a chance. Miloš values Ždralin almost as much as he values his own mother."

Konstantin smiled wistfully. "How is your mother? She is missed."

"My mother is in good health. She sends her love and letters. Ivan sent a slightly more ostentatious sign of his affection." Danilo gestured to an unsaddled Hungarian destrier tied nearby.

Konstantin walked over to the big chestnut stallion. "He didn't."

"He did."

Konstantin moved to his new horse and examined it. "Well, whatever he's asking me to do, the answer is undoubtedly yes."

Danilo smiled. "It's a gift, not a bribe."

"I hope that means things are well in Sivi Gora?"

"For the time being." Danilo looked around the mostly empty yard. One of Miloš's men had stayed to watch the animals. He lay in a pile of hay with his eyes closed and his face relaxed.

"And in the days ahead? Will Ivan have needs then?" Konstantin asked.

"As long as Murad reigns, he is a threat. For now, the sultan is busy subjugating the Bulgarians, but he intends to make us pay for beating his generals at Pločnik. We'll all be in need then." Danilo had lived as a hostage among the Turks for two years. He knew what they were capable of, and that knowledge frightened him. Victory at Pločnik had freed them, but sometimes, their liberty felt fragile and fleeting.

"Rivak will stand with Knez Lazar. That's why I met you here. You know that. "

"I do. And Miloš and I are grateful to count you a firm ally." Danilo patted his own horse, Dazhbog. Like Konstantin's, it was a gift from Ivan. "We hope Tvrtko will fall into the alliance with as much ease. But Bosnia is farther from the Turks, so the danger is not as great for him. And if the Turks distract Knez Lazar, Kral Tvrtko might be tempted to snatch up some of Lazar's lands."

"Or Ivan's lands. My brother lies between three giants."

Danilo well knew the precarious geography of Sivi Gora, but not all neighbors gave him cause for concern. "Knez Lazar won't turn on Ivan, not after Ivan's role at Pločnik. Kral Tvrtko is more of an unknown, which is why Ivan and Lazar send gifts for him as well."

Konstantin ran his hand along his new destrier. "That sounds diplomatic. Not a skill I would normally credit to my brother."

"The first time Ivan picked up a sword, he could barely wield it, and the first time he climbed on a pony, he fell off. He mastered those skills. He will master diplomacy as well."

"Good. Because even if he is safe from Knez Lazar and Kral Tvrtko, the Hungarians aren't to be trusted."

Danilo grunted his agreement. He had accompanied Ivan on patrols time after time to stop Hungarian brigands from attacking Sivi Gora's outlying villages and mining community. Hungarian nobles didn't send the raiders, but nor did they stop them. If Ivan made too strong a protest, it might provoke war. But too weak a response could embolden the enemy. A delicate balance with Király Sigismund and his Hungarian nobles, combined with concern over the Ottomans, shadowed Ivan's rule. "Miloš and I may approach them on our way back from Bosnia."

Konstantin frowned slightly. "Make an alliance with the Latin half believers?"

"If Murad attacks, we can't be picky about whose support we accept. We met with an ispán, Janos Bokori, over the winter. He didn't agree to an alliance, but he didn't outright reject it either. Knez Lazar wants us to try again, as does Ivan." Miloš and Danilo carried thoughtfully selected gifts for Tvrtko and more general gifts for Bokori because they knew so little of him.

"Surely Knez Lazar has his own emissaries without stealing Ivan's. It sounds as though you've been traveling all winter and all spring."

Ivan had said roughly the same thing to Danilo, asking him if he was sure he wanted to leave again so soon after returning from his last trip. "I volunteered for this journey. And for the previous ones. I'm more useful to our people out here than I am in Sivi Gora."

Konstantin turned his attention from the horse and focused only on his cousin. "Does Ivan never let you rest?"

"I am in good health. There is little need for me to mope about in Sivi Gora when Ivan can handle everything there himself." Župan Ivan couldn't be in two places at once, but Danilo knew his cousin's goals and needs well enough to act with confidence on Sivi Gora's behalf.

Konstantin folded his arms across his chest. "Danilo, ever since you were little, you and Ivan have been inseparable. Have you quarreled?"

"Of course not." There was no one on earth Danilo admired and loved more than his cousin Ivan.

"A quarrel with Helena?"

Danilo shook his head. His relationship with Ivan's wife had seen more than one strain. He'd frightened her on their first meeting, and it had taken him a long time to understand how Ivan could trust her so completely when she'd once broken a promise to him and crushed his heart. Yet they had come to respect each other, especially after Helena had befriended Danilo's timid wife. Helena had been the attending midwife when the time had come to deliver Tatjana. Neither Danilo's wife nor his child had survived. "What happened with the baby wasn't Helena's fault."

The delivery had been a difficult one, and Tatjana had been so delicate. But the double loss still felt raw. In Sivi Gora, Danilo normally slept in a room in the palace instead of in his empty home. And when emissaries were needed for diplomatic tasks all across the Balkans, he used the missions as a chance to escape.

"Are you unhappy in Sivi Gora?" Konstantin's gray eyes studied Danilo carefully. "There will always be a place for you in Rivak, should you desire it."

Danilo glanced at Miloš's man in the haystack. Tihomir looked to be asleep. "Sivi Gora is prosperous, and Ivan is a good župan and a good friend, but sometimes, I think my presence is difficult for him."

"How? You've been his best friend since he was old enough to toddle along after you."

"I think he feels guilty that his wife and daughter are alive and healthy and my wife and daughter are dead."

Konstantin bit his lip. "I am sorry for your loss, Danilo." It wasn't the first time Konstantin had expressed his condolences, and Danilo knew he meant it. Konstantin had lost several infants but not his wife. He could understand part of the pain but not all of it. And Konstantin would never have the guilt Danilo carried, the ever-present worry that the rumor the mercenaries had started was true, and the deaths were somehow Danilo's fault.

Danilo nodded his acknowledgment. His daughter had been born too early, and something inside Tatjana had perished with the infant. The fever had been but the final blow to someone who had already given up on life.

Konstantin was quiet for a few moments before changing the subject. "Does Ivan still obsess over defenses?"

Danilo smiled. "Until the walls of Sivi Gora resemble the Theodosian walls of Constantinople, he will keep building."

"Ivan's never been to Constantinople. How would he know what the walls look like?"

"His wife was born there. And it's not just walls. He's been buying cannon."

Konstantin nodded. "If Tvrtko won't help us, I'm afraid we'll need more than cannon. We need him as an ally, not an enemy."

Danilo worried about Tvrtko, too, but the past gave Danilo hope that their mission would prove successful. "He came to Pločnik and fought well."

"Yes. But many things can change in three years."

Danilo thought back to Pločnik, when the Serbs had thrown off their vassalage and won their freedom from the Ottomans. The battle had been hard-fought, and they'd been lucky. They had caught the Turks while they were scattered, and the Serbs had inflicted heavy losses on their enemy while suffering relatively light casualties themselves. Danilo had followed his best friend into battle, and he had seen Ivan rise to greatness. They had been triumphant, and that exhilaration had made it seem as if Sivi Gora would stand unthreatened for a hundred years. Danilo had married, and then Ivan had. And they had both been delighted with their brides, confident that their hard-earned happiness would last.

But it took only one difficult delivery to take a wife, and it would take but one failed battle to take their freedom.

Konstantin was right. Many things could change in three years.

Chapter Two
The Smuggler's Secret

The Adriatic Sea shimmered like polished copper in the light of the setting sun, but it offered little beauty for a slave. Iskandar bin Abdullah shouldered another barrel of salted fish and hauled it down the ramp of his Venetian master's ship currently docked in the port of Durazzo.

"Quickly now. I want the unloading finished before the light disappears," Signor Grato called to his workers and slaves.

Iskandar picked up his pace, at least while Grato could see him. The rotund man with whiskered jowls and ridiculous curled-toe shoes had owned Iskandar for two and a half years. In contrast to his master's red hose and thick doublet, Iskandar still wore the stained and tattered robes he'd been captured in after the Battle of Pločnik. He'd made numerous mistakes then, when he'd been a leader among the Ottoman raiders, choices he had regretted ever since. He shouldn't have been so sure of himself, shouldn't have underestimated his Serbian foes, shouldn't have given in to pressure from his men to ease their restlessness through pillage. At times, he also regretted begging for mercy when he'd been captured by his enemies. Ivan and Danilo had spared him, but there had been moments—so many of them—when Iskandar had been certain death would have been a better option than slavery.

A single hope kept him from giving in to complete despair. Since the time of Iskandar's purchase, he had imagined up twenty-seven ways to kill Grato, one for every scar his master's whip had left on his back. He had learned from his past mistakes. He would wait for the right moment, and then he would have his vengeance and escape his wretched condition.

As he unloaded barrels, Iskandar kept an eye on Grato negotiating with a merchant. A purse exchanged hands, and Grato put it inside his doublet next to his black heart. Then he turned to one of his employees, d'Artusio. "Bring the trunk. Use the Turk and the heretic."

D'Artusio waited until Iskandar unloaded another barrel, then gestured for him to follow. On their way back up the ship's ramp, d'Artusio motioned over the Bogomil slave with a branded face. Iskandar didn't know what was in the trunk, but it was heavily guarded, so it had to be valuable. He took one end, and the Bogomil took the other, and they walked it down the ramp and set it in the back of an otherwise empty cart.

"Climb in. We'll want you for the delivery." D'Artusio sat in the back with Iskandar and the Bogomil and kept his hand on the dagger at his waist. Grato called out a few instructions to the ship's crew and then climbed onto the cart, took the reins, and urged the horses forward.

Iskandar leaned into the planks of the cart as it jostled along. He'd sailed into Durazzo once before. He'd been newly enslaved then, chained on the ship until they'd sailed again. As they moved away from the waterfront now, he admired the red-tile roofs and the tall houses. It wasn't as splendid as Edirne or Venice, but Durazzo was certainly more impressive than any of the villages he'd pillaged as a ghazi.

Except, perhaps, for the last village he'd raided. The rough homes and little church had been unremarkable, but images of the woman he had briefly held captive there still haunted him. On the same day Iskandar had lost his freedom, he'd lost a piece of his soul to a maiden in that small village he'd taken. He didn't even know her name, but he remembered her face, lovely with the first blush of womanhood, hair like spun gold, and eyes with the depth and color of the sea on a cloudless day. Iskandar knew what it was for a woman's beauty to sear him to the core. It made any other form of beauty—in Durazzo or elsewhere—pale in comparison.

Iskandar's muscles had grown cold and stiff by the time Grato stopped the cart at a wide double-door gate, pulling Iskandar from his memories. Grato gestured to the gate. "Go knock."

Iskandar obeyed, something he had learned well over the last few years. Slavery had taken away all his choices save one: he could obey, or he could suffer a beating. But now, curiosity mixed with his resigned subservience. Grato owned his ship and transported goods for a profit, but normally, his business was with other merchants. This was a private residence, and it didn't border the waterfront.

One side of the gate swung open, and an armed guard examined Iskandar through narrowed eyes. Then he looked past Iskandar to Grato and d'Artusio.

His expression changed from hostile to neutral, and then he opened the other half of the gate.

Iskandar climbed back into the cart as Grato shook the reins. The guard closed the gate after they passed through, then walked ahead of the horses to guide them. The clip of horses' hooves echoed through the courtyard, past the villa's more public rooms, to a small, dark door in the back of the courtyard.

A narrow-faced man in a rich, fur-lined garment responded to the guard's knock. He pulled the door open and glanced at Grato. "Come."

D'Artusio motioned for Iskandar and the Bogomil to follow him with the trunk. Four torches lit the room they entered, but it was otherwise empty.

Grato took a key from a chain on his neck and unlocked the trunk. The man with the expensive clothing gestured for his guard to open the lid. At first, all Iskandar saw was pale linen, but it had to hide something else. Grato wouldn't have locked a trunk of ordinary cloth, nor would a load like that have weighed so much. The guard turned back the fabric, revealing five metal tubes. Hand bombards? Iskandar stepped closer, drawn to the weapons he'd heard of but had never before seen.

Grato cleared his throat, and d'Artusio took Iskandar and the Bogomil outside. But d'Artusio's curiosity must have been nearly as strong as Iskandar's because he went back in.

The fading twilight revealed a courtyard empty save for Iskandar and his fellow slave. When they'd first docked in Durazzo, Iskandar had deemed the port a poor choice for his escape. None of the other ships looked like they belonged to Muslims, and anyway, his destination wasn't along the coast. But now he reevaluated his options.

So, apparently, did the Bogomil, who started for the gate.

"If you wish to escape, it would be best to wait," Iskandar said. He was far from his old home in Edirne, but from Durazzo, the Via Egnatia led all the way to Constantinople. It passed through Ottoman lands, where Iskandar would be safe. But to travel so far, he needed not only his freedom but also coin. Freedom seemed available with a short walk across the courtyard, but a small amount of patience might yield coin as well.

"Why?" The Bogomil paused, but his eyes continued to flicker nervously around the villa.

"If you leave now, Grato will begin the search as soon as he comes out. If you wait, I'll help, and I'll make sure no one starts looking for us until daybreak." If the Bogomil tried to run now, Grato and d'Artusio would be far more vigilant, ruining Iskandar's chances of escaping later, after he'd had the chance to take Grato's coin.

"Why wait? This may be my only opportunity."

"You're a marked man. How will you hide the brand on your face when there's a reward for your capture?"

The Bogomil halted but didn't return to the cart. Iskandar picked up a fist-sized rock and hid it in the folds of his robes. Then he leaned against the side of the cart, playing the part of a tired slave at the end of a long day. If the Bogomil left, Iskandar would follow, but he hoped the man would wait for better timing.

The Bogomil came back eventually. "You have a plan? Something that will really work?"

Iskandar nodded. "I am a slave only because I was captured in battle. I know how to kill men, and I know how to blend in. I expect to use both skills tonight. Follow my lead, and we'll both earn our freedom." After years of waiting for an opportunity, the chance of escape seemed finally at hand.

Grato and d'Artusio came back outside before the Bogomil could ask for details. D'Artusio held a leather satchel. Iskandar expected grand payment for a trunk of hand bombards. Perhaps the satchel contained gold. He would find out soon enough.

Iskandar feigned slumber as Grato drove the cart toward the wharf, believable after all the work Grato had given him that day. The muscles of his arms were sore whenever he moved them, despite his long acquaintance with the labor demands of a slave. The skin of his hands was scratched, despite the calluses he'd long ago developed from hauling heavy cargo. Yet anticipation sang in his weary bones. After waiting far too long, freedom and coin were finally his for the taking. He would have liked a real weapon, but a quiet confidence settled on him, not unlike when he had gone into battle.

The night grew dark, and though the hour was not late, most people were off the streets, especially as the cart returned to the waterfront. Iskandar gazed around with half-closed eyes. Grato's ship was still a hundred paces away. D'Artusio stared across the water, and Grato guided the horses.

Iskandar caught the Bogomil's eye and nodded. The other slave tensed. Iskandar gripped the rock and swung it into the side of d'Artusio's head. The foreman slumped to the side immediately, and Iskandar leaped toward Grato. His master turned. Iskandar saw the terror on the man's face just before he smashed the rock into Grato's throat. Iskandar would have rather smashed his aquiline nose, but he didn't want to give Grato a chance to call for help.

Grato wouldn't suffer the same way he had made Iskandar suffer, but the punishment would be enough to satisfy Iskandar's thirst for justice. With his free hand, Iskandar grabbed Grato's throat and squeezed. Grato fought back, clawing at Iskandar's hand and gouging it with his heavy rings, but then Iskandar struck Grato's skull, and the master's resistance ended.

"Are you mad?" the Bogomil asked. "We'll be wanted for murder now."

Neither d'Artusio nor Grato was dead yet, but their deaths would be necessary. "Help me dump them in the harbor."

The Bogomil shook his head and climbed from the cart. Then he darted away, moving toward the buildings of Durazzo. Iskandar let him go. He wasn't running for the authorities. He was running away, but he wouldn't get far. Heretics weren't welcome in Durazzo, and with neither friend nor money, the Bogomil would have few options. Iskandar would have helped him, pretended to be his master until they passed through Bosnia, but Iskandar didn't need the heretic's assistance.

Iskandar took d'Artusio's cloak, tunic, boots, dagger, and satchel. Then he dragged him to the harbor and slipped him into the water. He did the same with Grato, only he took fewer pieces of clothing from him. He'd never cared for Grato's ostentatious fashion. Iskandar did, however, take the man's hat and the pouch. As suspected, Grato's purse contained gold coins. The satchel, in contrast, held only a single sheet of parchment. Iskandar couldn't read, but he kept it. Someone had considered it valuable.

The horses stamped and grunted as Iskandar unfastened them from the cart. He wasn't sure he could find a saddle to purchase overnight, but he would try. He fastened the dagger to his belt, wrapped d'Artusio's cloak about him, and donned Grato's hat, then led the animals from the waterfront as quickly as he could. He would wait and change into d'Artusio's serviceable tunic when he was farther away. Thus far, no one had noticed the two bodies dumped into the dark harbor, but that could change at any moment. He checked the scratches across his hands and wrists. They stung, but they bled only a little.

He slowed his pace when the smell of the harbor faded, and he forced his stride and posture to match that of an average man, one who had no master. He followed the main road, assuming that would give him the best chance of finding a caravan.

By the time the sun rose the next day, he had sold one horse, bought a saddle and provisions, and found a group of twenty travelers. At first light, they headed east. Throughout the night and morning, Iskandar had heard no talk of runaway slaves or murdered merchants. No one in the caravan seemed to doubt his tale that he carried a message from a Venetian senator.

As the morning grew warm and Durazzo faded in the distance, the feeling that he was again master of his own destiny slowly began to sink in. Grato and his whip were no more, and vengeance against Iskandar's other enemies—including the Serbs—was now within his reach.

Chapter Three
Two Wandering Artists

Maja Dinić ran her fingers over the small tesserae making up the newly completed mosaic of St. Sava. The village church was mostly dark, but candlelight reflected off the bits of glass and stone, showing each color, each shape, each angle.

"We should smash it," her younger brother said.

Maja shook her head. "No, we'll leave it." Long ago, her father had told her that life was like a great mosaic and each experience a tessera of glass or marble, limestone or ceramic. Some experiences were vibrant, others pale. Some were luminous, others dull. Some were light, others dark, but they all fit together to form a whole. Each was needful in its own way. Each had greater meaning and beauty only when complete. She believed her father, but at that moment, she craved something other than the dark experiences of grief and hunger, of being a victim of war and a victim of treachery. Would her life ever contain something as beautiful as the pieces of glass gilded with gold forming a halo around St. Sava's head? Or would her life's story always be pale, dull, and dark?

She took Luka's hand. She felt the same anger he did, but they had already appealed to everyone in the village without success. It was time to leave the church they had spent two years decorating with mosaics of the Savior and His mother, the apostles and the saints.

Luka pulled free of her grip. He had seen twelve winters and was perhaps growing too old to take his sister's hand. "We should smash half of it, then. Leave them only what they paid for."

"That would be blasphemous." She looked to her mosaic of the Virgin Mary. It had brought tears to the priest's eyes when he'd seen it, but the priest was not the patron and seemed to have no control over the man who had cheated them. She wasn't sure why they'd been given only half the promised payment. Was it because she was a woman? Because she was only nineteen? Because she was an orphan? Or simply because the town leader was dishonest and knew he could get away with defrauding two strangers?

Luka scowled. "They lied. This whole time, we've been giving their little village something to be proud of for centuries to come, and they swindled us!"

"Yes. They lied, and they cheated. But no one seems to care other than us. They ignored us when we complained of our payment, but they won't ignore us if we're caught vandalizing the church. They'll flog us or fine us. Or worse." Besides, Maja couldn't ruin her own work. She'd put a bit of her soul into the mosaics. Purposely damaging them might damage her.

She lifted the candle so it better illuminated the resurrected Lord on the inside of the dome. It was her best work yet, something her father would have been proud of. Now it was time to say goodbye and start over again. They'd managed with less before. The payment for the job was a disappointment, but they were not yet as desperate as they'd been after their parents had been killed. The injustice rankled her, but they would find work again, and she would negotiate terms for payment that didn't leave her and Luka so vulnerable.

They exited the church and loaded their donkey, Sinopia, with their tools and materials and a store of food. They left the churchyard and the village before dawn. They had come as outsiders, and for a time, they had felt welcomed. But now, again, they were wanderers with no home and no family other than each other. Their mother had taught them it was best to turn the other cheek. There were some things and some people Maja would never forgive. But a dishonest leader in an impoverished Bosnian village wasn't worth the grudge. Besides, in the new light of day, it was easy to believe their fortunes were about to improve. Nearly every village had a church, and Maja was confident she and Luka could make any of those churches more beautiful.

They walked all morning and came to another village that afternoon. But the destitute residents had nothing to spare for art commissions in the small chapel, so Maja and Luka set out again.

By evening, the skin of her feet blistered. Luka's mood grew sullen, and his pace grew slow. Maja took the lead rope in one hand and Luka's fingers in the other so he would keep a steady pace. He seemed too weary to fight the gesture. She had to stay positive, for his sake if for no other reason. "Come on. I wager the next village will have work for us. And fresh food." They had enough boukellaton to last several days, but better fare would cheer them both.

Luka pulled his hand free and folded his arms angrily across his chest. Apparently, he was not too tired to fight her hand-holding. "I still say we should have smashed that church. And we should buy a sword. People will think twice about cheating me if I'm armed."

The cost of a sword, even a poorly made one, was deterrent enough. And purchasing a sword wouldn't give either of them the skill to master its use. "We have to find more work before we purchase something like that."

"A weapon is a necessity out here."

"Only if you can wield it." The top of Luka's head came level with Maja's shoulders. A dishonest person might hesitate to swindle an armed man, but Luka still looked like a child. He might want to right wrongs and protect the defenseless, but desire wasn't the same as ability.

Sinopia brayed and slowed.

"We should let her rest a while." Maja stopped, and the donkey wandered to the side of the road to munch on the grass. Maja unloaded the packs with her father's tools. The hammers, chisels, and trowels were heavy but not nearly as weighty as the packs of materials she unloaded next. Most were already cut into tesserae, but some remained in larger pieces of limestone or glass, and a few were made of rare porphyry and lapis lazuli. She would find a place for them, somewhere, and they would be beautiful.

"I miss Mama." Luka adjusted his own bundle: clothing and a few ceramic plates. "And Papa. He wouldn't have let us be cheated."

"No. I don't suppose they would have cheated him." Her father's reputation as a master craftsman had been well-known, and he'd been a large man who had known how to use his fists. Not that his fists had done him any good when a band of Turkish ghazis had raided a village where he'd been decorating a church. The Turks had been driven back, eventually, but the Serb warriors who had defeated the ghazis couldn't reverse what the Turks had done. In a little church in a village near Pločnik, a mosaic remained unfinished, and two wooden crosses marked the graves of her mother and father.

Maja shook her grief off. "You will have to grow. When you are as tall as Father was, perhaps no one will cheat your sister."

"Or cheat me."

She smiled at his earnest indignation. Luka was good at cutting glass or stone into tesserae, and he was competent with borders, but Maja wasn't as gifted a teacher as her father had been. Maja's mosaics were much like her father's when finished, even if she took longer than he had to complete the work. But Luka was still learning, and his faces lacked life. He would improve with practice, of course, but she sometimes wondered if she would ever be a good enough mentor for him to fully learn his craft. She had never shared her lingering sense of inadequacy with him. He had enough to worry about without fearing that he might never become a master at his intended vocation. "Of course. No one will cheat you either, especially if you are tall and have a sword."

He smiled back at her. They were much alike, with golden hair and pale complexions that freckled and burned with too much sun. Their father had descended from Saxon miners, their mother from a captain of the imperial guard in Constantinople. Maja could still recall her mother's soft voice telling her stories of her grandfathers and great-grandfathers, always set in a beautiful city or a mysterious mine, while Mama combed and pinned Maja's hair.

When Sinopia seemed rested, they set out again. But it wasn't until the afternoon of their third day that they found a promising settlement large enough to include a church.

A priest nodded a greeting, then disappeared through the entrance, probably to prepare the evening service. Maja retied her sash and straightened her hair veil, then followed him inside, her eyes slowly adjusting to the dim light. Churches often had high windows to let in sunlight, but this one relied on candles. Churches were supposed to bring together all the senses for worship—color and light for the eyes, incense for the nose, and chants for the ears. But this was only a poor church. Maja smelled no incense, and the walls were largely plain. She could change that, could use the walls to tell stories of the Lord and His saints.

"May I help you, my child?"

Maja bowed her head and kissed the priest's hand. "My brother and I are mosaic artists. Would you have work for us?" She gestured to a damaged mosaic of a saint. Half the man's face was missing. Another panel was blank, and a third showcased a fresco, but the painting was of poor quality.

The priest pointed to the fresco. "We've just commissioned someone to paint the remaining walls."

The painting was new? Maja squinted at the fresco. "Art is supposed to be infused with the spirit of God. That looks as if it was done by an apprentice in his early years. Surely you would like something finer for your chapel."

"The artist is the son of the bishop's sister." The priest frowned at the painting. "Christ will have to be content with the efforts of our current artist."

"What of the mosaic? I could repair it."

"You?"

Maja gathered her thoughts. She'd already insulted the current artist, she was a stranger, and she was a woman. Those all gave her a disadvantage, but she needed work, and she knew she could do a good job—better than the painter. The villagers needed something beautiful, something magnificent to draw their thoughts toward heaven. "Yes. I have learned since I was old enough to hold a hammer. And I have limestone to make tesserae that will match the color of the saint's clothes and his face. Give me two days of trial. One to set the base layer of mortar, and one to set the upper layers and lay down tesserae. If you're not pleased with my progress, you will owe me nothing."

The priest walked to the broken mosaic and lifted his hand to the crumbling plaster. "It's been broken since I was a boy. But St. Cyril's face was complete, at least, until a few years ago. The artist plans to remove all the tesserae and use paint and plaster instead, but I asked him to wait until the other panels were completed before he tore this one down." The priest's voice hinted at nostalgia for the old artwork. "I will give you a chance. You can start in the morning."

Maja and Luka spent the evening in a local meroph's barn, surrounded by goats and sheep. Their bellies were full, and the coin purse only a bit lighter, so after sketching the planned repairs and sorting through her stone for the right pieces to fix the mosaic, Maja slept with contentment.

But the contentment disappeared the next morning when they arrived at the church with their tools.

The priest stood outside with a frown on his face, though the intensity of his expression paled in comparison to the ferocity of the man who stood beside him.

The paint-stained cuffs of the other man's tunic marked him as the incompetent artist.

"You'll have to leave. I've already been promised all three panels for my frescoes. There is no need for another artist."

"But it's foolish to replace the existing mosaic with a fresco. It's part of this village's history. It should be repaired." Maja would have felt that way even if another artist were to receive the commission. The sympathetic turn of the priest's lips suggested that he agreed with her.

The artist huffed and drew his nose into the air. "Any changes to the current arrangement would have to be approved by the bishop."

"Where is the bishop?" Luka demanded. "I'll tell him our work is better than your sloppy drawings and far more prestigious for the church."

The artist glared at the insult, then laughed. "The bishop won't go back on his promise."

Luka seemed ready to speak again, but Maja put a hand on his shoulder in warning. He hadn't been so angry as a boy, but watching the Turks slaughter their parents and dozens of other villagers, almost being enslaved by them . . . It had left him with a temper greater than his skill to defend himself, should he provoke an altercation.

The artist cast a final condescending look, then disappeared inside the church.

The priest watched him go. "I am sorry. I truly wanted to give you a chance, and I wanted the mosaic saved. But he has his commission from the bishop. He could paint blasphemy of the worst sort, and I'd be helpless to stop him."

Disappointment seemed to surround Maja like mortar around a tesserae. She swallowed it back. "Thank you for wanting to let us try."

The priest nodded, his gesture another apology.

"Where will we go now?" With a petulant pout, Luka shifted the canvas sack of tools from one shoulder to the other.

Maja didn't know. Sometimes she hated being the older sibling, the one responsible for everything. Her eyes stung, but she blinked rapidly to stall the tears of sorrow. She might be weary of being in charge, but that didn't change her duty. Crying would solve nothing. She had to be strong for her brother.

The priest stepped toward them. "I've heard they are building a new church in Sivi Gora. It's rumored that the župan is sparing no expense. He hired a master mosaicist from Constantinople. If you have skill, you might find work there."

"Where is Sivi Gora?" Maja asked.

"To the east and a bit to the north. In Serbia, almost to Hungary."

Maja had been to Hungary before. Luka had been born there during one of their father's commissions. The church had been Catholic rather than Orthodox, but her father's reputation had granted him the job regardless, and it had been a pleasant stay for their family. "Thank you. How far is the journey?"

Maja bought enough food to last the fortnight it would take her and Luka to walk to Sivi Gora. Nothing fancy. A few loaves of bread, cheese for the first few days, dried fish, and cereal they could boil into porridge.

And what if we make it there and no one will hire me?

Maja drove the thought from her head. She had to be brave, for Luka's sake, and perhaps for her own. Her father had never expressed concern over the next commission, the next key to providing food and shelter for his family, and nor had Maja's mother. But they'd had each other to share worry with, and Maja's father had been a man. It had been easier for him to find work.

"What's Sivi Gora like?" Luka asked the second day after leaving the village. She'd already told him all she knew, but she repeated it anyway. Sometimes he asked his questions more than once because he'd thought of something new to add to the discussion, and they had time enough to talk it over.

"I've never been there, but *Sivi Gora* means 'gray mountain,' so I suppose it's mountainous."

"And gray?"

Maja smiled. "Perhaps. But the inside of the church won't be, not if they hire us to decorate it." She would fill it with vibrant color that would make the images of saints, scripture stories, and the Savior come to life and draw the eyes upward, toward the heavens. If the župan agreed to hire her.

A nearby stream bubbled like the tinkling of glass tesserae.

"Let's stop here for a bit." She would refill their water bladders and give their donkey and themselves a rest. As she unloaded the heaviest of the packs off Sinopia's back, she told Luka what she'd learned from the priest. "Sivi Gora has a young župan who wants a beautiful church. There's a silver mine, which I suppose is how the župan is paying for said church."

"Are the Turks near Sivi Gora?"

So that was what Luka wanted to talk about: whether they'd be safe. Nearly three years had passed since the ghazis had slain their parents, but fear of the Ottomans had never really left them. "Closer than they are in Bosnia but still some distance. And if Sivi Gora is mountainous, that will make it harder for the Turks to get to." She took the waterskins off the donkey. "Stay with Sinopia while I fill these. Then we'll eat."

Luka nodded and pulled out the last of the fresh bread and soft cheese. She hoped he wouldn't inhale it before she returned. She normally gave him a larger portion of their food—he was still growing, and she wasn't—but she tired of the dried bread just as quickly as he did.

Maja picked her way down the bank to the stream through a grove of beech and chestnut. She walked along the bank until the water wasn't quite so shallow and filled both waterskins where the stream ran clear. They hadn't been empty, but she didn't want to run out of water, especially with the donkey to think of. She glanced back the way she'd come, trying to judge if it would be easier to bring Sinopia to the stream or use their bucket and bring the water to her.

"Hey!" Luka's panicked cry drifted down to Maja, but she couldn't see him from where she stood.

She left the water and ran. Noises came to her—a scuffle, a moan, a bray. What was happening?

She pushed through the last of the brush to see a pair of men running off with Sinopia. Maja almost ran after them, but Luka lay on the ground, unmoving.

"Luka!" She bent and turned his head, gasping when she saw the blood that covered the left side of his face. She pressed her hair veil into her brother's wound, wiping at the blood until she could clearly see the long cut across his forehead. He moaned a little but didn't open his eyes. "Luka?"

He managed another groan, but his eyes stayed closed. The thieves disappeared around a distant bend in the road. A bundle with her father's tools and one full of tesserae still lay under a yarrow bush where she'd left them. Most of the tools would work as weapons, but she didn't dare leave Luka, nor did she expect to win a fight against two grown men.

"Luka, can you hear me?"

He didn't reply. Helplessness welled up inside her. She had promised him that she would protect him, and she had done her best since the Turks had killed their parents, but she didn't know what to do for him now. It would take them until nightfall to return to the last village they'd passed, if she could carry him that far, which she doubted. The thieves had taken Sinopia, so she couldn't even put Luka on the donkey. The men had also stolen the bags with all their food and all their money. She could leave Luka and run for help, but what if the thieves came back? Or what if Luka's condition worsened and she wasn't there? And what if she found no help?

She looked in the direction the thieves had gone, then made her decision. She would stay with her brother and hope for the best. The old tunic she wore was already too short and ripped about the hemline. She tore another strip off the bottom anyway. Panic made her hands shake, but she repositioned her hair veil on the wound to stanch the bleeding, then tied the veil in place with the torn piece of tunic.

She checked the wound after a while. The blood seemed to have slowed, but bruises were growing on the side of his head. She went to the stream to collect the water bladders and fetched a cold rock to help with the swelling, but she doubted it would do much good. Finally, not knowing what else to do, she sang a lullaby her mother had sung to them when they were younger.

"*Alone was forced to wander through hill and over vale. I longed to find my freedom, where I'd be safe and well. But how I missed my true love, though he long was dead. I felt his voice was near me, running through my head.*"

The familiar words brought with them an old pain, reminding her of her loss. She couldn't lose Luka too. She sang, and she prayed, and then she prayed, and she sang.

And finally, Luka spoke. "Mama?"

"No. It's just me."

"I'm sorry, Maja. I tried to stop them."

She wiped a few tears from her cheeks. "I'm just glad you're still here. Everything else can be replaced."

"How?"

She didn't know. But they'd had little other than a letter of introduction when they'd left Pločnik, which had gained them their first commission as orphans in a country villa with a kind mistress. Maja had done good work there, and the lady of the house had allowed Maja the time and freedom she'd needed to experiment and improve her craft. But churches had always been her father's passion, so she had been eager to take their last job. She would have been less eager had she known how it would turn out.

Half the promised pay, and now even that was gone. Their reward for two years' labor had been stolen in a matter of moments.

Luka tried to sit and winced with the effort. He squeezed his eyes shut for a moment, then looked at their remaining bundles. "What will we eat?"

She didn't know that either.

Chapter Four
The Caravan Road

Iskandar traveled with the caravan from Durazzo along the Via Egnatia, following the Shkumbin River, passing by Lake Ohrid. As they drew near to Thessaloniki, the landscape grew more familiar. He'd been in these lands before.

Signor Contanto, a Venetian merchant with a chiseled nose and a gray-streaked beard, rode beside him.

"I was about my son's age when I left home to seek my fortune, though I traveled by sea rather than by land." The man's eldest son, Pascal, rode on the other side of his father. It was the lad's first journey away from Venice. Iskandar thought a lad so gullible ought to be at home with his mother a few more years, but perhaps he would learn best by observing, even when he didn't seem to grasp the strategies and negotiations his father and the other merchants employed.

"You seem to have found your way," Iskandar said.

Signor Contanto chuckled. Iskandar didn't like many Venetians, but he felt no contempt for Contanto. The man was cheerful and treated Iskandar with respect, and the food the family had shared with Iskandar was better than anything he'd eaten in years. "There are always new markets to explore, more profitable goods to trade. Our journey will end soon, but that does not mean we have to part. I could use a stalwart assistant. You speak Italian well enough. Can you speak Greek as well?"

"Yes." Iskandar didn't add that he could also communicate in Turkish, Vlach, Slavonic, and bits of Arabic. Contanto wouldn't offer him work if he knew Iskandar was a Muslim rather than the Rhodesian Catholic he'd claimed to be when he joined the caravan.

"That would come in handy. Think of it. The life of a merchant. Plenty of travel and, if my luck holds, a life of comfort. I would gladly give you work for as long as you wish it."

"I thank you for the offer. It is a generous one to make to a stranger. But I am afraid my purpose lies elsewhere." With the money Iskandar had taken from Grato, he could start over again in the sultan's capital. He also had the document from d'Artusio's satchel. He couldn't read it, but if Grato had traded a trunk of hand bombards for the parchment, it held significant value, and he intended to leverage that to his gain.

"I am sorry to hear that." Disappointment colored Signor Contanto's voice. "But perhaps you will change your mind before we part."

Iskandar didn't reply. He would break from the group soon and set off for Edirne. The Contanto family had done nothing to earn his hatred, and wealth tempted him, but not if it meant he must live among the Christians.

Ahead of them, someone in the caravan line shouted an alarm. Another screamed.

Iskandar scanned the landscape, finding the source of their terror: a pack of ghazis. For a moment, fear gripped Iskandar's stomach, but then a calm overcame him. These were his people, and they would be more interested in pillage than slaughter. If no one resisted, then perhaps no one would be harmed. And perhaps Iskandar would have company on his way to Edirne.

"Don't resist!" Iskandar shouted to the other members of the caravan. "Stay calm and cooperate, and you won't be hurt!"

The raiding party was only twelve strong. Had Iskandar wanted to fight, he could have organized the men of the caravan and given the raiders enough of a challenge that they might give up. But he preferred joining forces with them.

Pascal galloped away from the group, trying to escape. One of the raiders shot an arrow at the horse he rode, and Pascal was thrown to the ground when the gelding collapsed. Two of the raiders converged on the lad and dragged him back to the others.

The rest of the caravan waited, fearful but heeding Iskandar's call for cooperation. Signor Contanto's face hardened with rage as the ghazis brought his son back and kicked him in the stomach.

"His father is wealthy. He has most value as an *unharmed* hostage," Iskandar said in Turkish. The ghazis standing over Pascal paused, and everyone looked at Iskandar in surprise. The caravan he'd been traveling with didn't know his true origin, and the ghazis couldn't have expected to come across one of their own traveling with the Christians.

The leader rode closer to Iskandar and removed the scarf that had covered the lower half of his face. The skin was more wrinkled than Iskandar remembered, and the mustache showed far more gray, but the ghazi leader was a friend.

"Hasan?" Iskandar asked.

"Iskandar bin Abdullah. It is good to see you again. I feared the worst after Pločnik."

"Allah surely smiles upon us for our meeting to be thus. Peace be unto you, my friend."

"And unto you." Hasan looked over the caravan. "Why do you travel with Christians?"

"It seemed the safest way to reach Ottoman lands."

"You wish us to spare them?" Hasan asked.

Iskandar glanced at the carts, animals, and travelers he had journeyed with. "Take their supplies and demand ransom from their families, if you will. But I would be grateful if you left them unharmed. They have shown kindness to me."

The wrinkles of Hasan's forehead deepened as he thought. "They would fetch a good price in the slave markets, and it has been some time since we found a group so rich in wealth and so poor in security. I must provide for my ghazis."

Iskandar understood. He'd been in similar positions before. Some ghazis were loyal to a leader regardless. Hasan had been like that, first to Iskandar's father, then to Iskandar. But most ghazis would follow a leader only so long as he led them to success. If Hasan let the caravan go, he risked losing the loyalty of his men.

For a moment, Iskandar wavered between two choices. Signor Contanto had offered Iskandar employment, and Pascal had given him a poultice when the cuts on his hands had festered. That didn't mean he owed them anything. And yet, if an arrangement could be made that would help the family that had befriended him without taking from the ghazis, Iskandar wished to negotiate it. Allah, after all, approved of mercy.

"Signor Contanto, what would you be willing to pay for the freedom of your family and the other members of the caravan?"

Signor Contanto narrowed his eyes. "You were a spy, in league with them!"

"No." Iskandar had been a spy before but not recently. "I wasn't working with them before they attacked, but I am working with them now."

"Traitor!"

"Hardly. These are my people. And they know how much the group of you might bring in the slave market. But gold is easier to transport than slaves, if you can offer them money instead."

Distaste contorted Signor Contanto's face. "I have some with me. If it will buy our freedom, I will offer it all."

Iskandar shook his head. "They consider the caravan theirs now, not yours. You will have to offer something more. And you will have to give it to them quickly." As Signor Contanto considered his options, Iskandar continued. "I recommend swift agreement. I see lust in the eyes of the raiders. There are no women in the caravan, which puts fresh-faced lads at risk."

Signor Contanto's face darted to Pascal and then to Iskandar. "My son and I could get coin in Edessa."

Iskandar shook his head. He was willing to be fair with the Contantos, but he was no fool. "If the two of you leave together, you won't come back."

Contanto didn't deny Iskandar's prediction. "Can you guarantee my son will remain unmolested while I am gone?"

Iskandar spoke with Hasan before turning back to Signor Contanto. "Twenty pounds of gold and the members of the caravan will be granted their freedom, as long as you return within four days. I can guarantee their safety—and Pascal's—that long but no longer." The deadline was tight. They had passed Edessa two days before. But Signor Contanto would move more swiftly without the caravan, so long as he wasn't accosted by another band of brigands.

Signor Contanto nodded. He wasn't happy, but he was wise. This trip would be a costly loss, but he could rebuild his wealth after a setback. The same was not true of his family should they be divided and sold.

In the end, they let Signor Contanto and one other merchant leave for Edessa with four swift horses between them.

Iskandar glanced at the captured Christians as the two merchants rode off. He saw hatred there now that they knew Iskandar's true identity.

"You will stay until the ransom is paid?" Hasan asked.

"Yes."

"And after? Will you join us? We have much to catch up on."

"Gladly."

That night, while the hostages from the caravan spent their first night bound in ropes as captives, Iskandar and Hasan spoke over the campfire.

"After you began work with your sister's husband, I joined with a cousin." Hasan built the fire up, banishing the night's chill. "We had moderate success. Then he died, and I inherited leadership of these men. I thought you perished with Kasim at Pločnik."

"No." Tonight, Iskandar was grateful he had survived and endured. "Kasim died. I was captured. Bayezid sent no ransom for me, and I've been a slave ever since."

"Bayezid was in Anatolia. I doubt he received the request."

"Perhaps. Or perhaps he was disappointed in me. I tried to serve him, but I failed." Kasim had been loyal to Bayezid, one of Sultan Murad's sons, and Iskandar had offered his loyalty as well. But the two men he'd been ordered to execute had escaped, and then the Battle of Pločnik had been lost, and Iskandar was partially responsible. He had urged Lala Şahin Pasha to disperse the restless troops for pillage. And when they were dispersed, the Serbs had attacked.

"What will you do now? You were a fine ghazi in your time."

"Other than the Greek kastron that refused to surrender." Iskandar threw a twig into the flames. The town and its acropolis had fallen, eventually, but disappointment at that initial failure and all it had cost him still burned deep.

"That was bad luck. You would succeed, if you chose the path of a ghazi again. But I think your heart is set on something more important than raiding."

Iskandar frowned. "Some days, my heart is set only on revenge. The župan of Sivi Gora, and his half-Turkish cousin. Their crimes against me are many."

Hasan raised an eyebrow. "I remember the župan. He slew your father, and he broke the siege."

"He also captured me and sold me into slavery." Iskandar had begged for slavery over death, but that didn't ease the rage he felt.

"And the cousin?"

"He would have killed me in Rivak if you hadn't stopped him. He's responsible for helping the župan escape Erdine, he wounded me at Kırkpınar, and he cut free my captives after Pločnik." The last one was a minor offense, yet that one galled Iskandar the most. Iskandar didn't believe in witches, but he did believe the golden-haired girl he'd briefly captured in the small Serbian village had cast a spell on him. Desire for her consumed him, even years later. Iskandar had planned to take her as his bride, but Danilo had cut her free, and now she was lost to him. So was much of the potential he'd once had as a loyal follower of Bayezid.

"You have developed insight, Iskandar, to complement your strength of arms. That leaves you in a position to choose your own path. You could seek wealth. The lands around us are ripe for pillage. Join me, if you wish. I will gladly serve with you again. Or we can divide the ransom, and you can find your own followers. Or you could seek vengeance. I don't doubt you can disguise yourself and take revenge against your foes in Sivi Gora. But I think you are destined for something greater than pillage or revenge—glory and honor—and that path lies in Edirne, with the sultan's son."

Long after Hasan had retired to his tent, Iskandar stared into the dying embers of the fire. He wanted revenge, and he wanted wealth. But more than those, he wanted to be important. He wanted to have influence and see his people grow into something grand. Besides, service to Bayezid might include his other goals. Did Bayezid not grant his most loyal followers timar lands to support them? And would Bayezid not crush rebellious Serb župans like the man who ruled Sivi Gora?

Iskandar finally made his decision and drifted off to sleep. He didn't doubt he could be a successful ghazi or assassin. But he wanted more.

Chapter Five
Bosnia's King

Danilo sat in the great hall of Stephen Tvrtko, Kral of Bosnia, while servants brought bread, roasted goat, cheese, and a salad of sour cabbage.

The man beside him had a weather-beaten face and snowy-white hair. "Kral Tvrtko is powerful now, but I remember when he was deposed briefly, back when his mother was regent." The man squinted and studied Danilo. "That would have been before you were born, I wager."

Danilo shifted his gaze to the head of the table, where the kral sat with Miloš and Konstantin. "He seems to have long ago consolidated power." Tvrtko controlled Bosnia and parts of Serbia and seemed near the end of his campaign to take the Dalmatian coast from Hungary.

"Yes. Few would dare cross him now."

Danilo might have been wary of a man as powerful as Tvrtko if the kral hadn't three years ago joined the alliance with Knez Lazar that defeated the Turks at Pločnik. "Do you think he will fight alongside the Serbs again, should Sultan Murad attack?" That was why Danilo, Konstantin, and Miloš had traveled to Bosnia, to convince Kral Tvrtko to join their alliance.

The man fingered the ends of his white beard. "I believe he is willing but doesn't wish to pull too many of his troops from their work in Dalmatia."

Danilo nodded, sober. They needed Tvrtko's help, but Danilo understood the limits of military might. Tvrtko wouldn't wish to battle the Hungarians and the Turks at the same time any more than Ivan would.

After the meal ended but before the group dispersed, Miloš and another man approached Danilo.

Miloš gestured to the stranger. "I thought the two of you ought to meet. Danilo Darrasević, this is Emanuil Asen of Vidin."

Miloš wouldn't introduce the man without good reason, and the Asen name had a long history in Bulgaria. The Bulgar lands had been divided, with a Stratsimir the current tsar of Vidin while a Shishman was tsar of Târnovo. Danilo gave the man his full attention. "I'm honored to meet you."

"Miloš tells me you have the ear of Sivi Gora's župan."

Danilo didn't want to overstate his influence with Ivan, but nor did he want to downplay his authority and make the man lose interest.

In the hesitation, Miloš spoke. "Don't be modest, Danilo. You are Župan Ivan's most trusted adviser."

Miloš's words were true, but Danilo had been absent far too often of late to do much in the way of advising. Emanuil, however, didn't need to know that. "With the possible exception of his wife."

Emanuil smiled slightly. "Would you walk with me?" He motioned to the door leading to the bailey, and Danilo nodded.

"What brings you to Bosnia?" Danilo asked.

"Several reasons. Kral Tvrtko's wife is my kinswoman. I carry letters for her. I also seek information for my brother, Boyar Kalin. Like you, we were once subject to the Turks. Like you, we joined Knez Lazar and Kral Tvrtko at Pločnik."

"I remember the Bulgarian cavalry. You fought well."

Emanuil smoothed his mustache and beard as they walked into the bailey. The sun had slipped below the horizon while they'd dined, but the sky in the west still held dusky sunlight. "Yes, and for a time, we had our freedom. Then the sultan came for his revenge, and we are once again his vassals."

Danilo hoped the man wasn't spying for the sultan, but his words and his tone . . . He did not sound pleased to be a vassal of Sultan Murad. Before Pločnik, Konstantin, too, had been a vassal of the Turks, and Danilo remembered the burdens Rivak had been forced to bear. "Do the terms of your vassalage include military service?"

"They do."

"And has the sultan given any demands for the coming campaign season?"

"Not to my knowledge, though I have been away for more than a moon."

Danilo resisted the urge to fill the silence with words. As circumstances currently stood, Emanuil's brother would likely lead a force against the Serbs when the sultan next attacked. Danilo would gather as much information as he could but give away as little as possible.

"Does your župan really believe he can defeat the sultan?" Emanuil clasped his hands behind his back as they walked.

"By himself, no. If enough of us unite, yes."

"Unity, yes. Knez Lazar seems to be building quite the coalition." Emanuil glanced meaningfully back at the keep. "But I doubt he will convince all of Christendom to cooperate."

All of Christendom didn't have to unite in order to stop the sultan, but a great many of them would need to if they hoped to find victory. "Will he convince your brother, the boyar, to join our cause?"

Emanuil pursed his lips in thought. "We've seen what the sultan can do firsthand these past few years. If we rebel again, and if we fail . . . I imagine the consequences will be even heavier, and they are not at present light."

Danilo could understand the hesitation. Konstantin, too, had longed for freedom, but had accepted his vassalage as a necessity after the Battle of Maritsa had taken both their fathers and left the župa impoverished. Only when the right allies had come along, only when Rivak had built up its strength, only then had Konstantin won freedom from the sultan. If Boyar Kalin's situation had been similar, the heartbreak of reconquest must have been shattering. "It sounds as though we have a common enemy."

Emanuil gave a wry chuckle. "More than one. The sultan. And like Sivi Gora, we worry about the Hungarians. Tsar Shishman's portion of Bulgaria as well. Which is worse? Tribute to the Turks, conquest by the Hungarians, or the revenge of a rival?"

"I suppose that would depend on if you had a young son who the Ottomans might take as a janissary. On whether the Hungarians would force conversion to the Latin faith or allow us to continue worshipping as we currently do. On how driven for revenge your rival is and on whether he sees your family as a threat." Any option sounded bleak. Ivan shared two of the worries, which was why he kept building defenses and why Danilo traveled with Miloš to secure allies. The consequences of defeat were devastating.

"If we turn to fight one enemy, our other enemies might seize the opportunity to attack while we're engaged elsewhere."

Danilo understood. War on two fronts would mean weakness on all fronts. "What will your boyar do? I take it he does not wish to remain in the sultan's service?"

"Few of the sultan's vassals do. Perhaps your župan and my boyar could come to an understanding."

"What do you have in mind?"

"You have silver. We are near trade routes with the East. Closer relationships might benefit us both."

"They may." Sivi Gora already had merchants who brought goods from across the Balkans and beyond, but perhaps an agreement with Emanuil's boyar on some aspect of trade could be found, especially if it would bring Vidin into the alliance meant to stop the sultan.

"Neither of us wishes to battle two enemies at once. Perhaps Hungary feels the same. If your lands and my lands were allied, Hungary might hesitate to attack either of us, for fear of suddenly being at war with both of us. If Hungary were to attack you, we could cause them a great deal of trouble. And if they were to attack us, you could do the same. I speak of a defensive arrangement only, of course. My boyar isn't foolhardy enough to provoke a giant like Hungary."

"My župan also seeks peace with Hungary. I cannot speak for him in all matters, but we are always looking to form mutually beneficial relationships." Ivan wouldn't want Sivi Gora dragged into a war against Hungary, but if an alliance with a Bulgarian boyar would deter them from attacking, the risk of entanglement might be worth it. Danilo hadn't spoken with Emanuil long enough to trust him, but maybe, over the next few days, he could get a better feel for the man.

Emanuil ran his fingers along his beard again. "Then perhaps I shall visit Sivi Gora, and speak with your župan directly."

"I'm sure my župan will offer his finest hospitality to you."

Emanuil extended his hand, and Danilo grasped it in a sign of friendship. "Shall I expect to see you again in Sivi Gora?"

"That depends on the length of your stay. I'll accompany Miloš north when we depart Bosnia. As you know, if the sultan attacks, we cannot ignore Hungary. We don't expect aid, but we can hope for neutrality."

"In that case, I wish you luck." Emanuil studied Danilo a moment longer, then excused himself.

Danilo caught his cousin's eye across the bailey, and the two of them met each other near the stables.

"I see you've been making new friends." Konstantin glanced after Emanuil.

"Yes. Emanuil Asen from Vidin. Have you met him?"

Konstantin shook his head.

"He fought at Pločnik, but their freedom was short-lived. He seems wary of rebelling against the sultan again and losing. And he's worried about his neighbors in Hungary and other parts of Bulgaria encroaching on his borders if the Turks distract them."

"If he's here, I imagine part of him is willing to risk another confrontation with Sultan Murad. That, or he hopes Kral Tvrtko will launch a new attack into Hungary."

"I hope that's not the case." Danilo would be glad to see Hungary reduced to something that wasn't such a threat to Sivi Gora, but if the Bosnians escalated their conflict with the Hungarians, regardless of the outcome, they would be weaker when it came time to fight the Ottomans. "We need Kral Tvrtko's full forces, not their remnants after an all-out war with Hungary."

Konstantin looked toward the east. "I think the sultan will come this summer, and I intend to defend my lands, even if we're outnumbered ten to one. But I sincerely hope the odds will not be so much against us. An alliance with Kral Tvrtko looks favorable. I'll see what my men and I can find out about our new friend from Vidin."

A few days later, Danilo held back a yawn as Kral Tvrtko laughed at something Miloš said. Tvrtko, his chief advisers, and Danilo's traveling companions had gathered in the bailey. Dawn promised to chase away the chill well before noon, but for now, Danilo pulled his cloak tight and stamped his feet to keep them warm. Last night's feast had gone late. Danilo struggled to shake off the headache and the heavy eyes that went with a late night and an early start.

Kral Tvrtko's voice carried none of the weariness Danilo felt. "Tell Knez Lazar that I will stand with him against the Turks. If I do not come myself, I will send my general, Vlatko Vuković, and together we will defeat the enemy. Let the sultan send his minions. We'll be ready."

Miloš grasped Tvrtko's arm in solidarity. "We are glad for your alliance."

"And we are glad for yours. And for your gifts." Tvrtko moved to Danilo and made the same gesture. "I remember the men from Sivi Gora at Pločnik. I will be glad to serve with you again."

"And I will be honored to serve once more with you."

Next Tvrtko turned to Konstantin. "I also remember Rivak. A privilege to fight alongside you and your stalwart men."

"Thank you." Konstantin took the kral's arm and inclined his head in respect. "When the sultan comes, it will be my honor to stand with you."

They finished their farewells to Kral Tvrtko and his household, and then the men from Rivak, Sivi Gora, and Kruševac traveled east, grateful for the knowledge that Bosnia would be their ally.

Danilo rode beside his cousin. "I'm sorry you had to leave your family for so long, but I think our agreement will help keep Rivak safe."

Konstantin nodded. "Bosnia will join us. Perhaps Vidin too." Both Danilo and Konstantin had made opportunities to speak with Emanuil Asen before his departure from Kral Tvrtko's court, but his boyar's loyalties remained uncertain.

Konstantin turned to Miloš, who was riding behind them. "What will our numbers be?"

"Knez Lazar can muster five thousand," Miloš said as he guided his horse level with Konstantin's and Danilo's.

"Ivan has four hundred, if we count the mercenaries." Danilo wasn't ready to trust the mercenaries, not completely, but they had no love for the Turks, and Ivan paid them well.

"I'll call up my entire force." Konstantin frowned. "The last few years have been prosperous, but three hundred will be a challenge for us."

Miloš gazed across the fields that bordered their path. "War against Murad strains the coffers of everyone who resists him."

"Župan Dragomir will bring a few hundred more. And they're good men," Konstantin said. The old župan was Konstantin's neighbor and a kinsman by marriage. "Župan Nikola has promised five hundred. And Vuk Branković will bring a few thousand."

Miloš scowled at the mention of Vuk. "Yes, I suppose he will."

Like Miloš, Vuk was married to one of Knez Lazar's daughters, but the sisters had quarreled, and their falling-out had led to ill feelings between their husbands. Danilo had heard the stories around the campfire. They had made him grateful that his late wife's siblings, all brothers older than Tatjana, had experienced no similar strife.

"Will it be enough?" Danilo asked.

Miloš looked thoughtful. "I suppose it depends on how large an army Sultan Murad sends. Or perhaps he'll lead them himself. It may also depend on what the Bulgarians do."

The groups traveled and camped together the first day, but on the morning of the second, Konstantin's group divided from the others to travel a more southerly route.

Konstantin turned to Danilo before they parted. "Remember what I said. There will always be a place for you in Rivak, should you want it. And don't put up with any nonsense from Ivan's mercenaries about omens or curses. Any land that has your loyalty is blessed beyond measure."

Danilo watched his cousin and the Rivak men ride away, hoping Konstantin was right. Konstantin couldn't spend time worrying about omens and curses. He was a good leader and a good friend, but war would be a burden for him, even if they won. Rivak was less wealthy than Sivi Gora and more vulnerable to Turkish incursions. Konstantin wasn't worried about Hungary—Rivak was too far from the borders—but the nearer enemy was danger enough.

When their group, too, was ready to depart, Miloš mounted and urged Ždralin next to Danilo's palfrey, Dazhbog, as they followed the eastern road. "You can tell your župan that the meeting with Kral Tvrtko proved useful. Sivi Gora's western border is shared with a friend. As is its eastern one."

"Yes, and Kral Tvrtko seems confident we can defeat anything Murad throws at us." Danilo allowed himself a moment of satisfaction. Tvrtko's attitude was contagious. An alliance of Serbs and Bosnians had beaten the Ottomans at Pločnik. Surely they could do so again.

"He's coming off several victories. His general smashed an Ottoman Army led by Lala Şahin Pasha last summer."

Danilo nodded. News of the Bosnian victory at Bileća had made its way to Sivi Gora just before harvest.

"And his lands are farther from Edirne," Miloš continued, "so defeat doesn't scare him as much. Perhaps that's part of his secret—a lack of fear."

Danilo didn't say so aloud, but fear had been his companion at Pločnik. It hadn't kept him from fighting, but knowledge of its strength was a secret he tried to hide. "Now the trick is keeping the Hungarians at bay."

"Knez Lazar has made arrangements with them."

"Will they keep those promises? And extend their friendship—or at least an absence of hostilities—to Sivi Gora?"

Miloš thought for a while before answering. "Sivi Gora is small. Easy to escape notice. But it's also rich, and that makes it a tempting target."

"Which is why my župan builds walls and hires mercenaries." Danilo—and Ivan—considered Hungary as much a threat as the sultan.

"And why you will join me on my trip to Hungary?"

"Yes." It would take an extra fortnight, if the roads were good. It would take longer if they ran into poor weather or hostile bandits. No one waited for him, so the extra time didn't bother Danilo. But the other men had families. "Your wife won't be disappointed that you are gone for so long?"

"She knows I serve her father. Pride in my accomplishments will be a most fitting companion." A bit of mischief made its way into his eyes. "Besides, if I'm riding to Hungary, I can postpone dealing with the latest insult from Vuk's wife."

Chapter Six
The Hero of Pločnik

Maja's head spun as she trudged forward, her back bent under the heavy packs. Luka hobbled along beside her with an uneven stride. Every step he took looked like agony, and Maja wasn't even sure they were going in the right direction. Six days had passed since they'd been robbed, and though his bruises were fading, the cut on Luka's head was festering and made him dizzy whenever he stood. The thieves had struck him in the legs before they'd struck him in the head, and his right leg was swollen and tender whenever he put weight on it. Maja had wrapped the leg to help support it and had found him a long stick to help him balance, but he still winced with every step. Maja wasn't sure what else she could do. Her mother had always been the one to care for them if they were sick or injured. Now Maja wished she had paid more attention to healing work instead of forever running after her father to see which tesserae he could use next.

The day after the robbery, they had been given shelter by a kindly meroph woman. She'd even called for a healer, who had bled Luka to balance his humors, though Maja hadn't noticed any improvement. They had stayed with the woman for two days, Luka resting and Maja doing whatever chores the meroph gave her in exchange for food. But eventually, the garden was weeded, the fence repaired, and the roof rethatched. The woman, nearly out of food herself, had urged them to continue their journey, though she had sent them with enough food for a day. They'd made it last two, but even that had run out the day before.

That morning, they had scrounged new dandelion greens, but those had scarcely lessened their hunger before it had returned in force. They were making poor time. Luka needed rest often, and the packs Maja carried slowed her pace as well. She couldn't bring herself to abandon the tools or the tesserae, not while there was hope that they would someday find work again, so she continued to haul them with her. The thieves had stolen their extra clothing, so mornings and evenings were spent shivering, and nights were spent huddled together under whatever brush they could find to hold in their heat. For the present, the search for food was their overwhelming obsession, but they were poor hunters, she didn't know whether most plants were edible or poisonous, and it was too early in the year for nuts.

"I think I smell smoke." Luka lifted his head, searching the sky. "Maybe there's a home somewhere."

Maja had to sniff a few times before she caught the scent of wet wood burning. A home and a fire might mean food. Or danger, but the gnawing in her stomach helped spur her forward until a small tendril of smoke appeared. She and Luka followed the road around a curve and soon saw the first home of a village, then a second not far beyond. Neither of the homes looked inhabited, so she continued in the direction of the smoke. She'd seen plenty of villages like this one, with more empty homes than occupied ones. The Great Mortality had decimated village after village, and though that had been before Maja's time, most villages hadn't yet regrown. That would take generations.

"It always makes me sad to see the abandoned houses." Luka leaned heavily on his stick.

"That's because you love to create, and time is undoing all that work that someone once put into making a home."

Luka limped forward. "They could still be repaired. I never understood, in that last village, why more families didn't spread out into the empty houses. Some of the homes had a dozen people living there, with empty houses just down the road."

That Maja understood, because she and Luka had lived in one of the empty houses while they'd worked. "The hearth tax is paid per home. If two grown sons leave their parents' home, the family might end up with triple the tax burden."

"Did we have to pay a hearth tax?"

"Yes."

"Before or after they swindled us?"

"Before." When Maja and Luka had begun their work on the church, they'd been granted a residence and a living allowance sufficient for them to buy food, with promise of a larger sum upon completion of their mosaics. But the promised payment had been reduced thrice, with hearth taxes to the local nobleman and clerical tithes to the local church. And then with the swindle that had cut their already-reduced earnings in half. Maja's father had taught her how to cut tesserae, how to mix mortar, and how to arrange pieces of stone into the form of a divine face. But he hadn't prepared her for taxes and dishonest patrons.

Luka pointed. "That one looks like someone lives there."

"I'll check while you rest." Maja strode through the swinging gate of a fence. A fence in good repair, which was unfortunate, because she could have offered to fix one that was broken. Fences weren't the same as mosaics, but mosaicists had to be competent woodworkers if they wanted scaffolding so they could decorate walls above the level of their reach.

No animals wandered the village yard, but wisps of smoke escaped the chimney, so she wasn't surprised when her knock was answered by a middle-aged man.

"Yes?" His deep voice sounded worn, as if he'd been ill recently.

"Hello, sir. My brother and I would like to earn some food. Do you have any chores we could do for you?"

The man shook his head. "It still freezes at night. It's too early for spring planting."

Maja knew that quite well. She'd woken covered in a layer of frost more nights than she hadn't lately. "I have skill with wood, if your home is in need of any repairs."

He scoffed, as if he didn't think she was capable of repairing a home. "I've had all winter to repair my home. But spring is a hungry time. Not much of last year's harvest remains, and nothing new is yet growing. I can't give out food when I don't need any work."

Maja swallowed. She glanced back at Luka's gaunt face and made her decision. "A trade, then?" She pulled one of the trowels out of her bag and showed the man. It would be easier to replace than the chisel or hammer.

"I don't need something like that."

"Do you think anyone else in your village would have work? Or be willing to make a trade?"

The man crossed his arms and smiled as he looked her over from head to foot. "Our village was small to begin with. Then a fever swept through in the dead of winter, killed most everyone. All the other survivors left to start somewhere new."

Why would he smile while speaking of a fever that had killed or driven off all his neighbors?

"I'm the only one left, and it's been lonely. But that's to your favor, because I've thought of a way for you to earn some food." He reached for her blonde braid sticking out from under her hair veil—the fabric still stained by Luka's blood despite her attempts to wash it. The man's dirt-crusted fingers stroked her hair.

Maja froze as fear joined the hunger gnawing at her stomach, and it was suddenly hard to breathe.

The man jerked his chin up and tossed his words over her head. "Stay out here. I've a task for your sister, and then I'll feed you both." He dropped Maja's hair and took her hand, tugging her toward him.

Maja pulled back. She wanted food, but she hadn't intended to sell her body for it. "How much food?" she asked. She wasn't agreeing to the man's suggestion, but she was desperate enough to learn his full offer.

His lustful eyes wandered over her skin again, just like the Turkish ghazi had near Pločnik. "That depends a little on you."

"The answer is no." Luka hobbled up to stand at Maja's side. The man was big enough to give her brother another cut across the head, but Luka's expression showed rage more than fear.

Amusement pulled at the man's mouth. "Does the boy speak for you?"

Maja's throat was too dry to answer, but she nodded.

The man looked her over again. "You know where to find me when you change your mind."

"We won't change our minds," Luka said.

The man ignored Luka, focusing on Maja. "I give the lad two days, at most. When he dies, come back. I'll even feed you first." He chuckled and closed the door.

Maja swallowed back a swirl of emotions. Distaste. Humiliation. Fear. Disgust, for herself and for the man. And pride that Luka had stood up to someone three times bigger than he.

Her brother gave her hand a tug, but he didn't speak until they latched the man's gate behind them. "Don't ever do something like that, Maja."

She inhaled. His words were part rebuke, part plea. It had all happened too fast, before she could think anything through. Hard choices were best made when there was time to prepare for them. When thrown upon her, unexpected, they left her overwhelmed and uncertain. She swallowed a few times, trying to work moisture back into her throat. "I didn't suggest it. And I didn't agree to it." She glanced back at the house. "But what if that's our only option?"

"There's always more than one option."

"And what if the choice is him or watching you starve and die?" After seeing her parents slaughtered, Maja had vowed to protect her brother. When she had made that vow, she had thought it might mean killing the ghazis holding Luka captive, maybe dying in the process. Was lying with a man so her brother could eat any worse of a sin? She hadn't considered the offer because she was wicked, only because she was desperate.

Luka limped forward. "Don't ever do *that* for my sake. Besides, I'm not about to die." His stomach growled, as if pointing out the lie. "We'll find something."

Tears pricked Maja's eyes. She had tried so hard not to cry in front of Luka, but all those sensations remained. Horror, embarrassment, revulsion. And gratitude that her little brother had protected her when she hadn't been sure how to protect him. She used her hair veil to dry her tears. Luka had been brave. She would be too. "Yes, we'll find something."

The next day, little had improved. Luka's stride was slower, and he no longer spoke. Maja's stomach ached with a sharpness she'd never before experienced, and her head spun with dizziness. They had searched all the abandoned homes in the village, hoping that someone had left something behind that they could eat. But Maja suspected the man who'd offered her his bed had already gone through all the homes and taken anything useful.

They had walked until it was dark the night before because they hadn't wanted to sleep near the village. They had woken that morning before dawn, too cold to stay asleep. They had water, and they had each other. But food was nowhere to be found, and hope seemed almost as elusive.

They trudged on, resting often as determination faded into weakness. She found more dandelions to eat, but it was still too cold for them to be out in sufficient quantities to build up their strength. For today, perhaps, the meager harvest would keep them from becoming delirious.

When the sun approached its zenith, Maja heard horse hooves coming up behind them. Not so many days ago, she would have rejoiced at the sight of other travelers and asked them for food. Now fear lanced through her—Maja and Luka were even more helpless than they'd been when the first group of bandits had assaulted them. A glance behind showed seven men who looked like warriors. Or maybe brigands. Either way, that made them dangerous. She glanced at her bare ankles sticking out from the bottom of her too-short tunic. She didn't regret ripping it to make a bandage for Luka, but she wished the thieves hadn't stolen her good tunic, the one that properly covered her legs.

Maja and Luka moved off the road to let the riders pass, but the men slowed as they approached.

The one in the lead, a stately man with a touch of silver at his temples, gave them a look of concern. "Children, why do you travel alone so far from any village? Don't you know these parts are infested with brigands?"

Maja lowered her head in respect. She almost told them she was no longer a child but then thought better of it. It was wiser not to point out that she was an unescorted, unprotected maiden. Ghazis and merophs in abandoned villages both wanted something from her that she didn't want to give. Would warriors be the same? "We learned that the hard way, sir. We were set upon by thieves seven days ago and have had little to eat since. Could you spare some food? We have valuable stones with which we can trade." She hoped they would take the tesserae. If not, she would have to offer up her father's tools.

One of the other men had dismounted and walked to Luka, his eyes on the dirty bandage. "Has his wound been treated?"

She recognized first the voice, then the face. Shiny black hair, a neat beard, olive skin, and muscled arms. It was *him*. Her mind flew back to the last words he had spoken to them in a little village near Pločnik as he'd cut her, Luka, and a dozen village boys free of their ropes. *It's all right. You're safe now. The main Ottoman Army has been routed, and we'll chase the rest of these ghazis away soon. The priest is gathering everyone at the church, and he'll make sure you're cared for.* He had been covered in the blood and dust of battle, but his hands had been gentle and his words kind.

It had been the worst day of her life. She had seen her parents slain before her eyes, and though she hadn't understood the Turkish words spoken by her captor, she had guessed her intended fate—and feared it—by the way the infidel had looked at her and stroked her face and hair.

The Serb warrior standing before her now had lived in her memory ever since Pločnik as an angel who had saved her from a fate worse than death.

"His wound," the man said. "Does it need care?"

Maja drew her mind back to the present. "I washed it with water and dressed it with part of my tunic. A woman used a poultice soon after he was attacked, and a healer bled him to restore his humors. But he is still dizzy. And something is wrong with his leg."

"May I look at it?" the man asked Luka.

Luka must have recognized the man, too, because his eyes were wide, and he looked up with awe. But he wasn't so dumbstruck that he couldn't nod his consent.

Their hero from Pločnik folded back the makeshift bandage. Luka clenched his jaw, so despite the man's gentleness, it must have hurt. Maja took her brother's hand to comfort him.

Perhaps their one-time rescuer took it as a sign of worry, because he addressed her. "I promise I won't hurt him, least not any more than is needed to treat his wound."

"I know you won't."

One of his eyebrows drew up as if to question her sudden, absolute trust. Another of the warriors approached them with slices of boukellaton. The one she recognized from Pločnik spoke to her again. "Eat. I'll care for the lad. Your brother?"

Maja nodded. She took the offered food and did her best to eat with decorum. Had they given her anything less hard, she would have been sorely tempted to wolf it down in an instant. She had never before known hunger this fierce.

The man tending Luka drew a cry when he washed the wound with wine, but the oil he put on it next seemed to soothe the pain, and then Luka sat next to her, boukellaton in hand, as the man examined his leg and wrapped it in thick strips of cloth from one of the pack mules.

Luka didn't attempt to hide his hunger. He used their waterskin to drench the dried piece of bread, then ate it in four gulps.

The group's leader laughed at Luka's quick meal. "So you were set upon by thieves? How many?"

"Just two." Maja took the water from Luka and washed down the last of her barley loaf. She accepted another slice with gratitude when one of the men offered it. "I was filling our water skins, so we were separated."

"Have you no parents?"

"Dead, sir."

He frowned. "These are dangerous lands to pass through without weapons."

"The man who gave us directions forgot to mention that." The priest had been kind, so she didn't think he'd meant to send them anywhere hazardous. They had just been vulnerable and unlucky.

"Where are you going?" he asked.

"Sivi Gora. We are mosaicists, and we hope to find work at the new church being built there."

The leader smiled. "Do you hear that, Danilo? They want to decorate Župan Ivan's church."

Their savior from Pločnik now had a name: Danilo. Maja watched him for a reaction.

"You are walking to Sivi Gora?" Danilo folded his arms across his chest.

"That is our plan." Most villages were too small to invest in a mosaic for their church. That left towns and cities, and the chance to work on a church like the one being built by the wealthy župan sounded like an opportunity that came along only rarely.

Danilo looked along the horses and dismounted warriors, then gestured to their leader and slowly walked away. The man followed, and the two had a quiet conversation. When they returned, Danilo stopped in front of her. "I am also traveling to Sivi Gora, but we don't travel there directly. We ride to the border with Hungary. Eventually, our group will split. I'll head for Sivi Gora." He gestured to the leader. "Miloš and the others will travel on to Kruševac. I don't expect to reach Sivi Gora for at least a fortnight, but given your brother's injuries, it would probably take you at least that long to walk. If you like, and if you're willing to work, you can travel with us. You won't get to Sivi Gora any sooner, but you won't have to travel alone."

Luka looked to Maja to answer. For days, she had been begging God for help. He seemed to have granted it, so her decision was easy to make. "Thank you. Our hands are willing, and we would be glad to travel with a larger group."

"Do you cook?" one of the other men asked, a young one who had yet to grow a beard.

"A little." Maja could prepare porridge and pluck chickens. She could even bake bread, but only in an oven, and the group didn't look to have one among the supplies on their mules.

Danilo huffed. "The only thing we have to cook is boukellaton. The girl can fetch water, and the boy can help with the horses. Do you know how to groom a horse?" He looked down at Luka.

Luka hesitated. "I can learn."

The beardless man shook his head. "It doesn't sound like we're getting all that much from the arrangement."

Maja didn't want to be a burden, but she was desperate for them not to revoke their offer. She racked her brain, trying to think of something she could offer. "I can wash clothing. And draw portraits." She doubted the last would be helpful. "I can milk goats and make cheese or gather firewood and stir pots of soup."

Danilo held a hand out. "Don't be overly concerned with debts and payments. It is our duty to help a stranger in need. We only ask that you pitch in when you can."

"Then why did you insist they work for their passage?" the beardless one asked.

"There's a quote. From a saint, I think: When you find someone in need, offer them a way to earn their food and shelter. Then both giver and receiver are blessed."

"I've never heard that before. Which saint said it?"

Danilo shrugged. "Perhaps it wasn't a saint after all. Maybe it was only my župan."

Their leader, Miloš, broke in. "It's wise, regardless of who said it. But we'd best continue. I'd like to be clear of the forest before nightfall."

Maja and Luka finished their boukellaton and helped draw water from a nearby creek for the horses.

"Here, let me." Danilo took one of the heavy buckets from her as she stepped from the water's edge. "I didn't catch your names. I'm Danilo. That's Miloš, Tihomir, Darko, Viktor, Filip, and Ivo." He pointed to the other men in turn.

Maja would never forget Danilo's name. Not after he'd saved her twice. "Maja and Luka Dinić, but we want to earn our keep. We don't seek to live off charity."

Danilo smiled. Goodness, he was handsome, and he wielded the bucket as if it weighed no more than a twig. Each step with its weight had been a struggle for her, and she was stronger than most women. Or she had been before she and Luka had been robbed and gone hungry for so long.

"Your brother should rest until he's healed. The alignment of his leg hasn't been changed, but for it to still be so tender this long after the injury . . . It could be broken."

Broken? She was glad she hadn't pushed him any harder than she had. "But I'm not injured."

"Do you ride often?"

"No." She had ridden a horse before but never for long and not recently.

"Then let me draw the water. I expect your legs will be sore by the end of the day. No need to make your arms sore as well." His lips curved upward again, and he swung the bucket before a stallion, holding it with one hand while the horse drank and stroking the horse's forehead with his other hand while he spoke something soothing.

Not knowing what else to do, Maja watched as Danilo finished watering the horses, then repositioned the supplies until there were two mules without packs. He saddled them and brought them over to Luka and Maja.

"These two are gentle. They're trained to follow the group, so you won't need to guide them." He brought the smaller one to Luka and lifted Luka up. Then he turned to Maja.

"What should we do with our packs?" she asked.

Danilo took them from her. "Heavier than they look. What do you have in here?"

"My father's tools. And tesserae. And pieces of stone we could turn into tesserae."

"Tesserae. The bits that make up a mosaic?"

Maja nodded. "Yes. That's our trade."

Danilo fastened the tools onto the back of Luka's mule.

"Come on, Danilo," Filip called. "The rest of us are ready."

Danilo turned with a scowl. "We'll catch up." He fastened the other bundle on the back of another mule. Then he spoke to Maja. "This one's for you. Do you need help up?"

Maja shook her head. She had never been wealthy enough to own an animal for riding, but she had seen riders use stirrups to mount before. She thought through the process. She was on the left side, so she would need to put her left foot in first, then swing her right foot over. It worked fine in her mind, but when she tried it, her tunic made the swinging aspect of the mount difficult, and Danilo had to reach up to keep her from falling.

"Sorry." She felt her face go hot. She probably looked ridiculous.

"Are you on now? We don't want you falling off along the way."

"Yes, I'm on."

Danilo looked her over. "Hold on, then." He clicked his tongue and slapped the mule forward.

Maja lurched back but kept hold of the pommel. She thought she heard Danilo chuckling. He had a pleasant laugh, and though she was mortified to be the cause of it, the far more powerful emotion was gratitude. She had done everything she could to help herself and her brother, and none of it had been enough. Danilo had once again delivered her.

From time to time, Danilo checked on Maja and Luka as they rode that afternoon and evening. He also took his turn scouting ahead to check for danger and scouting behind to see if the mysterious man he'd noticed yesterday still tailed them. When he'd discussed it with Miloš, they'd decided not to provoke their shadow. Danilo caught a glimpse of him again when he scouted behind at the tenth hour but didn't pursue him. He didn't want to be led into an ambush. But he couldn't help wondering why the man was following them, trying to stay hidden.

They stopped to make camp at the eleventh hour. Danilo went to the artists. Since neither was accustomed to spending an entire afternoon in the saddle, they might need help dismounting. Luka winced as he crawled off and tottered as his feet found earth.

Danilo held out a hand to steady him. "How does your head feel? Any worse?"

"My legs are so sore that it's easy to forget my head."

Danilo wasn't a healer, but Ivan's wife was, and he'd seen her work often enough to know which warning signs he should look for. He felt the boy's forehead. The temperature seemed normal. He bent down to feel the boy's toes as well and to check their color. He tapped the lad's feet. "Can you feel that?"

Luka nodded.

Danilo looked up to see Maja watching them. She set her mouth and looked around as if trying to determine how to best get off the mule.

"Let me help," Danilo said. "Take your left foot from the stirrup and swing it over the mule's rump. You might have to hike your tunic up a bit."

She did her best to follow his directions, wincing as she moved. The mule stepped to the side, making her lose her balance, so Danilo reached up and caught her around the waist.

"There you are," he said when he'd lowered her to the ground.

"Thank you." She stumbled a bit, almost falling into him.

He offered her his arm. He didn't envy her. Danilo was on a horse most days, and his legs were weary. He could imagine how tender her legs must be when she wasn't used to riding.

While she was close, he let himself look at her more thoroughly. When he'd first seen her, back bent under the weight of her packs and ankles visible under her too-short tunic, he'd thought her younger. But she was certainly a woman, with golden braids, bright-blue eyes, smooth skin, and strangely inviting lips. Danilo had seen sacks of flour that sat a mule with more grace, and her legs wavered like those of a drunk, but she was beautiful.

He coughed lightly, trying to clear his head. He had other things to worry about, like who was following them. And what he could say to the Hungarian ispán Janos Bokori to gain his friendship, or at least his neutrality. And how they could defeat the army Sultan Murad would send against them. "If you walk around a bit, it should help with the soreness. As much as I'd like to say otherwise, tomorrow will probably be worse."

"It won't be as bad as seeing my brother lying on the side of the road bleeding." Maja steadied herself and released Danilo's arm. "Thank you for taking us. We're grateful to have your help again."

"Again?"

Her vibrant eyes studied him for a moment. "You don't remember us, do you?"

Danilo searched his memory. He was certain he would remember an introduction with someone as pretty as Maja, but she and the boy were strangers to him. "We've met before?"

Luka limped closer. "We were held captive by a group of ghazis. You cut us free after the battle near Pločnik."

So much had happened that day. The battle, the push to drive the ghazis away, his errand with Ivan to find Ivan's lost love. Somewhere in his mind was a vague recollection of cutting free a group of captives in a little village, but that had been nearly three years ago. "You were captives of Iskandar bin Abdullah?"

"There were several of them. We never learned their names." Maja folded her arms and grew still, as if fear of the ghazis still haunted her.

"Was their leader about thirty years of age, perhaps a bit more? Medium build and height? Black hair under a white turban and blue robes under leather armor? Favoring one arm because it had recently been wounded?" Danilo didn't enumerate Iskandar's other traits—sneaky, clever, persistent, and dangerous.

Maja's eyes widened, and she slowly nodded.

"I just remember the one Maja skewered with a spear." Luka mimed the thrust. "He had a scar on his wrist. I noticed it when he held his sword to my throat after I broke his nose with my elbow."

"Broken noses and impalements with spears?" Danilo smiled as he unbuckled the saddle on Maja's mule. "You two are a pair to be reckoned with." They seemed subdued now, but he admired their mettle.

"I should help. Tell me what to do." Maja reached for the saddle.

"Help your brother find a comfortable place to sit, then walk around a bit so you won't be quite so sore tomorrow. Just stay where you can see us and we can see you." He didn't think their pursuer would come close enough to harm Maja or Luka, but Danilo would feel better if they stayed nearby.

Maja seemed to hesitate. "The ghazi . . . Iskandar. What happened to him?"

"We took him prisoner. Then we sold him to a man from Venice."

She nodded, considering it. "So he may still live?"

"Yes. That concerns you?"

She looked to the ground, her shoulders tense and her jaw clamped tight, but not before he noticed a tremble. Worry? Horror?

He fought the impulse to comfort her with physical touch. Instead, he offered words. "Of course it concerns you. You wouldn't have asked otherwise."

She inhaled deeply. "I suppose he would have taken the boys as slaves or trained them as janissaries. But I think he intended to take me to his tent." Another shiver of fear shook her frame.

"Did he . . . ?" Danilo thought better of his question, especially with Luka listening to every word. "Did he hurt you?"

"He just scared me."

"Well, he's probably in Venice harvesting crops or shuttling rich merchants around the lagoon. He can't hurt you now."

She nodded. "Thanks to you."

"I am glad to have frustrated Iskandar's dishonorable intentions." Sometimes Danilo questioned their decision to let Iskandar live. He wasn't a threat now, and yet having Iskandar as a sworn enemy often darkened his mind the way an approaching storm cloud darkened the plains. He and Maja had something in common—Iskandar seemed to haunt them both. "I apologize for not remembering you. Much happened at Pločnik."

"You rescued many people that day. We had only one hero. After all the cries of panic and screams of terror, to hear your voice instead, speaking my language with kindness instead of fear . . . Being saved from slavery . . . It's not easy to forget."

The strength of her gratitude was almost tangible. It made him wish he could have done more, stopped the ghazis earlier, before they'd attacked the village. But had the Serb army dispersed to meet the raiders, they wouldn't have been able to defeat the main Ottoman force, and had the Serbs lost, the villages would have been pillaged in the aftermath. With either strategy, Maja's village had been doomed.

The camp around them was a bustle of activity as his companions erected tents and tended horses. The thump of a hammer pounding a stake into the ground drew Danilo's attention. He had been distracted by Maja and her brother for too long and needed to do his part.

"Here." He motioned for Maja to follow him to one of the other pack mules, where he retrieved a javelin. "Take this while you walk. Just in case you need to spear anyone."

She accepted it readily, with a slight smile. Her hands weren't the delicate hands of a noblewoman. They were covered with calluses, and Danilo doubted many noblewomen could stab a Turk, even in defense of a sibling. Fighting for the weak against an overwhelming enemy took spirit, and if the siblings' stories were right, she also had at least a bit of skill. He watched her walk to Luka. Spirit, skill, and, for the night at least, clumsy legs.

She wouldn't need a weapon while traveling with Danilo and the other six who rode with him. He would rush to her side in a moment if anyone threatened her, but maybe she needed to know she could protect herself.

Danilo was still smiling when he went to speak with Miloš, but he quickly schooled his features. "I saw him again."

"The same man as yesterday?" Miloš asked.

Danilo nodded. "I think so. Bearded, gray cloak, mail hauberk. He's trying to stay hidden. I couldn't tell if he knew he'd been spotted."

Miloš glanced around the tents. As he'd hoped, they'd made it out of the forest, where it would be harder for someone to infiltrate their camp. "We'll post double lookouts tonight. You and Darko take the first watch."

CHAPTER SEVEN
THE MUSIC OF HOPE

WERE DANILO REPORTING THE NEXT day's events to a župan, knez, or kral, he would have described them as uneventful. Yet that wasn't how they felt. He learned more about mosaics in one ride with the Dinić siblings than he'd learned in a lifetime of worshipping at churches in Rivak, Edirne, and Sivi Gora. And the sight of Maja wearing his cloak never failed to lift his mood.

He didn't see the spy on any of his scouting rides, but he shot a goose, and Tihomir, the youngest of Miloš's men-at-arms, snared a rabbit, so they ate well that night. The next day, they had poor luck and only boukellaton for their meals. Yet the new companions—full of gratitude and eagerness to help, made the meal feel like a celebration.

The next morning, when Maja directed her mule next to Dazhbog, Danilo smiled at her approach. She was getting better at controlling her animal, yet she seemed nervous.

"I think someone is following us," she said.

"A man wearing a hauberk under a gray mantle?"

Her mouth pulled with worry. "Maybe. I couldn't see him clearly. But you know of him?"

Danilo nodded, surprised she'd seen him when he hadn't. "We've noticed him off and on since we left Bosnia. He's never been close enough for us to question, so we're not sure who he's spying for."

Maja looked behind them. "You think he's a spy? What will you do?"

"What we've done every night. Post watchmen. You've noticed that Tihomir disappears for a few hours from time to time?"

"And you. You disappear on occasion as well."

"We're scouting ahead. Making sure no one intends to ambush us."

She looked behind them again, and he feared he'd aggravated rather than relieved her concern.

"I'm sorry," he said. "I suppose you aren't much safer with us than you were on your own. We have enemies. But I don't think this one is of the Ottoman variety. If I had to guess, I'd suspect a Hungarian."

"When I was young, my father made a mosaic in a church in Hungary." Maja kept looking about. If she continued, she might upset her mount.

"One that followed the Latin rite?"

"Yes." She turned her gaze on him, and her mouth pulled into a pleasant smile. "I got into a fistfight when one of the local boys called me a schismatic."

"Did you win?" He pictured her as a young girl, hands balled into fists and her graceful face drawn up in a scowl of indignation.

"Our fathers broke it up before it went very far. But later that night, my father told me that next time, I should punch harder. He said if you're forced into a fight and it's something worth fighting for, you have to do whatever it takes to win."

Danilo cast his eyes about and saw no sign of the spy. But he thought of Maja's words and of what it might take to win the next time they were forced to fight the Turks.

"Did you ever get into fights as a boy?" she asked.

"Not many. I grew up with cousins. Kostya was so much older than I was that we didn't get into scuffles, and he was intimidating enough to scare away any bullies who might have tried picking a fight with me. Lidija was also older than I, but we never quarreled. Ivan, on the other hand, was a year younger than I, and we were almost inseparable. But he got camp fever when he was four, and he was frail. He usually couldn't stay outside to play long enough for us to quarrel. Even on his good days, I was older and stronger, and it would have been wrong to swing my fists at him, no matter how stubborn he was."

"I would have liked to have cousins. I have Luka, of course. And I had a sister, younger than I. She died of a fever when we were small."

"I'm sorry." Danilo had no siblings, but when Lidija died in childbirth, it had been like losing a sister.

Maja shifted in her saddle again. "It was a long time ago. Did your frail cousin recover?"

"Yes. He's the one who captured Iskandar at Pločnik. Do you remember him?"

"No."

"Well, you'll meet him soon enough, as long as we aren't ambushed before we reach Sivi Gora. I'd best tell Miloš that our spy has returned." Danilo nudged his horse into a trot until he was even with Miloš. Maja stayed toward the back of the group, near Luka and the pack animals.

"She seems to enjoy your company." Miloš glanced back at Maja, then at Danilo. "Have you thought of remarrying?"

Danilo chuckled. He enjoyed Maja's company, admired her spirit, and had found himself gazing far too often at her attractive face and form, but he didn't have time for courtship. He had to figure out how to keep Sivi Gora and the rest of Serbia free when the Ottomans attacked again. "I'm cursed, remember? As is anyone who marries me."

"That rumor was nonsense. Sometimes women die in childbirth. If it's because of a curse, it's the curse that comes with being mortal."

"Be that as it may, we've only known each other a few days." She had memory of an earlier meeting, but he couldn't recall her face from the village near Pločnik. Even if he did remember, a quick conversation on the battlefield hardly counted as a proper introduction.

"Sometimes it doesn't take long. Besides, she has no sister to stir up contention. I think that rather balances out her status as a craftswoman rather than a noblewoman."

"I think most women get along better with their sisters than your wife and Vuk's wife. But, Miloš, please be careful what you say. She's had enough hardship. I don't want her reputation harmed by rumors."

"Would you deny an old man his right to tease?" Miloš raised one eyebrow in question.

"You aren't old." Miloš might have a few gray hairs in his beard and along his temples, but he still had strength and vigor. Danilo wouldn't want to cross swords with him. "But you should leave matchmaking to the women."

"I'll let my wife know. She'd be delighted to arrange a match between you and Maja. She could probably find a girl for the brother too. He's on the young side, but seems like he'll be sturdy enough once his leg heals."

If Danilo resisted, Miloš would only push harder. Danilo had married a stranger before, and it had turned out well, at least for a time. But what if he really was cursed? Best to keep the list of victims as it was now, with Tatjana and the baby. He wasn't sure he could take the heartache of finding and then losing another woman. "We'll reach Sivi Gora before we reach your lands. I'm afraid your wife won't have the chance to play matchmaker. And our spy is back. Maja saw him."

"Do you suppose Tvrtko sent him? Or Sigismund?"

"Kral Tvrtko knows our purpose and that we are of little danger to him. Why would we attack to the west when we expect war in the east? I'd wager it's the Hungarians. Sigismund has imperial ambitions, and he's unlikely to bring them to fruition unless he keeps his eyes on potential enemies."

"I've half a mind to capture him, whoever he is." Miloš frowned. "But that might make an enemy. And the purpose of our travels is to gather friends. We'll have to continue on as we've done. Cautious, so we don't provoke a hostile response."

Maja was relieved when they stopped early that night, though she worried about the spy. She managed to get off her mule by herself, and it took only a dozen steps until she could walk normally.

"Are you all right?" she asked Luka.

He climbed off his mount. "Sore. I always thought it would be nice to ride all day. Be a warrior. Now I'm not so sure."

Danilo came to check on them, as seemed to be his habit now. "Let's have another look at that head of yours, Luka."

Luka frowned but held still. It probably hurt, having the bandages changed, but Danilo had explained that it was important to keep the wound clean. It had made considerable progress since Danilo had begun tending it. He seemed knowledgeable about so many things—healing, riding, battles, religion, and how to make two frightened strangers feel welcome and safe.

Maja watched him treat Luka for two reasons: First, she wanted to learn in case there was ever a need for her to care for someone with a similar injury. Second, because everything Danilo did pulled at her interest.

Danilo had Luka sit so he could check his leg again too. As Danilo finished, Luka's stomach growled.

Danilo's expression twisted in amusement. "Hungry?"

Embarrassment colored Luka's cheeks.

"He's twelve. He's always hungry." Maja smiled at her brother, then sobered. "And the time since we were robbed has been difficult. They took all our food and all our money. One woman fed us, but most of the time, we had very little to eat."

Danilo stood and offered a hand to Luka to help him to his feet. "Tihomir and Darko went hunting. Perhaps they'll get lucky, and we'll eat well tonight. In the meantime, I'll grab you some boukellaton. Come on."

Luka limped after Danilo, and Maja followed Luka. Danilo stopped by Dazhbog and pulled two pieces of bread from his saddlebags. He gave one to Luka and offered one to Maja.

"I can wait." She hadn't meant to follow him like a beggar.

"I'm sure you can, but you don't have to." He held it out to her again, and those dark eyes of his held nothing but generosity. "You were almost starving for a week, weren't you?"

Maja accepted the bread, just as she had accepted kindness after kindness from him. Danilo seemed too good to be true, yet there he was, handsome, strong, attentive, and generous.

"Is that your bow?" Luka pointed to the long, polished shaft partially hidden by a bow case attached to the saddle.

Danilo nodded.

"Do you think you could teach me? If the Turks ever come near again, I want to be able to fight them."

Danilo considered the request for a moment before taking the bow from its case and stringing it. "It's not something you can learn in one evening, but we've some time on the road, and you'll be welcome to practice in Sivi Gora. Come on."

Danilo stopped at one of the packs and grabbed another bow. Then he took Luka to the edge of the campsite so any stray shots wouldn't interfere with the animals or the campfire Miloš and Filip were building. Maja was tempted to follow Danilo and her brother, but she also wanted to earn her keep, so she gathered firewood instead.

"Thank you, Maja." Miloš took a few pieces from her pile and added them to the kindling he'd just lit. Despite being the group's leader, he seemed to do as much work as any of his men. "You aren't interested in archery?"

Maja gazed at her brother and Danilo. "I am. I've seen the Turks, and I would very much like the ability to defend myself should I see them again. But I do not wish to be more of a burden than I already am."

"You're not a burden." Miloš poked the fire with a twig. Even a move as simple as that showed his ample strength. "It's a pleasure to have a young woman along. If you're interested, you ought to go learn. You'd be hard-pressed to find a teacher more able than Danilo." He looked up at her with a bit of a twinkle in his eyes.

Did he suspect that Maja was attracted to the man from Sivi Gora? She felt her face heat. Had she made her interest so obvious? But she would like to learn more about archery. Had she been armed the day her parents were killed, perhaps she could have prevented their deaths. And learning more about the skill could help her portray it better should she ever make a mosaic with an archer. It would be foolish, on both practical and artistic grounds, to pass up such an opportunity.

Danilo noticed her approach when she was still several paces away. He smiled in question.

"Do you . . . Do you think you could teach me?"

His smile deepened. "I can try." He handed her his own bow. It stretched from her shins to her armpits. "We'll start with shooting. I don't think you could string this one, but I don't want to take the other one from Luka just yet."

Luka looked back at her and grinned, then loosed an arrow. It flew into a tree about five paces away.

"Pull it back all the way to your ear. Otherwise it won't have enough force to break through Turkish armor."

Luka tried again, straining, but he made it to his cheek.

"That's better. Keep practicing so you build up the right muscles." Danilo turned to her. "Go ahead and draw it back. Without an arrow at first, but don't let the string snap. If there's no arrow to take the force, it damages the bow."

Maja nodded. "I understand. Tools must be properly cared for."

"That's right. Put your left hand here." He guided her hand to the center of the bow. "Hold it out." He lifted her hand and the bow, his touch firm but not overbearing. Something about his fingers on her skin made it harder to breathe, but she couldn't figure out why. "See how far you can pull the string back. But don't snap it."

She was gentle at first, not wanting to be rough with his weapon. But she hardly moved the string at all. His quickly smothered laughter convinced her to pull harder, but she still couldn't get the string to her face, and the more she pulled, the more difficult it became. She held it for a breath, then slowly released it.

"That might be a large enough draw to shoot someone without armor about ten paces away."

Maja tried again but couldn't go any farther than before.

"Tomorrow, I'll find a different bowstring. One that's not so tight."

"What will a looser bowstring do?" She glanced back at his dark eyes, a rich brown surrounded by thick lashes.

"It will be easier to pull back. But it won't launch the arrow as hard or as far. There are smaller bows in Sivi Gora. They might work better for you."

"Bows for boys?" Maja looked at Danilo's weapon. It was a bow for a man and best wielded by someone with a man's strength.

"This one does have a significant draw weight. It's not really meant for beginners."

Maja found herself watching his lips as he spoke. They were more expressive than most lips. Was there a way to capture them in a mosaic? She would have to ponder on it because it wasn't just the shape; it was more the way they moved.

"Here, I'll show you how it's done with an arrow." Danilo reached for his bow, and she handed it to him. "You find the slit in the wood of the arrow, back here, and slide it onto the bowstring. That's called nocking the arrow. Your hold supports the arrow next to the bow with the left hand, then with the right, you draw back and release." He loosed the arrow, hitting the tree precisely in the center.

"What about aiming?"

He frowned. "I suppose once you've done it for twenty years, the aiming part is more reflex."

"Twenty years? You can't have been taller than the bow when you started."

He lifted the bow slightly. "I didn't start with one this big. But I've heard that far to the west, they use bows as tall as a grown man. They're easier to build. Just one piece of wood. Yew, I think. But not easy to use from horseback."

"What is yours made of?"

"Maple, ibex horn, and deer sinew." He loosened the laces of his leather bracer and pulled it over his hand. "Put this on to protect your arm."

Maja slid it onto her left arm, the one that would hold the arrow. It was too large for her forearm, but she adjusted the laces so she could make the leather overlap, then pulled it snug.

Danilo nodded his approval and handed her the bow again. "Try nocking it." He passed an arrow over to her.

She slipped the back of the arrow onto the string, then pointed the tip at the same tree Luka was trying to hit. She pulled the string back, released, and the arrow shot almost straight up.

Danilo watched its flight. "Try again. This time, keep your shoulder straight, and don't drop your elbow. Like this." He stepped behind her and, with one arm, held the bow just below her hand. Warmth from his skin seemed to spread through her entire arm. Then he reached around and helped her draw the string back to her cheek. "Now release." His whisper was right next to her ear, and the ends of his beard tickled her neck.

The arrow hit the tree. He nodded and stepped back a bit. He had been so close. Normally, having a man right next to her would leave her feeling intimidated. But Danilo's arms, though strong, hadn't been threatening. There was something about him, some presence that she noticed even when he was distant from her. And if she was honest with herself, she liked it, whatever it was.

Danilo moved between her and Luka over the next while, encouraging them to hold their elbows in better positions and gently guiding her shoulder back. Danilo's bow was too powerful for her to use properly, but she gathered the basic idea, at least from an artistic perspective, and recognized how much effort it would take if she ever wanted to be a competent archer. Mastering the bow was a new ambition for her, but now that the ability to defend herself and her brother was suddenly a possibility, she would gladly sacrifice time and energy to attain it.

Darko and Tihomir returned from their hunt. Darko carried a pheasant and Tihomir carried a hare.

Tihomir paused long enough to watch Luka hit the tree, but only from about eight paces away. "Is Sivi Gora so desperate for archers that you're training artisans and women now?" He grinned as he spoke.

Danilo's mouth formed a charming sort of pout. "They've seen ghazis in action before. They'd like to be able to shoot back should they ever see them again."

Maja handed Danilo his bow and began loosening the borrowed bracer. "I thank you for the lesson. I should help prepare the food. I can pluck the pheasant at least." She would have rather stayed, would have rather had Danilo reaching around to help her draw back the arrow again and again, but she didn't want to shirk her promise to help the men who had welcomed her and Luka into their group.

That night felt like a feast. She hadn't intended to, but she found herself sitting by Danilo as they ate. Tihomir had offered her one of the juicy hare legs, and as she finished it, she realized that for the first time since finishing her last commission, hunger had kept its distance the entire day, until the enticing smell of roasting hare and pheasant had met her nose over the campfire.

When the meal ended, Miloš sent Darko and Viktor to stand the first watch. Though it was dark, no one who remained in their camp seemed eager to sleep.

"Did you bring your gusle, Danilo?" Miloš asked.

"No."

"You can use mine," Tihomir said. "I'm trying to learn because my wife loves music, but I'm not any good. Perhaps you can teach the gusle as well as you teach archery." Tihomir went to his pack and soon returned with the small wooden instrument and the bow to play it with.

Danilo accepted it and tested the string.

"Will you sing as well?" Miloš asked.

Danilo looked surprised. "I haven't sung in years."

"But you have a fine voice. I remember." Miloš adjusted his legs to a more comfortable position. "Perhaps it's time for you to start again."

Danilo seemed sad for a moment, then ran the bow across the gusle. Maja recognized the tune.

So did Luka. "'St. George and the Dragon.' Maja knows that one."

"You sing?" Danilo asked, still playing.

Maja felt her face go warm again. "A little."

"Good, we'll have a duet." Miloš chuckled slightly.

"But I've never sung for anyone other than Luka or my parents."

"I don't usually sing for groups either," Danilo said. "But Miloš is son-by-marriage to the most powerful man in Serbia, so I am in the habit of honoring his wishes."

Danilo started the tune over again, playing an introduction. He glanced at her, and she nodded, and then they both began. "Near a town, there lived a dragon; it lived down by the lake . . ."

After the first few lines, the nervousness faded. Danilo's voice was soft but pleasant, and it mingled with her own in comfortable melody. Then they repeated the cycle with Danilo singing a countermelody. For a time, Maja forgot everyone else, focusing only on Danilo and his voice, his mouth, his music coming from the gusle. It had been a long time since she had felt so carefree, so light, so happy. Darkness gathered around the circle of travelers, but the firelight shone on Danilo, and his timbre filled her ears and her heart.

CHAPTER EIGHT
BOKORI'S FORTRESS

THE NEXT FOUR DAYS TOOK the group on long rides, but Miloš always ensured they stopped while there was ample time to set up camp, practice archery, and sing around the fire. Danilo saw the spy the first day but not the second or the third, and the day after, their group reached the fortified city that projected Hungarian influence to the south.

As Hungarian soldiers lowered the drawbridge, it became clear that Janos Bokori, the local ispán, had spared no efforts to display his strength. Stone walls surrounded the town, and men in full battle armor patrolled their lofty height. Bokori commanded the garrison, collected the taxes, and acted as the eyes and ears of Király Sigismund. Anyone who entered his city would be completely at his mercy. Danilo glanced at Maja and Luka—Maja a woman of rare beauty only partially masked by her tattered tunic and stained hair veil, Luka a lad with a determination that might get him into trouble. Danilo was uncomfortable bringing them along but more uncomfortable leaving them alone.

"Why is everyone so nervous?" Maja whispered.

"Because we aren't sure what to expect." Danilo watched the drawbridge. "Knez Lazar is nominally Király Sigismund's vassal, but only to keep his northern border at peace while he deals with the Ottomans. And Sigismund knows it's an arrangement of convenience. Quickly made, easily broken. We're here to affirm Lazar's loyalty. And if possible, to gain Sigismund's help against Murad."

"Is the király here?"

"No. Just one of his ispáns. Janos Bokori."

Maja studied the walls of the fortress.

"Try not to draw attention to yourself. Ghazis aren't the only sort of men who might take advantage of an unprotected woman."

Maja drew the cloak he'd given her more completely around her body. Her ankles and lower legs still showed, but there was nothing Danilo could do about that now. He'd developed a fondness for her and her brother since they'd joined the group. Part of it was their obvious need for a protector, but there was more to it than that. Their gratitude, their eagerness to help, their hope of a new commission in Sivi Gora. It was contagious. The more they treated him like a hero, the more he wanted to be heroic. He hoped his desire wasn't sinful or vain, but surely any companions who made him want to be better were a blessing to cherish. He looked forward to the nightly archery lessons more than he should, and he enjoyed the singing. He hadn't sung since his wife died, not until Miloš had made his request, but sitting beside Maja around the campfire, the music came easily.

As they rode past the party of armed men who had come to greet them, Danilo glanced again at Maja and Luka. He hoped bringing them would prove the wiser of his options. Danilo tried to force a mask of calm but wasn't sure he'd succeeded. Bokori's men gave off an air of competence, but there was little welcome in their eyes.

Danilo no longer felt like singing.

Maja sat with Luka in the courtyard of Bokori's castle. Their horses had been cared for and their baggage stored away, and then Danilo, Miloš, and the others had gone inside. Just before he'd walked out of sight, Danilo had looked back at her. Maja hadn't had anyone other than Luka looking out for her since her parents had died. Surviving on their own had been difficult, and the weight of responsibility had often left her feeling worn, aged before her time, like a fresco that had been exposed to too much weather. She'd missed that reassurance that someone else cared enough to help.

"We passed a church." Luka gestured along the road that led from the castle.

Maja had noticed. She always did. And they normally stopped to view religious artwork whenever they had opportunity, whether it was at a village shrine or an enormous cathedral. Studying the works of others helped them improve their own skill. But Danilo had told her not to draw attention. Traipsing around the fortified city seemed unwise. They would wait.

"Maja, let's go look," Luka said.

"You're supposed to be resting your leg."

"But the church isn't far. Going there wouldn't be any harder than walking around our campsites has been. With the way Danilo wrapped it, it hardly bothers me at all, even when I put weight on it."

"Danilo said we should blend in. I didn't see anyone in clothing as worn as ours when we rode in. We'll stick out, especially if they hear us speaking Slavonic. Danilo doesn't think the city is safe for us."

Luka chuckled. "You like him."

She felt her face grow hot. "I am grateful for his repeated kindness to us and respect his judgment. We would be wise to show caution when he recommends it."

Luka was right. She did like Danilo. After he'd saved them from Iskandar, she'd formed an image in her head of a brave knight, good to the core, strong, handsome, and gentle. Meeting him again had only proved the image true.

"That's all?" Luka asked. "Just gratitude and respect? No suspicion that he might feel the same?"

She hadn't thought it possible for her face to feel hotter, but the temperature seemed to double. "He's just a good man trying to help a pair of strangers in need. Once we get to Sivi Gora, I doubt we'll see much of him." And perhaps that was just as well. She had seen how quickly those she loved could be stolen away. Love led to pain, if not through death then through knowing her growing affection was unlikely to be returned.

"So, can we go see the church?"

"No. We can trust Danilo's advice."

Luka sulked, and the shadows grew longer. Maja had every intention of heeding Danilo's suggestion, but curiosity called to her too. Did the church have any mosaics? Any techniques she'd not yet seen? Most of the recent churches she'd studied had been in small villages. Some of the artists might have been influenced by the great works of Constantinople, but most were decorated by men who had learned the craft from their fathers. A Latin church in Hungary might have an entirely different influence from what she was familiar with, and she hated to walk past it and never see it. Maybe Danilo could take her there later, but she didn't know how long the negotiations would last, and she wasn't sure she could ask yet another favor of him. He'd already done so much for her.

"That man keeps looking at you." Luka pointed toward the battlements but kept his gesture hidden from everyone but her.

Maja waited a few moments before gazing along the wall. She didn't dare stare at the man for long, but she noted his chain-mail hauberk and his dark-brown beard. Experience had taught her that when a man looked at her that closely, it usually meant trouble. But she didn't want Luka to worry. "No doubt he noticed the poor state of my tunic and wonders why such a poorly clad woman is traveling with such accomplished warriors."

"I don't think that's why, Maja."

Luka was getting harder to fool. She should have known better than to try. She sneaked another look. "When did you first notice him?"

"It's been a while. He's been there about half the time since the others went inside. His eyes keep returning to you."

That meant he'd been watching them for close to an hour. Suddenly, a visit to the church seemed wise. The building was along the main road, and several hours of sunlight remained for them to travel there and back. And while Danilo had told her not to stand out, he hadn't told her she couldn't leave. "Let's go see that church."

Surprise crossed Luka's face, but it was quickly replaced by excitement. He might long to be a warrior, but the same passion for art that had run in their father's veins ran in Luka's.

Two guards stood at the gate, but they said nothing as Maja and Luka left. The sun had burned away most of the clouds, and the town seemed brighter and cleaner in the unfiltered light as they followed the road from the castle to the church. Were she ever asked to make a mosaic of a Hungarian city, she would emphasize the angles of the buildings and cast it in warm sunlight.

The inside of the church felt spacious. High, pointed arches lined the sides, and the long ceiling of the nave showed ribbed vaulting. It wasn't the finest church she had ever seen, but it was far grander than any she'd seen in years.

"There's a mosaic," Luka whispered and pointed.

Maja glanced around the church, empty save for a few women praying and a man consulting with the priest under a crucifix. "Let's have a look."

Janos Bokori seemed determined to find them in breach of their earlier agreement. Danilo tried to hide his frustration as the summit stretched into its fourth hour.

"You met with Tvrtko," Bokori said.

"Yes. We made no effort to conceal our visit." Miloš kept his voice calm and placating, but he had to be feeling the same frustration. "We expect an attack from Sultan Murad. Kral Tvrtko has fought with us against the Turks before. We seek his help again."

"Tvrtko has also fought against Király Sigismund." Bokori crossed his arms. "You could be allying with each other to attack the Turks. Or you could be conspiring to turn against Hungary. How are we to know which?"

Danilo wished Tvrtko and Sigismund didn't have such a turbulent past. But he couldn't erase the wars between Bosnia and Hungary any more than he could wish Murad out of the Balkans. "If I may?" he said, asking permission to speak.

Miloš nodded. Bokori shifted in his seat to face Danilo.

With so many eyes on him, Danilo hesitated, but only for a moment. "The Ottomans are expanding. They will attack again. If we hold them now, that is to Hungary's advantage. If we fail, Sultan Murad will continue on to Sigismund's lands. And we are stronger with Bosnia's aid, so our alliance with Tvrtko is also to your advantage."

Bokori considered it. "If Tvrtko has a friend to the east, what is to prevent him from expanding to the west?" It was no secret that Hungary held ambitions for the entire Adriatic coast, lands that had recently fallen to Tvrtko. "And what is to prevent him from stirring up trouble among our other vassals?"

Danilo walked a fine line. Only last summer Tvrtko had encouraged uprisings against Hungary in Wallachia and Moldovia. "Tvrtko's commitment to Lazar will keep him from more expansion into Hungarian lands because his army will be needed against Murad."

"Yes, but Lazar and Tvrtko once stood with Király Sigismund's enemies, the Horvatis, when they rebelled against their rightful king. That makes it hard for Sigismund to trust them."

Danilo didn't argue the point, but he did his best to explain it. "You must remember that Király Sigismund was but seventeen when he came to the throne. No one knew if he would hold it. Many questioned him then, but they do not do so now that he has proved his ability to rule."

Miloš spoke next. "And Kral Tvrtko helped negotiate the release of Sigismund's wife when his enemies held her prisoner."

"Only because Mary's mother is Tvrtko's cousin." Bokori didn't seem impressed.

"Regardless of the past, one fact remains." Danilo spoke firmly. "Sultan Murad is expanding. If we do not stand together, we will all fall separately."

Bokori glanced at his clerk as if to make sure he was recording everything. "Very well. You have made your arguments. I will pass on the relevant details to His Majesty Király Sigismund along with your request for our neutrality."

"We would be glad of your alliance." Miloš managed to convey both respect and iron with his words.

"I will tell His Majesty that as well. Now you are no doubt weary from your journey. We will share a meal at sundown. In the meantime, you are left at your leisure."

Bokori stood, and as he did, everyone in the room followed suit.

As Bokori and the Hungarian contingent left, Miloš turned to Danilo. "You're right, you know. If we don't stand together, we'll fall separately. My only worry is that Hungary will step in and pick up what scattered pieces they can, because for now, we stand between them and the Turks. They won't feel their danger until after we've fallen."

"Surely Lazar's tribute is worth something to Sigismund." Župan Ivan had contributed to the payment, and Danilo knew each coin had cost Sivi Gora dearly—in pride as much as in wealth. But paying for peace with Hungary had felt like a gamble they'd had to take.

Miloš sighed. "Yes. We can hope his honor will keep him from going back on his word. But I hate for our success to hinge on the honor of a Latin half believer. Try to get on his good side tonight. If not Bokori, then one of his men."

Danilo nodded. The group broke up, and Danilo went back to the courtyard and glanced around, noting each person and animal. Where was Maja?

"They didn't lay the tesserae flat. They're at angles." Luka pointed to the golden halo above the head of Saint John the Baptist.

"But look at it as you walk. The sunlight reflects off part of it no matter where you stand." Maja gazed at it from another angle. The halo's glow wasn't as strong with the angled tesserae, but the pinpoints of brighter light against the golden mass was elegant in its own way. "I think I like it."

"Enough to do it?"

"Maybe. It depends on the lighting of the church and the quality of the gold gilding." Her fingers itched to try it. She could almost feel the tesserae in her hands, sinking into the plaster to create something of lasting beauty.

"Maja." Luka's whisper, urgent and alarmed, scattered all thoughts of artwork. "He followed us."

Maja turned toward the church entrance as the man from the castle strode through the door. She glanced around. She and Luka had been studying the mosaic for so long that all the praying women had gone. The man from the castle approached the priest, and soon he, too, had left them alone with the stranger. "Come on. There's got to be more than one way out of here."

Their perusal of the artwork had led them deep into the church, and the strange man was between them and the main entrance. She doubted he wanted to hire her and Luka as mosaicists, and she could think of few other reasons for his attention, none of them good. She took Luka's hand—he didn't resist—and pulled him past the pulpit. Pity they were forced to hurry. She'd been hoping to study the carved parapet.

The east of the church was lined with chapels. She darted into one of the brighter ones, hoping it would have an outside exit. Instead, an altar and a series of paintings depicting the life of the Virgin Mary met them. The light came from a plethora of windows, but there were no doors.

Luka grabbed a heavy candlestick from the altar and gripped it like a weapon. Maja almost told him not to, but then the man appeared at the entrance, and they were trapped.

"A word, my lady?" he said.

He was polite at least, but that didn't ease Maja's fear. She straightened her back, trying to project calm despite the tremors growing in her knees and traveling to her stomach. There was something innately intimidating about the man, beyond the long sword that hung from his belt. She hadn't noticed before, but he had a scar along his left cheek. And he was wearing a gray cloak.

Maja swallowed. "You may speak."

"You travel with Miloš Obilić and Danilo Darrasević."

It wasn't a question. Maja saw no reason to deny it. "Yes."

"Why?"

Maja hesitated. The man's words might have been polite, harmless even, but his eyes were threatening. Yet lying seemed likely to earn them even more trouble. "For protection. We have the same final destination."

The man crossed his arms and raised an eyebrow. "No other reason? You brought them no messages? No documents?"

"No."

The man walked closer. Maja instinctively stepped back, and Luka did the same.

"You carried nothing from a Venetian trader? You did come from the west, did you not?"

"Yes, we came from the west. But we passed through only small villages while seeking work. We saw no foreign traders."

"Are you sure?"

"Yes." Maja shuffled through memories, wondering what he could mean. She didn't think the arrogant painter had been foreign, nor did she suppose the bandits were connected to Venice, and the lustful meroph had claimed to be in his village all winter. In any case, none of them had sent Maja or Luka with a message. They carried no documents, only a few drawings of their father's. "Search our packs if you must. We don't carry what you seek."

"Your packs have already been searched. Perhaps I ought to search your persons."

"You can try." Luka stepped in front of Maja, his stride unsteady. "But you'll have to get through me if you want to touch my sister."

"Luka, don't." Maja tried to pull him back. His stolen candlestick was no match for the man's sword, and other than Danilo's archery lessons, Luka hadn't been trained to fight. They had nothing to hide, so perhaps the search would be over quickly.

The man laughed. "You might slow me down, whelp, but I doubt you'll stop me."

"He might not, but I will." Maja recognized Danilo's voice and saw him step into the chapel, his sword drawn. She'd never been so happy to see anyone.

The man with the cloak pulled his sword from its scabbard. "You wouldn't dare. Not in a church."

"Wouldn't I? This church follows the Latin rite, and I have no loyalty to Rome. I do, however, have an obligation to defend refugees who are under my protection."

The man took a step back.

"Perhaps it is time for you to leave," Danilo suggested.

The man looked between the three of them and glared. But he left.

Maja couldn't see the man's retreat, but Danilo's eyes followed him until his footsteps faded into silence. Then Danilo slid his sword into its scabbard and turned to Maja and Luka.

"Thank you." Maja wasn't sure what the man with the cloak would have done, but she feared it would have escalated into something unpleasant.

Danilo's face had been calm and hard while he'd threatened the spy, and his expression didn't ease now. "Why did you leave the courtyard?"

Maja was taken aback. She had been glad to see Danilo again, but he seemed angry. "We wanted to see the mosaics. And the man was staring at me. You told me not to stand out. I thought it would be best to get away from his scrutiny, but then he followed us."

An awkward silence stretched between them. Luka broke it by returning the candlestick to the altar. "We're sorry. We didn't mean to make matters worse."

Danilo sighed. "No. Of course not. And that's what I'll have to tell Miloš when I explain that I've made an enemy of Bokori's spy when I was supposed to be making friends. Come, please. Back to the castle."

Maja and Luka meekly followed Danilo from the church.

"What did he want?" Danilo asked.

Maja was grateful for his words because the silence had been deafening. She hadn't meant to complicate Danilo's mission. She had wanted to see the church, but more than that, she'd been scared of the spy. "He seemed to think we had a message or documents from Venice."

"Venice?" Danilo glanced at Maja.

"Yes. A trader or a merchant was supposed to have given them to us. But I don't know why the spy thought that, other than because we came from the west and met your party."

One of the other men they traveled with, Darko, joined them when they reached the castle courtyard. He grunted. "Glad it didn't take you too long to track them down."

"They wanted to look at the mosaics." Danilo's voice was calm, but Maja could pick out the slight strain of annoyance.

Darko chuckled. "Tatjana was like that when she was young. Always wandering off. Except she wanted to look at flowers, not pictures."

Danilo gave a halfhearted smile. "The spy who's been following us questioned them. Seemed to think they had papers from Venice. I should tell Miloš. Where is he?"

"In the great hall."

Danilo nodded and rushed off.

"Who's Tatjana?" Luka asked.

"My younger sister. Danilo married her." Darko gestured to Danilo's back as he disappeared inside.

Maja inhaled sharply, then tried to hide her reaction by looking around to make sure the spy wasn't nearby. She hadn't realized Danilo was married, but the more she thought about it, the more she chastised herself for not expecting it. Why wouldn't he have a wife? Most men were married by eighteen or nineteen, and she guessed he was in his mid-twenties. His family had to have status, or he wouldn't have been trained for warfare, so there wouldn't have been any economic reasons not to marry. And he was certainly attractive—but that was a thought she ought not have about a married man. She'd done nothing more than talk to him and sing with him, so she didn't expect there would be a penance. But she would have to retrain her mind. His pleasant face and strong muscles were not for her to admire.

Compounding her guilt was fear that she'd ruined the negotiations. Serbia couldn't stand against the Turks and the Hungarians at the same time. And there would be no peace with Murad, only submission. If her confrontation with the spy had unraveled all the work Miloš and Danilo had accomplished, all of Serbia would suffer.

What had she done?

"I'm certain it's the same man who's been following us. I got a good look at him four days back. Same hair color, same type of beard, same cloak, and that scar." Danilo crossed his arms and watched Miloš pacing the floor of the room they'd been assigned.

"And he thought we'd been given documents from Venice?"

Danilo nodded. "Documents or a message, and he was willing to threaten Maja and Luka to find out more."

"So you threatened him?"

Danilo felt heat rising in his cheeks. "Yes." Even in hindsight, he would do the same thing again. "I don't much care for spies."

"And yet you and your župan spied out key information before Pločnik."

"That was scouting, not spying."

"If you say so." Miloš clasped his hands behind his back. "What were they doing in the church in the first place?"

"They noticed him watching Maja and thought it best to leave. They didn't know he would follow. And as artists, they are naturally curious about the artwork in churches. Had they stayed, he may have questioned them in the courtyard."

"Perhaps. But perhaps we shouldn't have brought them with us."

Part of Danilo thought Miloš was right. His defense of Maja and Luka had created a problem, and if it derailed negotiations, it would be hard to justify their act of kindness in taking the pair into their group. Yet he couldn't have left them alone and defenseless. Even putting aside his friendship for the pair, there was a duty to protect those in need. "My župan always does what he thinks is right, regardless of the consequences."

A hint of a smile crossed Miloš's face. "Yes, Ivan and Lazar are alike in that. I will try to explain the situation to Janos Bokori. Perhaps I can smooth things over, explain that your actions are only a sign of a deep honor."

"Would you prefer I stay out of sight until we leave?" If it looked as though Miloš were punishing Danilo, perhaps it would calm potential resentment from Bokori.

"No. But see that you don't sit by the spy, whatever his name is, when we are invited to supper."

As it turned out, the spy wasn't at supper. Nor were Maja or Luka, but that was planned, and Miloš had insisted Tihomir eat with them, ensuring they would be safe and that they wouldn't wander. Danilo would have gladly traded assignments with Tihomir. Maja and Luka may have complicated negotiations, but they were easy enough company. He had been fearful when they'd disappeared—a multitude of misfortunes could befall a pair of orphans, especially when one was as attractive as Maja. Concern for them had made his words in the church terse, as had his failure to handle the situation with the spy in a more diplomatic manner. He was upset with himself more than he was upset with them, but he wasn't sure they would know that. He needed to explain. Perhaps apologize.

But instead of eating with the Dinić siblings, Danilo was stuck between strangers, picking at bland pork and drinking weak wine. He hadn't caught the name of the man to his left. The man had examined Danilo but seemed reluctant to engage in conversation. The man at his right was a soldier of some stature and seemed more willing to converse. But Danilo spoke no Hungarian, and the soldier spoke neither Slavonic, Greek, nor Turkish, the languages Danilo could use, so communication was severely limited.

Miloš and the others reported similar stalemates when they gathered after supper. The next morning, when they left the fortress, they were still uncertain of what Janos Bokori would tell his király. Would he recommend friendship? Alliance? Neutrality? Or would he recognize that his neighbors to the south were distracted and strike from the north while the Turks attacked from the southeast?

Chapter Nine
Ambush in the Forest

Iskandar stood beneath a tree, his horse tied farther back from the road. "Do you see that?" he asked.

Hasan squinted. "A cloud of dust. Someone travels this road."

They watched as the shapes drew near enough to divide into distinct forms. "Nine," Iskandar said. "More horses than riders." The presence of pack animals promised wealth. "Twelve of us. Nine of them."

Hasan clasped Iskandar's elbow. "You have brought us luck. First the caravan, then the document. Now another target."

The ransoms for members of the caravan had been large, and Contanto and the other merchant hadn't tried anything foolish. Before Iskandar had let them go, he'd asked Pascal to translate the document stolen from Grato, and he had learned who might be willing to pay for the letter's destruction: Ispán Janos Bokori. Ghazis were not known for using written documents to extract payments, but with the risk being so small and the reward likely to be so high, Iskandar had convinced Hasan and his men to join him for a detour into Hungary. None of them would object to more plunder, not when it was about to fall right into their laps.

Iskandar studied the length of the shadows. The group would be tiring as their day's journey neared its end, and Iskandar intended to take advantage of their weakness. "We'll set up an ambush."

Danilo glanced along the group. His eyes caught Maja's briefly before she turned away. Normally, she rode near him, but that hadn't been the case today, nor the day before when they'd left Bokori's fortress. She seemed to be avoiding him. That was probably his fault for being too hard on her and

Luka in the church. He'd been worried about her and frustrated by how the run-in with the spy might affect Hungarian cooperation. But Maja hadn't done anything wrong. She couldn't help it if the spy thought she was the most vulnerable member of the group, the easiest to question. Danilo had apologized, and she'd said there was nothing to forgive. Yet a strain remained between them.

Maybe it was for the best. Something about his time with Maja had made him feel happier than he'd felt in years. He was attracted to her, but more than that, he admired her. Yet when it came to Maja, his emotions were like an inexperienced horseman, galloping along more quickly than was wise. He didn't have time for a woman, and even if he did, there was the curse to think about. Maybe Konstantin and Ivan were right, maybe there was no curse. But if there was, it would be foolish to pursue anything more than a polite acquaintanceship.

Tihomir nudged his horse next to Danilo's. "Are you familiar with the road ahead?"

"No. You?"

"No. I suppose I should try to find a place to stop for the night."

"I'll go." Danilo had taken the last scouting trip, so it was Tihomir's turn, but riding ahead would give him more time to sort out his feelings for Maja.

Tihomir smiled. "I don't mind going. Perhaps Maja is growing tired and needs encouragement."

Danilo huffed. "I doubt she wants it from me." She had been friendly and warm for most of the journey, but that had likely been prompted by gratitude. Since the incident at the Hungarian church, the friendliness had vanished. She was still polite, but she was holding back the earlier warmth and hadn't participated in the nightly archery lessons with Luka. Nor had there been any singing.

Tihomir tilted his head, pantomiming deep thought. "If I were the only unmarried man in the group, traveling with an extraordinarily beautiful woman, I would find reasons to talk to her."

"Would you?"

"I would. But since I am married, I'll leave that pleasure to you. And I'll go look for a campsite."

Tihomir pushed his horse from a walk to a trot, leaving the group behind. Danilo watched him until he became a speck, then disappeared into a copse of trees.

Danilo looked back at Maja. She was laughing at something her brother had said, so Danilo decided to leave any attempt at reconciliation until later. Strange how an impending conversation could make him almost as nervous as an upcoming battle. At least with battle, one didn't have to worry about where one stood with the opponent. There were no questions as to who was enemy and who was ally. Words spoken with women were not always so clear-cut.

They rode through little-traveled lands now, so Danilo doubted they'd see anyone, but as he approached a copse of trees, he strung his bow. Tihomir hadn't turned back to warn them, so the area was undoubtedly safe, but for Danilo, worry always accompanied an inability to see clearly. His eyes moved from ground to trunk and from branch to shadow as they rode. Nothing stirred. Even the birds were silent, startled by the riders.

The road narrowed between the trees. Miloš led them, with Danilo behind him. Maja and Luka were a few horses back, in the center of the group.

Danilo caught movement to his left. He drew and nocked an arrow, but in the few moments it took him to do that, the movement disappeared. Had it been only a bird? Only his imagination?

"What was it?" Darko asked.

"I'm not sure. Maybe nothing."

Darko drew his sword. He was Tatjana's brother, so Danilo knew him well, and they had long ago developed a mutual trust.

Danilo guided Dazhbog off the road, into the ground between the chestnuts and the evergreens. Something about what he'd seen made him uneasy.

"Now!" The single word was shouted in Turkish.

"We're under attack!" Danilo yelled. He turned his horse around, back to the group. He ought to have rallied to Miloš, but he rode toward Maja instead. Miloš was capable of defending himself. Maja was not.

His horse responded to the pressure of his knees. With his hands, he shot first one arrow at a turban-headed bandit, then a second arrow before the first had even finished its flight. Cries filled the air as the Serbs scrambled for weapons and the bandits attacked.

Two men were taking the pack horses. Danilo shot them both, all the time moving closer to Maja and Luka. One of the raiders rode next to her, and she whipped him across the face with the ends of her reins. A moment later, Danilo's arrow plowed into the man's chest.

Without Tihomir, their group was only eight strong, but Maja and Luka had no real weapons. Turkish shouts ordered men to converge on the bowman. Danilo wished he had his shield. As the first arrows rained around his stallion, Danilo dismounted and ran to Maja.

"Get down. They have archers." Danilo didn't bother telling Luka the same thing. He grabbed the boy about the waist and dragged him off the mule.

Danilo found more targets for his arrows. But Darko lay on the ground bleeding, and Viktor had been taken prisoner. How many Turks were there? With the trees, the panicked horses, and the shouts all around him, he couldn't tell.

One Turk came at him with a scimitar. Danilo drew his own blade and met the strike. He dropped his bow, using both hands to push the man back. Maja screamed behind him. He turned and rushed at the man trying to haul her away, stabbing him in the stomach. Danilo yanked his spathion out just in time to block the next attack from a Turkish scimitar.

Danilo saw who held the blade and gasped.

Iskandar bin Abdullah.

Iskandar was supposed to be a slave, not a ghazi. How had he escaped his fate? Danilo brought his blade around. Iskandar parried, then riposted. Danilo felt the strength of the blow from his wrists to his shoulders.

Iskandar was a skilled swordsman, but Danilo was no laggard. He met Iskandar's thrusts, and then another of the bandits joined the attack. Danilo continued the fight, always moving away from one or the other so as not to face strikes from both men at the same time. But then a third enemy joined the fray.

Danilo blocked one blade, then another, but he couldn't do more than throw a hand up to slow the shield barreling toward his face. It smacked him in the head, turning everything white and then black for a moment. Danilo stumbled and felt his knees hit the ground before the world returned to color again. Iskandar disarmed him, and another ghazi held the point of his blade against Danilo's neck.

Danilo fought to fill his lungs with air. He thought the ghazis might run him through, but the fight was over, and the bandits had won. Miloš, Viktor, and Filip knelt on the ground with their hands clasped on the back of their heads. So did Maja and Luka. Two of his other friends lay on the ground, one wounded, one dead. Tihomir remained missing.

Iskandar stood in front of Danilo, a smirk of deep satisfaction growing on his face. Then he threw up a shield and bashed it into Danilo's face with enough force to send him into the dirt. As the agony spread across his forehead, Danilo's fuzzy mind heard the next orders.

"Tie him up."

Iskandar couldn't believe his luck. With one ambush, he'd captured the woman of his dreams and his bitterest enemy. The ghazis took the captives back to their own camp. The scout and one other Serb were dead. Another was likely to die before nightfall. That left the boy to sell, the woman to take, and four Serb warriors to ransom. Except Iskandar didn't plan to ransom Danilo. The Turkish half-breed would have a different fate. Someone had to pay for the five ghazis who'd been killed in the raid, the wounds inflicted on three others, and the years Iskandar had spent as a slave.

Some of the ghazis looked through the supplies and tended the horses. Others stripped the warriors of their armor. It seemed armor and animals would be the most valuable things they received from the ambush, until the ransoms came in, because the packs carried little of interest.

Iskandar gazed on the golden-haired woman. She stood before him, her hands bound in front of her. He caressed the golden strands of her hair, feeling their smoothness. She turned away, her jaw set in defiance. The years had been good to her, melting away the last of girlhood into something even more lovely. She may have resisted capture, but spirit only made Iskandar all the more eager to tame her. Desire for the woman was almost more than he could bear.

"I want her as my portion," Iskandar declared to the other ghazis.

"Why should you get first choice?" Mustafa asked.

"Because I set the ambush. And she was mine before, until she was taken from me. The ransoms for the others will more than compensate for her value."

Mustafa looked almost as unhappy as the Serbian girl, but he didn't say anything more.

Iskandar pointed to Miloš. "That one is married to a daughter of the most powerful man in Serbia. Think what a man like that can raise if his life depends on it." Iskandar pointed to another of the captured Serbs. "He's of noble birth as well. Not worth quite as much but worthwhile all the same."

Iskandar stepped to where Danilo lay on the ground, bound in chains. Unlike the other captives, Danilo would have understood every word, even those spoken in Turkish, and his eyes focused on Iskandar with fiery loathing. "I have one other request. I want this one impaled. The sooner the better."

Mustafa raised his eyebrows. "What of his ransom? You would take the woman *and* squander the coin we could gain from a hostage? We did not ambush the group for the joy of seeing someone impaled. We fought and were wounded with the promise of a reward."

"Sometimes revenge is more satisfying than ransom. Even were I to request half the wealth of Sivi Gora."

"Would you get it?" Mustafa asked. "That much?"

Iskandar eyed Danilo, waiting for him to protest or beg, but the prisoner didn't speak. "What would your cousin give for your safe return? Half his treasury? More?"

Danilo ignored him.

"Perhaps the better question is what *wouldn't* he give for your life?" Iskandar chuckled. Which would be more satisfying? Beggaring Ivan or impaling Danilo? If ransomed, Danilo would live. No matter how high the ransom, there was the possibility that Danilo and Ivan would seek revenge, eventually. But there would be no return from death. Killing Danilo would end the threat from one enemy and wound the other's soul so deeply that he would be forever marked. "No matter. I prefer impalement." He turned to one of the other ghazis. "Find me a pole."

Mustafa's hands fisted, and he looked ready to protest, but Hasan motioned for him to wait. He stepped forward and inclined his head with respect. "A word please, Iskandar?"

Iskandar nodded and walked a few paces away. He feared he wouldn't like what Hasan had to say, but Hasan had long ago earned Iskandar's esteem. He'd made the hajj to Mecca, he'd served Iskandar's father, and he'd helped set Iskandar on the path to recovery after Danilo's cousin had left Iskandar without money, followers, or his full health.

"Iskandar, I know you wish revenge, but the potential ransom is too great. It is within your right to forfeit your share in exchange for the man's death, but your share is only a seventh part of the ransom. The other six shares are not yours to risk."

"I have my shares from the caravan ransoms. I can use those to compensate the men, and I can forgo any payment we receive for the document."

"You would give up everything you have to see him dead? Don't be foolish. What you've taken gives you a chance to start over. Think of the comfort you can have, the influence you can wield."

Hasan's words were wise, as always, but hunger for Danilo's death was strong. "There will be other groups to pillage."

"That is uncertain and can't be set against current shares. Mustafa is not the only one who resents your claim on the girl. Don't waste the man's ransom, not if you want their loyalty. Or perhaps you would prefer to share the woman? You must compromise on something. You can't take the woman *and* slay someone worth such a large ransom. It would not be fair to the rest of us. You can have one or the other, but not both, or you'll spark mutiny."

Iskandar's eyes fell on the woman again, and her beauty made the blood sound in his ears. She would be his and his alone. And with the money he wrung from Župan Ivan, he would have a fine home for her and servants to cater to her needs. She might be scared of him now, but that would change. She would come to respect him, come to love serving him. One day, she would worship him. Iskandar nodded. "The woman will be my sole portion, and we will ransom the župan's cousin."

The lines of Hasan's shoulders relaxed, and Mustafa's posture shifted to something less hostile.

Iskandar strode to Danilo and kicked him in the side with enough force to break ribs, and he hoped he'd succeeded. Danilo winced as his body folded inward.

"Know this: You owe your life to the fact that your cousin is wealthy and devoted to you. Were the prospects for your ransom any less lucrative, I would impale you here, tonight. But I doubt your cousin will pay any less if you have a few broken bones or missing teeth. So don't get comfortable. I'll be otherwise occupied tonight, but your turn will come."

Chapter Ten
Iskandar's Camp

Ropes hugged her wrists, but Maja still kicked and elbowed Iskandar as he dragged her toward a tent. Luka watched in horror. Danilo and the others watched, too, but none of them could help her. They were all wounded, some severely, and all were chained.

Iskandar shoved her inside and pulled her to a large cushion in the center of the tent. "Stop struggling. Just sit."

The ghazi spoke Slavonic? Maja hadn't expected to understand his words, wasn't sure she wanted to. He pushed her again, and she fell onto the quilts and pillows.

Iskandar left her there while the other ghazis followed them into the tent. Iskandar spoke in rapid Turkish to first one, then another of the men. Maja glanced around at the trunk and table, hoping to find a sign that her fate was something other than what she feared. The sides of the leather tent were unadorned, but the carpets were rich. The design seemed more Italian than Ottoman, as if the tent had been plundered.

She moved to the edge of the cushion, planning to duck under the side of the tent and flee, but Iskandar turned the moment she moved and hauled her back to the center. He continued to look at her often, but there seemed to be tasks he had to attend to with the other men. She supposed he was the leader. She didn't understand the language he and his men used, but she followed most of the gestures and recognized the items they brought from the packs. They were dividing up the loot.

The ropes burned her skin as she tried to twist her hands free, tried to reposition the knots so she could untie them, but fear made her fingers shake, and a secure hand had bound the ropes. The light between the flaps of the tent slowly disappeared. Eventually, darkness consumed the day in the same way dread consumed her heart.

The last of Iskandar's ghazis held Tihomir's armor in his hands. She'd seen his body, and she mourned his loss. The ghazis had killed another of Miloš's men, too, and wounded all the others, Darko severely. All the men had been kind, offering to protect two helpless artists. Perhaps those still alive would be ransomed. Eventually, they could return to their lives, albeit with a reduced fortune. But what would that mean for their plans to defend Serbia from Sultan Murad? War was expensive, and ransoms could cripple a land for years. Luka would likely be sold as a slave. Would she ever see him again? And what would the future hold for her?

She didn't want to think about that. She had to get away. She owed the warriors any help she could give them, and she had to rescue Luka. But above all, she had to escape from Iskandar.

He sent the man with Tihomir's armor from the tent and came to sit beside her on the cushion. She scooted away.

"You captured my heart outside Pločnik. Allah smiles upon us to have brought us together once again," he said.

Maja stared at him. She had captured his heart? She'd never even spoken to him.

"I don't know what the intervening years have brought you, but obviously, you suffer." Iskandar brushed his hand along her skirt. "Your clothes are ragged. You're thin. And you've been forced to travel with a pathetic band of would-be warriors."

The men she traveled with weren't pathetic. She liked them all. One in particular she liked more than she should. She shuddered, remembering how Iskandar had kicked Danilo. There was more to their history than Pločnik, and she feared that put Danilo at a greater risk.

Iskandar untied the ropes around her wrists. "What is your name?"

Maja rubbed her wrists and didn't answer.

"Come, you are to be my wife. I wish to know your name. I am Iskandar, named after the great conqueror. And you, my love, are to be my next conquest."

Maja stood and stepped away. The tent wasn't big enough to grant her sufficient distance from him. What was coming might be inevitable, but she wasn't going to make it easy for him. What she really needed was a weapon, and surprise.

Iskandar left the cushion and followed her, and this time, there was nowhere for her to go. He took her shoulders, not roughly but firmly. She tried to twist away but his grip was solid.

"My mother was not a willing bride either. But she came to respect my father. He provided well for her and gave her a son. In time, you, too, will see how lucky you are. You will have food and fine clothing. You will be taught the true faith. I will give you great pleasure, and you will give me children."

Iskandar was delusional. Maja felt a stab of sympathy for his mother, who might have faced exactly what Maja did. But Maja would never follow that path, never respect Iskandar. How could someone whose greatest joy came from religious mosaics be happy with someone whose beliefs called those images idols? She was content with plain tunics and simple bread, and she could never deny her faith. Nor did she believe love could grow from a union forced by abduction.

Iskandar pulled her in and kissed her mouth. When she tried to turn away, he held her head, and when she kicked him, he pushed her onto the cushions of his bed and followed her there. Then his lips were on hers again, urgent and domineering. His weight pressed down on her, and despite all her attempts to push him away, she couldn't get enough leverage to free any of her limbs.

"Wait!" She heard the desperation in her own voice.

He paused, his mouth on her neck.

"If this is to be my wedding night, I wish to wear my best tunic. My traveling clothes are, as you say, in tatters. It's not dignified for a bride. If you want my cooperation, I want my baggage brought to the tent, and I want a moment to prepare. I want my comb and water for washing."

"You are beautiful no matter what you are or aren't wearing. Your smell is intoxicating, and your hair is like spun gold. There is no need for water or a comb." His mouth moved on her neck again and followed her movements even as she squirmed away.

"I insist." Maja wasn't as strong as he, not physically, but she would do anything to delay what was coming. "Would you deny a maiden this simple request?"

Iskandar caressed her cheek, then his fingers ran down her neck. "If it will please you that much, I will fetch your saddlebags."

"Thank you. Mine are the ones made of canvas instead of leather."

Maja had been planning to escape while he was gone, had hoped her brief politeness would deaden his suspicion, but he tied one end of a rope to her ankle, and the other to a trunk. As soon as he was gone, she tested the trunk, but she couldn't lift it, let alone carry it. She saw no knives nearby, but she attacked the knots with her fingers.

Danilo lay on the ground with the other captured Serbs—other than Maja. He tried not to think about Maja and what Iskandar would do to her. As much as Danilo wanted to, he couldn't change anything while chains held his ankles and wrists.

"He's gone," Miloš said.

Danilo looked to where Miloš had been cradling Darko's head on his lap. Danilo hadn't had a chance to fully examine Darko's wound, but he'd seen enough that he wasn't surprised, only saddened. The man left behind a wife and three children. Danilo's marriage had made them brothers, so Darko's death was the loss of a kinsman.

Danilo's head still pounded from the skirmish. And his eyes kept turning to Iskandar's tent. Maja was inside. She had relied on Danilo for safety, and he'd failed her.

"Danilo." Miloš's voice was a whisper. "Most of them have gone to sleep. Get the guard over here."

Danilo met Luka's eyes and whispered to him. "Come closer so there's more slack in the chains."

Luka obeyed, moving slowly so their fetters wouldn't rattle.

Other than Iskandar, who was digging through the captured baggage, only one other Turk hadn't retired to a tent.

"Some wine, please," Danilo called to the Turkish guard.

The guard drew closer and folded his arms across his chest. "You wish wine?"

"It's our tradition to drink to the memory of our fallen comrades. Or keep the wine for yourselves and bring us the plum brandy. Darko would approve of the rakija over the wine. It's the finest drink in the Balkans."

The guard huffed. "You are at liberty to ask for nothing."

"Your prisoner is a great man." Danilo gestured to Miloš. "If his family is to pay a ransom for his safe return, they will expect him to be treated with honor."

"In comparison to what you can expect, his treatment will be quite favorable. But that doesn't include wine or rakija."

Danilo waited until Iskandar moved away carrying several packs. Maja's? He forced himself to focus on what he could do, not on what he couldn't. "Why not? It was ours, and it's of no value to you, unless you plan to partake." Danilo assumed everyone in the group was Muslim and, therefore, forbidden to drink alcohol. But conversion among roaming ghazis didn't always run deep enough to overcome basic thirsts.

The guard took a step toward Danilo and bent to face him. "None of you are great men. Wealthy, perhaps, at least until your ransom is paid. But the sultan will trample you under his feet, and then you'll be little better than slaves. So get used to your chains." The guard kicked Danilo's thigh, then turned to walk off.

He didn't get far. Danilo lunged forward and tackled the man's legs. He fell to the ground, and Danilo crawled desperately to smother the man's cries before he alerted the rest of the camp.

"Get the keys," he told Luka.

Iskandar had tied multiple knots, and Maja had managed to get only the first undone by the time he returned.

"Your bags, my flower."

While he laid her things on the trunk, Maja retied the knot so he wouldn't know what she'd done. She smiled up at him, trying to portray innocence. Her heart pounded with fear. Where had he learned to tie such tight knots?

Iskandar bent to untie her, seeming to have no difficulty with the ropes.

"You'll turn around while I change?" Maja asked.

Iskandar raised an eyebrow. "If you wish."

She took a bag from the trunk to the table, where Iskandar had placed a bucket of water. She washed her face while she thought, then dug through her pack. All her spare clothing had been stolen by the bandits she and Luka had met on the side of the road. But her father's tools hadn't been taken, nor divided as part of the pillage. She gripped the handle of his hammer. It was hardly a war hammer, and she was hardly a warrior, but it would have to suffice. Iskandar had trapped her in a corner, but that didn't mean he'd won.

She heard his footsteps behind her.

"Come, you've delayed long enough. I've been waiting nearly three years for this."

She stayed still until his footsteps stopped and she could feel his breath on the back of her hair and his hands on her waist. Then she twisted and swung the hammer into the side of his head.

Iskandar collapsed, and he stayed on the ground.

Maja's hands shook. She allowed herself a few deep breaths. She wasn't sure she could free the others, not with chains binding them and six other Turks wandering the camp, but if rescue was beyond her skill, perhaps she could go back to Janos Bokori and convince him to launch a rescue mission. They hadn't seen the spy since they'd left the fortress, but maybe he was out there, somewhere, with a fast horse. Miloš was wealthy enough to make a rescue worth Bokori's time.

A grunt sounded outside the tent, and Danilo burst through the flap, a blood-darkened scimitar in one hand.

He glanced at the unmoving Iskandar lying on the floor in a spreading pool of blood, then at her. "What happened?"

She showed him the hammer she still held.

"Are you all right?"

Maja still couldn't speak. She managed a nod, then ran into Danilo's arms when he opened them. Her body trembled with the aftermath of what Iskandar had almost done to her and what she had done to him. Danilo's arms were strong and steady, and she wanted to stay there, despite their hurry. Or she did until she remembered Danilo was married.

She stepped back, ending the embrace. "Thank you. That's the second time you've rescued me from Iskandar's bed."

"It looks as though you rescued yourself this time."

Iskandar still hadn't moved. Maybe she had killed him, but she was too frightened to check. "Luka?"

Danilo took her hand and pulled her toward the flap. "He's helping Miloš get horses, but there are a few ghazis still about the camp and only one sword among us, so we have to be quiet."

"Wait. I need my bags." Maja ran to the pack on the trunk.

"These as well?" Danilo went to the table.

"Yes."

Danilo scooped up her things and led her outside. She took the bundles from him so he'd have both hands free for fighting.

Luka almost knocked her over when he rushed to her.

She held him tightly, but only for a moment. "Take this." She handed him one of the packs, and he fastened it to a mule.

Danilo helped Filip onto a horse, then Viktor. Both were wounded. So was Miloš, but he had gathered all the animals from their group and from the Turks, so the enemy would be unable to pursue them with any speed.

"Where's Darko?" Maja asked.

"He bled out."

The group of warriors had been cut nearly in half, and of those left, only Danilo was healthy enough to wage battle, and he, too, was injured. Flight was their best option.

Danilo helped Luka onto one of the Turkish horses, then escorted Maja to the stallion that had belonged to Tihomir. "Come, I'll help you up. Did Iskandar . . . ?" He paused. "If he hurt you, riding might—"

"He didn't."

"Good. Because we have to ride hard, regardless of pain. And because no man should take a woman by force." He gestured to the saddle and helped her mount. After seeing the skirmish, watching her friends be captured and killed, and then being taken as pillage, she was exhausted, and fear still shrouded her. But she would ride as fast and as long as Danilo ordered.

"Is Iskandar dead?" Danilo asked.

Maja shook her head. "I don't know."

"I'll make sure." Danilo took a step toward Iskandar's lair, but then a ghazi emerged from one of the other tents. For a moment, he only stared, but then he sounded the alarm. Another ghazi appeared, then a third, and one of them launched an arrow at the group. Danilo ran to Dazhbog and mounted, and the group galloped into the night.

Chapter Eleven
Bokori's Treason

Maja was ready to fall off her horse when they finally stopped during the fourth watch of the night, and she had the feeling that Danilo would have pushed them harder, only Viktor had already tumbled from the top of his horse. An arrow had pierced his side during the initial ambush, and though Danilo and Miloš had treated it, the wound made the journey difficult for him. Worry that the ghazis might steal other animals and come in pursuit remained, but exhaustion pressed all of them, and eventually, they surrendered to the need for sleep.

Maja slept next to Luka. When she woke, the sun was high, and despite her lingering weariness, she couldn't fall back to sleep. Luka still breathed heavily beside her. She sat, looking around. Miloš, Viktor, and Filip still slept. Danilo stood over the baggage, sorting through their things. A large bruise marred his left temple. Eventually, he noticed her gaze and smiled.

Rather than speaking loud enough to wake the others, she stood and smoothed her hair, then walked over to him.

"How are you this morning, Maja?"

"It seems I have missed most of the morning."

He glanced at the sun. "With good reason. We rode most of the night. If we're not interrupted by any more spies or ghazis or bandits, I think we can get to Sivi Gora in three days. We'll have time to recover then."

"And Miloš? How far is he from home?"

"Kruševac is farther to the east. We'll find a group to send them with once we reach the main road." He frowned for a moment. "My weapons have been stolen, and I am but one man, but I hope to offer them some protection until better options appear."

Maja picked up a long scimitar, one she assumed he had taken from a ghazi. "You have a sword as well."

"At present, you have it. And after seeing how lethal you can be with an artist's hammer, I hesitate to take it back."

"Lethal?" She went over the events in her memory. "The hammer didn't pull from my hand, so I don't think it went deep enough to kill him. I wish it had. You arrived moments after he fell. And I was terrified of him. I . . ." She had needed time to tuck all her emotions back inside after nearly experiencing the thing she'd most dreaded for three years. But now she wished she knew whether Iskandar remained a threat or was a ghost. "I'm sorry I didn't check. And then it was too late."

Danilo shook his head. "I should have made sure he was dead at once, but at the moment, getting you to safety seemed more important. I'm sorry you put your trust in our company and ended up as Iskandar's prize again."

Danilo didn't need to feel guilty about their capture. It hadn't been his fault. "Had Luka and I gone our own way and run into another set of thieves, I imagine they would have treated me much as Iskandar intended to." The meroph they'd begged for food hadn't been so different from Iskandar. "Or we would have starved."

"Still, I can't help but think that's not the first time I've failed you."

"What?" She had no claim on his protection, and he'd shown nothing but kindness to her and her brother.

"At Pločnik. Iskandar's group killed your parents and dozens of other villagers. If Ivan and I had been just a bit earlier, we could have saved them."

She had wished for the same thing before—so many times. But she'd spoken with the priest in the village, and he'd explained the strategy. The warriors had needed to defeat the main foe first. Only when that threat had ended could they chase ghazis. Danilo and his friend held no blame for her parents' deaths. "If you would have taken just a little longer, you would have been too late to save my brother and me. He would be a janissary, and I would be Iskandar's concubine. You can't hold yourself responsible for the weight of the world, Danilo."

He didn't respond to her comment. "You don't have any weapons among your things, do you? The ghazis took all of ours."

"Other than my father's hammer and chisel? No. I suppose you could fling tesserae from a sling, but I doubt they'd do anyone much harm." She went to her packs and opened them. Maybe something she had would be of more use than she supposed. She put aside the bundles of sorted tesserae and marble scraps she'd begged from a sculptor. She showed Danilo her father's trowels and other tools. Useful in close combat, but only if the opponent had nothing better than a knife or his fists.

Then she opened her second bag and found a leather satchel tucked inside that she didn't recognize. "Do you know what this is?"

"It's not yours? It was on the table with your comb."

"No." She opened it and found only a single sheet of parchment, which she pulled out to better see. She couldn't really read, though she could recognize some words, and she'd written verses and names in her mosaics before. Yet some of the letters on the document were completely unknown to her. "What language is this?"

Danilo took the paper when she handed it to him. His lips pulled to the side in a pleasant sort of pout as he read, and his dark eyes had a mysterious intensity. She pushed away the urge to brush his skin with her fingers and reminded herself he was married. She looked away. The rest of the group still slept.

"Hungarian, I think. With a Latin script," Danilo said. "Besides Slavonic, I know Greek and speak Turkish, but I can't read this." He sat down again and rubbed his neck, then his face, sighing.

Did he have any idea how simple motions like that emphasized his strength and made her heart beat a little more quickly? She would have to start avoiding him again, but that would be more challenging in their smaller group.

"How are you?" she asked. "Iskandar was rough with you yesterday." She couldn't see the skin beneath Danilo's clothing, but evidence of Iskandar's mistreatment showed on Danilo's face.

"He's been rougher before. Nothing broken this time, not even the skin. But when I get back to Sivi Gora, I think I'll sleep for a week."

"Didn't you rest when we stopped?"

"Someone had to keep watch."

"I'm awake now. I'll keep watch." She glanced around at the quiet camp. "What do I do?"

Danilo chuckled softly. His laughter was like music. "Wake me if you see anyone or anything unusual. I don't suppose you'll be alone for long. Someone else is bound to wake up soon."

"Yes," a deep voice said. "Someone is bound to wake up soon. Why did you let me sleep so long?" Miloš stood and stretched.

"Because a ghazi put an arrow through your thigh. And you are, after all, a great man."

"Bah. If you treat me as though I'm feeble, it might become true, and I don't want that. I'll stand watch."

"It might be better if we leave." Danilo set to work packing away supplies, then stopped when he got to the parchment from Iskandar's tent. "Do you read Hungarian?"

Miloš took the letter. "No. But I recognize the signature. Janos Bokori."

Maja stood on her toes to see the paper again. "But it came from Iskandar's tent. Why would he have a letter from Bokori?"

"Perhaps the answer lies with what is written." Miloš scanned the parchment. "I can sound out the words, but I can't tell you what they mean."

"I understand Hungarian. My father worked there when I was young." Maja had been pleasantly surprised by how much she remembered of the language after a day surrounded by it at Bokori's fortress.

Danilo seemed to give up the idea of sleep and instead listened as Miloš sounded out each word. Maja did her best to translate, and they gradually pieced together the meaning.

To His Majesty, King Charles V of France,

We remember fondly the betrothal of Catherine, firstborn child of my late king, Louis, to your son, Louis, heir to the dukedom of Orleans. With the deaths of Catherine and her father, Hungary is in need of a leader from a strong, noble family. Mary, our current sovereign, is but a child, and her cousin Charles of Naples threatens to take her throne. You were once amenable to a union between your noble house of Valois and the house of Anjou. We beg you to consider Mary for your son's wife and help us defeat our common enemy. Mary's betrothal to Sigismund of Luxembourg can easily be disregarded. He has yet to reach manhood and lacks the strength to claim his throne or keep it secure. Our regent, Elizabeth, widow of my king, eagerly requests an alliance. I hope to visit you in person to discuss these matters further.

Your servant,
Janos Bokori

Miloš handed it to Danilo. "Hide it away."

"What does it mean?" Maja asked.

Danilo took the letter and hid it back in the satchel, then put it into another pack. "It means that Janos Bokori, who claims to be a loyal follower of Király Sigismund, once conspired with Queen Mary's mother to cut Sigismund out."

"It's what the spy was looking for." Maja thought back to her interrogation in the church. Of course Bokori would want the letter back—to destroy it before someone showed it to Sigismund.

Miloš nodded. "I'll wake everyone. We need to leave as soon as possible. Not a word to the others about the letter."

Danilo began loading the horses. "Don't even tell Luka," he told her.

"I won't. But why not?"

"If Sigismund learns Bokori was disloyal, Bokori stands to lose his position. What do you think he would do if he learned we have a letter that can ruin him?"

"I suppose that depends on how ruthless he is. Given how his spy acted . . ." Maja understood the need for secrecy.

"He might go so far as to have anyone who knows of the letter's contents killed. So we ride now." Danilo adjusted the straps of Dazhbog's saddle.

"But if he was looking for something from Venetian merchants, how did a Turkish ghazi come by it?"

Danilo helped her saddle one of the stolen Turkish horses. "I'm not sure. But if Iskandar knows we have it, I doubt that bodes well for us."

Danilo said goodbye to Miloš, Viktor, and Filip two days later when they found a large group of traders traveling through Kruševac. "Perhaps this group won't push you as hard as I have."

Miloš took Danilo's arm in farewell. "You pushed with good reason. I suspect we'll see each other again soon. In the meantime, look after her." Miloš looked toward Maja and lowered his voice. "A widower could do worse, you know."

"I thought we had agreed to leave the matchmaking to your wife."

Miloš grunted. "If she can stop quarreling with her sister long enough to arrange it, perhaps that will be the case."

"I think we will all have larger problems to worry about this coming summer than matchmaking and sibling rivalry."

"Yes, including that letter." Miloš frowned. "Danilo, those words are a weapon. Be careful with it. Use it in your favor, or it will be used against you."

"As you say. Godspeed, my friend."

"Godspeed to you as well."

Miloš and his men said their goodbyes to Maja and Luka, and then the artists joined Danilo, heading north, away from the main road. With only three riders and five horses, they were vulnerable, but they would reach Sivi Gora the next day. Danilo was worried, but only a little.

He glanced behind him from time to time, watching the other group grow smaller and smaller and keeping an eye out for spies or ghazis. Miloš had given Danilo the option of continuing on to Kruševac, where Miloš or Knez Lazar could arrange an escort back to Sivi Gora for Danilo and the Dinić siblings, but that would mean more time away from Sivi Gora, and Ivan needed to hear what Danilo had learned while away. Danilo just hoped he wouldn't come to regret his choice.

As the sun began to brush the horizon, Danilo sneaked a glance at Maja. She caught his gaze for a moment and quickly looked away.

The more he'd tried to speak with her, the more things had grown awkward between them. He'd tried to be no more than friendly, despite Miloš's suggestion that he should court the pretty artist. It seemed she was not interested in courtship. With few exceptions, she'd been withdrawn ever since leaving Hungary.

Perhaps it was just as well. He'd once told Ivan that he intended to remarry only if his match could somehow make Sivi Gora stronger. Maja would make Sivi Gora more beautiful when she decorated its church, but she'd bring no military or trade alliance. Even if she'd been an heiress, Danilo was too busy for romance. The sultan would come for his revenge, and Danilo needed to help his župan prepare.

He rode forward, trying to convince himself that he didn't mind Maja's aloofness, that he hadn't been worried to distraction while Iskandar had had her in his clutches, that he hadn't enjoyed holding her for those brief moments in the tent, that he had no interest in watching her wake in the morning over and over again.

He tried to convince himself—and utterly failed.

Maja woke with a start, chilled, soaked in perspiration, and gasping for breath. Luka lay beside her, still asleep in the moonlight. Iskandar was nowhere to be seen, unlike her dream, but the fear remained, her limbs quivered, and a quiet sob escaped her throat.

"Maja, are you all right?" Danilo stepped closer and sat next to her. He'd been awake when she and Luka had prepared their bedrolls, and she supposed he'd been keeping watch ever since.

Maja inhaled and exhaled a few times before she could answer. "Just a dream." Her voice shook. She sat and held her hands so they'd stop trembling. "I don't think I'll be able to fall asleep again for a while. If you wish to rest, I can keep watch." She caught the warble still clinging to her voice.

"A dream, or a nightmare?"

"A nightmare. With Iskandar." She bent her knees and leaned forward, hiding her face in her arms. She tried to stop the tears, but the dream had seemed so real, so painful, so full of horror of the worst kind.

Danilo pulled a blanket around her to keep her warm, then ran his fingers up and down her back. "He can't hurt you now. He's either dead or still recovering from the headache you gave him."

She wiped at her tears, but more came. "He remembered me from Pločnik, three years later. He won't forget me now, not if he's still alive."

"I will get you safely to Sivi Gora, and then I will talk to every man in the garrison to make sure Iskandar never follows you through the city gates."

Maja wanted to be safe so badly, but as long as Iskandar lived, he was a threat. She shook with fear as she remembered his words. How he had called her his bride and told her she would someday bear his children and join his faith. "I hate him," she whispered. "And I hate that even though we escaped from him, he still has the power to haunt my dreams."

Danilo put an arm around her, and she leaned into him as if he were an oasis where neither ghazi nor nightmare could intrude. There in Danilo's arms, she felt safe. He held her for a long time, his mere presence giving her the comfort she was so desperate for. Her tears dried, and the sound of a distant creek helped calm her heart. Then, gently, Danilo kissed the top of her head. The simple motion made her feel as if she stood in the light of the sun. She basked in its warmth, letting it drive away the chill of fear.

She looked up to meet his gaze. Those dark eyes of his held her for a long moment, and then her focus fell to his mouth. She wanted to feel his lips on her skin, not just on her hair. The distance between them closed, slowly, but with a pull that made their joining feel as inevitable as the sunrise. He brushed a finger across her cheek, then along her jawline, and the warmth of his breath mingled with her own.

Then she stiffened and pulled away as embarrassment and shame replaced the brief peace she'd felt in his arms. She should not have been in his arms at all.

"Maja?" His eyes and mouth pulled with surprise.

She stood and stepped away, drawing the blanket around her more tightly because the night's chill had sunk in again. "I can stand watch if you wish to rest."

"Maja?"

She heard the question in Danilo's voice but didn't respond.

He sighed. "I'm sorry. I only wanted to offer comfort, and then . . . well, I didn't think you would mind."

That was the problem. She hadn't minded, not soon enough. "I think your wife would mind."

"My wife?"

"Yes, your wife." Even now, the horizon in the east was growing gray instead of black. The sun would rise, and before it set again, Danilo would return to his family. Yet he had almost kissed her. And heaven forgive her, she had nearly welcomed it.

"I mourned the required time for Tatjana. Longer." Danilo looked into the distance. "I do not think she would begrudge me new affections."

Maja grasped on to his words, trying to decipher their meaning. "Mourned? Is she not waiting in Sivi Gora for you?"

Danilo shook his head. "My wife died a year and a half ago."

Maja inhaled with surprise. Embarrassment still spun in her chest, but it was joined with other emotions now. Compassion for a good man who had suffered a significant loss. Relief that her attraction for Danilo was not sinful. Worry that she had hurt him when he had already experienced enough hardship.

She watched him for a moment, seeing the sadness in his expression and the grief in his posture. Eventually, she sat beside him again. "What happened to her?"

The fingers of his right hand rubbed the fourth finger of his left hand. She supposed he must have worn a ring there at one time, but the finger now was bare.

"Childbirth." He spoke the word softly, slowly. "The baby was to be our first. Tatjana fell ill with a fever, and then the baby came, earlier than expected. It was a long delivery, a hard one. Our daughter was too small, too early. And

Tatjana . . . She was so exhausted, so heartbroken to have lost the baby. I told her that I needed her to fight, to get better, to stay with me. Begged her not to give up. But the fever never left. She died a few days after the baby."

Maja knew what it was like to lose two family members in quick succession, and it had almost broken her. She placed her hand over his. "I am sorry for your loss. For both of them."

He nodded, his eyes on their hands. They stayed like that for a long time, as the world around them grew light and the shadows retreated. She hoped she could give him comfort in his grief the way he had given her comfort in her fear.

Eventually, he shifted his hand so he was holding hers. "How long have you thought I was married to a living wife?"

"Since Hungary."

He pondered her response. "And that's why you stopped riding next to me and ended most of our conversations early?"

Maja nodded. Her face felt hot, and she hoped the dawn was still distant enough that he wouldn't notice the flush of her skin.

"And is that what drove you away when we were sitting together before?"

She nodded again.

"Is that the only thing?"

He had rescued her again and again. He was kind, strong, and brave, and she could search all the paintings from here to Constantinople and not find a face or form that attracted her more. "What other reason could I have?"

His mouth moved in that motion that always drew her eyes—not quite a smile but tinged with humor, not quite a pout but holding a plea. "Do you believe in curses?"

Curses? She wasn't sure why he asked or what she believed. "My mother always said that God is stronger than a curse."

Danilo swallowed. "I hope your mother is right, because half of Sivi Gora's garrison believes I'm cursed and say that's why Tatjana and the baby died."

She could hear the guilt in his voice and instantly wanted to deliver a tongue-lashing to the half of the garrison who had placed such a weight on him. That, or create a large panel of the last Judgment Day and place likenesses of the guilty parties among those souls in hell. "I have a hard time believing that anyone as wonderful as you could have earned a curse."

His grip on her hand shifted, and his gaze fell to her mouth. This time, if he wanted to kiss her, she wouldn't pull away. Yet something seemed to hold him back, and she suspected it was her earlier reaction. The hand not holding hers caressed her cheek. "Maja, has anyone ever kissed you before?"

His question brought with it pain over fresh memories. "Just Iskandar."

Danilo shook his head. "Iskandar didn't kiss you. He attacked you. If you didn't want him to kiss you, he was doing it wrong."

Maja's pain eased, and she leaned into his hand. "How is it done right? Will you show me?"

Danilo's mouth lifted into a smile, and she closed her eyes as he drew near. His hand slid from her cheek to her hair, and his other hand cradled the small of her back. His lips met hers with a gentleness that surprised and delighted her. The warmth, the comfort, the longing, it grew and spread and left her breathless. Not so long ago, she had woken trembling from a nightmare, but this . . . Danilo's mouth against hers was a dream of the most beautiful sort. It also left her trembling, but with pleasure and anticipation.

He ended the kiss but kept his face near hers, and awareness at his closeness made her skin tingle.

She wanted to lean into him, wanted to repeat the splendor and the power she'd just felt. "Again?" she asked.

He repeated his kiss, now with an added fire that seemed to rival the new light of dawn. Her arms wrapped around him, drawing him closer, and his mouth sent her soaring.

"Why is someone as marvelous as you kissing someone like me?" she mumbled.

His smile made her eyes track his mouth again. "You asked me to, remember?" He brushed his lips softly along her cheek until his mouth was next to her ear. "And because you have become very dear to me over the last fortnight. Regardless of what happens when we reach Sivi Gora, I want to see more of you, Maja. You've reminded me of what joy feels like."

Joy. He'd named the dominant emotion she felt in his presence, though she also felt safety, comfort, and awe at his goodness. There was also surprise that her hero from Pločnik was even more incredible than she'd imagined and that, somehow, he seemed to want to be near her as much as she wanted to be near him.

Luka yawned and turned in his sleep. Maja knew her brother's sleeping habits well enough to know he would soon be fully awake.

"I'll get the horses ready." Danilo, too, seemed to realize Luka's eyes would soon find them. "If we leave with the sunrise, we can be to Sivi Gora by midday, and I'd very much like to show you my city, Maja."

Chapter Twelve
The Trail to Sivi Gora

The road curved around a hill and passed through a thick copse of trees.

"Will we be able to see it soon?" Luka asked.

"No." Fresh blossoms and fuller trees had changed the view since Danilo had ridden the opposite way to join Miloš for the journey to Bosnia, but Danilo knew this path. They were still an hour's ride from the gates. "It won't be visible until we're nearly there. The terrain is too full of hills and vales. But it's a beautiful city. I think you'll both be happy there."

He glanced at Maja and returned the smile she gave him. He hoped she, especially, would be happy in Sivi Gora because he didn't want her to stay only for the time it would take her to decorate the church. Their shared kiss still surprised him. He hadn't kissed Tatjana until the week before the marriage ceremony. But he couldn't deny the draw he felt to Maja, not even when he considered the poor timing. War was coming. Falling in love again would be foolish. Yet denying it would only be cruel for them both.

The morning was windy, not unusual for springtime, but the sun warmed them as their path continued over the uneven ground. Danilo could barely keep his eyes open after not sleeping at all the night before and sleeping very little every other night since they'd escaped Iskandar. When they had traveled with Miloš after leaving Iskandar's camp, he could have asked the others to take equal turns standing watch, but the other men had been wounded, Luka was inexperienced and injured, and Maja needed what sleep she could get in between the nightmares. The previous night, with just the three of them, had offered even fewer options. But now Danilo was almost home. Perhaps he'd sneak into the city so no one would know he was home until he'd settled the Dinić siblings and had the chance to sleep. Then, after a rest, he could deal with reports and inquiries and treasonous letters from dangerous Hungarian ispáns. And when that was completed, he could work on sorting out his feelings for the pretty mosaic artist riding beside him.

A slight whistle and swoosh sounding almost like the wind teased his ears for a moment. Then an arrow slammed into Danilo's side.

He grunted and swayed in the saddle. His ribs burned, but he stayed upright and guided Dazhbog off the road into the trees. He couldn't see who had shot him, but another arrow might be on its way.

"Get off the road." His voice was too quiet, but even his whisper had taken effort.

"Danilo?" Maja spotted the arrow. Panic widened her eyes and threaded her voice with fear. "Danilo!"

He wanted to tell her not to worry, but that seemed dishonest. Danilo panted with the pain. "Can you climb?"

"Yes."

"Then scramble up that tree with Luka. Take this pack with you and hide it." He climbed off his horse, wincing, and patted the bundle with the letter from Bokori.

She dismounted and ran over to him. "But how deep did the arrow pierce you?"

He waved her away. "Just go." He could still breathe, so the arrow couldn't have gone in too deep. Danilo pulled on the hilt of the stolen scimitar, making sure it wasn't stuck in its sheath. He longed for his own sword or a bow, but weapons and armor had been the first thing Iskandar's men had divided among themselves.

Luka's legs disappeared into a cloud of beechwood leaves. Maja handed the pack up to him but seemed to hesitate before following her brother up the tree.

"Go," Danilo urged.

"But what are you going to do?"

"Fight back, as soon as I can see him." Danilo gritted his teeth and took a shallow breath.

"Don't you need help?"

"You can best help by staying safely out of sight and keeping that letter from whoever attacked us." He caught a glimpse of a horse and moved for a clearer view of the rider.

"But you're bleeding!"

Danilo didn't look back at her. "Disappear, and stay quiet. If anything happens to me, stay hidden until it's safe, then get that letter to the župan."

He walked forward along the edge of the road, hoping that when the attack came, it would be farther from Maja and her brother. He risked a quick glance at the arrow still stuck in his ribs. The off-white fletching had been attached in neat, straight lines, made by someone with skill. Having an arrow protruding from him would limit his movement, but if he yanked it out, the bleeding would be worse. He thought a moment before deciding agility was the greater need. He would have to risk the bleeding.

He yanked and nearly doubled over in agony. He'd forgotten to factor in pain. It was so intense that he had to close his eyes, and that was dangerous. He reconsidered his options. He would have to fight with the arrow still sticking from him because his pull on the shaft hadn't brought it free, and another attempt might bring him to the ground.

He listened, but other than Dazhbog and the horses stolen from the Ottoman camp, the wind was the only sound. Where had the archer gone?

A twig snapped behind him. Danilo pivoted to see two men trying to sneak up on him. Their dress suggested they were bandits: no armor, unruly hemlines, unkempt hair. Danilo gripped his scimitar and ran at the closest one, a man armed with a spear, bow, and quiver. The man pulled his spear back in preparation for a thrust, but Danilo anticipated and dodged to the left, then swung the scimitar across the man's belly, just below his ribs.

The second man was on him almost immediately, and he carried a well-made spathion. Yet his movements were hesitant, as if he'd only recently stolen the sword and wasn't confident in its use. Danilo said a prayer of gratitude because with an arrow protruding from his body, he wouldn't have been a match for a competent swordsman. The man hewed the blade toward Danilo thrice, and each time, Danilo met the strike. But the blows made the burning in his side flare. The man cut toward him again, and Danilo blocked, pushed, and cut the man across the neck.

More noise came from the road now as two more men, these two on horseback, rode into sight and charged toward Danilo. He grabbed the injured man's bow and nocked an arrow onto the string. He shot one, then the other, but by then, another rider was approaching him, and the man with the spear and bow, though dying, was aware enough to roll onto his quiver, keeping the arrows out of Danilo's reach. Danilo could have finished the man off, but he didn't have time.

A woman screamed. Maja.

Danilo couldn't help her while being attacked. He preferred a spathion to a scimitar, so he plucked up the sword from his other defeated foe and ran toward his newest attacker, thrusting his sword up and ripping into the horse's neck. When the horse tumbled, he traded blows with the rider.

The bandit parried Danilo's cut and struck back hard. The vibrations from the clash of blade on blade sent tremors down his chest, hitting his injury and making the pain explode. He stepped away. He needed just a moment. But the bandit wasn't about to relax his attack. Danilo threw his blade up just in time to block the next blow.

One of the men Danilo had shot with an arrow drew out a dagger and joined the fray. Neither handled their weapons with more than average skill, and one was wounded, but so was Danilo, and he was weakening. And there was Maja to think about. She wouldn't have screamed if she didn't need help.

Both men ran at Danilo at once. A flash of sunlight glinted off something metallic that dropped from above and hit the wounded man on the head. Danilo didn't pause to see what had fallen. He drove his sword into the other man's belly and then turned to finish off the one who'd been hit in the head. He slid his sword into the man's torso and let him fall to the ground next to the shiny object. A mortar trowel.

Danilo stared at it, then looked up. Maja sat in the branches above him, but the tree he'd sent her up was some distance away. "How did you get over here?"

"I've been scrambling around on scaffolding since I could walk. But a group of them have Luka surrounded, and more are riding this way."

Danilo shoved aside the partially disemboweled man with the quiver and took the arrows, then rushed back the way he'd come.

Four bandits had Luka between them. Blood streamed from the boy's nose, but he was still kicking and punching, trying to resist as the men fought to tie his wrists. A fifth brigand led the horses around—the ones the bandits had ridden and Danilo's and the Dinićs'. Several of the brigands mounted. Danilo nocked an arrow and sent it flying into one of the men's backs. He hit a second man before one of the bandits pulled Luka in front of him as a shield and the rest ducked behind trees.

Danilo tried to keep his breathing shallow because of the pain in his side, but he was thirsty for air. Perspiration dotted his forehead, and his throat was dry.

He heard branches scratching together above him and glanced up to see Maja. "The group coming toward us. How many riders?" he asked.

"Seven."

Danilo wasn't sure he could slay the three that still held Luka, then fight off seven more. With the debilitating wound in his side, it seemed unlikely. But even if this were a fight he couldn't win, waiting would only make it worse. He needed to attack now, while there were only three enemies. Soon there would be ten.

Movement stirred the branches above him.

"Maja, wait." If the bandits had pulled Luka from the branches, they could pull Maja down too. And there were things they could do to Maja that they were unlikely to do to her brother.

She didn't stop. She might have a few more trowels, but Danilo doubted they'd do much good. She'd been lucky to hit one bandit. She was unlikely to strike a second.

One of the bandits noticed the other group. But instead of calling out a greeting, he called out a warning. Another of them dragged Luka to the horses. Danilo shot the man in the leg—he couldn't get a clear shot at anything else. Luka elbowed the man and broke his hold, running to Danilo on legs still clumsy from his injury. The other bandits didn't pursue. They mounted their horses, grabbed reins for the animals they were stealing, and rode off. Danilo shot one man, and he fell, but Danilo let the others go so he could cut Luka's hands free and prepare for the next attack.

Luka grabbed a fallen branch and held it over his shoulder like a weapon. Danilo wasn't sure how helpful the boy would be, but there wasn't time to send him into hiding. Danilo nocked another arrow and moved toward the bend in the road, where he could best launch his shots at the new group about to fall upon them.

Maja watched the first group ride off with all their horses while the second group rode closer. She'd thrown her father's hammer at one of the bandits and a trowel at another. She still had another pair of trowels and her chisel, embedded in a block of wood. And tesserae, but most were too small to be used as weapons.

The thundering hooves of the second group slowed, and as they came around the corner, Maja waited for Danilo to shower them with arrows. He'd been awe-inspiring despite his wound, but she was scared for him. This group wasn't divided into smaller pairs of men, and they wore chain mail and carried lances and swords. Their armor was just as good as the type Danilo had worn before it was stolen, and because the ghazis had stolen his, he was left not only wounded but also vulnerable.

Danilo put a hand on Luka's shoulder and said something she didn't catch. Luka lowered his branch, and they walked toward the horsemen. Did Danilo mean to surrender? She supposed he had little choice, but it made her nervous. What would this group do to them?

The lead rider leaped from his horse. He said something, but at that distance, the words were unintelligible over the sound of leaves scraping against each other in the breeze. He reminded her of a youthful St. George, vigorous, comely, and armed with multiple weapons. Only a helmet protected his head, though, not a halo of golden tesserae—and she suspected his intentions were not at all holy. The man rushed to Danilo, grabbing his shoulder and eyeing the arrow.

The man mumbled something, and Danilo muttered something back, but Danilo's expression seemed grim. Of course it did. They were being captured. The men now surrounding them weren't ghazis, but that almost made it worse. Iskandar's men had seemed able and eager for plunder. The brigands, too, had seemed greedy for anything they could steal. But these men . . . they seemed far more proficient, focused, and lethal. She couldn't detect the greed, but the skill with which they rode, handled their weapons, and controlled the situation suggested that of all the armed groups she'd seen since leaving Hungary, these were the most dangerous.

The St. George look-alike called to one of the other men, who began digging through a saddlebag. When the man next to Danilo fingered the arrow, Danilo winced.

Maja climbed from branch to branch, then to another tree, wanting a better look. Dancing spring foliage blocked her view of what happened next—whether Danilo was helped to the ground or forced to the ground—but when the branches shifted again, he was on his back, looking over at her.

He held her gaze. "You can come down now. But be careful."

Maja felt seven pairs of eyes look toward her. She had thought Danilo would want her to hide and take Bokori's letter to his župan, but if Danilo and Luka were both prisoners, she preferred to remain with them, come what may.

She climbed back to where she'd left the packs. Luka walked over to meet her so she could lower the bags to him. With so many men about, she had to take care not to show too much of her legs as she climbed down. When she reached the ground, she gathered her fallen tools and put them back in her pack. She avoided the dying brigands but picked up one of the spears now lying on the ground. Luka and Danilo were both injured. One of them might need a walking stick, and if she kept a few trees between her and the men of the new group, perhaps she could chisel off the point and hide it for future use.

The armed men had all dismounted and were gathering the few horses the brigands did not take, checking the bodies on the ground, and setting up a perimeter. Danilo spoke with the St. George look-alike kneeling by his side. The newcomer had taken his helmet off, and he was younger than she'd first thought.

"You look like a skewered partridge." The man turned to collect supplies from one of the other warriors. "I'm going to apologize in advance."

"For what?" Danilo asked.

"This." The man poured wine over Danilo's wound.

Danilo gasped and hissed through his teeth. "You could have warned me."

"Brace yourself again." This time, the man took a dagger out, rinsed it with wine, and stuck it into Danilo's skin, sliding it beside the arrow.

Maja's jaw dropped. Outnumbered or not, she wasn't going to stand by while Danilo was tortured. She pointed the end of the spear at the man with the knife, its tip level with his nose, only a handspan away. "Stop hurting him!"

All around her, men drew swords and stepped closer, threatening her as if she were a villain. The man with the knife in Danilo's side looked at the spear, then at her, his eyes seeming to calculate whether or not she would strike.

"Maja, put it down." Danilo reached for the shaft and pointed it away from the other man. Danilo's breathing was uneven, but his face was calm. "The arrow has to come out, or it might tear more flesh when I ride home. And he's not hurting me. At least not more than he has to. This is the župan of Sivi Gora."

The župan eyed her for a few moments, then went back to his work. He studied the wound, applied lateral pressure with his knife, and yanked the arrow free. He was hurting Danilo—she could tell by the way Danilo's jaw tightened and his eyes squeezed shut—but she supposed the župan was also healing him. It just didn't look like it.

Embarrassment heated her face. She had threatened *the župan*, the man she hoped would hire her for his church. And all he had done was help Danilo. But it hadn't looked like he was helping, at least not at first.

"Two of the bandits rode off," Danilo said. "One of them is wounded."

"We'll catch them later." The župan helped Danilo into a sitting position and wrapped a bandage around his wound.

"Do you know who they are?"

"We have a few guesses." The župan looked up as a tall man with high cheekbones approached after questioning one of the dying brigands. "Cyril, what did you learn?"

Cyril glanced at Danilo, then at the župan. "It's as we suspected, lord."

The župan swallowed and nodded.

"And what did you suspect?" Danilo asked.

"I'll give you the details later." The župan tied off the bandage. "They attacked the mine last night. Killed one of the men garrisoned there and injured some of the miners."

Danilo ran a hand along the bandage. "Give me a quiver, and I'll come with you."

"You most certainly will not." The župan put his helmet back on. "You'll go back to Sivi Gora, and Helena will stitch you up."

"You said yourself it didn't go deep, but I'll have someone at the garrison look at it."

"Go see Helena. Don't make me insist."

Danilo frowned but didn't argue.

"I should have sent you with a small army when you left. I'm sorry."

Danilo offered a one-syllable laugh. "Diplomats don't travel with small armies."

"An entourage of a few dozen, then." The župan glanced at Maja and Luka. "Although it seems you did gather a few friends."

Danilo caught Maja's eye. "Yes. But it's a long story, and those bandits are getting farther and farther away."

The župan stood, and one of his men brought his horse. "Goran, ride in with Danilo and his friends."

Danilo accepted the župan's help to his feet. "I don't need an escort. Just give me a good bow and a spare quiver."

"Take Goran, and a bow. Just in case." The župan handed his own bow and quiver to Danilo, then he turned to one of the other warriors. "Adamu, ride ahead and inform Dama Helena that Danilo is wounded and she should prepare to tend to him."

One of the warriors mounted and galloped off.

Danilo protested. "That leaves you with only five."

"Against two, one of whom is injured. I think we can handle it. Go on. You can tell me about your journey tonight."

Danilo seemed to resign himself to obeying.

The brigands had taken most of the horses, but two remained. One of the warriors handed Maja the reins of one and offered the other to Danilo.

"Go ahead and mount up," Danilo told her. "Luka too. It looks like you'll have to share."

Maja climbed on first, then Luka mounted behind her. Danilo still stared at the other horse when they finished.

The župan hadn't yet mounted his own horse, and he seemed to notice Danilo's hesitation. "We can fetch a wagon."

"I can ride."

The župan helped Danilo onto the horse and then scrutinized Danilo's pained expression. "Are you sure you wouldn't rather have a wagon?"

"I'm fine." Danilo adjusted his grip on the reins. "Go catch your bandits. They took Dazhbog, and I'd like him back. He's my favorite horse for long journeys."

The župan smiled and thumped Danilo's horse on the rump, sending it down the road. Maja urged her horse to follow. She turned to watch the župan's group mount and ride off in the opposite direction.

Luka watched them as well. He probably wanted to join them. Maja studied the other warrior, Goran. He rode beside Danilo, and they spoke quietly enough that she couldn't understand them. She supposed now that they were back among Danilo's friends, he wouldn't have much time for her. And she would miss his attention, because her fear while watching him fight had been much more than casual interest for a friend.

Chapter Thirteen
Refuge

By Maja's estimate, an hour passed before they turned a bend and an enormous wall came into view. The bottom fourth was made of large stones, and the upper portion was made of brick. Hexagonal towers dominated either side of the road where it wove into the town, with matching towers protruding from the wall every twenty paces or so. Sivi Gora was a fortress. Maja would have liked to study the walls more thoroughly, but she instead followed Danilo and Goran through the gate.

Danilo turned back and met her eyes. "Just stay with me until we get everything sorted out. I'll talk to the župan and the artist at the church as soon as I'm able."

After everything else that had happened, he remembered her art? She smiled her gratitude. The road they traveled was straight, and she could already see the cupola of the church above the homes and shops. People on horseback and foot crowded the streets. Those who walked carried packs on their backs or led donkeys and mules. It must be market day.

Sivi Gora gave the impression of contentment. Surely there were beggars somewhere, but none were within view. Many of the people wore simple clothing, but hers was by far the most tattered in sight.

She wanted to stop when they reached the church. The exterior was beautiful, and curiosity about the interior, where she might be given a wall to fill with tesserae, was almost consuming. But a glance at Danilo and memory of his wound encouraged her to ride on. Filling a church with mosaics could take years, so there would be plenty of time for her to look later.

They passed more homes—larger homes—before reaching a palace. Several grooms approached as they passed the guarded gate. The paved courtyard was decorated with potted plants and fountains, and the walls were made of pale limestone blocks that shimmered in the sunlight.

Maja surrendered her horse to a groom but kept the pack with the letter. It was too dangerous to leave it with anyone else.

The man who had ridden ahead of them came from the home and motioned them to follow. Danilo turned back as though to make sure Maja and Luka were there, then followed the man inside. He led them to a nearby room with wide windows and several beds and tables.

An elegant woman entered the room right behind them. She was dressed like an empress, with curly brown hair beneath an ornamented hat and a dalmatica covered in intricate embroidery. “Danilo! How bad is it?”

“Barely more than a scratch. Hardly worth bothering you over, but Ivan insisted I come to you rather than someone at the garrison.”

She put an apron on to cover her dalmatica with the elaborate roundels and pushed up the sleeves of her tunic. The tunic was plain in decoration, but it looked like silk. Without hesitation, she unwrapped the bandages and examined the wound, apologizing when Danilo winced.

“Take off your tunic and lie down.” The woman went to a ceramic bowl to wash her hands.

Danilo stripped off his tunic, so he was left wearing only his trousers, and sat on one of the raised beds. Goodness, his chest and arms were muscled. That much definition would be a nightmare to put into a mosaic.

The woman washed his side with water, then with wine. She glanced up at Maja. “I don’t believe we’ve met. I’m Helena.”

“The župan’s wife,” Danilo added.

“Pleased to meet you, Dama Helena. I’m Maja Dinić, and this is Luka.” Maja gestured to her brother, who sat on another of the beds. Maja continued to study the woman’s clothing and the way Danilo’s blood now stained her hands. “Why is a župan’s wife tending to the wounded?”

Dama Helena smiled. “Because I have more experience than anyone else in Sivi Gora.”

Danilo grunted. “Only because you haven’t let anyone else have opportunity to gain experience.”

Maja watched Dama Helena carefully to see if she’d scold Danilo for such a statement, but she merely wiped her hands and grabbed a needle and thread.

"Will he be all right?" Maja asked, subtly reminding the woman that Danilo was injured, hoping that would make the woman less likely to punish him for impudence.

Dama Helena dabbed the needle and thread with wine. "It didn't go deeper than muscle. I expect it will heal, but I'll strongly recommend rest. As will your mother."

"You haven't told her yet, have you?"

"I assumed it would be better to wait until after you were bandaged."

Danilo seemed to relax for an instant. Then his eyes caught the needle, and he tensed again.

As Dama Helena stitched and Danilo clenched his teeth and squeezed his eyes shut, a little girl, about a year old, sneaked into the room on unsteady legs. She was beautiful, with round cheeks and tight, dark curls that came nearly to her chin. Her clothing suggested she was no servant's child, and she walked first to Dama Helena, then Danilo.

"Sofija, you shouldn't be here." Dama Helena glanced from her hands, sticky with blood, to the little girl, but went for the bandages instead of the child. "Over the last fortnight, she's become very good at escaping her nursemaid."

Danilo smiled. "Are you surprised by that?"

"Knowing her father, I shouldn't be." Dama Helena placed one end of a bandage on Danilo's side. "Hold that while I wrap."

"Should I take her?" Maja asked as the little girl patted Danilo's healthy shoulder.

"Up?" the child asked. "Up?"

"Not now, Sofija. Just hold my hand." He took the little girl's hand in his own. But only for a moment. He soon released his grip and reached to tickle her instead. The little girl shrieked in pleasure and pulled away, sitting on a rug just out of reach.

"Hold still." Dama Helena looked over Danilo's face, then his chest. "Your bruises look older than this gash."

"They are. We ran into ghazis."

"This far west?"

"Yes. Led by Iskandar bin Abdullah."

Dama Helena's hands froze. "Iskandar?"

"Mm-hmm. Had he not stolen my armor and weapons, I doubt this would have happened." Danilo gestured to his wound.

"Does Ivan know?" Dama Helena asked.

"Not yet."

The little girl sneaked close enough for another tickle, and Danilo obliged. "She's grown since I left."

Dama Helena smiled. Something about the woman's gesture suggested she was the child's mother. "You were gone a long time. And you were missed. But you are not allowed to take her to the range for at least a week. I don't want you pulling on a bow until this is healed."

"Do you often take her to the archery fields?" Maja asked, confused as to why Danilo would take the župan's child to his training.

"Not with my approval." Dama Helena finished tying the bandage and took the blood-soaked rags away.

Maja raised an eyebrow in question at Danilo.

"It's an uncle's right."

"She's your niece?" Maja looked at Sofija, then at Dama Helena. The resemblance was unmistakable. "And the župan's child?"

"Ivan's my cousin, not my brother, but close enough."

"Not the frail cousin you grew up with?" She remembered him telling her of Kostya and Ivan but never would have guessed that a warrior as robust as the St. George look-alike had once languished with poor childhood health.

"The same."

That explained why Danilo could speak so familiarly with the župan's wife. He was family. As Sofija tried to climb onto Danilo's chest, Maja took a deep breath. Danilo wasn't married, and he had shown affection for her that morning, but he was still completely forbidden to her. The župan's cousin. Kind, brave, handsome, and as far above an artist as the dome of a church from its foundations. Had she known, she never would have asked him to kiss her. Kinsmen of lords only formed lasting relationships with women who offered more than calloused hands and mortar-splattered tunics.

Dama Helena came round the bed toward her. "Maja, are you well?"

Maja forced a smile for Dama Helena and felt Danilo's eyes on her. "Yes. I am only weary from the journey. I was worried for Danilo, but it seems that under your care, he will recover, and I am glad for that. But some of the bandits were rough with my brother." She turned to Luka, grateful to divert the woman's attention elsewhere. "Would you mind helping him?"

Luka turned from where he'd been examining the carved-stone window frame. "It's only a bloody nose, Maja. I just need to wash my face."

"Let me see it." Dama Helena approached Luka, and he held still for her while she prodded his nose and asked a dozen questions. He wouldn't have let Maja examine him that closely, but Dama Helena carried authority. "You're right. Nothing serious. But I noticed you were limping. What happened to your leg?"

"Some bandits broke it, I think," Danilo said from his bed.

Dama Helena guided Luka through several movements, then she adjusted the bandages. "It may have been broken, but it seems to be mending. Rest it as much as you can, especially if the pain worsens. For now, come. I'll have someone show you to the bathhouse. And then we'll find a place for you to stay."

They couldn't stay in the palace—they were mere craftsmen—but Maja and Luka had no money for an inn.

Maja hesitated, uncertain what to do.

Danilo tickled his niece again. "Can we find them a place near the church?"

Helena thought for a moment. "A week ago, I delivered a baby on a street with several empty homes. Near where Matthias's family lives."

"The homes are in good condition?"

"I expect they could be made so within a few hours."

Danilo nodded.

"I'll have someone look into it." Dama Helena led Maja to the hall and called to a servant. "Maja and Luka Dinić rode in with Danilo. Please treat them as honored guests. Get them food, a bath, and clean tunics."

The servant nodded. "This way, please."

Maja took another glance at Danilo, then looked pointedly at the pack with the letter inside.

Danilo caught her meaning. "You can leave it here."

Maja smiled in farewell, then followed the servant. She hoped Helena's definition of honored guests matched her own, because she couldn't currently afford a bath, a room, or a fresh tunic. She'd be in debt before she mixed her first batch of mortar.

"Tell me about Maja," Helena asked as she plucked Sofija from Danilo's chest, where the little girl had climbed.

Danilo's head hurt and so did his side. He wasn't in the mood for conversation, but he answered Helena anyway. "She and her brother were robbed. We came across them about a week later, and they were nearly starving. They're mosaicists. Someone told them Sivi Gora's župan was building a church, so they planned to come here for work. We let them travel with us for protection." Danilo huffed, then regretted it as the ache in his side flared. "Not that we were able to keep them safe. It seems Iskandar developed an obsession for Maja at Pločnik. She and her brother were among a group of captives Ivan and I set free. But slavery didn't do much to weaken Iskandar's fixation."

"I had hoped Iskandar was out of our lives for good."

"So had I."

Helena pulled Sofija to her until the girl squirmed, then she set the toddler down and straightened. "Is it wrong that I wish he were dead?"

"If it's wrong, it's a sin we share."

"Sometimes I wonder . . ." Helena trailed off. "He could have been dead, if it weren't for me."

Ivan had nearly killed Iskandar just after Pločnik. But Iskandar had bought his life with information about where to find Helena.

"Ivan wouldn't change what happened in that village, not if Iskandar led an army to Sivi Gora's gates. Nor would I."

"Wouldn't you?" For a moment, Helena's expression made her look not like the wife of a župan but like a frightened refugee.

"The trade was worth it. I just wish Iskandar hadn't escaped or been set free." In chains, Iskandar was harmless. At the head of a group of ghazis, he threatened everything. "Of course, he might be dead. Maja hit him in the head with her hammer."

"Did she really? I'm impressed."

"From what she remembers, it didn't crush the skull, but maybe he bled out. Or maybe it became infected." Danilo gritted his teeth, wishing he'd made certain Iskandar was dead. "I should have checked, but I had only one stolen scimitar, and they had bows, and most of us were injured. We had to flee."

Helena folded her arms. "So you're the hero who rescued Maja? Twice? No wonder she's smitten with you."

Danilo grunted. He certainly hoped Maja was smitten with him after the kisses they'd shared that morning, but he hadn't been planning to discuss it with Helena. "What makes you say that?"

Helena's arms relaxed. "The way she looked at you. The way her face turned pale when she found out you're a member of the župan's family."

"Maybe it was the blood." Although Maja hadn't seemed squeamish about blood before.

"That was after I finished the stitches. I suspect the shock had more to do with societal norms. A soldier courting an artist would be common enough. A member of the župan's family courting an artist is far less common."

Danilo rubbed his eye. "Why couldn't a župan's cousin court an artist?"

"I didn't say he couldn't. Only that it would be rarer. But . . ." Helena's face fell. "Are you planning to court her?"

Danilo sighed. The answer was unequivocally yes, but everything felt fresh and fragile, too early to discuss. "The last fortnight, I've been ambushed by ghazis, tracked by a Hungarian spy, and shot by brigands. What's more, I suspect the sultan will turn west this summer. It's hardly an ideal time to court someone."

Helena bit her lip as if considering whether or not to say something.

"What?" Danilo asked.

She shook her head. "I don't suppose Ivan has returned yet, or he would have come to check on you. But you should rest. I imagine he'll want to talk with you as soon as he rides in." Helena took Sofija and exited the chamber, leaving Danilo to ponder what Helena wasn't telling him.

CHAPTER FOURTEEN
A BULGARIAN ALLIANCE

SLEEP CAME EASILY, AND WHEN Danilo woke, his hearing returned before he felt like opening his eyes. He recognized his mother's voice first.

"He'll do anything you ask, so perhaps you ought to ask less of him."

"Who else could I have sent?" The second voice was Ivan, his best friend, his cousin, and his župan. "There are a limited number of people who have my full trust, and I can't send you or Helena."

"What if he'd died?"

"Then I never would have forgiven myself. But, Aunt Zorica, I did what I thought was best at the time. And he didn't die. Give him two days, and he'll be showing me up on the archery fields again. Isn't that right, Danilo?"

Danilo smiled before cracking open his eyes. They hadn't slept in the same room for years, but Ivan still knew him well enough to tell when he was awake. "Three days, unless you've fallen out of practice while I was away." He glanced at his cousin, who was holding his sleeping daughter.

Ivan looked down at Sofija and brushed a curl from her face. "Lately, she won't nap unless someone holds her."

"I warned him he'd spoil her." Danilo's mother's tone held more teasing than reproof.

"Like you spoiled me all the times I was sick?" Ivan asked.

"She's not sick anymore."

"Is it so awful if I want to hold her while she sleeps? For a time, I feared she wouldn't see the next morn." Ivan shifted the sleeping child.

"She was sick?" Worry nagged at Danilo, but Sofija had seemed fine earlier, so she must have recovered.

His mother smiled as she looked at the little girl she'd long ago claimed as grandchild. His mother was not yet fifty, and though the years had given her plenty to grieve over, her face had aged but a little. A few wrinkles extended from her eyes, but her fair complexion remained clear, and the brown of her hair was still rich and vibrant where it peeked from her hair veil. "She was only in great danger for a day or two."

"Was the illness widespread?"

"No," Danilo's mother said. "'Twas a fleeting fever."

Danilo said a prayer of gratitude that he hadn't come home to a death. He knew the pain of losing a child. Losing little Sofija would have cut them all to the core. He changed the subject before his memories grew too heavy. "Is that a new tunic, Mother?"

She looked at the embroidered cloth and then at Ivan. "I keep telling my nephew that he doesn't need to purchase so many clothes for the ladies of his court, but when it comes to fashion, he stopped listening to me years ago."

Ivan smiled. "I promised a dying man that I would see that his family was provided for. His widow embroiders tunics. I simply ensure that she always has a place to sell her crafts."

His mother smoothed the cuffs, thick with blue and gold thread. "If she didn't know you would buy them, perhaps she would make something more affordable and sell it to the merchants instead of the župan. You did give her a house. Many would consider that fulfillment of your vow."

She sat on the edge of Danilo's bed. He pushed himself up so he was sitting.

She put a hand on his knee. "I am glad you've returned, mostly in one piece. What can I do to help you? Food? Another pillow? A clean tunic? Or shall I pull Ivan away so you can rest more before he starts bombarding you with questions?"

Danilo smiled. "I have much to tell my župan, but there is a matter of importance I would be pleased to leave in your capable hands. I traveled with two others. Artists who hope to decorate the walls of the new church with mosaics. We found them after they were robbed. They lost everything, other than their tools. They need a place to stay, clothing, bedding, food."

His mother nodded, then kissed his forehead and stood to go. "I will make sure they have everything they need, and I will leave you to Ivan's pestering." She had a mother's worries, but she also understood the importance of Danilo's most recent journey.

Ivan scowled, though there was no coldness in the expression. "Aunt Zorica, I would never *pester* Danilo."

She smiled at both of them. "See that you don't. He's had a rough trip."

Ivan shifted his sleeping daughter as Danilo's mother left. "If you want me to go, you can fill me in on everything later."

Judging by the angle of the light coming through the windows, Danilo had slept long enough. If he slept more now, he might have trouble sleeping through the night. "Stay. Did you catch the bandits?"

"Yes. Philippos is tending to Dazhbog. The men put up a fight. I had hoped to question them, but . . . well, they won't be attacking the mine again."

"Bandits, new tunics, and Sofija falling ill. Did anything else change while I was gone?"

"The weather. Didn't you notice that the last of the snow has melted from the mountains?" Ivan glanced out the window. "And there's a new commander for the mercenaries."

"Hensel is gone?"

"I asked him to leave."

"Why?" There was something Ivan wasn't saying. "The men respected him, and he was a good warrior."

"He insulted my best friend by starting rumors of a curse."

The curse again. Danilo had known one of the mercenaries had started it, but he hadn't suspected Hensel. "I thought you were going to let that go."

"I was, until Philippos confirmed it was Hensel. I couldn't know and not act."

Danilo followed Ivan's gaze to the courtyard. "Are you sure that was wise? Hensel was an asset, and you know what we might be up against if Murad turns his eyes to the west."

"Is it better to do what is wise or what is right?"

Danilo knew better than to answer.

"Besides, I couldn't trust him. Not when he told lies about you." Ivan seemed to hesitate.

"And?" Danilo prompted.

"And he didn't go quietly. He promised revenge. He gave the bandits you saw today their information about when to attack the mine."

A contingent of the Sivi Gora garrison was stationed at the mines. Most of the men rotated between the mines and the town every few weeks, and when they returned, they brought with them the silver dug from the mountain. The schedule wasn't regular enough to allow an ambush . . . unless someone like Hensel revealed inside information. "Did they get one of the silver shipments?"

"They tried. Killed one of the garrison, hurt some of the miners. Cyril confirmed it with one of the men you wounded today. Hensel told them when to strike. I increased the size of the guard after his threats. If I hadn't, the bandits might have gotten away with it."

"Do you suppose Hensel was always disloyal? Or did he turn when he was dismissed?"

"Goran and I went over the accounts. Nothing seemed amiss as far as payments go, but that doesn't mean he hadn't been scheming." Ivan shifted his daughter again. "Aunt Zorica was right. I'm paying for not making Sofija nap in her own bed. My arm is about to fall off. How was your journey? Helena said you ran into trouble before today."

Danilo told Ivan about Iskandar, Tvrtko, Bokori, and Bokori's spy. At about that time, Helena came in with a tray of bread and skorup. Danilo pointed to the pack Maja had brought into the room earlier. "We found something significant about Bokori. A letter that proves he once conspired to cut Sigismund out from his promised bride and the throne of Hungary."

Ivan studied the pack. "Does he know we have it?"

"No. We inadvertently took it from Iskandar, though I have no idea how he came to have it. But the spy was suspicious when we met with Bokori."

"Who knows?" Ivan asked.

"Us. Miloš Obilić. And Maja."

"That could be useful." Helena offered refreshment to Ivan, then to Danilo.

"Or dangerous." Ivan shifted Sofija again so he could eat. "If Bokori knows we could ruin him, he may be tempted to raze Sivi Gora to the ground."

"That depends on how you play it. Handled correctly, it could keep Bokori under obligation to leave Sivi Gora alone." Helena placed the tray on the nearest table. "We have only to issue a few threats that word will leak out should anything happen to Sivi Gora or its leaders. Even if the letter is destroyed, rumor could make Sigismund lose faith in Bokori. He'll be obliged to be on our side in any negotiations."

"I didn't know you had such a devious side." Ivan looked at Helena with admiration.

She chuckled. "I grew up in Constantinople. I would have to be either blind or deaf not to have picked up a few things about conspiracy and intrigue."

Ivan reached around to grab another piece of bread smeared in creamy skorup. "We can't send him a letter. It might be intercepted. And the *threat* of turning Sigismund against Bokori is more useful than actually turning Sigismund against Bokori."

"He might come to us. Or send his spy. The man followed us from the time we left Bosnia. He may have tracked us from Hungary, and I just didn't see him." Danilo found his eyes drawn toward the pack. "Which means we need a safe place for that letter."

"What did the spy look like?" Ivan asked. "We can warn the guards to be on the lookout in case he tries to enter the city."

"Can Maja sketch him?" Helena suggested. "She's seen him, and she already knows about the letter, so we wouldn't have to explain why we wish to block him at the gates."

"The overprotective mosaicist who threatened me with a spear?" Ivan raised one eyebrow.

"She did what?" Helena seemed aghast.

"She thought I was hurting Danilo." Ivan propped a leg up on Danilo's bed.

"So she threatened Ivan with a spear and may have killed Iskandar with a hammer? Have you brought us an artist or an assassin?" Helena's tone held more teasing than worry.

"Does she draw?" Ivan asked.

Danilo didn't know.

"Most mosaicists outline their design in the mortar before they place their tesserae." Helena walked to the doorway as if to call someone to fetch Maja.

"I'm not sure we should involve Maja any further. Blackmailing Hungarian ispáns could turn dangerous." Trouble seemed to follow Maja readily enough without adding to it.

"She's already made an enemy of the spy, hasn't she? And of Iskandar?" Helena met Danilo's eyes with a plea. "Bokori's man will suspect her regardless because she rode in with you. One drawing won't make any difference when it comes to the threat from Bokori, but it might keep him out of the city, and that makes Maja safer."

Danilo nodded his consent.

Helena smiled her thanks. "I'll ask her to come now. Bokori's man could already be here."

"Will you take the letter too?" Ivan asked. "Put it somewhere safe."

Helena went to the packs.

"It's in the top one, in a leather satchel." Danilo nodded when she found it, and then Helena left.

Ivan shifted Sofija again.

"Let me take her." Danilo held his arms out.

"You don't mind?"

"No."

Ivan stood and gently laid the slumbering girl in Danilo's arms. She was warm, the way sleeping children were, and a cross between a sigh and a coo escaped her lips as she was repositioned.

"She's perfect, you know." Danilo shifted Sofija's weight so it didn't aggravate his wounded side.

"I know." Ivan cupped the girl's hair in his hand. Then he straightened and gazed at Danilo for a long moment. "Aunt Zorica is right. I've been working you too hard. I'm sorry."

"Send me where you need me, Ivan. That's what I'm here for." Danilo was hungry for purpose, and serving his župan was a worthy cause.

"But what about you? Don't you need anything?"

Danilo shook his head. There was nothing Ivan could give him that he hadn't already provided. Danilo had fine stallions, armor, clothing, and weapons. He ate as well as Ivan, at least when in Sivi Gora. Ivan had even given him a beautiful home, though Danilo had spent little time there since Tatjana's death. Regardless, they didn't have the luxury of worrying over petty needs right now. Murad would strike soon. Danilo was sure of it.

Danilo looked up as Helena brought Maja into the room. The bathhouse had erased all the grime of the journey, her blue tunic was clean, with a bronze belt to cinch it at the waist and emphasize her pleasant shape, and the hair peeping from beneath her hair veil was neat and straight. For a moment, Danilo felt self-conscious. He needed to use the bathhouse himself, trim his beard, and put on clean clothing.

Maja smiled shyly at him and went to the table. She sat on the stool and took the piece of vellum Helena offered, then drew with a quill pen and sepia-colored ink. Danilo sat up straighter to watch her movements. She'd been pretty before, in an innocent, unsophisticated way. Now she was stunning.

"Is this how you remember him?" Maja asked when she was done, handing the vellum to Danilo for inspection.

He forced his eyes away from the attractive mosaicist to the work she'd done. The scar was there, and the proper thickness of the beard, and the look of his eyes. "Yes. It's a good likeness." Danilo glanced at Maja again, appreciating her talent as well as her beauty. He hesitated to make his next request, but he wanted her safe. "Can you do the same with Iskandar? A few members of the garrison would recognize him, but most would not."

Maja's shoulders stiffened, and for a moment, Danilo regretted asking her to draw the man from her nightmares. But Maja picked up her quill again and set her jaw with determination.

"If a drawing will keep Iskandar outside Sivi Gora, I will create as many of them as you would like."

"One should be enough." Danilo prayed his request wouldn't curse Maja with another nightmare. He didn't expect to sleep near enough to offer her comfort should the ghazi haunt her dreams again.

She handed the drawing to him when she finished. The Iskandar in the image looked more menacing than the spy, but the likeness was accurate.

Danilo handed both sheets to Ivan. "She's good. You should hire her for your church." He kept his gaze on Maja and was pleased to see her muscles relax now that Iskandar's face no longer stared back at her from the sketch.

Ivan took the vellum. "I'll speak with Arcadius tomorrow. In the meantime, I'll have these sent to the gate. And there's something else I wanted to talk to you about."

"I'll have Cyril take the drawings." Helena turned to Maja. "I believe your brother was hoping to visit the church. I'll arrange for someone to escort you there."

"I'm surprised they haven't gone already." Danilo would have liked to take them himself, but he didn't want to make them wait.

Color rushed to Maja's cheeks. "How long will your recovery be?"

"Not long. I don't plan to train with the garrison right away, but I do plan to be out of bed in time for a hot supper."

Helena cleared her throat. "If you would be so good as to take it easy for at least a few days, I think that will benefit you most in regard to a complete recovery." She glanced at Sofija. "I'll take her to the nursery so she doesn't disturb you when she wakes."

Danilo did his best to ignore the pang in his side when he lifted the girl up to her mother's arms. Then he watched Helena, Sofija, and Maja leave the room.

"I haven't seen you smile that much at anyone older than Sofija since . . . Well, it's been a long time." Ivan studied him with a penetrating, hazel stare. "I take it Maja is not just an artist you've taken pity on?"

Danilo and Ivan had secrets from each other only when they were apart, so Danilo told his cousin the truth. "I've grown fond of her."

Ivan looked thoughtful. "Fond of her, like that time at the harvest celebration when we both decided Sveta was the prettiest girl in Rivakgrad, but neither of us dared dance with her because we were afraid of her uncle? Or fond of her, like Kostya was when he met Suzana on the day of their betrothal?"

"It wasn't as immediate as what Kostya felt for Suzana, but it's been a fortnight now. Maja is beautiful, but more than that, she has an artist's soul. The way she sees the world makes everything more vibrant. She has spirit and a strength that's seen her through hardship after hardship. So yes, I care for her a great deal." Their shared kisses that morning crossed his mind. He hadn't meant to fall so deep so fast, but something about Maja and their time together had made what happened feel almost inevitable.

"Do you wish to marry her?"

Danilo grunted. He needed time to sort out the future with Maja, and Maja would have a great deal of say in what happened. "I think the sultan is sending another army west, so this isn't the best time to discuss marriage."

Ivan leaned forward. "Danilo, I would rather give you privacy when it comes to matters of the heart, but . . . because the sultan is sending an army, I've been trying to build alliances. And that includes marriage alliances."

The first hint of worry lapped against Danilo. "Marriage alliances involving me?"

"You are the most prominent unmarried man in Sivi Gora."

"Unless people believe in a curse."

"That ridiculous rumor was limited to the garrison and the other patrons at their favorite taverns. It hasn't affected what Bulgarian diplomats think of you, and Emanuil Asen, in particular, found you impressive when he met you at Kral Tvrtko's court. He stopped here on his way back to Vidin. He suggested an alliance formalized with a marriage between you and his niece. In exchange, his brother will stand with us against the Turks and against the Hungarians."

Danilo almost asked why Ivan hadn't discussed the matter with him first, but Danilo had been gone, and Ivan had asked months ago whether a new wife for Danilo could be part of his diplomatic options. At the time, grief for Tatjana had still clutched his heart strongly enough to make any change, even marriage to a stranger, seem as though it might be an improvement. "Is his army large?"

Ivan shrugged. "What really matters is if your heart is already taken. I want you to be happy. You haven't been since Tatjana died, and I thought maybe another wife would change that, even if she was a stranger. It worked for Kostya. And it worked for you before, when you married Tatjana. But if you care for Maja, I would not ask you to give that up."

"And the alliance?"

Ivan frowned. "I can send a letter explaining that plans have changed. Marriage isn't the only way of establishing an alliance."

Danilo swallowed. He understood the benefits of an alliance with Emanuil Asen's brother, Boyar Kalin. He also understood how Ivan's desire to see him happy again might have made a marriage alliance seem like the best decision, even with other options available. He glanced at the pack Maja had left in the room. He hadn't known her long, but the thought of giving her up was painful. "I will do whatever you ask, Ivan. But if the choice were mine, I would pursue Maja."

Chapter Fifteen
A Sundering

That evening, Danilo found Helena waiting for him when he exited the bathhouse.

She motioned to his side. "How does it feel?" She closed her eyes briefly. "And tell me how it really feels, without softening it like you would for your mother or the men."

Danilo had never before had Helena tend to one of his injuries, but he'd heard from other members of the garrison how thorough she could be. Complete honesty would be the quickest way to pass her verbal exam, and then he could find the Dinić siblings. His mother had undoubtedly ensured all their basic needs were filled, but he wanted to make sure they were settled and comfortable. "The warm water helped, but it still aches when I move it."

"A sharp ache on the wound?"

"More widespread. I feel it, but it doesn't hurt any more than my head did after Iskandar knocked his shield into it."

"May I feel your forehead?"

He nodded his permission, then sat on a nearby bench so she didn't have to reach as high.

"It feels normal, and I am pleased. Will you let me know if the pain worsens? Or if you feel feverish? Or if the wound changes color or swells?"

"I will."

He expected Helena to dismiss him, but instead, she sat beside him on the bench. "You seem in better spirits than I expected."

"It's not a serious wound."

Helena looked at the paving stones of the courtyard. "Not about the wound. Did Ivan tell you that Emanuil Asen paid us a visit after he met you in Bosnia?"

"Yes, and I'm glad it went well. We need all the friends we can find."

Helena bit her lip. "Did Ivan explain your role in that alliance?"

"The proposed marriage? Yes, but marriages aren't the only way to seal an alliance. We'll come up with something else."

"Ivan will call off the marriage?" Helena looked ill.

"Yes. I haven't known Maja long, but I have grown fond of her. Enough so that Ivan doesn't need to play matchmaker."

"Danilo . . ." Helena swallowed. "Ivan had hoped that a new bride would bring you joy, but the discussion with Emanuil wasn't merely about finding you a wife. It was about Boyar Kalin's army of one thousand men."

"That large?" It was equal to the combined armies of Konstantin and his two closest neighbors. Double what Sivi Gora could muster.

Helena nodded. "Yes. One thousand more for our side, and one thousand less for the sultan's. You see the significance? It could mean the difference between victory and defeat . . . the difference between Sivi Gora's survival or its destruction."

Dread crept in fully now. An alliance with Emanuil Asen and his brother was not something to turn down. "We both want the same thing: safety from the Ottomans and safety from the Hungarians. Marriage isn't the only way to make an alliance."

"No, but Emanuil Asen was quite insistent. He wanted *you* to marry his niece. Probably because he knows how much Ivan relies on you, and if his niece, as your wife, has your ear and you have Ivan's ear . . . we would be unlikely to forget our obligations."

Helena wasn't merely filling him in on what Ivan hadn't said. She was trying to convince him to change his mind. "You want me to marry the Bulgarian, don't you?"

Helena looked up. Tears pooled in the corners of her eyes. "I want Sivi Gora to survive. And I'm not sure it can without this alliance."

"You would have me give up Maja for a stranger?"

Helena blinked away her tears. "Neither of us expected you to find someone else. We wouldn't ask it of you if it weren't vital, but you've only known Maja for a fortnight. Surely it is not too late to end your pursuit of her and do what is best for Sivi Gora instead."

Danilo clenched his jaw. Helena had said *we*, as if she spoke for Ivan, too, but Danilo had already discussed the alliance with his cousin. "If Ivan wants me to marry the Bulgarian instead of pursuing a woman I have come to deeply admire, then he is my župan, and I will obey him. But I spoke with him before I went to the bathhouse. He made no such demand."

Helena shook her head. "Has he ever *demanded* that you do anything? He would give you Sivi Gora itself if you asked for it. And if you marry a woman with no money and no army, it will cost him just as much. He can't save Sivi Gora without that alliance. You'll cost him his land. And he won't be the only one who suffers because of it. If you love him as much as he loves you—"

"You have no right to question my loyalty and love for Ivan." Danilo bristled. "I'm not the one who crushed his heart."

Helena turned as if she'd been slapped. The silence between them stretched out for the length of several heartbeats before she spoke. "I would not have done it had there been any other choice. I didn't want to hurt Ivan. And I don't want to hurt you or force you to hurt Maja. But my choice was about survival for my people. And you are facing the same choice, Danilo. Will you put your wants over the needs of everyone else in the župa?"

He finally saw it. The desperation in her plea, the fear in the stiffness of her shoulders. "You're scared of what's coming?"

She looked at her hands and nodded. "I've lost a home before. I don't want to lose Sivi Gora too. Not after everything Ivan has done to make it great. Not when I have delivered most of the children who are under the age of three. Not when I have a husband and a daughter whom I love with my whole soul. I know I ask much, but I'm not asking you to do anything I haven't done myself. And as the husband in a marriage, you would hold far more power than I did as a slave in my enemy's harem. I wish you could follow your heart and follow your mosaicist. But if we lose the coming war, our future is measured in mere moons."

Danilo rested his forearms on his knees. The more he considered the possibility of not pursuing a future with Maja, the more he realized how much he wanted it, even after so short a time. But if Sivi Gora were defeated, any happiness he and Maja might find together would be far too brief. She, too, would suffer if Sivi Gora fell.

As Danilo wrestled with his thoughts, a trio of mercenaries walked past on their way to the bathhouse. Mercenaries who might not be trustworthy because Hensel, their former leader, had spread rumors of a curse and an omen. An ill omen that meant Danilo would be the cause of Sivi Gora's downfall. Danilo's hand trembled. The omen had seemed ludicrous when he'd first heard it. He would never betray his cousin or the people of Sivi Gora.

Unless the omen had meant this: the pull Danilo felt for a woman and the consequences that would follow if he pursued her instead of agreeing to marry a stranger whose father commanded an army of one thousand men.

Defeat seeped into Danilo's muscles and settled into his bones. "The Bulgarian woman. Do you know anything about her?"

Helena's voice held no triumph at Danilo's changed manner. Maybe they understood each other better, now that they had both faced the same choice. "Ivan made sure she shares our faith. Emanuil Asen did not remember her exact age, but he assured Ivan she is not older than twenty and five. She has never been married before."

Danilo nodded. Once, Ivan's grandfather had suggested Ivan marry a Hungarian woman who was double his age, Catholic, and a widow barren to her first husband. Ivan had ensured Danilo would not face a similar arranged marriage. Had it not been for Maja, perhaps Danilo would be content with the Bulgarian stranger. "Where is your husband?"

"Probably in his antechamber." Sorrow touched Helena's mirthless expression and imperfect posture. "He did not ask me to speak to you. You know Ivan. He will do anything for those he loves. But if he insists on throwing away this alliance to make you happy . . . I fear we are doomed."

"I understand." Danilo stood. He would talk to his cousin and tell him that the alliance was more important than anything else. And he would hide his feelings so Ivan wouldn't know just how much sacrificing a chance with Maja hurt.

The church in Sivi Gora wasn't the largest one Maja had ever seen, but it had taken only moments for it to become her favorite. Now, on the morning of their second day in Sivi Gora, she studied it again. Even incomplete, it drew the eyes toward heaven. Three rows of columns divided the long nave, and the high windows of the clerestory shone with bright morning sunlight. It was different in the morning than in the late afternoon, as they'd seen it the day before, but that only made her love the church more.

Luka nudged her gently with his elbow. "Is that the župan?"

Maja pulled her eyes from the windows to the men walking toward them from the direction of the sanctuary. Župan Ivan, his hands clasped behind his back, walked beside another man with gray streaks in his beard. The župan wore mail over his tunic, and even in the church, he kept a sword buckled at his side. They were too distant for her to understand their words, but the murmur of conversation reached her only moments after she saw them.

A third man strolled behind them, his eyes drawn to the clerestory, as hers had been. Danilo. He, too, wore armor, so the items stolen by Iskandar's men must have been replaced. The župan slowed, and Danilo joined the other men. Not long after, Danilo turned his gaze to Maja and Luka and motioned for them to join the group.

"I think he wants us to come over," Luka said when Maja didn't immediately start for the others.

Maja nodded as a double dose of anticipation swirled inside her chest. The župan had promised to talk to the mosaicist in charge of the church. She already loved the church. Few things would give her greater pleasure than filling its empty walls with tesserae. The only thing that might exceed that yearning was the desire to see Danilo again.

The župan turned to them when they drew near, making Maja glad that today she wore a clean tunic of the proper length, wore a hair veil that wasn't stained, and carried no spear.

"Arcadius, I'd like to introduce you to Maja and Luka Dinić. I think they're the solution to the concerns you expressed about the anticipated length of your project."

"How is that, Župan Ivan?" The man's voice was deferential, but it also held confidence, even if his Slavonic was accented.

"They are mosaicists and can assist you with the work. I know it was a great hardship for you to consent to working away from Constantinople for so many years. This will shorten the time until the church's completion."

"I do indeed miss my home, lord, but . . ." Arcadius scrutinized Maja and Luka. "You wish me to use local talent?"

"I do indeed," Župan Ivan said. "Naturally, your compensation will remain the same, and you will be the senior mosaicist."

Arcadius cleared his throat. "They seem very young."

"We've decorated churches before," Luka said. "As well as villas."

Arcadius lifted his chin. "And the results?"

"Maja's mosaic of the Virgin Mary was beautiful enough to make the priest cry."

Maja put a warning hand on Luka as defensiveness hardened his posture and tone.

Arcadius smirked. "Yes, well, rural priests are easily overcome." He turned back to the župan. "As much as I look forward to seeing the church completed, the use of a woman mosaicist is certainly . . . unconventional."

The župan gave a polite smile. "Your reputation, Arcadius, is renowned. But when all the work is completed, both men and women will worship here. Provided they are qualified, I see no reason not to use both men and women for the decoration."

Arcadius glanced at Luka. "And boys, apparently."

Luka stiffened beneath Maja's hand, but he clenched his jaw rather than striking back verbally.

"And how are they to be compensated?" Arcadius asked.

"That will be arranged with them privately. Give them a fortnight, and we can see how things play out." Župan Ivan gestured toward the narthex. "Come, tell me about your plans for John the Baptist. He is my family's patron saint. In the meantime, perhaps Luka can fetch his tools. He and Maja seem eager enough to begin."

The župan led Arcadius away.

"Are you ready to start today?" Danilo asked.

Luka grinned. "It's been weeks since I've cut tesserae or mixed mortar. Trust me, I'm ready. Come on, Maja, let's get our tools."

"Actually, Luka, is your leg recovered enough that you could fetch them without Maja's help?" Danilo asked. "I've a few things to discuss with your sister."

Luka nodded and hurried off, eagerness making his steps light and his expression happy.

Maja felt much the same, though she wasn't entirely sure if that was due to the prospect of starting work on the church so soon or because of the man who stood at her side. Maybe both.

She turned to face Danilo. His beard had been trimmed since their last meeting the day before, and not a hair of his head seemed out of place. "How is your wound?"

Danilo grunted. "No worse than the day before, so I suppose it is healing."

"I noticed your new armor." He'd never stopped looking like a warrior, not when he'd worn only a simple tunic, not when he'd worn nothing at all over his chest and arms, but the armor highlighted his strength and skill, two things she loved about him, though that list was extensive and growing with each new day. "It looks as though you have a spathion instead of a scimitar now, so your weapons have also been restored. Did the župan recover your stallion?"

"Yes. Dazhbog is safely in the palace stables. Are your accommodations acceptable?"

Yesterday, after their time at the palace and their visit to the church, their escort had taken them to a small townhome a quarter mile from the church, and had given it over for their use. While they'd been in the church, someone had brought in baskets of food, bedding, and several pieces of clothing for both of them.

"It is far more than I expected." Her smile faltered. "I have nothing to complain about, but I do wish to know the terms of our staying there." She needed to plan for the hearth tax and the clerical tithes that would be owed. The home contained all they might need in terms of pots and blankets and jars of olive oil. But they still had no money. The župan had insisted Arcadius give them a fortnight's trial. Maja was confident in her abilities, but she hadn't forgotten the fresco artist who had refused to share the empty walls of a village church with a mosaicist. A resentful senior mosaicist could create all manner of challenges and drain the joy from the work. Or end her employment on a whim.

"The home is for your use while working on the church. You'll also receive a monthly salary. The items inside the home are a thank-you for keeping me company on my journey."

She and Luka were in Danilo's debt, not the other way around. "In that case, you must allow us to host you as our first guest as soon as you have an evening that doesn't require your presence at the palace."

Danilo's feet shifted, creating more space between them. "Actually, Maja, I fear that would be unwise, and that's why I asked Luka to fetch the tools himself. So I could give you news before you hear it from someone else."

Worry tightened her throat. She'd come to care a great deal for Danilo, and she'd thought those feelings were reciprocated. But his current posture didn't invite her closer. Instead, it seemed to erect a barrier between them. "What news?"

He didn't speak right away but ran a hand through his silky black hair. "I didn't expect to meet someone like you while I was away. Ivan and Helena didn't expect me to meet someone like you while I was away either, and so they acted as if things would be the same when I returned. That my heart, so bruised from losing Tatjana, would still be unattached and unspoken for. So my župan arranged a marriage for me."

Maja inhaled in shock. "You are betrothed?"

"I soon will be. But I didn't know. I wouldn't have . . . Things would have been different had I known. Yesterday morning, when I held you . . . when I kissed you . . . I thought I was free, free to follow my feelings, free to court you."

Maja swallowed as pain crept into every part of her chest. For one brief, beautiful day, she had imagined that she and Danilo would again trade smiles over archery practice, use their voices to create harmony, share more kisses, more laughter. She should have known better, should have known that it was too good to be true. Danilo was like a gold-gilded tesserae: fine, rare, and reserved for specific locations. Halos, crowns, jewelry for the nobility. They weren't used with dull sandstone to create a field or a floor, no matter how much the dull sandstone might admire the sparkle of the gold. "Your cousin is forcing you to marry?"

His lips pulled. "It's more complicated than that. Sivi Gora is small, and we face threats from several directions. We're desperate for allies. This is one way to get them. And you didn't see it because you drove my grief away, but I have been lonely since Tatjana died. Maybe if things had been different, I would have been glad to return home to news of a marriage alliance. Instead, I find myself mourning what might have been, what I realized I wanted just as the possibility of it was taken away."

Maja's eyes stung, but she did her best to blink any tears away. Crying would help no one. "Who is she?"

"A stranger from Bulgaria. I've yet to meet her. But the marriage is meant to secure a military alliance. Her father commands a significant army."

Armies. That was what all of Serbia needed, more than they needed artwork that reminded them of God. Danilo wasn't rejecting Maja because he didn't like her or because he was above her station. It wasn't personal . . . but that didn't make the growing wound hurt any less.

"I'm sorry, Maja." The way Danilo said her name nearly made her weep. She hadn't imagined the tenderness he'd shown her. It was still there. In a world at peace, she could have hoped the moments they had shared would grow into love. But the world was not at peace.

"I won't be able to make all the promises I had hoped to make with you," he said. "But I promised you'd be safe in Sivi Gora. This alliance will help make that true. And I'll make sure Arcadius is fair with you. You'll have your work. I can promise that, at least."

She inhaled deeply, hoping she could speak without tears. "Thank you for helping my brother and me find safety, and a church where we can work, and a home where we can live." She swallowed. "I hope the stranger can bring you the joy I wish I could give you."

She meant her wishes sincerely. He deserved to be happy. But the words seemed to burn her throat.

He laid a hand on her arm. A gentle touch, one she would have followed closer and turned into an embrace had circumstances been different.

"Forgive me," he whispered. The pressure of his hand increased for just a moment, and then he released her arm and walked away.

She watched him until he disappeared into the narthex, and then she turned her eyes to the church. It was still beautiful, and she knew that as soon as the first batch of mortar was mixed, the empty walls would again call to her, as if begging for her to gild them in color and texture. Yet she also knew that she would trade it all in a heartbeat if it meant she could instead have a future with Danilo.

Chapter Sixteen
Edirne

Almost three years had passed since he'd left the city, but Edirne was much as Iskandar remembered it. As the seat of the Ottoman sultanate, it was a center of trade and, more importantly, power.

Upon his escape from slavery, Iskandar had thought to reach Edirne without wealth, with only his past service to recommend him to the sultan's son. His time with Hasan had given him hope of coming as a wealthy supplicant. Riches from the caravan combined with proceeds from the mysterious letter ought to have changed his fortune. But now, again, he was destitute. And it was all Danilo's fault.

Hasan was dead, and Mustafa had abandoned him, taking most of the supplies and most of the coin while Iskandar recovered from the gash in the side of his head. The Serbs had stolen all the horses and stolen the golden-haired woman he now claimed as his bride, so Iskandar had made his way east on foot for most of the journey. He'd stolen a horse outside of Niš and had made better time after that.

He dismounted as he reached the busy market and led the stolen animal through the crowd. His stomach rumbled. He had only a few coins left, but he was at the end of his journey, so he bought a loaf of cheap, coarse bread from a baker.

Most of Iskandar's associates had fallen at Pločnik. His half sister was probably still in Edirne, but she was a widow now. He doubted Saruca still lived in the same large home her late husband had provided for his wives. That, too, was Danilo's fault. Or Ivan's. Either way, hatred for the Serbs burned in Iskandar's chest, and it burned more fiercely when his head ached, as it often did in the wake of the woman's assault.

He used his last coins at the bathhouse and changed into his spare clothing. He needed to be presentable if he was to meet the sultan's son. He wasn't certain he could gain an audience with Bayezid, but he would try. The sultan's other living son, Yakub, wasn't an option. The wily prince was unlikely to forget how Iskandar's patron, Kasim, had turned on Yakub and thrown his support to Bayezid and how Iskandar had followed Kasim's lead. That bridge was burned.

Iskandar didn't approach the palace directly. He remembered enough of Bayezid to know where he preferred to spend his afternoons. The fields where the sipahis trained were near the palace, and though they were walled off, the walls weren't formidable enough to hold out someone like Iskandar.

He found a tree that grew near the wall and used it to swing himself over. He landed hard behind the stables.

"Halt!" someone cried.

Iskandar cursed his luck. No one should have seen him. But he straightened his shoulders and stood to his full height. He had served with sipahis before, so he knew their ways.

A soldier in a loose split-leg robe, turban, and leather boots pointed his spear at Iskandar. "What are you doing here?"

In a flash of inspiration, Iskandar came up with a plan. He wouldn't approach Bayezid seeking pity. He would approach the prince offering service. "I bring information from the west. For Bayezid."

"You should seek him at the palace, then."

"Is he there now? I recall that Bayezid enjoys riding in the afternoons and showing the sipahis that his skill exceeds their own."

The soldier lowered his spear a bit. "Who are you?"

"A ghazi who once served the sultan's son. And, Allah willing, I will serve him again."

"Come." The soldier motioned Iskandar to walk in front of him. "Left," he ordered when they reached the front of the stables. He continued giving directions until they were at a small fountain.

The man motioned a guard over, and the two of them spoke in whispers. When the guard left, Iskandar sat with the soldier in the late spring sun. Mist from the fountain cooled him, compensating for the sun's glare, because no breeze stirred the air.

At last, the guard returned and stood before Iskandar. "You will follow me."

He led Iskandar past the training grounds, through a gate, and into a lush garden full of spring blossoms and rushing water. The air was noticeably cooler. The man leading him stopped, and Iskandar followed his example.

"You will give me your sword," the guard said.

"Will I get it back?"

"That is Bayezid's decision, not mine."

Iskandar surrendered his scimitar and consented to a quick frisking of his robes. A chance to speak with Bayezid was a boon, but an audience was not the same as a position. That he had yet to earn.

The guard pointed him forward.

Iskandar followed the directions, walking along the paved path until it turned a corner. There, on a bench, surrounded by part of his entourage, sat Bayezid.

Iskandar took a few more steps before lowering himself to his knees. "Peace be unto you, Great One."

Bayezid didn't return the greeting. "Iskandar bin Abdullah."

"You do me great honor in remembering my name." If Bayezid remembered Iskandar, did he also remember all their past dealings? His worry, already high, grew.

Bayezid huffed. "What do you want?"

"My lord, I humbly beg to be allowed into your service once again."

"The last time I gave you an order, you failed."

Iskandar hadn't really expected Bayezid to forget the disaster when Danilo and Ivan had slipped away after Bayezid had ordered that they be executed, but Iskandar had hoped time would soften the magnitude of his failure. "I will gladly hunt down the men you ordered executed and kill them now, if it will prove my loyalty or in any way further the interests of our people."

Bayezid stood, towering over Iskandar's kneeling form. "You can't undo the damage they caused at Pločnik. But I don't want two petty Serb nobles. They aren't important now. I want all of Serbia. And I doubt you can give it to me."

Bayezid turned his back to Iskandar in dismissal. Iskandar knew he should go, and the eyes of Bayezid's attendants urged him to be on his way, but Iskandar was desperate. "I have skills you can use. I can spy out the enemy and find their weaknesses. I can bring you information no one else can."

"You are not the only man who can spy." Bayezid faced Iskandar again. "Why would I use you when there are a score of others who would be just as effective and who haven't failed me in the past?"

"Because taking me into your service will irritate your brother Yakub. My sister's husband, Kasim bin Yazid, once served Yakub. And I served Kasim. But Kasim decided to support you instead, as did I. Accepting me as a loyal follower will remind Yakub that a great sipahi leader like Kasim chose you over him."

Bayezid's scowl softened ever so slightly, and he turned to his attendants. "Leave me. All of you."

The men obeyed, though some of them left only reluctantly. When Bayezid and Iskandar were alone, Bayezid spoke again. "I will give you one chance to prove yourself. My father is sending a message to Lazar of Serbia. The delegation leaves tomorrow. If you are as skilled as you claim, you will find a way to travel with them. My brother is no doubt sending a spy. You will be mine. Report what you see. You have disappointed me in the past, but if you help me gain my goal, I will shower you with riches until the end of your days."

"And your goal, Great One?"

"I wish to be the next sultan."

Chapter Seventeen
The Bulgarian Bride

Danilo waited before the palace with his mother, Ivan, Helena, and a few other guards and officials as the small contingent from Bulgaria entered the palace courtyard. Emanuil Asen dismounted a bay stallion and strode to the group to offer his greetings.

"Welcome." Ivan grasped Emanuil's hand in friendship. "How was your journey?"

Emanuil smiled. "Swifter than planned, for which we are grateful."

Their arrival was sooner than Danilo had expected, and though he took Emanuil's hand in greeting, he couldn't muster enough enthusiasm to overcome his worry. The carriage that waited in the courtyard held the woman he was to marry. Curiosity drew his eyes to the cloth pulled closed over the windows, but more than that, dread swirled in his gut. Ivan had told him as recently as that morning that if the woman was repulsive, they could find another way. But opportunities to gain an ally with one thousand men while denying the enemy the same number were few and far between. Rejecting whoever waited in the carriage would feel a lot like proving Hensel's omen about the downfall of Sivi Gora true.

"Come, let me introduce you to my niece and her companion." Emanuil walked to the door of the carriage and motioned for Danilo to join him. Danilo held his breath as Emanuil opened the carriage door and offered his hand to someone inside.

The woman Emanuil drew forth was beautiful. Her exposed brunette hair caught the light, as did her painted mouth. She smiled at Danilo and placed a red hair veil atop her head. Then she studied Danilo as if she were pleased with what she saw. Perhaps Danilo didn't have to worry about whether the Bulgarian bride would find him appealing, because the cast of her eyes suggested she would like nothing better than to loop her arm through his and go for a private stroll. So different from shy Tatjana, who had blushed and stammered at their first meeting. And from Maja, who had looked at him like he was a hero rather than a delectable morsel to be consumed.

Emanuil watched the exchange with a knowing look. He released the woman's hand. "Stanimira is my niece's companion. She speaks Slavonic more easily than Ekaterina does and can help with the adjustment."

Emanuil reached into the coach again. Small fingers grasped his. The arm that followed was sleeved in embroidered silk, but the figure wore a cloak with the hood pulled over her head so Danilo couldn't see her face until she had been helped onto the paved courtyard and cast her soft brown eyes up at him from roughly the height of his elbow.

"Danilo Darrasević, may I present my niece, Ekaterina."

She bowed slightly, a stiff, practiced motion. Freckles caressed her nose, and her skin was otherwise clear, still too young for blemishes. Her gown was elaborate, but the body beneath it was a child's. She didn't smile, and the hand not in her uncle's grasp pulled nervously at the fabric of her skirt.

Emanuil's niece wasn't a woman. She was a girl.

Shock turned Danilo mute for several long moments. Then he returned the girl's bow. "Welcome to Sivi Gora, Ekaterina."

Three paces away, Ivan's face had gone pale. Both he and Danilo had learned to disguise their feelings while they'd lived in Edirne, but Ivan had never hidden his as well as Konstantin, and Danilo could read the surprise and the worry in his expression.

"Not yet twenty and five." Ivan's whisper to Helena was barely audible. "I daresay not yet half that."

Danilo's mother seemed to hear, too, and knew how to ease the growing tension. She stepped forward and offered her welcome to Ekaterina and Stanimira. "I am sure you are weary after your journey. May I offer you food and a place to rest?"

The girl's eyes widened, and she looked to Stanimira, who spoke to her in Bulgarian. Slavonic and Bulgarian were not so very different from each other. Some of the words were the same. Yet it seemed differing languages as well as age would complicate any relationship with the girl.

Ekaterina nodded to Danilo's mother and followed her inside, as did Stanimira, but not before the woman gave Danilo a glance best described as sultry.

Helena nudged her husband with her elbow, and Ivan stepped toward the guests. "Our grooms will care for your animals. If you will follow my wife, she will see that you are shown to your quarters, where you may freshen up and rest before supper."

Ivan gestured to the palace entrance. Emanuil paused before Helena. "Dama Helena, a pleasure to see you again. My men and I thank you for your hospitality. Given the situation in Vidin, we will not impose on you for long."

Helena responded with a polite, diplomatic smile. "Come. Sivi Gora is pleased to host you once more, no matter how short or long your visit."

As Emanuil led his entourage inside, Ivan walked to Danilo, grasped his shoulder, and leaned his head next to Danilo's ear. "I will find a way to fix this."

Danilo shut the door of his bedchamber in the palace and let out a sigh. He had agreed to marry a stranger in the hope of saving Sivi Gora from the Ottomans and the Hungarians. But he had thought his agreement meant marriage to a woman, not a girl.

He tried to picture life with a bride so young. They would have separate bedchambers for years. She wouldn't be old enough for him to confide in or ask advice from. With the exception of his fortnight with Maja, the time since Tatjana's death had been lonely. Marriage to Ekaterina wouldn't change that, not for a decade. She would be more like a daughter than a wife.

Ivan had vowed to fix the situation, and Danilo trusted Ivan to try, but not every problem had a solution, at least not without a cost, and if the cost of rejecting Ekaterina was the loss of Sivi Gora, then Danilo would have to go through with the marriage.

He went to a tall table, poured water into a bowl, and washed his face. No one had mentioned when the betrothal ceremony would take place, and Danilo assumed Ivan could delay it for a few days, at least. Unless Emanuil insisted it happen before he leave. If that were the case, Danilo's unhappy fate might be sealed as early as tomorrow. He slapped the table with his palm. He was trapped. He could reject the child bride and ruin the military alliance. Or he could marry her and hope that in time, the relationship wouldn't seem as dismal as it did now.

"Does something trouble you?"

Danilo spun around in surprise. He'd thought he was alone, but a woman emerged from behind his bed curtain.

Stanimira, his intended's companion.

"What are you doing here?" Danilo had his own home beyond the palace walls, but he used this chamber often enough that he considered it his. Had one of the servants confused whatever hosting plan his mother and Helena had arranged and lodged a Bulgarian guest here by mistake?

"I was resting. Until you woke me." She sauntered toward him. Her level of undress seemed to prove her assertion that she had been napping. Her hair was uncovered and undone, falling around her shoulders in gentle waves. Only a thin tunic covered her body, and the neckline was far lower than was customary. But her expression wasn't sleepy. It was hungry, and not for food.

"One of the servants must have put you here on accident. I'll leave," Danilo said. They could sort out bedchambers later.

"You don't need to leave." Stanimira continued her approach, and her sweet perfume met his nose. "I've been waiting for you." She stood before him and placed a hand on his chest. Her smile grew. "I saw how you looked at me in the courtyard. I think you're delighted to find me in your bedchamber."

His bedchamber. There hadn't been a mistake when the servants had given the guests their rooms. She had sought out his bed. "Last I heard, I was supposed to marry Ekaterina, not you."

Stanimira ran a hand down Danilo's arm. Her red lips were only a handspan away from him.

"Yes, but Ekaterina is young and inexperienced. She doesn't know how to please a man. Surely you'd rather have a woman than a girl in your bed?"

Danilo couldn't back away because the table was behind him, but he stepped to the side. She was right; he didn't want a girl. But Stanimira wasn't the woman he wanted, and even if she were, he wouldn't stoop to illicit affairs. "You should return to the room you were shown to when you arrived."

She gave him a coy smile. "Ah, you prefer discretion. Perhaps that is wise. In time, Ekaterina will be grateful if few people know that I am your mistress. I'll return tonight."

"Don't come back. You are not my mistress, nor will you become my mistress."

She walked to the bed and sat on the edge of it, her hands resting on the mattress and her knees splayed wide. "Does that mean you plan to consummate your marriage with Ekaterina?"

"No. Not while she's so young. Maybe in time, years down the road."

"Ten years? Five?" She gave him a sympathetic smile. "That's a long time to wait for your wife to grow up. But I am willing to help you pass the time, and I know you find me attractive. Your gaze in the courtyard said so."

She was alluring, but she wouldn't be his wife, and thus far, beauty was the only quality he'd found to admire in her. "I apologize if my eyes lingered too long on you. I assumed you were my future bride. Since that is not the case, I will leave. You may finish your rest, but do not return to my bedchamber."

She chuckled as he strode to the door. "Don't you see? I am meant for you as much as Ekaterina is."

That gave him pause. Emanuil had presented Stanimira to Danilo's view as if he wanted Danilo to admire her. Only after Danilo had been given a chance to see every lovely curve and shiny lock of hair had Emanuil clarified that Stanimira was the companion, not the intended bride. "So Emanuil brought his niece to bind Sivi Gora to Vidin through marriage. And knowing his niece's age, he brought you to be my mistress?" He didn't say so aloud, but he suspected her assignment included spying on him, or influencing him, and thereby influencing Sivi Gora.

She stretched on the bed like a graceful feline and smiled. "Emanuil said you were young and strong. He failed to mention that you're also clever. I think we shall get on very well, Danilo, because I am meant to be your consolation."

"Why did you agree to a scheme like this?" Curiosity kept him in the room a while longer.

She patted the bed beside her. "Come sit, and I will tell you."

"I can hear from where I stand."

She shifted positions, allowing more of her skin to show. "Emanuil gave me a generous allowance for my time here. I get to live in Sivi Gora, where the streets are clean and the Turks are far away, and I only have to please one man instead of every man who wanders into the brothel."

"In my family, we honor each vow we make, and we do not take mistresses. I think it best if you return to Vidin with Emanuil." Danilo strode to the door.

"If I return to Vidin, who will translate for Ekaterina? I suppose you will still marry her?"

Danilo paused. "I will do as my župan asks, but I think a scheme so elaborate suggests that both sides want this alliance to work. We don't need a wedding when we have a common enemy. Or is there something else I haven't figured out yet?"

She brushed her hair over her shoulder. "Come join me, and I will whisper the answers to all your questions."

Stanimira was almost enchanting, but Danilo doubted Emanuil had shared all the details of his scheme with her.

Danilo left his bedchamber and walked down the hall to Ivan's antechamber. A guard waited outside, but he let Danilo pass. They always did. And when they didn't announce him, Danilo had learned to knock or pull down on the door so the hinges squeaked, warning Ivan and Helena that someone was about to enter. But today, his cousin was engaged only in conversation with his wife.

Ivan looked up from the chair where he sat. "I plan to talk to Emanuil, but he put me off until after supper. Now Helena and I are trying to figure out what kind of father sends his daughter off to a foreign land to marry a stranger when she is still a child."

Helena folded her arms. "A desperate father."

Ivan frowned. "If they are that desperate for our friendship, our mutual enemies will be sufficient to keep us allied."

Helena shook her head. "It doesn't make sense to insist on a marriage when we have other reasons to form an alliance. There must be another motive."

"I wouldn't think her old enough to be an effective spy. If he's desperate for an heir, she's likely too young to produce one, even if . . ." Ivan glanced at Danilo and looked away, but Danilo could finish the thought without hearing the words. Even if the marriage were consummated, which it wouldn't be, not for years.

"Ekaterina is not meant to be the spy," Danilo broke in. "I believe that task is for her companion. And I suspect the reason Emanuil delayed your discussion was so there would be time for me to enter my bedchamber and find Stanimira waiting in my bed."

Ivan shifted in his seat. "So she is a seductress and a spy rather than a companion for the young Bulgarian lady?"

"Attempted seductress," Danilo clarified. "She freely admitted that she is meant to be my mistress. I didn't confront her about being a spy. I doubt she would admit to it. I want Boyar Kalin's army to fight with us when the sultan comes, but it is hard to trust a man who searched Vidin for the prettiest Slavonic-speaking harlot he could find and then sent her to gather information on us."

Helena walked to the window. "If Emanuil arranged a spy and lied about his niece's age, did he also lie about the size of the army?"

"He didn't *exactly* lie," Ivan said. "She is most certainly not yet twenty and five."

Helena looked back. "He misled."

"I'll confront him after supper." Ivan stared out the window. "At the very least, we can postpone the betrothal until after we've had confirmation of the army's size. Maybe by then we'll have a resolution that is not quite so distasteful."

"Would you like me to ride to Vidin and verify the army's size?" Danilo didn't relish another long journey, but leaving Sivi Gora would give him much-needed space from three females: the one he was supposed to marry but could not love while she was only a girl, the one trying to seduce him, and the one who'd stolen a large piece of his heart before she'd started creating mosaics in the church.

"Are you well enough for a ride that long?" Ivan motioned to Danilo's side. "You haven't been training, so it must still hurt."

"I will begin training tomorrow. If I am not on the road to Vidin."

Ivan shook his head. "Stay. I'll send someone else. You need to have a say in your fate."

Maja ran her fingers along the loose tesserae, feeling for just the right one. She found the proper size of green glass and pressed it into the mortar, finishing the leaf on the border she'd been assigned.

A glance behind her revealed that the chief mosaicist observed her, as had become normal since he'd been forced to hire her. Arcadius had been given little choice but to accept Maja and Luka, but that didn't mean he trusted their abilities. Maja had thus far been working only on borders—something most apprentices could complete in their early years. Her previous commission had involved an entire church, and she longed to create something more meaningful than ivy. She supposed a period of testing was warranted, but Arcadius seemed eager to see her fail. The constant scrutiny made her nervous. And that made her slow. It was infuriating, but she kept hoping he'd relax in another day or so, when he'd seen she was competent at her work.

At least, she thought her work was adequate. Was Arcadius so skilled that he saw flaws where she couldn't?

Arcadius grunted and crossed his arms. "You and your brother can clean up today. It's too late to start a new panel."

"Yes, sir."

He turned and left.

Maja ran her fingers over the vine she'd created around Arcadius's mosaic of Saint John the Baptist, feeling for uneven tesserae. She glanced behind her to make sure Arcadius had disappeared from sight, then reached up to smooth one of the blue glass pieces he'd used as part of the saint's robe. The mortar underneath was beginning to harden, but she managed to push the protruding corner flat.

"How dare you even touch the work of a master mosaicist from Constantinople, queen of cities and bastion of Christianity. You, a lowly Serb." Luka imitated Arcadius's accented Slavonic perfectly.

"Shh." Maja held her finger to her lips. "He might still be able to hear you." The scaffolding they stood on was halfway up the wall of the church, about ten cubits above the floor. She wasn't sure how far their voices might carry. And even if Arcadius had left, there was the stonecutter, Petar, still about somewhere, as well as a few penitents praying throughout the nave, and she didn't want any of them to hear. "Besides, you forgot my most significant defect. I'm a woman."

"Woman or not, at least your tesserae are even. And have you seen his portrait of Saint Sava? If he really looked like that, it's no wonder the patriarch of Constantinople made the Serbian church independent—he probably didn't want to see a face so hideous ever again."

"Autocephalous, not independent." Maja turned to the mosaic of Saint Sava. "It's not that bad. Of course, it's not that good either." Her father had done mosaic portraits of Saint Sava before. He'd usually made him younger, with a normal-sized nose, and given him kind eyes instead of a glare. "But you know how Arcadius feels about Serbs."

"A Serb is paying him."

"Yes. Trust them to pay you and defend you but don't let them touch the tesserae. Speaking of which, would you rather clean up the stones or the mortar?"

"The stones."

Maja gathered her things and climbed from the platform. With tools and pails in hand, she headed for one of the side doors, passing a man who knelt before Arcadius's mosaic of Christ hanging on the cross. The image had been completed before she and Luka had arrived in Sivi Gora, and though she preferred her father's style, it was a good mosaic. Better than the image of St. Sava. She meant to leave the man to his prayer, but though the sun had long ago dipped beneath the level of the windows, enough light remained that she recognized the familiar black hair and muscular shoulders of Danilo. And with that recognition came pain because no matter how much she admired him, a future together was out of reach.

She watched him for a few moments, sensing sadness and a plea in the way his hands clasped together and his lips moved silently. He needed comfort, and she wanted to give it to him. But that would only hurt. She could never forget the way he had saved her from Iskandar—twice. Nor the joy she had felt, all too briefly, when he'd kissed her. Yet the wisest course of action was to move on and pretend she hadn't seen him.

She was about to do precisely that when a piercing clatter sounded behind her, making her flinch, even as she realized what it was: a trowel dropped from the scaffolding. She glared at her brother, but she'd dropped tools before too. It might have been an accident.

"Maja?" Danilo's voice came from behind her.

She inhaled and tried to calm the twist in her heart before turning to him. "Hello, Danilo. I am sorry we disturbed you."

He glanced at the platform, then at her. "I was almost finished anyway. How goes the work?"

"We finished this one today." Luka moved to the edge of the platform so more of the image was visible.

Danilo studied the mosaic of John the Baptist with rough tunic and thin legs. A golden halo about his head proclaimed his holiness. "Did you work on him?"

Luka's chuckle drifted down. "He'd look better than that if Maja had made him."

Danilo raised an eyebrow and looked not at Luka but at Maja.

Maja's face went warm. "Arcadius asked me to work on the border. I did the vines."

Danilo nodded at the mosaic. "The vines are extraordinary."

The small compliment was like sunshine, and she couldn't hold back a smile. "Thank you. How has your healing progressed?"

"Well enough." He motioned to Maja's pails. "Do you need help?"

"Oh, um . . ." Maja wasn't sure what to say. He had helped with everything on their journey, but surely the župan's cousin, soon to be betrothed to a Bulgarian boyar's daughter, oughtn't stoop to washing mortar from pails. "They aren't heavy." She ought to use her work as a reason to step away, but his eyes held her. "I'll rinse them out before we leave. It can wait, if you would like to see any of the other mosaics. You've seen Christ on the cross and John the Baptist. Arcadius has also made an image of St. Sava."

Luka scoffed from the scaffolding. "You should let Maja redo that one. His face at least; otherwise, he'll scare the children."

Maja felt her cheeks warm. "Luka, shh. Someone might hear. Other than us and Danilo."

The smile on Danilo's face told her he was amused rather than insulted. "I would be interested in seeing more of your work."

Maja looked at the pails. "So far, my work here has been limited to vines and borders."

"That's all?"

"Perhaps it is not so unusual. He is the master mosaicist. I am an untried woman with less experience than he."

Danilo studied the vines again. "I am not an artist, but I think you have proven yourself."

"I hope that with time, Arcadius will share your opinion."

"I could talk to him now." Danilo looked around, but Arcadius had already left for the night.

She was tempted to accept Danilo's help yet again. But he had already made it possible for her to work in a beautiful church, and Maja wanted to *earn* Arcadius's trust, rather than using a friend to force an opportunity. She didn't want to be like the painter in that small village who had won his commission only because he'd been the bishop's nephew. Besides, something troubled Danilo, and she didn't want to add to his burdens. "I have been here less than a fortnight, and there are still many walls in need of tesserae. I can be patient a while longer."

Danilo nodded. "Let me know if your patience does not yield the work you are capable of." He reached for her pails. "In the meantime, I'll help you clean. It so happens I am avoiding the palace for the night."

Maja let him pull the pails from her hands. Wisdom told her to find an excuse to flee. But she had missed him, and washing out pails at the side of the church might be her last chance to talk with him. She walked toward the side door, and he followed.

Once outside, she scooped out the excess plaster from her pails. "We heard a group from Bulgaria arrived today. Is that why you're avoiding the palace?"

He nodded.

"And your bride? Did she arrive as well?"

"She did, though Ekaterina is not the reason I will sleep elsewhere tonight."

Maja dipped the first pail in a large barrel of water. "Then what drove you away?"

"Ekaterina's companion. I think she's a spy, selected for her abilities to seduce."

Maja watched Danilo's face as jealousy twisted in her chest. "Has she tried to catch your eye already?"

Danilo folded his arms. "She was waiting in my bed when I went to my bedchamber this afternoon. I told her not to return, but I'm not entirely sure she won't."

"Have you told the envoy from Vidin? Surely he doesn't want his niece's companion trying to seduce his niece's intended husband." Danilo didn't answer right away. Maja studied his expression and thought she understood part of it. "He knows?"

"Ekaterina is very young. Twelve. Thirteen. But she looks as if she could be ten. So in addition to bringing a bride, someone thought they would also bring me a convenient mistress."

Maja rinsed out her second pail. "What will you do?"

"I don't plan on allowing the companion to seduce me, but beyond that, I'm not sure." His voice was soft. "I had hoped for inspiration. That's why I came here." He glanced back at the church.

"If you wish to pray longer, I will do my best not to drop any tools and ask Luka for the same care."

"I will pray more, eventually, but no matter who the bride is, we need the army that alliance will bring us. That's a duty I can't escape. I can, however, insist her companion return to Vidin. I wouldn't put it past her to set her sights on the župan. Not that she would get far. Ivan will never love any woman other than Helena."

Maja used an old cloth to wipe the mortar from her trowel. "And you? Can you love again after losing your wife?"

Danilo sat on one of the steps. "When Tatjana died, I wasn't sure. Everything seemed so bleak for so long. I didn't know if the pain would ever end, if it would ever soften enough to let in happiness or love. Then I met you, and it was like the coming of spring after a long winter." His gaze was like a caress as his eyes pored over her face. "Thank you for helping me learn that love is possible after heartbreak, because everything seems very bleak again, and my only hope is that someday Ekaterina will grow up, and maybe I can fall in love with her then, but I expect many lonely years before that happens."

Maja sat beside him. "Will you take a mistress?"

He shook his head. "There is only one woman I would consider, and you aren't that type of woman, and I'm not that type of man."

Maja looked at her hands lying in her lap. "I almost was, once. After we were robbed. We were so hungry. A meroph offered us food if I would . . . I suppose I wouldn't have been his mistress, not exactly. It wouldn't have lasted so long. I didn't agree to it, but I needed time to think it through, weigh the cost of falling into sin against the risk of starving to death. Luka rejected the arrangement at once, and he was right. As are you. I decided that day that I would give myself fully only to a husband."

"And I admire you all the more for it." Danilo took her hand and gently rubbed the dried mortar from her skin.

"Poor Ekaterina." Maja swallowed against an overwhelming sadness. "I doubt she'll ever know just how lucky she is to have you."

Danilo's lips pulled into a sad sort of smile. "She has my sympathies as well, though for different reasons. She's young to be forced into a foreign land, to be married to a stranger when she is still but a child. I know the pressure to marry for the good of a family, or of a people, but I have a hard time understanding how a father or uncle can marry away a girl her age."

"Maybe they want to protect her. Send her far away from the Turks. Marriage to a good man who is a Christian, even when a child, is better than being forced into an Ottoman harem, which could also happen while she is a child."

"That could be part of it."

Maja would have relished any reason to become Danilo's bride, but that didn't mean Ekaterina wasn't dreading it. Maja envied the girl's fate, but she felt no anger toward the girl herself. "She's probably feeling sad and overwhelmed and lost. You should get her a kitten, or a puppy."

Danilo leaned forward. "Ivan and I were given a puppy shortly after our fathers were killed at Maritsa. We loved that dog. Ekaterina is older than we were then, but maybe it will still work. A marriage with her is not what I seek, but I should show her what kindness I can. It's not her fault we're being forced to marry."

Maja looked at her tools. She would have to depend on them to distract her in the coming months and hope that eventually her feelings for Danilo would fade. "Luka will wonder where I am."

"Then let me walk you back to your brother. And thank you. It's not fair of me to seek your advice and comfort, but I am grateful that you've given it."

He stood and offered her his hand to help her rise. His touch was everything she wanted, and the way his breath caught suggested that he, too, was affected when skin was placed against skin. They would have to avoid it in the future. She pulled her hand free and opened the door to the church.

"Where will you sleep if you do not sleep in the palace?" she asked.

"My home. It's been a long time since I slept there, but maybe Tatjana's ghost won't be quite so strong now that I am haunted by other regrets. It's a nice home. Ivan gave it to me."

"About the župan, I've been meaning to ask something."

"Yes?" Danilo followed her along the nave to the scaffolding.

"Arcadius said that we are to depict his grandfather, Župan Đurad Lukarević, above the entrance to the nave, offering up this church to Christ, as is customary for the patron. Is Župan Đurad Lukarević your grandfather too?"

"No. Ivan inherited these lands through his mother's line. His father and my mother were siblings. I have no claim on Sivi Gora, but Ivan and I have been close since we were infants. I followed him when he inherited."

Maja nodded. "Is not your cousin equally a patron of this church?"

"Ivan and his grandfather planned it together. But Ivan was elsewhere for a time, so he missed the first two years of its building."

"Shouldn't Župan Ivan appear in the panel with his grandfather if he helped plan it? He'll see its building to completion." The foundations were vital, of course. Maja knew that. But it was the windows and the artwork, the long columns and high arches that people would remember and admire.

"I was there when Ivan gave Arcadius his instructions. His grandfather is the official patron, and him alone."

Maja would have to obey the župan's wishes, but it felt wrong for him to be absent from the artwork when he was commissioning it. "Could we add his likeness somewhere else? Assuming I earn Arcadius's trust, I could suggest we place the župan and his wife as the bride and groom at Cana. Or show them being resurrected with the righteous. Or we could place him in his favorite scripture story."

Danilo tilted his head to the side, thinking. "When we were little, he was fond of Daniel in the lion's den. But now I'm not so sure."

"Any others? If I am ever given work beyond a border, I'll want to fill the church with images he and his family will love."

"My mother's favorite is the story of Christ healing the woman with a blood disease. There was a fresco of it back in Rivak, in the chapel in the grody, where I grew up. It's Suzana's favorite, too, I think."

"Suzana?"

"My cousin Kostya's wife."

Maja nodded, imagining the lions and the woman from the scriptures. "Images of healing will also honor Dama Helena's work."

Danilo glanced at all the empty panels, and a smile lit his face. "If you wish to honor the župan and his wife, show Dama Helena as Esther, begging for the life of her people. And show Ivan as David, trying to slay a giant. Give Goliath a Turkish turban."

Chapter Eighteen
Spies in Sivi Gora

The next morning, Danilo met Ivan on the archery fields. He drew his bowstring back to his right cheek and loosed the arrow. It flew straight into the target on the other side of the field. His recently healed wound was still tender but only a bit, and he didn't want to let his aim deteriorate with a longer recovery.

"How do you feel?" Ivan asked.

"Well enough."

Ivan watched him make his next few shots, as if to verify that Danilo could make the movements without wincing. Then Ivan glanced down the field, squinting, and began his practice. "I'm trying to convince Emanuil that we can form an alliance without your marrying Ekaterina."

Danilo paused his practice. Hope seemed to flutter within his reach, but he worried that it would fly away like a butterfly if he tried to grasp it too tightly. "Any progress?"

"He's agreed that Stanimira will return to Vidin with him, so long as we find someone who speaks Bulgarian to translate for Ekaterina."

"Good. We don't need a spy. Or a seductress." Danilo loosed another arrow.

"I asked Father Dmitar to find someone as soon as possible."

"I don't suppose Ekaterina will also return to Vidin?"

Ivan nocked another arrow. "No. Boyar Kalin is set on a good marriage for his daughter, but if we can find a bridegroom more prestigious than a župan's cousin, Emanuil thinks his brother will accept a change, so long as the bridegroom is Christian and not in danger of immediate Ottoman invasion."

An enormous burden lifted from Danilo's shoulders. "I might not have to marry her?"

"You don't have to marry her. Regardless of anything else."

"But if we want Boyar Kalin's army . . ."

Ivan grunted. "Then we had better find a substitute. In six years, she could marry Marko, assuming Kostya and Suzana agreed to it."

Ivan's nephew was only nine. Church law allowed boys to marry at fifteen, girls at twelve. Would Marko at age fifteen be happy with Ekaterina at age eighteen? Danilo didn't want to marry her, but nor did he want Marko to be stuck with an unwanted match. Danilo didn't know the girl well enough to judge if they would be suitable for one another. He had yet to have a conversation with her without the aid of a translator, and he preferred to avoid the current woman changing his Slavonic words into Bulgarian ones. "Will Emanuil wait that long?"

"No, but I'll find someone, even if I have to make him the heir of my silver mine." Ivan's arrow hit the target, but not in the middle, something he's always managed from this distance before. Most of his cousin's arrows were clustered around the target's center, but the cluster wasn't as tight as usual. Was the pressure affecting Ivan's aim?

Danilo watched Ivan's form for the next three shots. It was perfect, the same familiar motions Danilo had watched day after day for years as they'd practiced. But the result was substandard. Ivan's aim was still accurate enough to stop an enemy soldier, but where before his shots would debilitate, if not kill, now they would only wound. Danilo might expect that type of decline from an aging man, but Ivan was only twenty and four years old.

Danilo didn't want to insult his cousin or question his skill. They walked in silence to the other end of the field to collect their arrows. Only then did Danilo see a frown of disappointment on Ivan's face.

"I'm up to sparring if you are." Danilo wasn't really sure he was ready, but he wanted to know if Ivan's swordsmanship had declined the same way his marksmanship had.

"Are you sure?" Ivan pulled his arrows from the target. "Helena will scold us both if you reinjure yourself. I don't want to overwork you while you're healing."

"Try me."

"Right-handed or left?"

"Right." Danilo wasn't feeling so much recovered that he wanted to practice with his off hand, though they made consistent efforts to keep that skill up.

The two sparred, sword against sword. Their breathing was hard, and their strikes were too. Ivan was the most skilled swordsman Danilo had ever crossed blades with, and he seemed as sharp as ever. Or was Danilo simply flagging because he'd practiced less on his journey and was still recovering from his wound?

Ivan pulled back after they had worked up a sweat. "You should probably stop and see how it feels tomorrow. You don't want to overdo it on your first day back."

"No. And I want to find a puppy this morning."

"A puppy? Why?"

Danilo returned his practice sword to the rack. "It might help Ekaterina feel not quite so alone when her uncle and the companion he hired return to Vidin. I don't want to marry her, but that doesn't mean I want her to be miserable."

Ivan nodded. "It's a good idea."

Danilo almost kept quiet, but he didn't want to take credit for something he hadn't thought of. "In truth, it wasn't my idea. I went to the church yesterday after supper. I didn't realize Maja was still there, but she was working past sunset. She suggested a small animal as a present." Danilo shook his head in frustration. "The more I see her, the more I want her."

Ivan nodded. "I'll find someone else for Ekaterina to marry. I promise. But it might be best if Emanuil and his contingent remain ignorant of your passion for a mosaicist. They're leaving later today, but I doubt Stanimira is the only spy. You'll be careful?"

"I can avoid Maja for the present, especially if it means the chance of having her for a lifetime." Hope remained that fragile butterfly, but now it seemed to have landed within his reach, and if he and Ivan did everything right, they might be able to catch it.

"Ivan!"

Ivan put his practice sword away as one of the grooms, Philippos, ran across the field to them.

"What is it?"

"A messenger from Knez Lazar." Philippos handed Ivan a sealed piece of parchment.

Ivan broke the seal and read the message. "Is the messenger still here?"

"Yes."

"See that he's treated well. And see that the Bulgarians learn as little as possible of him."

Philippos nodded and ran off, back toward the palace.

"What does it say?" Danilo asked.

"I've been summoned to a war council." He read over the letter again. "I'll need to leave tomorrow if I'm to make it on time."

"Would you like me to come with you?"

"Of course I would." Ivan stared at him for a while. "But I've asked a great deal of you lately. Are you sure you want to leave again so soon?"

"If Knez Lazar has called a war council, I'd like to find out why." Danilo could guess the reason. The sultan had chosen his campaign for the summer, and he would be coming west.

Two days after Danilo's visit to the church, when Maja had spoken to him after his prayers and he had helped her clean her trowels, Maja and Luka watched him ride out with the župan. The group was twenty strong. Two were more boys than warriors, but they wore the same chain-mail hauberks and scaled-leather cuirasses. According to rumor, the men rode to Kruševac, Knez Lazar's chief city.

Danilo rode next to Župan Ivan. He didn't scan the crowd of townspeople, so he never saw her. She wished he had stopped by, just for a moment, so she could send her greetings to Miloš and the others from their journey. She would never be able to repay her debt to them.

Gratitude should have been her primary emotion when it came to Danilo, too, but she also felt attraction, admiration, and a longing to be with him. She wanted to watch him think through something she said, wanted his touch, wanted to pry away some of the grief and worry that weighed him down. And foolish as it might be, she wanted to look at him again. She liked his dark eyes. Were she to put them in a mosaic, she would choose a warm hematite for the pupil and a translucent umber for the iris. His skin would be of pale brown marble rather than pink, and she would show him armed with both bow and sword.

She sighed and turned toward the church when the group passed a corner and disappeared from sight.

"You like him." Luka swung the pail with their tools back and forth as they walked. His stride was almost normal now, and he said the pain was mostly gone.

"I don't think that's any of your concern."

"Admit it."

"Were mother here, she would tell you to stop teasing your sister. And were Father here, he would tell you to prepare a few hundred tesserae for him."

"But they aren't here. And I don't suppose you would have talked to Danilo for that long the other day if you didn't fancy him. You don't talk to Arcadius or Petar for that long."

Maja felt her face go hot. "I needed to ask him about the mosaics and his župan."

"You took your time getting around to that."

"Then I made a mistake. A flower may admire the sun, but the sun will always be out of reach. Danilo will soon be betrothed to a Bulgarian child whose father commands a large army." The day before, she and Luka had watched the party from Bulgaria ride out. According to the stonecutter, the young Bulgarian bride had not gone with them, but the carriage had contained a woman of extraordinary beauty. Maja hoped that meant the spy had gone with the party, but that still left the girl Danilo was meant to marry in the Sivi Gora palace.

"What?" Dismay pinched Luka's face.

"You haven't heard the gossip? They need a marriage to seal an alliance because without the alliance, they aren't sure they can defeat the Turks again."

Luka was silent for several long moments. "How long have you known?"

"The day after we arrived."

"And you didn't tell me?" Hurt showed in the lines along his frown.

"I meant to. But it hurt so much that . . . well, I never got around to it. When you were happy, I wanted to bask in everything good that's happened to us since we came here. And those times when you were frustrated with Arcadius or in pain from your wound, I didn't want to make things worse."

"So you held it all inside?"

Maja nodded.

Luka put a hand on his hip. "Maja, I know you think you're responsible for me, but we're family, and I'm the oldest friend you have. You can tell me when your hopes shatter. You don't have to bear it all alone."

She swallowed back emotion. Sorrow over Danilo's impending betrothal. Pride and gratitude at Luka's determination to support her. Next time she received news that hurt, she would share it with him. "You know, a mosaic is made up of hundreds of shattered pieces of rock and glass. Somehow, it's still beautiful."

"That sounds like something father would say."

Years-old grief sharpened and stung. She missed her father and her mother. Were they here, she would have long ago confessed her hopes and disappointments when it came to Danilo. But regardless of what her father had always said, sometimes life was not like a mosaic. The wall of a church was smooth, but life was unpredictable. When she created an image, she could pick the size and color of each tesserae. But life was given as much as chosen. A mosaic could be sanded, but for her, life was both chisel and grinder, ever chipping and cutting her.

Maja looked behind her even though Danilo's group was long gone. As she turned back, a man on the street made her pause. She stared. He was clean-shaven now and wore no gray cloak, but she recognized the bearing, the nose, the eyes, and the scar from when he'd followed her into the church in Hungary. Bokori's spy was in Sivi Gora.

She turned away so she wouldn't attract the man's attention. "Luka, the Hungarian spy is here."

Her first thought was to tell Danilo, but he'd ridden off. Perhaps a fast rider could catch him—someone other than Maja or Luka; their horsemanship still left something to be desired, and they owned no horse.

For a moment she considered reporting to the gate. There would be guards there, and surely one of them could catch up with the župan's group. But why would they listen to Maja?

"What should we do?" Luka asked.

"You're going to go to the church, and you'll tell Arcadius that I had urgent business at the palace."

"What?"

"I don't know who else to tell, so I'll have to find Dama Helena." She had seemed kind the day they'd ridden in, she knew about Bokori's spy, and she would have the power to do something about it, whether that involved rounding up the guards, sending a messenger after the župan, or finding a different option.

"I should follow him and see where he goes, so we can find him again." Luka looked over his shoulder.

"So he can threaten you again after he's gotten you alone? No, as soon as he recognizes you, he'll know he's been discovered. Go to Arcadius, and then stay out of sight."

Luka seemed reluctant to agree, so she walked him to the church and saw him safely inside before she rushed to the palace.

After a swift walk, she reached the gate leading into the palace courtyard. One of the guards met her at the entrance and stood in front of her, blocking her path.

"I'd like to see Dama Helena, please."

The guard crossed his arms and frowned. "And you are?"

"Maja Dinić. Please, it's a matter of some urgency."

"It always is. Someone giving birth?"

Maja was confused for a moment before remembering that Dama Helena was a midwife. "A different matter."

"Wait here." The guard motioned a page over and whispered something in his ear. The boy ran off, disappearing inside the palace.

Maja waited, hoping Dama Helena would see her. As a midwife, Dama Helena would have to be accessible, but Maja wasn't one of her patients.

Eventually, the page reappeared and came to stand next to the guard. "She'll see you. Follow me."

The first time she'd been in the palace, Maja had followed Danilo to a room on the first level. The page led her a different way now, to a different room. Dama Helena's audience chamber?

"Wait here," the page said.

Maja watched the page leave, then looked around the room. An icon of the Virgin Mary graced one of the walls, a geometric mosaic covered another, and the scent of freshly cut spring blossoms wafted from a terra-cotta amphora.

"Maja?" Dama Helena appeared from a different door.

Maja bowed. "My lady."

Dama Helena walked over to her. "No need to be so formal. I am glad to see you again."

"I wish I brought happy news."

The smile faded from Dama Helena's face. "What's wrong?"

"Bokori's spy is here. I saw him not far from the church this morning, just after the župan and his group rode out. If we hurry, perhaps a messenger can catch them?"

Dama Helena placed a hand on her waist as she thought. "He's only one man. We needn't disrupt a war council just because he's wandering the streets of Sivi Gora." She paused again for just a moment, pacing across the room. "The first four people I've thought to tell rode out this morning. But we'll manage. We'll have him watched. Not by you or Luka. I suspect he'd recognize you. And he may search for you." She walked back to where she'd come from and stopped a servant. "Please send for Christophoros. It's urgent."

The servant nodded and rushed off.

Dama Helena came back to Maja. "How goes your work at the church?"

Maja hesitated. "I am very grateful to have work, my lady."

"But?"

Maja stuttered, wishing she hadn't sounded anything other than thrilled. "B-but nothing. I'm grateful for the work, as is my brother. Arcadius is slow to trust my abilities, but I'm sure that will change."

"Is he? How?"

Maja wished she hadn't brought it up. She'd already looked foolish when she'd threatened Dama Helena's husband with a spear. Now she was compounding her earlier lapse with apparent ingratitude. Yet lying would be even worse. She glanced at the doorway, willing someone to interrupt her before she made a bad impression on the župan's wife. "In my last job, I did everything. The picture of Christ Pantokrator in the dome, the images of the Nativity, the wedding at Cana, the Sermon on the Mount, the Crucifixion, the Resurrection. Here Arcadius has asked me to do the borders. But I've been working only a fortnight, and he is more experienced than I, so I will be patient."

Dama Helena nodded. "I am a healer and a midwife, but there have been times when I was not allowed to help, even when those who needed help were very dear to me. I understand that frustration, that helplessness."

"You?"

"Yes. It surprises you?"

Maja nodded, studying the woman more closely. She was beautiful, her tunic was so fine its cost was probably close to a year's wages for a working man, and she lived in a palace with a powerful husband she had seemed quite fond of and a much-cherished daughter. "Looking at you, I can't imagine much pain in your life."

Dama Helena gave her a wry smile and walked to the mosaic. "What do you see between my fingers?" Dama Helena placed her hands on the border so that a handful of golden tesserae were visible.

"Tesserae, gilded in gold."

"And now?" Dama Helena moved her hands.

"Black ones."

Dama Helena let her hands fall to her side. "The black ones make the gold ones shine the better for the contrast, do they not?"

"Yes, my lady."

"Do not believe that because all you see is the gold that there has not also been blackness."

Maja took the gentle rebuke to heart. She knew very little of Dama Helena. Her life now did indeed seem perfect, other than the threat from the Turks and a Hungarian spy wandering her city while her husband and his most trusted warriors were all absent. "I'm sorry, my lady."

"You don't need to apologize. My life now is indeed very blessed. I have a loving husband and a healthy baby, and Sivi Gora prospers." Dama Helena lifted her fingers to the mosaic again and ran them along the thin line of gold tesserae, then into the green and black ones. "But we cannot see the future. It would be foolish not to enjoy the moments when everything seems well. It would be equally foolish to expect the good moments to last forever."

Maja wanted to ask Dama Helena about her past, but a man clothed in armor came into the room and stood before the župan's wife. The two of them spoke in another language. Greek? Maja didn't understand any of it, but the man's posture and professionalism gave her confidence. Here was a man who could set a trap for a spy, if that was what his orders were.

The man bowed to Dama Helena and rushed from the room.

Dama Helena turned back to Maja. "May I ask for your help?"

"Yes, my lady."

"Good. We're going to find the spy. And blackmail him."

Maja pushed the final tesserae into the plaster decorating a wall in an isolated room in the palace. Dama Helena looked on with approval.

"Normally, my work is better than this." Maja wiped her hands on a cloth and began helping Luka with the cleanup. "I'm not used to completing anything so fast." Maja studied the simple geographic design of mixed blues and umbers. Behind the small mosaic, on a shelf made from a missing brick, lay the letter from Bokori. They'd covered the shelf with first wood, then plaster, then the new lunette.

"I think it's lovely." Dama Helena clasped her hands behind her back. "I hope we never have need of the item, because I would hate to destroy the mosaic. Come."

Maja and Luka followed Dama Helena from the room, carrying their tools and the extra tesserae with them. Maja wasn't sure how long the lunette would last. They'd used only one layer of plaster rather than the normal three. But after finding the spy and pointing him out to Christophoros and the soldiers who accompanied him, there had been little time to spare.

"Leave your things here." Dama Helena motioned to the same room where she had stitched up Danilo's side. "If you prefer, you can return to the church or to your home, but if it doesn't frighten you, let us show Bokori's man that you are under our protection."

Maja didn't want to see the spy again. She remembered how helpless she'd felt at the church in Hungary. But she was already developing a love for Sivi Gora and its ruling family. She wouldn't back out now. "I'll come."

"As will I." Luka placed the last of their equipment on the ground and straightened his shoulders. Sometimes, Maja wished he were still younger because then she could exclude him from matters like this. But he was growing up, and as hard as it was, she had to let him.

Dama Helena led them from the room. She paused outside an elaborately carved set of wooden doors. "And now we must hope I have chosen wisely." She pushed the doors open.

The chamber inside was large. Sunlight from multiple windows showed rich tapestries, thick rugs, and a carved pair of chairs set on a dais at the room's head like a pair of thrones. Dama Helena gestured toward a bench set against the wall. Maja and Luka went to sit there.

Standing in front of a hearth, surrounded by guards, was Bokori's spy. At the sound of the door, he turned and glared first at Dama Helena, then at Maja.

The tunic Dama Helena wore under her dalmatica reached the floor, so her feet were hidden. She ignored the man and walked with such grace to the raised chair that it looked as if she were floating, and then she lowered herself with the elegance of an empress sitting on a throne. Instead of the kind face Maja was accustomed to seeing, Dama Helena's eyes were hard now, and her face looked made of stone, beautiful still but stern.

"You may approach." Dama Helena's voice was cold and unwelcoming.

If the spy was intimidated, he hid it well. He didn't step forward at once, perhaps as a form of defiance. He gazed around the room, pausing as he looked over Maja and Luka. Maja tried to mimic the confidence and coolness she saw in Dama Helena, but she didn't think she succeeded.

The spy finally strode forward. Two of Sivi Gora's soldiers flanked him as he walked, showing that the spy was clearly at their mercy. Maja hoped the display of force wouldn't backfire.

"You are Janos Bokori's man, are you not?"

The spy didn't answer.

"What are you called?"

"Vadas."

Dama Helena kept her face impassive. "And what do you hunt in Sivi Gora?" When he didn't answer, she continued. "No matter. I know what you seek, for I have seen it."

The slightest hint of worry crossed Vadas's face—a small frown, a noticeable swallow.

"We have no desire to stir up trouble between Bokori and Sigismund. Just as we have no desire for trouble with Hungary."

"If Sivi Gora has no desire for trouble, then those who live here ought to avoid interference with things best forgotten." Vadas kept his voice calm, but contempt showed in his eyes. Maja recognized that look. She'd seen it from him before. "The great wealth of Sivi Gora's mine makes it tempting. And the small size of its population makes it vulnerable."

"Our walls give us protection, and our mines pay for mercenaries. Anyone foolish enough to strike will find us capable of fighting with a fierceness that will bleed them white."

Vadas raised his chin. "Do you threaten us?"

"I only inform you that should you make us an enemy, you will find us a formidable foe. I advise you to tell your master this. We have made numerous copies of a certain letter, penned before Sigismund was crowned. Copies are being delivered to our allies with instructions to forward the letters to Sigismund should Hungarian forces ever attack our lands. I'm sure Janos Bokori can imagine what that will do to his lord's faith in him."

"You expect me to believe that?"

"You watched the župan ride out this morning, did you not? And our Bulgarian friends ride out the day before? Both parties carried multiple copies of the letter."

"A copy offers no proof."

"Is proof needed, or mere suspicion?" Vadas didn't answer immediately, so Dama Helena continued. "Hungary would be wise to leave Serbia in peace. A weakened Serbia will put the Turks at Hungary's door. We can be allies rather than adversaries. It would be prudent for Bokori to tell his lord exactly that."

"Would an ally speak thus to me?"

Dama Helena's face softened ever so slightly. "I told my men to treat you well. Did they offer you refreshment?"

"Yes, my lady."

"Did they beat you?"

"No, my lady."

"Mistreat you in any other way?"

"They detained me."

"You are free to leave the palace whenever you wish. And you may return to Hungary whenever you like. But several of my men will accompany you until you leave the gates of Sivi Gora."

Vadas stood for a moment, peering at Dama Helena as if hoping to see a weakness. But her face held firm, showing authority as plainly as the ornate embroidery of her clothing showed wealth. Finally, he bowed. "I shall depart at once, my lady, and give Bokori word of our conversation."

He turned to leave, and several soldiers followed him from the room. Maja watched him go. Only when she turned back did she notice that Dama Helena's hands were shaking.

The next afternoon while Maja and her brother stood on scaffolding to apply the base layer of mortar to a panel, Luka tapped her shoulder and motioned toward the entrance of the church. Dama Helena strode regally across the church floor, her eyes examining the walls, both blank and decorated. Behind her stood a pair of soldiers. Bodyguards?

Maja finished smoothing her load of mortar, then wiped her trowel clean, thinking that after their work to thwart Bokori's spy the day before, Dama Helena might wish to speak with her. But Dama Helena approached Arcadius instead.

Maja went back to her work, disappointment and embarrassment almost as thick as the mortar she arranged with her trowel. Why would she think the župan's wife might wish to talk to her again? Dama Helena had been friendly, but that didn't make them friends.

But Maja hadn't made much progress on the base layer when Dama Helena called to her from the foot of the scaffolding. "Will you come down for a moment, Maja?"

Maja handed the trowel to Luka and climbed to the floor. Arcadius stood beside Dama Helena, looking decidedly unhappy.

"Yes, my lady," Maja said.

Dama Helena quirked her lips, perhaps as a reminder that Maja wasn't to be so formal. But Dama Helena was the župan's wife. Maja wouldn't be showing the proper respect if she didn't address her formally. "I wish to see your work under less rushed circumstances."

Maja looked at the vine bordering the mosaic of Saint John the Baptist.

"Not a border."

"Then, my lady, you would have to travel many days to a small village church to see my last work."

Dama Helena smiled. "Follow me." Dama Helena walked into the narthex, and the soldiers and senior mosaicist followed her. She gestured to one of the empty panels. "You are to decorate that one. Take as much time as you need, and let me know when you've finished."

Maja stared at the empty panel, excitement bubbling up inside her like water in a spring. The wall was completely blank. The possibilities were nearly endless.

Arcadius cleared his throat. "My lady, are you sure you want to risk an untried artist here? These panels are among the first worshippers see. What if her work is less than satisfactory?"

Dama Helena's mouth pulled into a straight line. "Her work in the palace was satisfactory. There is no reason to suppose her work in a church will be any less so. Besides, if I gave her a panel elsewhere, you would tell me I shouldn't do so because it is too close to the altar and sanctuary. I wish to see what a woman artist can do, and you will indulge me in my request."

Arcadius looked to the ground. "Yes, my lady."

"Thank you." Dama Helena's thanks carried a hint of dismissal.

Arcadius left.

Maja couldn't control the enormous smile pulling at her face. "My lady, you do me great honor in allowing this. Thank you. Do you have any requests?"

"I will trust your judgment." Dama Helena gestured to one of the guards, and he left. The other stayed. "And I wish to apologize that circumstances have come between you and Danilo. None of us wanted to hurt either of you. I hope circumstances will change, but that's something I can't promise. The only thing I can promise you is the opportunity to make this panel beautiful, regardless of what an aging master mosaicist from Constantinople says."

Maja would have chosen Danilo over the panel, but she understood the stakes that rendered that choice impossible. "Thank you, Dama Helena."

Dama Helena smiled sadly. "I know I have no right to ask you for anything, but I would prefer discretion from you and your brother where the spy is concerned."

"Did he leave yesterday?"

"Yes."

"And did the župan really travel with copies of . . . ?" Maja didn't finish her thought, not wanting to reveal something she shouldn't in front of the remaining guard.

"To my knowledge, my husband has never told a lie. The same cannot be said of me, not when my home and those I love are threatened." Dama Helena looked to the entrance. The first guard had returned with several other men. They were dressed in workmen's clothes, but their posture suggested they were warriors. "These men will keep you safe if Vadas returns. I doubt that's his real name, but I suppose it will do as well as any other when we discuss him."

Maja glanced at the men in surprise, then back to Dama Helena. "My lady, surely two artists are unworthy of such concern."

"Are you? I drew you in deeper than I ought to have when I let Vadas see you. But your presence gave me courage, and I needed to be very brave yesterday. I hope I've made Bokori cautious rather than set in motion something I won't be able to predict. I would have rather planned it with Ivan." Dama Helena crossed her arms, and for a moment, she looked vulnerable. "Or with Danilo. Which is another reason for the guards. If something happened to you, Danilo might never forgive me."

After Helena left, Maja spent the afternoon finishing the base layer of mortar she'd begun for Arcadius. In her mind, she began making plans for the panel Dama Helena had given her. That level was generally reserved for stories from the scriptures, and Danilo had given her several suggestions. At the end of the day, Arcadius called in Petar, and all of them arranged the scaffolding so Maja could work the panel she'd been assigned. She wanted to dance and sing in celebration of Dama Helena's gift, but she did her best to remain decorous.

"Most irregular," Arcadius complained. "The župan's wife shouldn't be involved in the church's artwork. It's her husband's place, not hers."

Petar raised an eyebrow but didn't speak, not until the work on the scaffolding was finished and Arcadius had left the narthex. "Dama Helena gave you this panel to test your skill?"

Maja nodded.

"She'll do a good job," Luka said. "When she finishes, it will be the best mosaic in the church."

Maja tried to silence Luka with her eyes. She doubted the stonecutter would be impressed by her brother's boasts.

Petar crossed his arms in contemplation. He was not yet thirty, with short-cropped hair, and his stance made the large muscles of his arms more prominent. "Hmm. When I saw her come in, I thought she had come to warn you off."

"Warn me off?"

Petar nodded. "I've seen the župan's cousin talking to you. I can't imagine the župan's family allowing something like that to proceed, least not for long." Petar looked to the blank panel, then to Maja. "Look, you're young. Be careful. Men in power are used to getting what they want from naive young women, but men like that *use* women like you. They don't marry them."

Maja stiffened. "Danilo has been perfectly honorable toward me."

"So far, maybe." Petar glanced to where the two guards relaxed, well out of earshot. "She assigned them to you, did she?"

Maja nodded.

"Why?"

Maja couldn't tell Petar about the spy, so she said, "I'm not sure."

"Have a care. Perhaps the cousin's intentions are, as you say, honorable. But that could be equally dangerous for you. People like the župan will do anything to protect their family, and an unfavorable match could easily be seen as a threat. You don't know if those men are guards to protect you, spies meant to besmirch your reputation, or assassins."

She was relieved when Petar went back to his carvings along the outside doors of the church and she and Luka were free to gather their tools and finish for the day. Confusion at all that had happened still swirled round her. Dama Helena had no reason to ruin Maja, because Danilo had already agreed to accept his marriage, despite its dismal chances for happiness. But if Petar had noticed Danilo speaking with her, would a Bulgarian spy have seen the same thing, and would that ruin an alliance vital to Sivi Gora's survival?

Chapter Nineteen
The Sultan's Threat

Dozens of male voices created a low murmur along the stone walls of Knez Lazar's grody as the war council gathered. Danilo stood with his cousins, Ivan and Konstantin, and for a moment, the threat of war retreated behind a steady flow of memories and news about family.

Miloš approached the group and greeted Danilo with an embrace. "I am pleased to see you again."

"And I you. Have you recovered?"

Miloš nodded. "Yes, as have Viktor and Filip. How are Maja and Luka?"

Danilo did his best to school his face. Thinking of Maja was pleasant, but that wasn't his purpose at the moment, and he wasn't yet free to pursue her. "They are in good health and have begun work on the church, as they intended."

A mischievous smile crossed Miloš's face, but he didn't push the subject further. His expression changed to something more serious as he greeted Konstantin and Ivan.

A guard slipped through the crowd and approached Knez Lazar, seated at the head of the hall. The guard bent next to Knez Lazar's graying hair to whisper in his ear. Knez Lazar's expression hardened, and then he nodded. He gave a few instructions, and the guard left the room as swiftly as he'd come.

Knez Lazar stood and motioned for Vuk and Miloš to join him. The three conversed in whispers.

"What do you suppose that's all about?" Ivan asked.

"Family council?" Konstantin crossed his arms. "I hear two of Knez Lazar's daughters got into some sort of argument again. Last time, they pulled their husbands into it. Something about which husband was the better warrior, Vuk or Miloš."

Ivan frowned. "They can both kill Turks, can't they? Isn't that enough?"

Konstantin seemed almost amused. "One would think that having so many daughters with which to form marriage alliances would be an asset. Seems to be more of a headache for Knez Lazar lately."

"Speaking of marriage alliances . . ." Ivan rubbed the back of his neck. "Do you know any župans with a young son or a nephew they wish to marry off?"

"Why do you ask?" Konstantin relaxed his arms.

Ivan fidgeted with his dagger's sheath. "That Bulgarian you and Danilo met at Kral Tvrtko's court stopped at Sivi Gora on his way back to Vidin. We felt a defensive alliance could benefit both of us, as we are both threatened by the Ottomans and the Hungarians. It's meant to be sealed with a marriage alliance, so my first thought was to gain a wife for Danilo."

Konstantin glanced from Ivan to Danilo, studying their expressions and undoubtedly finding nothing joyful in either. "But?"

"But the bride is very young, and Danilo would rather pursue someone else."

Concentration furrowed Konstantin's brow as he studied Danilo. "If there's a new woman in your life, why didn't you tell me about her when we were last together?"

"It happened after we parted."

Konstantin turned to his brother. "And why did you arrange a marriage for Danilo without asking him first?"

"He did ask me," Danilo said. "But that was before I left. None of us expected things to happen the way they did."

Ivan shook his head. "I regret it, Kostya, but Boyar Kalin has a thousand men. And he and his brother were slightly misleading when it came to the age of the bride. I made a mistake, and it's not your responsibility to fix it, but Danilo and I would be grateful for your help. If Boyar Kalin receives a better offer for his daughter than the cousin of a župan, maybe we won't have to choose between having his thousand men on our side or freedom for Danilo."

Konstantin grasped Danilo's shoulder. "There's little I wouldn't do to see you happy again, and it just so happens that most of the people I would need to speak with are gathered in this room. I'll see what I can do. How young is she?"

"Twelve," Danilo said. "But she looks younger."

"Twelve. I suppose that's easier to work with than a woman of forty." Konstantin walked along the hall to speak with Župan Dragomir, the leader of a župa that bordered Konstantin's lands.

"Is Župan Dragomir's youngest grandson married yet?" Ivan asked.

"I can't remember." But Danilo hoped the answer was no. The grandson of a župan and brother of the heir would offer significant prestige. And because Ivan and Konstantin's sister had married another of Župan Dragomir's grandsons, a kinship tie with Sivi Gora remained.

Knez Lazar ended his conversation with Vuk and Miloš. He cleared his throat, and all conversation in the room ceased. "A delegation has arrived from Sultan Murad."

The sudden intake of breath was echoed around the room as surprise and worry spread among the Serb nobility. Danilo kept his eye on Miloš. Of the three men at the head of the hall, he was the one Danilo knew best. Miloš crossed his arms and set his face, revealing nothing. Not long after, the heavy doors leading into the great hall swung open, and a group of six emissaries in flowing Turkish robes and clean Turkish turbans strutted into the room. Danilo's eyes riveted on one of the men. Iskandar.

Ivan noticed too. "So, he's still alive after all."

Alive, and a servant to the sultan. That was dangerous. Iskandar scanned the room and stopped when his eyes fell on Danilo and Ivan. A sneer crossed his face, and one hand went to the hilt of the sword hanging from the sash about his waist.

"I'm glad Maja isn't here," Danilo whispered.

"I wish she would have swung her hammer a little harder." Ivan folded his arms and lifted his chin in defiance. Iskandar might have noticed the surprise, but he would find no fear from Danilo or from the župan of Sivi Gora.

Iskandar wasn't the main emissary. He stood at the back of the group. The leader, a man dressed in a blue robe with gold embroidery and a green sash, stepped forward and bowed curtly to Lazar.

The Serb knez nodded in return. "Welcome, messengers of Sultan Murad."

"Peace be unto you," the messenger replied. His Slavonic was spoken with an unnatural cadence, but each word was clear.

Danilo gritted his teeth. *Peace be unto you* was a common greeting—he'd heard it time after time during the two years he and Ivan had been in Edirne—but he doubted the Ottomans meant to leave Serbia in peace.

"We bring a message from Sultan Murad, leader of the Divinely Protected Well-Flourishing Absolute Domain of the House of Osman."

"Speak your message." Vuk's voice was polite, but only just.

"The sultan says, 'Lazar, we cannot both rule Serbia. By Allah's will, Serbia is to be mine. Deliver to me the keys of all your cities and the tax revenues for the past seven years. Give me these, or meet me in battle. On Kosovo's plain, we will decide who is to be master and who is to be servant.'"

Not a sound echoed through the great hall when the messenger finished his speech. The audacity stunned Danilo. No negotiation, little justification. Just a simple demand. Turn over Serbia, or fight for it. Danilo's cousins watched the emissary with stern gazes, as did the other members of the war council. Konstantin and Ivan would fight, and Danilo suspected Knez Lazar and most of the other nobles in the hall would as well.

Kosovo Polje. The field of blackbirds. Major caravans passed through those lands, joining east to west and north to south. It was no surprise that Murad wanted it for his own, but if Lazar's mind was like that of his nobles, Murad would find the Serbs reluctant to relinquish it.

Knez Lazar stood, his posture erect and majestic, and when he spoke, his voice carried his intent to every corner of the hall. "Who is Murad to demand our lands, our heritage? We will not give them over meekly. Tell your master that we will fight."

In his dealings with the Serbs, Iskandar had found them brave but stubborn to a fault. Loyal but predictable. Strong but finite. Lazar's reply didn't surprise him. He would have been disappointed had the knez agreed to turn over the keys and the revenues. Better to slaughter the troublesome race than to try to subdue them. Iskandar remembered well their recent rebellion at Pločnik and doubted the Serbs would ever be loyal, no matter how great a victory the sultan won.

The Ottoman delegation would leave soon, but Iskandar had another task to accomplish first. He found Miloš Obilić in the stables, seeing to a majestic stallion.

Upon noticing Iskandar, Miloš glared. "You? What do you want?"

"I wish to make you an offer."

"We've had dealings before, and they've not left me eager for more. I am currently lamenting the fact the Maja's hammer didn't drive itself through your skull. You'd best leave before I follow her example." Miloš wore a sword and dagger, and the horse looked as though it would trample Iskandar should he get too close.

Maja. So that was the bewitching woman's name. She'd not been as meek as Iskandar had first supposed, but that wouldn't deter him. Now he hungered for her all the more. She would be his one day, and if taming her involved pain for pain, then so be it. "Where is Maja?"

"That's not your concern."

Frustration burned in Iskandar's chest, not unlike a smoldering fire. But there would be time for him to search out information on Maja later. Once all Serbia was under Ottoman control, she would be his. But for now, he had a task. "I am here to bargain. To make a deal."

"A deal? Let me guess. Lands in exchange for peace? Submission to postpone slaughter?"

"Not exactly."

"What, then?" The Serb's expression seethed with unconcealed hostility. "And be quick. I am not sure how long I can contain my loathing for you."

"Join the sultan. Turn on Lazar, and help the sultan wrest all of Serbia from him. In exchange, Sultan Murad will reward you generously. Honor, wealth, peace. All will be yours."

Miloš was silent for a moment. And then he laughed, and the noise was long and loud and full of derision. He stopped abruptly. "Go away before I run you through with my sword."

Iskandar nodded his head and left. He hadn't expected Miloš to betray Lazar, not really. Iskandar walked slowly from the stables, ensuring that multiple grooms saw him and would know Miloš had spoken with an Ottoman messenger. That would be enough.

"That's ridiculous. Miloš would never make a deal with Iskandar." Danilo had spent more time with Miloš than either Konstantin or Ivan. He knew Miloš was loyal.

The groups from Sivi Gora and Rivak were traveling from Kruševac to the main road that led from Belgrade to Constantinople. The next day, they would split. Konstantin and his men would ride south to Rivak. Ivan and his men, including Danilo, would ride east to Sivi Gora. They would meet again in Kosovo.

"But why would Iskandar have gone to see him?" Ivan pulled his horse, Triglav, closer to Dazhbog.

"Are you certain they met?" Danilo supposed Iskandar could wander where he wanted, but surely Iskandar was wise enough to know he'd made an eternal enemy of Miloš when he'd attacked their group on their way home from Hungary.

Ivan nodded. "Philippos was sure of it."

"And you trust the groom that much?" Konstantin asked.

"I trust Philippos completely." Ivan's comment left no room for argument. "He said Iskandar asked Miloš to turn on Knez Lazar and promised Murad would reward him. Miloš laughed and told him to leave. And Iskandar was asking after Maja."

Alarm flared in Danilo's chest. "He knows her name?" She was safe in Sivi Gora, for now. Surely Iskandar wouldn't be foolish enough to return to Ivan's city. He'd left as a slave. Knez Lazar might respect Murad's emissaries enough to grant Iskandar freedom of movement, but Iskandar would have no such privilege in Sivi Gora.

Ivan seemed to notice Danilo's worry. "I'll clarify with Philippos, but that's what it sounded like."

"Well, I suppose Iskandar had to try someone," Konstantin said. "He knows we'd run him through if he made us an offer like that." Most of the Rivak contingent rode behind the Sivi Gora group, but Konstantin rode with his brother and cousin. "Vuk isn't so sure Miloš can be trusted."

"What?" Danilo's concern for Maja shifted to concern for Miloš. "I trust Miloš nearly as much as I as trust the two of you."

"Well, that's good enough for me." Ivan glanced at Danilo. "Iskandar was no doubt trying to make trouble. He has a talent for that."

"Of course." Konstantin looked thoughtful. "He'd want to create dissension. But I fear Serb unity is already less than perfect. Vuk rarely misses a chance to slander Miloš. You've heard about what Mara did?"

"Mara?" Ivan asked.

"Vuk's wife. She slapped her sister, Jelena, cut her cheek with a ring. When Miloš noticed the blood on his wife's face, he asked Vuk to reprimand Mara for striking her sister. Vuk refused."

The thunder of galloping hooves kept Danilo from asking more about what had happened between Knez Lazar's daughters. Ivan had set more men than normal to the task of scouting, and Adamu was riding back toward them.

"What is it?" Ivan asked as Adamu halted his horse near Ivan's side.

"Hensel is back, with a few friends. He's upset about something." Adamu reported to Ivan, but his eyes slipped to Danilo. "Killed Cyril and then rode off. I killed one of them, but there are still two out there, maybe more."

Danilo had a good idea what *something* Hensel was upset over. Maybe it didn't matter if Danilo was cursed or not. The rumor and its backlash were taking on a life of their own. Who needed curses when mere mention of them was sufficient to cause discord?

"If he's willing to strike out at us here, he'll keep attacking until we stop him." Ivan fingered the hilt of his sword. "Can we catch them?"

"Maybe." Adamu looked back the direction he'd come. "They'll have a decent lead, but the ground is good for tracking."

Ivan glanced at Danilo with a questioning look.

Danilo knew what Ivan was asking. Part of him wanted to forget about the curse, but Hensel had already set brigands on the men guarding a silver shipment from the mine, and now this. Cyril had a family back home, and they needed justice. "I think we had best pursue."

"I'll come too," Konstantin said. "We'll have to take Adamu, of course. Maybe a few others, but not many if we want to catch him. We can leave Goran and Bojan over the rest of the men."

Ivan and Konstantin gave orders to their men, then Danilo, his cousins, and seven others galloped after Sivi Gora's former captain of the mercenaries. They brought an extra horse for Cyril's body.

Adamu slowed the horses when they approached the grove of trees where Hensel had set the ambush. Two bodies lay on the ground. Hensel's arrow had driven through the armor to pierce Cyril in the center of his chest.

The other body lay three paces from Cyril. Danilo expected a stranger, or perhaps one of the mercenaries who had left when Hensel had been dismissed, but the face that stared back at him with dead eyes was one he remembered. He motioned his older cousin over. "Do you recognize him, Kostya?"

Konstantin dismounted and crouched to study the face. "His nose is crooked. I suppose I broke it when I chased him out of that Bosnian tavern."

Danilo gritted his teeth. "I shouldn't be surprised to find him conspiring with Hensel. He knew about the omen and the curse, and Hensel's the one who started those rumors."

"Did Hensel send him to spy on us?" Konstantin asked.

Danilo shook his head. "I don't know. But if so, I imagine Hensel was reporting to someone else. The question is, Who?"

Ivan and Adamu collected Cyril's body and remounted. "The sooner we catch Hensel," Ivan said, "the sooner we can ask him."

They continued their pursuit as the sky changed from blue to a golden pink and then to ever deeper shades of purple. Eventually, Ivan pulled on his reins. "We should stop. We can keep looking once the moon rises, but we'll be vulnerable if we continue in the dark."

The men dismounted to give their horses a rest. "Did he say anything to you while you fought?" Ivan asked Adamu.

"Only that he hoped Sivi Gora would fall to the Turks and that . . . well, the rest doesn't matter."

"It might." Ivan waited for Adamu to continue.

"It was rubbish. He said Sivi Gora's ruler was already swayed by one Turk, so the Ottomans would feel right at home, and the peasants would hardly notice the difference."

Danilo folded his arms across his chest as hatred for Hensel burned inside him. But more than that, guilt pinched his breath. If he hadn't come to Sivi Gora, Cyril would still be alive. It wasn't Danilo's fault, not really. He couldn't control prejudice. But a new weight settled over him. Cursed or not, he was bad luck for Sivi Gora.

An arrow whistled through the air and slammed into Miladin's stallion. The horse reared up, then lost its balance and collapsed onto Miladin's legs. As the horse thrashed its own legs in panic, Danilo and the others took shelter behind the animals not yet injured.

Danilo nocked an arrow and looked over the back of his horse, searching for their assailant. He assumed it was Hensel.

"Do you see him?" Ivan asked from beside him.

"Not yet. You?"

"No." Ivan squinted at a tree in front of them.

Danilo saw movement in the distance and pointed. "That might be them." Hensel was too far away to hit with an arrow in such low light, but Danilo intended to get closer. He mounted his horse.

"I'll come with you." Ivan slipped his boot into the stirrup and eased into his saddle.

Danilo nodded and spurred his horse forward. Ivan matched speed with him. Knowing their opponents were armed, they purposely took an indirect path that would obscure their approach with trees. But when they reached the spot Danilo had last seen movement, no one was there.

"Where did he go?" Ivan gripped his sword in one hand and scanned the nearby landscape.

A few rocks and trees offered shelter, but the surrounding area was clear. If the men had tried to slip away completely, Danilo would have seen them.

Dazhbog whinnied. There. A dark form tried to slink away. Danilo whipped an arrow into his bow, drew it back, and released it. The man cried in pain. Then another shadow moved behind Ivan. Danilo nocked another arrow and spun to release it. The shadow fell.

Ivan turned to stare at the form, mere paces from him. "How did I not see him?"

Danilo jumped off his horse and rolled the body over. Hensel. He still breathed but didn't try to speak. Danilo heard Ivan join him, and they both watched the life fade from the man's eyes. The other man, when they found him, was also dead. Danilo rarely regretted his long-honed accuracy with the bow, but that night, it might have been better had he aimed for something less vital than the heart. With no survivors, they could ask no one who Hensel had reported to.

Ivan walked around the boulder where Hensel had hidden. The former mercenary's ambush had almost killed the župan. "It's dark tonight, isn't it?"

Danilo glanced at the moon, not yet fully over the horizon. Clouds obscured its light, so he supposed Ivan's description was partially accurate, but they'd hunted men through darker nights than this. Or was Ivan being figurative? "What should we do with the bodies?"

"They killed Cyril. We'll search them, and then we'll leave them for the crows."

When they got back to the others, Danilo dismounted next to Miladin. "How is your leg?"

"Bruised but not broken." Miladin grunted. "I'll be ready to fight at Kosovo."

"Can we win against the sultan?" Adamu voiced the worry they all had at the back of their minds.

Konstantin led Miladin's injured horse around and patted its forehead. "It doesn't matter. We've worked too hard and bled too much to surrender our freedom without a fight. When I was seventeen and the new župan of Rivak, I had to swear allegiance to Murad, the man whose army had just killed my father and my uncle." He glanced at Danilo as he mentioned Danilo's father.

"I had to fight in his wars and impoverish my župa to pay his tribute for years. I would rather sacrifice all than repeat that humiliation. If my choice is between slavery or death, then I will risk death."

Chapter Twenty
Descending into Doom

Danilo and the others had a short journey back to the camps Goran and Bojan had erected for the men of Sivi Gora and Rivak. When the horses were cared for and the men settled, Konstantin joined Ivan and Danilo around a campfire.

"Župan Dragomir is reluctant to make any binding plans without discussing the matter with his wife and his two remaining grandsons," Konstantin said, "but Todor is unmarried, and seems to have the patience to teach a betrothed our language and our customs. I imagine the boyar will be as content with him as he would have been with Danilo, so watch for a messenger to bring you word. If there's time for messengers."

Hope that had sprouted when Ivan had vowed to find another groom for Ekaterina grew into a physical relief. He wasn't free to openly court Maja, not yet, but now it seemed like that might, with time, be possible.

Two days later, when they reached Sivi Gora and rode through the gates, Danilo was tempted to stop at the church to see if Maja was inside. But he didn't want rumor of his affections reaching Vidin prematurely. Besides, it was his duty to follow Ivan to the palace. Battle was coming, and preparations would begin immediately.

They rode into the palace courtyard, and as they were dismounting, Helena appeared in the palace entrance. "Ivan?"

As soon as she spoke, her husband grinned and walked over to her. Danilo helped Philippos with the horses, allowing the župan a few moments with his wife.

When he finished caring for the animals, Danilo found Ivan and Helena in Ivan's antechamber. Coming back to Sivi Gora had brought contentment, but when he heard what Helena had to say about Vadas the Hungarian spy, a cold dread seeped into his blood. It seemed Sivi Gora had not been uneventful while they'd been away.

"Did you scare him or anger him?" Ivan asked.

"I hope I made him cautious and convinced him that any attack on Sivi Gora will lead to Bokori's downfall." She looked out the window. "I wish I knew how closely they are tied. I assume Bokori would trust Vadas with information about the letter only if he commanded his full loyalty. But it would be nice to be certain, just as it would have been nice to consult with you before I acted."

Ivan reached for her hand. "You did well."

She grasped her husband's palm and smiled first at him, then at Danilo. "Maja did well also. She and Luka recognized Vadas and told me he was here. They also helped hide the original letter. I had several copies made, and I'm hoping you'll have good suggestions for where they should be stored. Rivakgrad, I think. And perhaps Kruševac. We ought to consider Vidin, too, though I am uncertain how much we can trust Boyar Kalin and his brother."

Danilo tried to hide his irritation that Helena had drawn Maja into the plot. He folded his arms and suppressed the angry grunt that wanted to escape.

"What?" Ivan asked him.

Danilo didn't want to pick a fight with Ivan or Ivan's wife, so he tried to take the acid from his words. "The more Maja is involved, the more she becomes a target."

"Yes." Helena frowned in apology. "I felt it was a needed risk, but to make up for the added danger, I've assigned guards to look out for her."

Danilo nodded. "Good men?"

"Yes. Trustworthy, skilled, and passionately in love with their own wives." A hint of a smile formed on Helena's lips.

It had been a long time since she'd teased him. For a moment, Danilo could almost forget the hurts of the past and the dangers of the future. They couldn't expect a messenger from Župan Dragomir for many days, but hope that Danilo would not have to marry a child bride was growing.

"Perhaps you should supervise these men," Ivan suggested. "Take a shift or two."

"Is that my dismissal?" Danilo asked. They would be in Sivi Gora only a week before they marched away to war. Danilo was determined to be at Ivan's side whenever he was needed. But Ivan would want time alone with his wife, and Danilo intended to give them as much privacy as he could.

"Only if you want it to be. If I need you, I suppose I can find you at the church, examining the progress of our new artists? Discreetly, of course, in case Emanuil left spies behind." Ivan's mouth pulled half in question, half in jest.

"Actually, I was planning to check on my mother, like a dutiful son."

"Send her my love. I will also visit her, but it might not happen until after supper."

Danilo nodded and left his best friend with his wife. Before he even closed the door, he could hear the murmured *I missed you*s. Danilo had never met two people more in love than Ivan and Helena, and he was happy for them. What must it be like to so completely fill another person's heart and have that person in return fill yours?

Danilo had loved Tatjana, but theirs had been an arranged marriage. They had shared tender feelings, marital intimacy, and a pride in Sivi Gora. Their marriage had begun pleasantly and grown better with each succeeding month, but she'd been taken before their lives had fully woven themselves together, and sometimes, he mourned that he'd never had a chance to see what their love might have grown into if they'd had more time.

Danilo's mother was easy to find. She sat in the palace garden, enjoying the soft sunlight and embroidering a tunic that looked as though it might fit Sofija. Danilo knelt before her and kissed her hands.

"I am glad to see you safely returned," she said.

"It is good to be back, but I fear we will depart again soon."

"Oh?" She set her needlework aside.

"The sultan told Knez Lazar to hand over the keys of all the cities in Serbia and seven years' worth of taxes or meet him in battle at Kosovo."

"So the men of Sivi Gora will ride to Kosovo?"

"Yes."

His mother studied her hands, not meeting his eyes. "Rivak too?"

"Yes."

She took a deep breath. "Then I must say extra prayers for my son and my nephews. And for Serbia." She motioned for him to sit beside her on the bench. "I have watched many men ride off to wage war against the Turks. And I must remind myself that some have returned."

Unspoken was the fact that some had not returned. Her husband and her brother. Danilo's father and his uncle. Others, too, some when Danilo was a child, some more recently. At least she would know soon. They would leave to fight against a crescent storm within the week, and most open battles, like the one they expected at Kosovo, were decided the same day they began.

She reached over and took his hand. "I will miss you. Am I right to assume this will delay any betrothal to Ekaterina?"

"There will be no betrothal before we march to Kosovo. With a little luck, not after either, not to her. Kostya has nearly convinced Župan Dragomir that Todor ought to marry her instead of me. Župan Dragomir just needs to convince Dama Isidora and Todor."

His mother inhaled with satisfaction. "Which will maintain the alliance with Boyar Kalin, and leave you free to marry someone better suited to you?"

He nodded.

"I'm glad. I like Ekaterina, and I think she will grow into a fine woman, but you need a wife who can be a companion and a friend from the beginning of your marriage. I suppose that news explains why you seem more at ease today. I'm glad for it. You have been wandering for too long."

"What do you mean?" Danilo had traveled throughout Serbia, Bosnia, and Hungary, but he hadn't been wandering; he'd always had a destination in mind.

"Danilo, you have always been a loyal servant to your župan. First to Kostya, now to Ivan. I love them as much as you do. Kostya was older when those boys were orphaned, but Ivan was still so young. He's more like a son to me than a nephew."

"And he is more like a brother to me than a cousin."

His mother nodded. "Yes. And to serve a man you love is a blessing. Your faithfulness is admirable, but there must be more to your life than loyalty to your župan. You need something else to make it complete."

"I am content."

"Are you?"

He didn't answer right away. When he had married Tatjana, he had wanted love and a family. And he supposed that desire was still there, buried under the rumor of a curse and the knowledge that a battle was coming. "It seems a poor time to pursue any goal other than victory over the sultan."

His mother picked up her embroidery again. "My son, the Turks have been a threat to Christendom since before your birth. And regardless of what happens at Kosovo, they will remain a threat. Do not let a powerful enemy make you postpone happiness just because the enemy exists. There will always be threat, and there will always be evil. If you let them take you away from what you most want, what you most need, then you have given them an extra victory."

He watched her needle move through her cloth, and his thoughts turned to Maja. His mother wasn't pushing him to a specific person, just to a defined destination: happiness. And for him, happiness had always been found in familial bonds. His family, including Tatjana, had been chosen for him. He had made key decisions for himself before—when he'd followed Ivan, first into temporary exile, then to Sivi Gora. Would pursuing a woman he selected for himself bring him joy or simply add another complication to a summer already filled with threat? "Did your marriage with my father bring you happiness?"

Her fingers stopped for a moment. "Yes. I loved him enough to spurn a match that would have been more sound politically. That decision had consequences, but I don't regret it. I loved Darras, and my brother, too, was happy to have Darras join our family. Your father and I had so many differences: our religion, our language. Even small things, like how he was always hot and I was always cold, but that didn't seem to matter."

"He died a Christian, didn't he?" Danilo remembered attending church with him.

"Yes. He was baptized just before our betrothal."

"Did he convert to please you? Or to please Uncle Miroslav? Or to please God?"

His mother turned the cloth in her hands, checking the underside. "I wondered that myself for years." She looked up at Danilo. "Not long after you were born, he told me that he became a Christian because the story of Jesus touched his heart. In his despair, he felt his Redeemer guiding him, lifting him up. And in his joy, he recognized the Savior's hand. He converted because he came to trust and love the Lord even more than he came to trust and love my brother or me."

Danilo nodded. He wished he knew more about his father, born Muslim but a Christian in his memory. There were times when Danilo felt like an outsider, but that feeling must have been even stronger for his father, who hadn't been born a Serb. His father had consciously chosen the life he had lived. Danilo had been born into it, but his mixed heritage had always given him two paths he could pursue. Knowing the sincerity of his father's decision gave Danilo more confidence. He was Serb not only by destiny but also by choice. "So, my father made his decision, and never looked back."

"No. He never looked back. Before he rode away to Maritsa, he told me not to worry for him, because regardless of what happened, he had turned his soul over to his Redeemer, and the Lord would keep it safe."

Danilo smiled, grateful to know his father had been at peace with God when it had come time to meet his death. Danilo, too, wanted that assurance when his life drew to a close. He just hoped that time was still far distant.

"You've always known you had a Redeemer, Danilo. You're different from your father in that way. But you also need something. Decide what it is, and be not afraid to seek it."

Danilo didn't stay in the garden long after that. He went to the bathhouse, and he went to supper. But after that, instead of listening to the gossip in the garrison or sitting in while Ivan and Goran organized supplies for the coming campaign, he walked along the wall. A cool wind seemed to greet him, to pull him from one tower to the next, clearing his mind and allowing him to ponder.

What did he need? There was nothing of worldly value that he didn't already have, nothing he couldn't get simply by asking. He had the love of a family. His mother had cared for him enough to follow Danilo from her home in Rivak to a new land, one she wasn't tied to. And all because Danilo had followed his younger cousin. There wasn't anything Danilo wouldn't do for Ivan, and he knew the same was true in reverse. Few people were blessed with a friendship as deep and true as his with his župan. Danilo should be content, but his mother was right. He'd been wandering since Tatjana's death, and not just along the wall.

He glanced behind, back toward the palace. For a moment, the shadows played tricks on his eyes, and he thought he saw someone, but he must have been mistaken because the wall was clear.

"Danilo?"

He turned toward the guard in the next tower. "Yes?"

"Is it true? Did the sultan really challenge Knez Lazar for control of Serbia?" Marjan was one of the younger guards, with a feathery, newly grown mustache.

"Yes, Marjan. It's true."

"What did Knez Lazar say?"

"He said we will fight. And we will."

Marjan relaxed against the crenelated edge of the battlements. "What was it like, at Pločnik? I was too young to go then."

Danilo thought back. The Ottoman commander had underestimated his foes, and when he had let his ghazi raiders disperse for pillage, dividing his forces, he'd left the remainder of his men vulnerable, and the Serbs and their allies had crushed them. But it hadn't been easy. "The thing about the Turks is they're tenacious. They attack, and if they don't break through, they retreat and attack again. Over and over again, until their opponent scatters. But we didn't scatter before them. We held, and then we scattered them."

The sentry stood taller. "If it is my privilege to ride with Sivi Gora's army, then I will do my best to see that the same thing happens at Kosovo. We'll scatter them again."

Danilo grasped the lad's shoulder, pleased with his confidence, his hope. In truth, the coming battle made Danilo nervous. He didn't think Murad would repeat the mistakes of Lala Şahin Pasha, the Ottoman commander at Pločnik. Knez Lazar would have an alliance of Serbia and Bosnia, Vidin as well, but Murad could draw men from a vast empire and from his numerous vassals. Luck had played a role in Pločnik. Danilo expected Kosovo to be very different.

He bid Marjan good night, then continued to the towers that made up the gatehouse. There he climbed down into the streets of the town, descending into the darkness just as he felt the Serbs were descending into their doom.

CHAPTER TWENTY-ONE
DAVID'S FIELD

MAJA SANG TO HERSELF AS she imagined what the field of battle had looked like that day long ago when David had slain Goliath. Had the open area where they'd met been grassy, as she was depicting in a mix of cobalt-green and chrome-green tesserae? Or had it been dry and brown, like ocher marble and umber glass? Maja glanced at the stones she'd made in the corner of the mosaic with large gray and brown tesserae. They were sharp to represent danger, because slaying a giant had been no easy task, and dull to match their real-life counterparts. She didn't regret the bright grass. David had been fighting for a promised land, not a desolate one.

Sunlight had long ago disappeared, so she worked by candlelight. She didn't mind the long hours. She would finish the landscape tonight, with tesserae she had sorted into the right colors before the sun had gone down. Tomorrow, she could start on David. She would give him hazel eyes, like the župan. But David would have to be a younger version of Župan Ivan. David hadn't been old enough to grow a beard, and she had always pictured him as a slim man in his teens, not yet come into the full strength of manhood.

She continued her work and her song, a bittersweet ballad that matched the mood of her heart. "*I looked widely for my dear one, the one I planned to wed. I found him in the churchyard, burying the dead. He said, 'Touch me not, my lady, the curse is on me too. And soon I'll go to join them, though it means leaving you.*'"

Something in the shadows shifted, and she stopped singing and spun around. Maybe she shouldn't have sent the guards and Luka to their beds.

Her fear vanished, though, when she recognized the face looking up at her from the ground. Danilo.

"How long have you been there?" she asked.

He smiled softly. "Long enough to know that your song isn't very cheerful."

She caught the glint of his eyes in the candlelight. Goodness, she loved those eyes. She could stare into them for hours and not be bored, though wisdom suggested she turn her gaze elsewhere rather than on a man forbidden to her. "I heard the Great Mortality hit Sivi Gora hard. A song about the plague seemed appropriate."

"Yes, Ivan's grandfather lost his wife and six of his seven children. The other families of Sivi Gora didn't fare much better."

"Perhaps I shouldn't sing about it if it still haunts the inhabitants." She glanced back at the mosaic taking shape on the wall behind her. "It seems we have to immortalize hardships either in song or in art. Perhaps to remind us that they can be overcome."

"Then maybe I should learn your song. Hardships are common these days." He glanced around the empty, dimly lit narthex. "Helena said she arranged guards for you. Why are you all alone?"

"I spread too much mortar. If I don't finish this section tonight, it will be too dry tomorrow. Both guards have families. I didn't want them to miss their suppers or time with their children because I overestimated how much I could do." Besides, Vadas had left long ago, and she'd seen nothing since his departure to give her fear. "And I've learned that Luka is easier to live with if he gets his sleep, so I sent him home as well."

Danilo frowned. "But what if Bokori sent another spy? Or Sultan Murad, Emanuil Asen, or a renegade mercenary? Goodness, a drunken member of the garrison could be a threat to a woman all alone, especially this time of night." He stepped closer to the scaffolding. "Would you like some help?"

Maja glanced at her mosaic. She didn't want to trust anything, even a blade of grass, to someone not trained as an artist, especially not in the nave of a church. But the thought of him climbing the scaffolding to keep her company was appealing. She battled what she wanted—Danilo close to her—with what was wise—distance because he was meant to marry another, and Petar's warning still lived in her head.

A small gray tessera lay on the edge of the scaffolding. Should she push it with her toe and give him something to retrieve and a reason to climb up to her?

"I can't leave you here alone when your work against the Hungarian spy has placed you in danger." Danilo spoke into the silence. "I won't try to put anything into the mortar, just as you wouldn't expect me to hand you my bow if bandits came through the door and attacked us."

She glanced at his bow hanging unstrung at his side. "I wouldn't mind shooting your bow again, if it weren't so hard to pull back."

"It has to have a heavy draw weight to make it through Turkish armor."

Maja remembered him telling Luka much the same thing. How many Turks had Danilo killed? She ought to feel some sorrow or horror at the death of anyone, but it was hard to conjure up pity for the people who had slaughtered her parents and nearly enslaved her and her brother. Only Danilo's intervention had prevented that on two different occasions. She knew any lasting relationship with him was impossible. And yet, tonight, he was just below the scaffolding, and she doubted he would leave after what he'd said about the dangers of her being alone. She had no other escort home.

Ignoring wisdom, she shuffled as if she were going back to her work and bumped the tessera from the scaffolding.

She feigned surprise as it fell to the floor below.

Danilo turned at the sound as it struck the ground. He walked over to it and picked up the small piece. "Should I bring it up to you?"

"Please."

She watched him climb the scaffolding, and when he arrived, she accepted the small bit of gray marble from him. "Thank you."

"You're welcome." He smiled at her, then looked over the partially completed mosaic. "What will it be?"

She walked along the scaffolding, pointing out the underdrawings she had already made. "Here's David." She walked a little farther, to the outline of a large man in profile. "And this will be Goliath."

"How much do you need to finish tonight?"

"The grass." Maja put the gray stone he'd retrieved with a pile of similar-colored tesserae and began with the green ones again.

Having someone watch her while she worked usually made her nervous, and Danilo was no exception. But feeling his eyes on her hands also sparked a different emotion, one that made everything in the nave seem more vibrant, more alive. Part of her wanted to hurry so as not to keep him waiting. And part of her wanted to slow down to make their time together last. This stolen evening with him might be their last together, and regardless of the pain their sundering would bring, for the moment, she was greedy to have him near her side.

He sat on the scaffolding, content to watch, even without much speech, though he answered when she asked after Miloš and the others from their previous journey. When he told her that Iskandar still lived, she pushed a piece of glass too far into the mortar and had to draw it out, wipe it clean, and insert it again. Iskandar had ruined many things, but she wouldn't let him ruin David's landscape. The candles shrank, and the grassy field took shape in undulating waves of mixed green glass. Through it all, Danilo's presence made her feel both safe and unsettled because he was still the hero she'd imagined him to be, but no matter how much attraction she felt for him, no matter how easy it was to converse with him, she could only ever admire him from afar. Like the saints of tesserae, with their gold nimbuses, or David with his sling—at the moment only an underdrawing—he was legendary but distant. When she put the last piece of glass into the mortar, completing the field, she felt strangely disappointed to be finished.

Danilo seemed to recognize her task was complete and stood to study the partial mosaic more carefully. "You do good work."

"Thank you." She glanced at his face, wondering if he was just being polite, but he seemed sincere.

He stood back a bit to see it from a different angle while Maja put the unused tesserae into canvas bags. "And this is also a beautiful view."

She glanced up to see him looking in her direction. She turned to see the blank wall behind her. "That's only the first layer of mortar. It's nothing but lime and sand, crushed bricks and chopped straw."

"I wasn't talking about the wall."

Maja felt her face grow warm because it seemed he had been referring to her.

Danilo returned to his seat on the scaffolding. She wanted to sit beside him, close enough that she could raise her fingers to feel each curve of his face and touch those expressive lips. She was far too fond of him.

"Maja?" Danilo asked. "Did you push that tessera to the ground on purpose?"

"Was it that obvious?"

His mouth pulled with humor. "I think your talent with artwork far exceeds your talent for acting."

Maja felt her face grow even hotter. "I'm sorry. I shouldn't have tricked you."

"Don't be sorry. I wanted an excuse to join you. I've been thinking all night, before I came here and since. And I'm not going to marry Ekaterina."

Joy flickered inside her chest as if a torch had just been lit, but the flames soon died down. "What of the alliance with Vidin?"

"Ivan is pursuing other grooms for Boyar Kalin's daughter. We still need that alliance, but Ivan plans to find a way to cement it while still allowing me to court a woman of my choice."

She opened her mouth, but no words came out, at least not at first. Was he suggesting that he intended to court her? For a moment, hope released an all-encompassing giddy sensation. But should Danilo escape marriage with a child bride, a mosaicist was hardly an appropriate replacement. "And who is the woman of your choice?"

"Have I not made my preference obvious?" He met her eyes and held them.

"Danilo . . . I'm not sure that's wise."

He looked away. "Because I'm cursed?"

"I don't believe in curses."

"Then you have some other reason that I shouldn't pursue you? Some other concern about the idea of *us*?"

Maja swallowed. Knowing that he felt some of what she did gave her satisfaction and hope, but it wouldn't change their circumstances. "Danilo, you are handsome, kind, and a fine warrior. And you are the župan's cousin."

He glanced at his hands. "But despite those things, there's something holding you back?"

"The last one, Danilo. You are the župan's family. I'm a mere artisan. The more I see you, the more I want to see you. The more I talk to you, the more I want to tell you everything. But it will have to stop eventually, won't it? And that will hurt. The longer we fool ourselves, the greater the pain will be when it ends."

"Why would it have to end? I think we could be happy together. There are empty walls throughout the city that you could fill with mosaics, so you won't want for commissions. And as for my family, my mother has urged me to think of my own needs, Ivan found your threat with a spear amusing, and Helena's quite fond of you."

"As a friend. Not as a suitable woman for marriage into her family."

Danilo shook his head. "My first marriage was to please my family. Assuming we can make the alliance with Boyar Kalin work another way, and I think we can, I can court whomever I like. Ivan wouldn't deny me that. He'd be pleased to see me wed again, as would my mother."

"Even if the woman in question were common instead of noble?"

Danilo reached for her. She walked forward, and he took her hand, drawing her down next to him on the scaffolding. "You'll find that in Sivi Gora, we're more interested in noble character than in noble birth. And I do not think I would use the term *common* to describe someone who's rescued herself from a Turkish tent, defended me with a spear, and turned an ordinary wall into a field of glittering grass."

He released her hand and ran his fingers over her palm. She felt something in each caress, from her skin all the way to her heart. Her breath caught in her throat just from knowing he was next to her, protecting her, touching her, wanting her. The hour was late enough that she ought to feel tired, but instead, she felt a heady rush as she focused on the man next to her, the man she'd been in awe of since Pločnik. Did he really have room in his heart for her?

His fingers whispered along her wrist. "I can't openly court you until everything is settled with Ekaterina and Vidin, but will you wait for me?"

She felt her smile growing so large that it might split her face. "I will wait."

A shadow shifted below, and Maja's attention turned to the lower level of the church.

"Did you see something?" he asked.

"No." She stared into the dark corners of the church. "One of the candles must have sputtered." She turned back to Danilo. "I shouldn't be so easily startled. Especially with you here to keep me safe."

"It's getting late. I should walk you home." He helped her to her feet, grasping her hand again, releasing it only so they could climb from the scaffolding.

She gathered her tools, and he blew out the candles. Then he took her hand, and they walked through the deserted streets of a sleeping Sivi Gora. They didn't speak, but there was no reason to. They had each other, and for the moment, that was all that mattered. They slowed as they reached the home where she and Luka had been staying since their arrival.

"May I call on you?" Danilo asked. "It will have to be in secret until all is settled with Vidin, and I have much work to do before we march to Kosovo, but I don't want to waste what little time we have."

"You may. I'll not spread more mortar than I can fill these next days, knowing I might have a visit from you to look forward to."

He brushed a finger along her cheek and stared at her lips, and she wondered if he would kiss her. She could barely breathe at the thought of his mouth on hers, their arms around each other and their bodies close. There was an unspoken desire between them, something deeper than friendship, more intimate than courtship. Even now, she could feel it—powerful, persuasive, persistent.

He pulled away suddenly, and disappointment surrounded her like mortar surrounded a tessera. She'd wanted him to kiss her again.

"What was . . . ?" The angle of his head changed, and he pulled her closer to him, next to the courtyard wall. But his motivation seemed to be something other than affection, because the mood had shifted. He was tense and wary. "Stay here," he whispered. A glimmer of moonlight shone on his drawn dagger as he left her side.

More spies? Was that what he'd seen? And was that what she'd noticed in the church? Both enemies and uncertain allies would have reason to watch Danilo. Or perhaps Petar's words were true, and despite Danilo's rosy prediction, the župan didn't want his cousin to court someone like her.

A muffled cry was followed by the scrape of boots along paving stones.

"Danilo, no!" The voice was one she didn't recognize, and though the words were Slavonic, they sounded accented.

Curiosity pulled Maja from her hiding place.

Danilo held a young man against the wall, someone she recognized from the palace.

"Philippos?" Confusion filled Danilo's question. "Why are you spying on me?"

The young man glanced first at Maja, then back at Danilo. "I was just following orders."

"From whom?"

"From Župan Ivan."

Danilo released Philippos and took a step back. "Ivan wanted you to follow me?"

Philippos nodded.

Maja studied Danilo's face. Confusion and hurt were visible even in the dim light.

"Why would your cousin have you followed?" But even as she spoke, her previous fear was confirmed, and any hope she'd felt that the way ahead for her and Danilo would soon be open quickly shattered.

Chapter Twenty-Two
May the Sun Light Your Path

Danilo went to see Ivan the next morning. He'd not slept at all the previous night, wondering what on earth he'd done that would make his cousin want to spy on him. Ivan had told him to be discreet with Maja, and Danilo had obeyed. And before that, he'd been willing to give her up if that had been what the župa needed. Ivan had no grounds for suspicion, and if mercenaries were spreading false rumors again, Ivan ought to have asked Danilo about them directly rather than resorting to tails.

"Good morning, Danilo." Ivan glanced up from a pile of papers and waved him into the antechamber. "You're just in time to give your opinion on whether I should hire more mercenaries or order more cannon. Neither will be here before we head to Kosovo, but if we take a loss, it would be nice to have replacements coming. I want both, but then I'd have to raise a special tax to pay for them. Do you think the merchants would agree to it without much complaint?"

"You trust me to advise you?"

Ivan looked up from his papers again, confusion at Danilo's tone furrowing his brow. "There is no one I trust more."

Danilo felt sick inside. Ivan had been his best friend since they were boys. Danilo had followed him and sacrificed for him, and until yesterday, he'd always thought Ivan returned that loyalty. But now Ivan wouldn't even tell the truth about what had happened. "If you trust me, why are you spying on me?"

"I'm not spying on you, Danilo. If you were to betray me, I'd rather die than live with the knowledge that a man I revered like a brother had turned on me."

"Then why did you have Philippos follow me?"

"You caught him already, did you?" Ivan walked to the window and stared out. His back was to Danilo, he was unarmed, and there were no guards about. Apparently, Ivan didn't expect Danilo to stab him in the back this morning. "He tailed Niketas for a fortnight and was never discovered. Managed to tail a few people in Kruševac too."

"Why did you have Niketas tailed?" Niketas was a Greek soldier, but he'd served Ivan well since his own lands were taken by the Turks not long before Pločnik.

"It sounded like good training for Philippos. When he succeeded at that, I had to give him someone harder. I couldn't very well warn you, or it wouldn't be a real test for the lad."

Danilo let out a frustrated sigh. "You had him tailing me so he could become good at tailing people?"

"Yes."

"I might have killed him."

Ivan spun to face him. "Is he all right?"

"He'll have a few bruises. I realized who it was before I sliced him with my dagger. But what if I hadn't?"

Ivan swallowed. "I assumed you would recognize him. You've always had eagle eyes."

Danilo sat on a bench and rubbed his temples. Only now that the truth was known did it hit him how much he'd dreaded a confrontation with Ivan. He'd feared he would be pushed off a cliff, so to speak, and now he was free to draw back from the edge. "What precisely are you doing with Philippos? And why?"

"He wants to be more than a groom. And a spy sounded like a useful asset. Bokori's man has certainly been of service to him. And if you possessed any less virtue, Asen's spy might have wrapped you around her finger, and then he'd have the ear of my top adviser."

"So you want spies of your own because the Hungarians and Bulgarians both have them?"

Ivan nodded. "I wish we lived in a world where espionage weren't needed . . . but since that is not the case, it seemed wise to start with someone young, someone willing, someone I already trust."

Danilo shook his head, trying to grasp what it all meant. "You're training spies, hiring more mercenaries, and perhaps ordering more cannon. Ivan, what's going on?" A war was coming, but the battle would be over before

Philippos was trained, before the mercenaries arrived, and before the cannon could be cast.

"I want to leave Sivi Gora secure if I don't return." Ivan walked over to sit next to him. "I have no son, and Sofija is but a baby. Helena will govern well—she loves Sivi Gora, and the people love her—but I want to smooth the way for her as much as I can."

Danilo huffed. "What kind of talk is this? Of course you'll return."

"I had a dream, Danilo. I saw Helena weeping over my body. You were there, too, but seemed in good enough health, which is why I'm planning on your help. You'll know how to keep the city secure. And you'll have wisdom when it comes time to find a good husband for Sofija. Someone she can love. And someone who can keep Sivi Gora strong."

The room seemed to grow colder. Danilo shook it off. "Are you certain you were dead? Perhaps you were merely hurt or asleep."

"If I were alive, she would have been trying to mend my wounds. If I were asleep, I don't imagine she would be weeping."

"It was just a dream." Danilo enunciated each word.

"It's repeated itself. Five times."

"So you're giving up because of a dream?" Danilo looked at his friend, then at the doorway, where little Sofija was toddling into the room. Part of whatever she had most recently eaten was still smeared across her mouth.

"I'm not giving up. I'm just preparing the best I can in case the dream proves true." Ivan turned to his daughter as she babbled something Danilo didn't understand.

Danilo tried to think of something encouraging to say. A dream was just a dream, but the repetition was unnerving. And the Ottoman Army would be vast and skilled. Kosovo would be no picnic in the meadow. "I understand preparing for the worst, but that doesn't mean you shouldn't fight for the future you've worked so hard for."

"Oh, I'll fight. And I intend to sell my life dearly."

Sofija drew closer. "Up?"

Ivan stood and scooped his daughter into his arms. He scrutinized her face and gently held her chin. "What have you got on your face?"

Hadn't Ivan noticed the red preserves before? It was too much like the day before, when they'd ridden into the courtyard. Ivan hadn't reacted to his wife until she'd spoken. Something was wrong with Ivan. He'd almost missed Hensel sneaking up on them in the dark, and his archery had grown sloppy—but not from lack of practice.

Danilo stood and walked to the window. "Does she still like birds?"

"Yes."

For the first time in his life, Danilo lied to his cousin. "There's a pretty one in the tree across the courtyard."

Ivan joined Danilo at the window. "Do you see the bird, Sofija?" He pointed outside, trying to get his daughter to look.

Danilo looked from his cousin to the empty tree and then back again. "Ivan, there's no bird."

"Then why did you say there was?" Ivan's eyebrows scrunched together in confusion.

"Can't you see for yourself?" Danilo whispered.

Ivan's gaze fell to the floor, and he seemed to hold his daughter to him more tightly. "Not as well as I used to."

"When did this happen?" And why hadn't Ivan told him?

"It's been gradual."

"You can't go to war if you can't see." The task of battling the Turks would be difficult enough without that disadvantage. If Ivan had had repeated dreams of death and couldn't see clearly across the courtyard, he ought to stay in Sivi Gora.

"It's only things in the distance that are blurry. I can still see well enough to read. And I can still see well enough to stop a Turkish scimitar or stab my lance into a Turkish sipahi. I can compensate for it. I'll leave the archery to others and use more scouts." Ivan shifted his daughter. "Just don't tell the men. I don't want them to fret or fear that they're being led astray."

Danilo blew out a breath full of worry. "Does Helena know?"

"She figured it out. Ironic, isn't it? I married the most beautiful woman I've ever seen, and now I can't even be sure it's her from across the hall."

"What if it gets worse?"

"Like I said, it's been gradual. I'll see well enough to fight at Kosovo. After that, it might not matter."

Danilo returned to the bench and sat, tilting his head back so it rested against the wall. Ivan was vulnerable and determined to go to Kosovo—and possibly die there—regardless of his weakness. Danilo knew Ivan well enough to doubt anyone could change the župan's mind, but he tried to think of any argument that might sway him.

A knock sounded on the cracked door.

Philippos stuck his head inside the room and glanced from Ivan to Danilo. "I, um, came to make my report. But it seems Danilo beat me to it."

Ivan's expression went from sober and determined to amused. "Yes. I'd have you try Goran next, but I doubt he'd notice, even if you tailed him until harvest time. Come in. I'll think of someone new for you to tail soon."

The young man stood before Ivan's desk. He glanced at Danilo, a little wary after the previous night's encounter. Danilo was frightened to think of how close he'd come to seriously harming the lad. "Are you injured? I was a little rough with you last night."

"I'm fine, sir." Philippos forced a smile. "Was Maja all right? I didn't mean to scare her."

"She was startled but otherwise fine." He supposed Philippos had seen the entire evening. Perhaps it was just as well that he hadn't kissed Maja, especially not the way he'd been tempted to kiss her.

"Were you with Maja last night?" Ivan set Sofija down, one corner of his lips turned up in interest.

"I was." He almost listed the reasons: he had needed to warn her that Iskandar still lived, and she had been alone, and he hadn't wanted to leave her without protection. Neither was a lie, but he had also wanted to see her again, and then he'd wanted to stay.

Ivan studied Danilo for a moment, and Danilo expected more questions about Maja, but instead, Ivan turned the subject back to Philippos. "And who would you suggest Philippos practice tailing next?"

Philippos stood straight, eager for his next task. The lad had seen only fifteen winters, but Danilo had long ago noted his intelligence and absolute devotion to Ivan. "How good are you, Philippos?"

Red colored his cheeks. "Obviously, I still have much to learn, or you wouldn't have seen me last night."

"But you tailed Niketas and, I suppose, Iskandar?" That would explain why Philippos had reported to Ivan on Iskandar's meeting with Miloš in Knez Lazar's stables.

Philippos nodded.

"And neither saw you?"

"No."

Danilo folded his arms. "Maybe it's time to use him instead of just training him."

"For?" Ivan asked.

"What if Hensel left a few men behind? Or what if he was reporting to someone else?" That seemed more likely, given the reach he'd had. He—or his accomplice—had arranged for someone to spy on Danilo and Konstantin when they'd met in Bosnia. The crass mercenary had possessed a tongue too loose and provocative to blend in and listen, but it took foresight and resources to arrange for a spy, even a poor one. Hensel had also given information to brigands trying to steal a silver shipment and, most recently, ambush the groups from Sivi Gora and Rivak on their way home from Kruševac. He was dead now, and perhaps any connection to his accomplice or master was broken, but Hensel wasn't their only adversary. "Bokori might have sent a replacement whose face we don't know. Asen, too, when we sent Stanimira away."

"But if they are strangers, how will I know to follow them?" Philippos asked.

"If some of the mercenaries were working for Hensel, they'd be with the garrison, but I'm not sure who they'd report to now that Hensel is dead." Ivan shifted a stack of papers so they would be out of Sofija's reach. "Anyone reporting to Asen might try to contact his niece."

"Surely she's too young to be a spymaster." Danilo couldn't picture it, but in truth, he'd spoken very little with the Bulgarian girl once meant to be his bride.

"Helena has spent more time with her than I have." Ivan played with Sofija's fingers. "Says she has a sharp mind. Having people constantly underestimate you could be an advantage for a spy."

Danilo nodded.

"So I should look for any strangers wishing to contact Ekaterina?" Philippos asked.

Ivan nodded. "For now. Or people you recognize but who are suddenly crossing paths with her more often than they should."

The corner of Philippos's mouth pulled up, as if he relished the new assignment. "I'll see what I can find and report to you later." At Ivan's nod, Philippos excused himself.

"So," Ivan said, "how was your time with Maja?"

Danilo almost laughed. "We ride to war in a few days. You think you won't return. We have at least three entities who might be spying on us. And you wish to know if I enjoyed my evening with Maja?"

Ivan folded his arms, watching Sofija grab at the dust motes shimmering in the light from the window. Danilo wondered how well he could see his little girl.

"When storm clouds gather, sometimes there is comfort in seeing a bit of sunlight shining on a friend. And there is no one I would wish sunshine on as much as I would wish it on you. Whether or not I return, I want you to be happy. If Maja can help ensure that, then there is little I won't do to make sure you and she have the chance you need."

Chapter Twenty-Three
Shadows of Secrecy

Maja startled awake with a sob. The images in her dream had felt so real because three years ago, they had been real. Her father, struck down by a Turkish ghazi when he'd tried to defend his wife, children, and apprentice. Her mother, killed as she'd tried to help Maja and Luka escape. Luka plucked from her side by a terrifying raider who towered over them both. The sickening sound of her spear piercing one of the enemy, then the horrifying moments when she recognized Iskandar's intentions.

She climbed from her bed and went to the window, where fresh air pulled at her skin. If only it would pull away the fear that still clung to her mind. Luka slept in the other bedchamber at the back of their home. She could wake him, but it hardly seemed fair to deprive him of sleep just because she sought comfort.

A door creaked. So Luka was awake. Good, because she wouldn't fall back asleep anytime soon. They could have a meal in the middle of the night together, and then maybe thoughts of Iskandar and all the horrors he'd poured on her village would depart for a time.

She wrapped a shawl around her shoulders and pulled the door to her bedchamber open. The soft glow of a single candle showed the table, cupboards, and a mess strewn across the floor. A man stood over the wooden trunk where they kept their tools, a man far larger than Luka. He blew the candle out, and the room was plunged into darkness.

"Who are you?" Her voice shook.

The man didn't answer, but she heard his footsteps, and they were coming closer. She stepped toward the table and grabbed one of the stools, holding it by the seat so she could use the legs against the intruder.

The footsteps slowed, and the way they echoed . . . he was within range. She swung the stool around and connected with something. Someone grunted and cursed. But then she felt the stool ripped from her hands. She screamed, and then she was shoved against the wall so hard that everything turned black.

Danilo yawned as he and Goran reviewed the lists they'd drawn up of which men would march to Kosovo and which would stay to protect the city and the silver mine. Danilo pointed to one of the names. "Can we switch him? His wife is with child."

"So is Adamu's wife."

"Yes, but neither of us will convince Adamu to stay. He's been looking out for Ivan since we were boys. And his wife's mother lives with them, so if there are complications, Slavica will have help. Besides, we need him on campaign with us."

Goran nodded and hid a yawn himself. They'd suspected war would come this summer, but they hadn't been able to make some of the preparations until they'd known when the campaign would begin, and Murad's timing meant that much of the preparations had to happen in a matter of days. They could have rushed through the lists, but deciding who marched to war and who remained in Sivi Gora would shape the strength of their army in the field. It might also determine which women would be widowed and which children would be fatherless by harvest time. Neither Danilo nor Goran took their responsibilities lightly.

Voices, louder than they ought to be for this time of night, echoed along the barracks courtyard, then Michel, one of the soldiers on duty, opened the door. Luka was with him.

"Someone broke into our home." Luka's voice was strained, as if he'd been running. "And whoever it was hurt Maja."

Worry made it hard for Danilo to breathe. "How badly is she injured?"

Luka shook his head. "I don't know. I couldn't wake her."

Danilo grabbed his weapons, then a torch from one of the sconces on the wall. "Goran, we'll have to finish tomorrow. Michel, Luka, come with me." Michel wouldn't have been Danilo's first choice, but he wasn't sure whether he had time to find anyone else.

Danilo ran to the Dinićs' home. His ears told him Michel and Luka followed. When the home came into view, he slowed and handed Luka the torch so Danilo could draw his sword. The door wasn't latched, so he breezed inside. The front room was lit by a single candle that burned on their small table. Maja and Luka had little in the way of worldly possessions, but what they had now lay strewn about the floor. Blankets and clothing were furled along the floorboards, spilled bags of tesserae made untidy piles near an open wooden chest, and one of the stools lay on its side.

Maja's crumpled body faced away from him. He knelt beside her and scanned for blood, and when he found none, he laid a hand on her forehead—still warm. The light was too dim for him to see a heartbeat, but he felt one when he slid his hand to rest on her neck.

"Luka, light a few more candles or a lamp. Michel, hand me one of those blankets, then take the torch and check outside."

Luka reluctantly moved to do as he was asked, finding a lamp and illuminating the room more fully before returning to Maja's side.

Michel took one of the blankets from the ground and handed it over. "What am I looking for?"

"Anything that doesn't look as it should. Signs of break-in, someone lying in wait."

Michel nodded and left the home.

Danilo draped the blanket over Maja and called her name a few times. He held her shoulder but didn't shake it. Helena had told him that when people were injured in the head, it was sometimes best not to move them.

"She wouldn't answer me either." The worry on Luka's face and in his voice spoke of a misery the boy could barely contain.

"What happened?"

Luka swallowed. "I heard her scream, so I came out of my bedchamber, but it was too dark to see anything. I thought maybe she'd had another nightmare."

"Did you hear anything?"

Luka hesitated. "Just the door slamming shut. Maja didn't answer when I called, and she wasn't in her bed. I went back to my room because I had a candle there, but it took a long time for me to light it because my hands were shaking. Then I saw her, and . . . I was afraid she was dead. I couldn't wake her."

As Luka spoke, Danilo examined Maja's hands. Bruises were forming on her palms and on some of her fingers. One along her temple, too, and when he felt beneath her hair, he found a lump there.

"Come sit and hold her hand." Maja didn't need her brother's hand, but Danilo suspected the opposite might be true. Danilo took the lamp and looked into the other rooms. Nothing looked out of place in either bedchamber. He brought a cloak from a peg on the wall and wrapped it around Luka.

A sound that was part whimper, part moan escaped Maja's throat.

"Maja?" Danilo called her name again, but no other signs of responsiveness followed.

Michel came back inside.

"Did you find anything?" Danilo asked.

"No."

Danilo nodded. He would examine everything himself when the sun came up. "Now I need you to go to the palace and tell Dama Helena she's needed."

Michel's brow furrowed. "You wish me to ask Dama Helena, wife of the župan, to come here in the middle of the night?"

"Yes. Tell her there's been a break-in and an injury in the home of the mosaicists, and I guarantee she'll be willing to come." Danilo wouldn't impose on Helena without good reason, especially not on a week like this, when so many preparations were needed, and waking Helena would likely mean waking Ivan as well. But Helena was a midwife. She was used to having her sleep interrupted. And Maja still hadn't stirred.

"I can't just march into the palace and go to the župan's bedchamber. Or to his wife's bedchamber."

Danilo reminded himself to have patience. "There will be guards on duty. They know what to do in a situation like this."

"If you say so."

"I do. And, Michel? Hurry." Danilo glanced at Luka and didn't finish his thought, but he hoped Michel would understand and obey. Maja had been stunned and unresponsive for a long time. She should have woken by now, unless the injury was far more serious than it looked.

Michel left reluctantly. Danilo studied Luka. The fear they both shared that Maja would never open her eyes again . . . or that if she did, some part of her would not be the same, was almost palpable. Danilo tried to swallow it back. Her breathing was steady, and the lump was significant, but it didn't seem any larger than when Danilo had first discovered it.

"Is anything missing?" Danilo asked Luka. Whoever had broken in had been looking for something, but Danilo couldn't figure out what.

Luka seemed reluctant to leave his sister's side, but he stood and straightened the stool, checked the cupboards in the kitchen, and went to the items strewn about the trunk. While he inventoried the tools and supplies, Danilo watched for any sign of change in Maja. Anger at whoever had harmed her burned, but not as strongly as fear pricked along his skin. He'd finally let himself care deeply for another woman, finally gained the hope that he would soon be able to pursue Maja the way he wanted. Now it seemed just as likely that he would have his heart crushed again. He whispered desperate prayers while Luka put the spilled tesserae back into bags.

"All the tools are here," Luka said. "If some of the tesserae are missing, it is only a few. I don't think the thief took anything."

No doubt because it had not been a thief but a spy.

"Maja," Danilo whispered. "Please, come back to us."

Pain pounded in Maja's head, accompanied by a swirl of murmured voices. A chill gripped her, sinking into her bones. Soft pressure along her hand made her instinctively grasp whatever warm object had come into contact with her skin.

"Maja?"

She tried to focus on the voice, but pain and a heavy weight of exhaustion made even opening her eyes too challenging a prospect. At least for a while. But she needed to do something, needed to go somewhere. The remembered urgency mixed with the pain, but she couldn't remember what or where.

"Maja?" That voice again, pleading with her. Deeper than Luka's. She still couldn't remember what or where, but she remembered *who* that voice belonged to. Danilo. His hand, too, she suspected, clutched her own.

Words wouldn't come when she tried to speak, but with time, she forced her eyes open. Danilo and Luka came into focus, both of them leaning over her with worry pinching their mouths, then relief showing in their eyes.

"Are you all right?" Luka looked as if he'd been crying.

Maja swallowed. "I think so." Except that her head hurt, and she was cold.

"How is your head?" Danilo asked.

"How do you know my head hurts?" Could he read her mind?

"It's bruised." His gaze shifted from her eyes to her temple. "Do you remember what happened?"

The memories came slowly, distorted, like a mosaic viewed from too close. Only when she backed away did it all come into focus again. "I had a nightmare, and then I heard something out here. I thought it was Luka, but it was a man instead. He blew out the candle before I could see him. I tried to defend myself with a stool, but he yanked it away. And then . . . that's all I remember."

"Do you have any idea who it might have been?" Danilo asked.

Maja's teeth started to chatter. It was so cold, and her answer did little to warm her. "My dream was about Iskandar. What if it was him?"

Danilo felt her forehead. "Can you move your head and arms?"

She nodded and forced her head and limbs to move, proving they were not seriously injured. Danilo scooped her up off the floor.

"Your bed will be warmer than the floor," he said.

She almost protested. She was capable of walking herself, but she still felt weak, and even the small movements had left her dizzy. Danilo didn't lay her in bed directly. Instead, he sat on her mattress and pulled her in front of him so her back was against his chest.

"Grab some extra blankets, Luka." When Luka complied, Danilo pulled them around her and wrapped his arms in front of her. Sitting against him like that . . . it felt intimate. More intimate than was safe when attraction to him was so strong, but she also felt the warmth of his body, and the shivering slowed, then stopped.

"I don't think it was Iskandar." She heard Danilo's words, but she also felt them along her back. "Whoever broke in was looking for some*thing*. Iskandar would have been looking for you. And he wouldn't have been scared off by Luka."

Maja nodded. Warmth from Danilo's body and the logical reason as to why the intruder couldn't have been Iskandar helped calm her fear. But she didn't move away. She would happily let Danilo hold her as long as he was willing. "Maybe it was one of Bokori's men, looking for that letter. Or someone from Vidin who doesn't want an alliance with Sivi Gora, looking for a token or some other proof that . . ." Maja didn't finish because Luka was with them.

She felt a brief chuckle from Danilo. "Well, if he was looking for evidence that I don't plan to marry Ekaterina, we can hope he is not currently watching us. But where was your guard?"

"I sent him away. After last night . . ." She chose her words carefully and purposely did not look at her brother. "After last night, I thought anything

I had seen to cause fear was just Philippos. If the župan and his wife wish to spy on me, their guards can do so during the day. I wanted to sleep in peace. Not that it mattered. Iskandar has a habit of infiltrating my dreams."

Danilo adjusted his hold, running his hands along her arms. "I guarantee Philippos was not the one who ransacked your home."

"No," she agreed. "The man with the candle was larger. Taller than Philippos or Luka."

"It wouldn't have been one of the guards either, and not just because you sent them away." Danilo glanced at the candle. "Will you find more light, Luka?"

Luka nodded.

When he left the room, Danilo continued. "Ivan and Helena aren't spying on you, or on me. Philippos was following me as part of his training. Ivan didn't warn me because that would have ruined the challenge. And the guards were assigned to protect you, not to spy on you."

"You're certain?" She hated to question him, but all day, she'd been convinced that the župan, in either desperation or in a carefully crafted plan, was making sure she and Danilo did nothing that might compromise the military alliance.

"I'm certain. Ivan is working to find someone else for Ekaterina to marry. He's determined, and I'm determined, and I hate that we have to keep it secret a while longer, and I hate that so much depends on others, but please don't give up on me. Wait just a while longer. Tonight has made it even clearer to me that I don't want to lose you."

She turned her head so she could see him. "I will wait, and I will be every bit as determined as you and your župan."

His embrace tightened ever so slightly, and he pressed a kiss into her hair. Despite everything else that had happened that night, she felt safe and content in his arms. She trusted him. If he said a way would open that allowed them to be together, she would wait for him to make it so.

Luka returned with another candle. "Do you think Dama Helena will come soon?" he asked.

"Dama Helena is coming?"

Danilo shifted so she was sitting beside him. She wasn't cold anymore, but she instantly missed his close embrace. "You hadn't woken for . . . I don't know. It felt like a long time. And she is the most experienced healer in Sivi Gora."

"I didn't think the guard would go when you told him to." Luka folded his arms. "Can they disobey you?"

"Not really." Danilo adjusted the blankets around her so they covered her back as well as her front. "But Michel's obedience is reluctant. He was one of Hensel's friends, and I hear he has called me a Turk before, though not within my hearing. I'm not in the habit of losing my temper, but I am proficient enough with weapons or my fists that few men will insult me to my face. And my position means few will disobey a direct order."

Sadness and anger mingled together at the thought of others judging Danilo by his skin rather than by his kindness. "We live in a time when warriors are highly valued. I understand why, and I am grateful for your abilities, but I am sorry if you must rely on your skill and position rather than immediate acceptance from others in the garrison."

"Some people find differences hard to ignore." He gave her a melancholy smile, the movement of his lips drawing her attention to their admirable form.

Maja shifted her gaze to his eyes. "Tesserae are defined by color, by size, by luster. A man is defined by his choices, not by the color of his skin. By his integrity, not just by his skill with a weapon. And by the courage in his heart rather than the luster or comeliness of his features."

He smiled. "Are you a poet or a mosaicist?"

Maja felt her face heat. "I'm sorry. I shouldn't have said anything."

He gently touched her shoulder. "Don't be sorry. Your mind is beautiful. Thank you." His eyes were riveted on her face, and it was hard to breathe, but the tightness was alluring. If not for her brother's presence, she would have surrendered to that invisible force that pulled them together, and she wouldn't have stopped until her lips met his. But Luka was in the room with them, and then a knock at the door drew Danilo's attention.

Dama Helena and her armed escort entered, and she examined Maja's wounds and tested her sight and balance, then recommended rest. She also insisted on guards who would not be so easily dismissed.

Luka went to his own bed, and Danilo borrowed a blanket and said he would guard the two of them for the rest of the night. Maja fell asleep knowing he lay just outside her door.

She didn't go to the church the next day, but the day after, with her head no longer so tender and all the dizziness in the past, she and Luka arrived early. She was eager to make up for lost time, and her work would help her find the patience she needed to wait until the time was right for her and Danilo.

She paused in the doorway of the narthex, studying the colors of the sky and musing over which types of stones and colors of glass would make the most accurate depiction of a summer sunrise. Petar arrived while she was still listening to the birds and watching the sky.

"Are you all right? Your brother said someone hit you."

"Yes, but I am recovered."

Petar nodded. "I'm glad you're better. Do you know who did it?"

"No. It was too dark, and it happened too fast."

He crossed his arms. "Well, take care up on those scaffolds. It's not a good place to be dizzy, and if that bruise on the side of your head is any indication, whoever broke into your home hit you hard."

She followed Petar into the church. "I'll be cautious. I promised Danilo that I would stay on the ground if I feel the slightest bit dizzy."

Petar stopped and turned to her. "Danilo?"

Maja felt her cheeks go hot. "He was at the barracks when Luka ran for help. He's been investigating what happened."

Petar lowered his voice. "Others may believe that, but I think someone as important as the župan's cousin has far more pressing matters to attend to in the days before the army marches to war, unless he is taking a *personal* interest in the case. As a friend, I will repeat my warning: Take care. Those who play with fire are bound to end up with burns."

She almost argued. Yes, Danilo was taking a personal interest in her plight, but that was because he cared for her, not because he planned to use her. She'd felt his sincerity when he'd helped the night of the attack, when he'd prepared a meal for her the next morning, when he'd pleaded with her for caution on the scaffolds. Maja would be patient and quiet because all the secrecy, all the waiting—Danilo was worth it.

Chapter Twenty-Four
The Pain and Pleasure of Farewells

Early on the morning of their departure for Kosovo, Danilo bid farewell to his mother, checked on the army's progress, and then went to find his cousin. The last few days had been a rush of preparations and training. He had stolen a few moments with Maja but never for long and never while alone. Nor had a messenger from Župan Dragomir arrived, so Ekaterina was not yet betrothed to someone younger, someone not already in love with another woman.

Danilo reached Ivan's antechamber, and through the cracked door, he spotted Ivan with his family. He stepped back, out of sight, to give them privacy, but the image of Ivan balancing his daughter on one hip and cradling his wife in his arms didn't immediately fade. Perhaps it was easier for Danilo to make this journey, knowing his family was already dead. Many people liked him, but that deeper love, the kind that made loss such an agony, that was something Danilo shared with few others. His mother. His cousins and their families. And perhaps Maja.

Ivan's voice carried into the corridor. "Women risk their lives to bring children into the world, and men risk their lives to keep those children free."

"Promise me you'll be careful. I need you, Ivan." Helena's voice cracked.

"Helena, you are the love of my life, and you are the best thing to ever come to Sivi Gora. I love you, and I love my city, and I know you are strong enough to deal with whatever might come. Keep the city safe. Keep Sofija safe. And if I am able, I will return to help you."

"Ivan—"

Danilo didn't hear the next words, just muffled sounds and some of Sofija's babbles.

"Let me ride out with you," Helena said.

"You'd have me repeat my farewells and feel this pain all over again? I think it would be easier if you watched from the walls."

"Will you see me on the walls?"

"I'll know you're there. That will be enough."

Ivan's footsteps sounded, drawing near. Danilo stared out a window until the footsteps stopped beside him. He glanced at Ivan, who was breathing hard and wiping a tear from the corner of his eye. Guilt at catching his friend in a vulnerable moment crept across Danilo's chest, but he was only following Ivan's request from the night before on where to meet him.

"Is everything ready?" Ivan asked.

"The men are assembled. Philippos has Dazhbog and Triglav saddled and waiting for us. Korab and Stribog are ready to be led." Ivan and Danilo would ride their palfreys to Kosovo, then use their warhorses when they battled the Turks. "Goran already has the baggage wagons outside the gates."

"Good." Ivan strode through the hallway toward the palace doors.

Danilo followed, taking long strides to keep up. "Ivan, are you sure . . . ?"

"Sure of what?"

"Are you sure you want to go?"

Ivan's mouth pulled wide, but it wasn't exactly a smile. "Want to go? Nay. But it is my duty. And our cause is worth dying for. It may also be hopeless, but that doesn't make it any less deserving of my full devotion and every last drop of my blood, should it be required."

"Did you tell Helena about your dream?"

Ivan sighed. "I couldn't. Perhaps that makes me a coward."

"You, a coward? Don't be ridiculous. Besides, it was just a dream."

Ivan met his eyes for a moment as they entered the courtyard. He didn't agree; that was plain from his expression. But nor did he argue, perhaps because he sensed a more urgent conflict of opinion in need of his attention.

Philippos held the reins to three horses with his right hand: Ivan's, Danilo's, and his own. With his left hand, the lad held the lead ropes for the two destriers.

Ivan took his palfrey from Philippos and gave the lad a stern look. "Put your horse away. We've already had this discussion. You are not coming."

"But I'm good with the bow. And someone needs to look after your horses. You'll be busy directing the army and coordinating with all the other lords. You need someone dependable to assist you."

"I also need someone dependable here. And you're too young for the type of battle we'll have at Kosovo."

"I could stay in the camp."

"You could. But would you?"

Philippos frowned. "I'm only trying to serve you. Don't send me away."

Ivan's face softened. He placed a hand on Philippos's shoulder. "If you truly want to serve me, stay and look after my wife and my daughter. I need to know there is someone like you, loyal to them, capable of doing whatever is needed, should I not return."

Philippos looked at the ground. "As you wish, my župan. I will serve Dama Helena as diligently as I have served you."

Ivan wrapped the lad in a hug. "Thank you. God be with you, Philippos."

Danilo mounted Dazhbog, and Ivan mounted Triglav. Philippos handed them the lead ropes for their warhorses.

As they rode through the courtyard gates onto the main road, Ivan turned around and glanced at his palace and his groom. "There are a lot of young men in Sivi Gora, but that one is my favorite, even if he is stubborn."

The weight of Ivan's goodbyes sat heavily on Danilo, so he took the chance to lighten the mood. "Skilled and stubborn. He's exactly like you were at that age."

Ivan smiled softly. "Have I changed?"

Danilo thought of saying that his friend's skill had grown and his stubbornness had softened into determination, but the mood was still too heavy for his liking. "Yes. You've added slyness to the mix."

Ivan chuckled. "Oh, Danilo, I'm going to miss you."

The weight was back, black as a moonless, overcast night, a feeling that they were riding to their doom. "It was just a dream."

Ivan merely raised an eyebrow in response.

"Then I'll trade you fates," Danilo blurted out. And he meant it. He would die if it meant Ivan could live.

Ivan looked at the pommel of his saddle. He cleared his throat and blinked his eyes. "I don't think that's our choice to make. And anyway, I've had more happiness in these years with Helena than most people have their entire lives. I'll be content with that." He glanced along the wall, and Danilo followed his gaze, picking out Helena amid those who watched. "Is she there?" Ivan asked.

"Yes. If you wave now, she'll see it."

Ivan turned, and anyone looking would assume he could see the beloved wife he waved to. It wasn't until they reached the new church that Ivan spoke again. "Besides, you can't trade me fates. You have unfinished business here to return to." Ivan motioned toward the church, and Danilo spotted Maja standing in the doorway to the narthex. She smiled as she met his gaze, and the heavy emotion melted away.

"How did you know she would be there?" Danilo asked.

"Lucky guess. In truth, I can't see her well enough to recognize her, but you should say goodbye. I can tell you about my speech to the men later. Kostya has always been better at speeches than I am, so I plan to steal a line from him about how it's better to die free than to live a slave."

"My place is at your side, Ivan. Besides, there might be a Bulgarian spy watching." He couldn't let his guard down and give someone from Vidin a reason to ruin the alliance as the army left for campaign. "I hate all the secrecy and sneaking around."

"Of course you hate it. You've always been a man of the highest integrity. Although you didn't seem to mind all the secrecy and sneaking around when we were in Edirne."

"That was different. Rebelling against the sultan had been our goal since we were boys. Ekaterina, on the other hand, is an innocent party."

"You aren't hiding your feelings from her. You're hiding them from her father and uncle, and I hope they will be good allies, but they're hardly innocent parties. Besides, they'll have to march before a messenger could arrive from Sivi Gora, and Murad will have spies to report any rebellion in Vidin. Once they march, it's too late for them to turn back." Ivan fingered something tucked into his belt. "It's a long ride to Kosovo, and the wagons move slowly. I have every confidence in your ability to catch up."

Danilo's gaze fell on Maja again. Unfinished business indeed.

"Take this." Ivan handed him something.

Danilo reached for the offered brooch. "You're giving this to me? Why?"

"So you can give it to Maja. It's not really from me. Helena thought the glass matched Maja's eyes. Best not to argue with a župan's wife. Wouldn't you agree?"

Danilo studied the jewelry. A piece of smooth blue glass lay at the center, set in gold, with clusters of pearls around it. Perhaps the brooch was Helena's apology for pressuring him to see the significance of the alliance with Vidin. Maybe it was also a sign that she now approved of Danilo's intention to court Maja.

"Don't you think you'd regret it, if you didn't say goodbye? Hand me Korab's lead rope and go."

If Danilo never returned to Sivi Gora, he would indeed regret not saying goodbye to Maja. He slipped the brooch into his coin purse, then he tossed his destrier's lead rope to Ivan and pulled on Dazhbog's reins. "I'll catch up to you." He dismounted and led his palfrey back to the church.

Maja smoothed her tunic and wiped the dust from her hands as he approached. The portion of the bruise visible on her temple had faded, but it still showed.

"Is anything wrong?" she asked.

Danilo glanced over his shoulder at his cousin and the other men riding out to battle. "Other than Murad's army and hostile Hungarians? No. I just wanted to say goodbye. And tell you that I hope to see you often if I return."

"I very much hope you will return and that I will see much of you when you do." She met his eyes. Helena was right. The glass of the brooch matched Maja's eyes exactly.

"Ivan seems to think I'll return. But he's a župan, not a prophet."

"Regardless of his title, I hope he's right."

Danilo winced. "I don't. He thinks I'll return, but he doesn't think he will."

Maja's mouth opened slightly, and she looked toward the city gate with concern. "Then I hope he is partially wrong and that both of you return safely. But I have seen Turkish raiders before. Only small bands, and they were frightening enough, so the thought of an entire army is truly terrifying."

"We'll be armed with more than chisels and broken spears."

Despite his attempt at levity, Maja folded her arms, and something about the movement made her seem smaller, more vulnerable. "You'll look out for yourself, won't you?"

"I'll do my best because I very much wish to return. In the meantime, I have something for you." He took the brooch from where he'd tucked it into his coin purse and handed it to her.

She held it in both hands. "It's beautiful." She looked from the brooch to Danilo's face and back again. "But it's too much . . . I can't accept it."

"I think you had best accept it. I'll be disappointed if you don't. And what's more, Ivan and Helena will be disappointed. It's best not to upset a župan's wife when she's set on matchmaking, even if the match is to remain secret a while longer."

Maja swallowed, meeting his gaze. She ran her fingers along the clustered pearls of the brooch. "But I have no gift for you in exchange."

"None is needed."

She glanced at his mouth, then a smile spread across her face. "Actually, I've thought of something. Come." She took the reins of his stallion and tied the horse to a piece of uncut masonry that matched the church's floor, then she took Danilo's hand and led him to the deserted alley at the side of the church.

She stood before him, her eyes downcast as if she were suddenly shy. Then she stepped closer, stood on her tiptoes, and pressed her lips to his. Her mouth moved slowly, uncertainly, as if giving him the chance to step away. But he didn't want to pull back. He put his hands at her waist and guided her closer. Her mouth was like wine—delightful, sweet, and refreshing—but the more he kissed her, the more the thirst grew, and the more he drank it in, the more he knew her lips would soon intoxicate him completely.

He straightened but didn't pull back completely. Exhilaration pulsed through his body at being so close to her, at tasting her affection and knowing it mirrored his. Ivan and Helena were right. Maja would make him happy. And unlike the German mercenaries or the gossipy tavern maids, Maja seemed to accept him completely, just as he was. He could make her happy too.

Her eyes were still closed, and her chest rose and fell in deep breaths. He ran a finger over her lips, then along her cheek and down her jaw. "Thank you for your gift, Maja. There have been a lot of goodbyes today, and this one was by far the most pleasant."

He took the brooch from her and pinned it to her outer tunic. "You know, you're a lot like a jewel: beautiful, unbending, and resilient." He took her hand and kissed it. "Be well while I'm gone. Finish your mosaic. And light a few candles for us soldiers." He brushed her cheeks with his fingers a final time, then turned to go.

She grabbed his hand and held it.

"I can't stay."

"I know," she said. "But do your best to come home."

Do your best to come home. If he came back to Maja, Sivi Gora would finally feel like home, for the first time in years.

Chapter Twenty-Five
A Call for Sacrifice

Iskandar made his way through the vast Turkish camp on the south of the Llapi River. The Serbs were gathering on the north, and battle would come soon. Iskandar passed a score of camels, groups of men sitting around cooking fires, and numerous tents. Most of the men were Ottoman, but Sultan Murad's Christian vassals had also sent their required men, and mercenaries from Genoa waited, too, ready for battle. No one could defeat such a vast host. Victory was assured.

Armed guards stood outside Bayezid's tent when Iskandar arrived. "I'm here to report."

"You'll have to wait. He's meeting with Evrenos."

Iskandar waited until the meeting between the sultan's son and the general ended. Then the guard called him in. Iskandar bowed low when he entered the tent and saw Bayezid. "Peace be unto you, Great One."

Bayezid waved him up. "Your report?"

"The rivalry remains. Splitting the division into a catastrophe will be simple."

Bayezid motioned for him to sit. "Lazar's sons by marriage?"

"Yes. Two of them have been bickering, according to my source. Vuk Branković suspects Miloš Obilić."

Bayezid released an amused huff. "Miloš is the one you met with?"

"Yes. And he turned me down. But we have the manpower to win without a traitor. Fear of a traitor will be enough, and I sowed that fear in Kruševac."

"Perhaps." Bayezid's eyes had a hard look to them. "You have underestimated them before. The Serbs are fierce warriors, as are their allies from Bosnia."

"Allah will grant us victory. Of this, I am sure. Especially if you are to lead us."

Bayezid smiled. "My father, the sultan, will command from the center. I'll have control of the right, with Evrenos. My brother will hold the left."

"Then may he who is on the right hand of the sultan be showered with success. I pray you will allow me to fight with you."

"Is that what you most wish? To serve me? Or do you still seek revenge on the Serbs who have wronged you?"

Iskandar didn't answer immediately. Danilo and Ivan would be with Lazar's army, but how would he find them amid the thousands of men in the enemy host? And was punishing them worth it if it meant appearing less loyal to Bayezid? "Defeating their army will be vengeance enough. Until the battle is finished, my place is by your side."

After the battle was done, perhaps he would seek out his enemies—if they survived. Their deaths would be sweet to him, regardless of how they came about. He wanted them dead with an intensity that consumed him, but first, he had to prove himself to the sultan's son. After his place was secure, he could seek vengeance and follow the other longing that consumed him—seeking out the elusive Maja. He hadn't forgiven her for striking him and escaping from him, but desire for her still burned, perhaps even stronger now that he had been so close to having her. That also would have to wait. He would have patience, but he would not forget about the wrongs he sought to avenge, nor the woman he would soon claim as his own.

Since making camp on the north of the Llapi River on the wide Kosovo plain, Danilo had seen and heard dozens of reports on the enemy that gave him worry and few that gave him hope. The scouts said the Turkish host was so large that if it were to rain, no drops would reach the ground. They would all be caught by men, horses, or camels. An exaggeration, but only a small one.

Yet a visit from Konstantin, Župan Dragomir, Emanuil Asen, and a fourth man in Bulgarian-style armor promised an exception from the steady stream of ill news.

Konstantin gestured to the man Danilo had not yet met. "Boyar Kalin, this is my brother, Župan Ivan of Sivi Gora, and my cousin Danilo. They are currently hosting your daughter, Ekaterina."

They all exchanged greetings. Danilo watched Konstantin for any sign as to what had been decided about Danilo's obligation to Ekaterina, but Konstantin's expression offered no clues.

Finally, when everyone had been introduced and refreshment offered and politely declined, Župan Dragomir spoke. "Boyar Kalin and I had a long discussion, and we have determined that a union of our families would benefit us both. If Danilo is not opposed to the change in plan, Boyar Kalin's daughter will marry my youngest grandson."

Danilo tried to keep his smile neutral, but he wanted to burst into a shout of joy. "I have no objections. I wish Todor and Ekaterina a happy union. I am pleased that two valued allies have found an arrangement that will benefit both their families."

Boyar Kalin nodded. "Now you must excuse me. I need to consult with some of my men before I join Knez Lazar."

Konstantin led the group from the tent, and Danilo turned to Ivan and finally released the grin he'd been holding back. No more obligation. No more secrecy.

Ivan returned Danilo's smile. "I suppose this means you and Maja will be married before harvest time now that the final obstacle is gone."

"She has to say yes."

"She will." Ivan said the words as if they were fact.

"I think she might." Danilo felt the joy of promise, but then he sobered. "Ekaterina wasn't the final obstacle. There's still the sultan's army to deal with, and his host is far larger than ours."

"They may outnumber us, but that doesn't make our cause less worthy." Ivan looped his belt around his tunic and tested his sword in its sheath.

"No." The dark foreboding was back again, seeping through the tent and penetrating Danilo's chest.

"Better to fight them in Kosovo than at the gates of Sivi Gora." Ivan stuck a small dagger into his boot.

"Sivi Gora's walls will stand for a hundred years." That was what they had said as they'd watched them being built.

"I hope so," Ivan said. "Will you come with me?"

"To the meeting with Knez Lazar? If you wish."

Konstantin waited for them as they left the tent. He wore his armor and his sword, but not his helmet or shield. They didn't expect an attack—not yet—but they didn't want to be caught without weapons if they were surprised. He studied Danilo's face. "I expected you to look happier after that meeting with Župan Dragomir and Boyar Kalin."

"I would be elated were it not for the vast army across the river."

Konstantin placed a hand on the hilt of his sword. "I think it will begin tomorrow. And I am glad for it. I spent years as a vassal of Murad. I would rather die than repeat that shame."

Danilo remembered the yearly tributes paid to the sultan, the fear of the child tax, and the seasons when Konstantin and the warriors had been called away to fight the sultan's wars, battles that gave them only casualties with no chance of glory. Only three years ago, they had thrown off that burden, and now the freedom they had earned was again at risk.

Knez Lazar's tent was large and filled almost to bursting by men with war on their minds. Vuk Branković stood beside the knez. Lazar was Vuk's father-by-marriage and his lord, but Kosovo belonged to Vuk. He would command the right wing. Tvrtko's general would take the left. Danilo and his cousins expected to serve with Lazar's men in the center.

Knez Lazar nodded to Vuk, and Vuk lifted his hands, calling for silence without words.

When the last conversation ended, Lazar spoke. "My brave nobles, tomorrow is St. Vitus Day. And tomorrow we battle our mortal enemy. Soon we will struggle for the very soul of Serbia and for the security of Christianity. And if we are to be martyrs, as was St. Vitus, then how blessed we shall be to serve our Lord with our deaths. All must die. Do not fear it, for Christ has already conquered death. It will have no sting for His true followers. How much better to fight with the sword, to struggle against shame, than to submit to slavery. If we are to die, then we will die for a cause so glorious that we shall be remembered forever. I have had a dream, my brave nobles."

Danilo glanced at Ivan, wondering if Lazar's dream had been like Ivan's, but his cousin stayed focused on the knez.

"In my dream, a gray falcon flew to me from Jerusalem with a letter from the Virgin Mary. The falcon turned into the prophet Elijah and offered me a choice. He said, 'Knez Lazar, where will you have your kingdom? On earth or in heaven?'"

Lazar folded his hands together and continued. "A kingdom on earth will last but a while. But a kingdom in heaven will last the eternities. Is there a question of which we should seek? No, my brave nobles. Tomorrow we will saddle our horses and gird on our swords. We will drive out the Turks, if we are able. But first, we will dedicate ourselves to God. I have built a church of silk and brocade. There we will hold communion. If it is to be our last communion, then more blessed are we. Do not fear martyrdom, my brave ones. Fear not to sacrifice your bodies for the heavenly kingdom, for you are to be soldiers for Christ."

Knez Lazar's words sounded throughout the tent and beat a steady doom on Danilo's heart. He didn't want to die. He didn't want his cousins to die. And he didn't want his people enslaved by the Turks. He didn't want to choose between a heavenly kingdom or an earthly one. He wanted both. Peace and safety from the Turks now and salvation in the world to come.

Danilo sat through the council as they discussed how the men would be arranged the following day. Sivi Gora's men would be held in reserve, to be put into battle wherever the fighting was hottest. Unless the Turks made mistakes, they could expect heavy casualties. He glanced at Ivan, wondering how his cousin could seem so calm.

When the war counsel finished, Danilo went with the others to a scarlet tent to receive the Eucharist.

"Are we all to die?" he asked Ivan. "Is there no hope?"

"Of course there is hope. But there may be death as well." Ivan turned to him. "It's not our deaths themselves that we must offer up, just our willingness to sacrifice *all* for the sake of our people. I worry about them, Danilo. I will always believe. And there are many like me, who will always stay true to Christ and His church. But what will happen if the Turks take our lands? How many will believe then, when their belief costs them higher taxes? When their belief leaves their children vulnerable to the sultan's levies that fill his army with janissaries? I do not seek death. But if by giving my life I can keep my people free of the Turkish yoke, I will give it. And if that isn't possible but I can instead give them something to hold on to when their souls are threatened, then I will give my life for that. I am their župan. I owe it to them and to God."

They prayed in the tent turned into a church. Danilo finished first and suspected Ivan would be a while longer, so he didn't wait. If these next days were to be his friend's last, he would do what he could to ease Ivan's burden. Danilo knew Ivan's wishes well enough to begin the preparations without him.

Miloš found Danilo outside the tent. "Danilo, I am glad to see you before the battle." He gazed toward the Ottoman camp. "We will need good men like you when the time comes."

Danilo didn't feel like a good man at the moment. He felt selfish. He was surrounded by willing martyrs, but he wanted life—for himself and for his people. "I'll be ready to strike against them with all my strength."

"Yes. Me too." Miloš bit at his lip. "I hope it will be enough, but I wonder."

"Don't tell me you've had a dream too." First Ivan, then the knez. Danilo didn't want to hear about any more dreams of death.

Miloš shook his head. "I don't need dreams to tell me how this will end."

"Are we doomed?" Hearing Knez Lazar, listening to Ivan, seeing the vast army waiting to battle against them . . . they all combined to make hope fade and doom seem inevitable.

"No, but this battle will be the worst we've seen yet. Not everyone will walk away from it. But I hope you will, my friend." Miloš grasped his shoulder. "I may not be a dreamer, but I can imagine. And I can almost see you and a pretty little mosaicist being very happy together."

Danilo remembered Maja's kiss, thought of the way it had felt to hold her in his arms. He longed to have a woman like that by his side, but he knew how easily death could keep them apart. "If I'm alive."

Miloš slapped him on the back. "Leave that to God. Follow the knez, follow your župan. And if you survive, live a life full enough to make those of us who don't survive proud."

Those of us who don't survive. The wording of Miloš's last sentence caught Danilo's attention. "You haven't seen your own death, have you?"

"Not exactly." Miloš smiled. "Don't worry about me, Danilo. If my death can help my people, I will gladly give it. Sometimes, we serve our cause best with our deaths. Other times, we serve our cause best with our lives. I am prepared to give either."

"As am I." Danilo said the words, and he meant them. But he preferred life.

CHAPTER TWENTY-SIX
THE FIELD OF BLACKBIRDS

DANILO STOOD NEXT TO HIS destrier, holding Korab's head so he wouldn't panic when the cannon blasted. Ivan stood beside him. They wore chain-mail hauberks, lamellar corselets, and iron helmets. They carried swords and daggers, maces and lances. Danilo also had his bow, already strung, and a quiver of arrows. He would fight in the first line of warriors rather than with Sivi Gora's archers, but he didn't like being without his favorite weapon.

Sivi Gora's horsemen were positioned behind the juncture between Knez Lazar's men and Kral Tvrtko's Bosnian army, to be held in reserve until the needs of the battle dictated their orders. Lazar had honored Sivi Gora with the assignment, saying there were few groups he trusted better to turn the tide of battle when it needed turning. He remembered how they'd fought at Pločnik and was grateful for their skill. Danilo didn't doubt they'd be committed before long. He tried not to think about how many of them might be dead by nightfall. In the meantime, they waited, for the battle and for their role in it.

"I guess we'll see if paying for all those artillery pieces was worth it." Ivan's face was set, showing determination instead of fear, calm instead of panic.

Danilo felt anything but calm. He didn't think his nerves showed, but unease and restlessness churned in his stomach. Part of him was grateful for every moment of calm, and part of him was eager for the battle to start. When it began, there would be something other than the suspense to focus on.

A boom sounded, then another and another. The artillery barrage had commenced.

"I hope it works." Ivan squinted into the distance.

Danilo watched as a group of enemy soldiers scattered when a round shot bore into them. The blast sent up a plume of dust, and a handful of men were overturned, but the Serbs and their allies were outnumbered almost two to one. Killing a few Turks with each round of artillery wasn't enough. They needed something more effective.

Ottoman cannon responded. The balls whistled as they passed overhead. Danilo found himself ducking ever so slightly as the projectiles shrieked and then exploded. One hit nearby, falling among the Bosnians, killing horses and wounding men. If the Serb artillery was largely ineffective, at least the Turkish volleys were no more potent.

The cry of wounded men assaulted Danilo's ears, reminding him that the damage done wasn't insignificant, not to the men who'd been hit. The scent of cannon blast assailed his nostrils. He patted Korab's forehead and spoke in whispers to calm the animal. Nearby, other animals strained at their reins and snorted their discomfort.

A battle of archery followed the artillery exchanges, and the main force of Serbs charged forward.

Ivan signaled for his men to marshal themselves into ranks. He spoke to his group of two hundred mounted warriors. Their foot soldiers were elsewhere, likely already engaged. "Every enemy you slay gives our people another day of freedom. We will go where the fighting is fiercest, and battle where the foe is strongest. Show them no mercy, for if they succeed, they will enslave your children and carry off your wives, ravish your lands, and leave you less than a man. And be not afraid, for our cause is just. They can slay our bodies, but if we are valiant, they cannot touch our souls."

The fight taking place in front of them was difficult to follow. Dust choked the air, and the clash of weapons beat a steady doom across the fields. As the sun crept higher and higher in the sky, Vuk Branković held the right wing of the Serb forces and advanced, but only a little. Knez Lazar's forces in the center held their ground, but the Bosnians on the left were pushed back.

"I think Tvrtko's men might need our help before much longer," Danilo said. He wasn't sure Ivan could see that far in any detail.

Ivan nodded. "We'll be ready if Knez Lazar calls us there. He said to wait for his signal."

While he waited, Danilo took shots at any Turks who broke through the line and came within range. Releasing arrows was almost as natural as breathing for him. Nock, draw back, and release. He aimed, of course, but not consciously. Time and practice had made the skill a reflex. Most of the Turkish horsemen wore hoods and tunics of mail, with plumed round helmets of iron. At this distance, Danilo's triple-bladed arrows easily sliced through their armor.

Ivan called to his runner. "Get Danilo more arrows. He'll empty his quiver if the sipahis keep coming through."

Danilo smiled at his cousin. "Best to strike them down when they're unable to strike back, wouldn't you agree?"

"If you can see that far."

Danilo emptied his quiver and a replacement while they waited for their next task.

A group of twenty, led by Miloš, cantered toward the group. "A group of Turkish archers is trying to turn our left flank. We're to drive them back."

Danilo grabbed another quiver of arrows and positioned himself at Ivan's side. His cousin may have foreseen his own death, but if it was within Danilo's power, he intended to stop it. He wasn't sure how or when, but he would do anything he could to change Ivan's fate.

The group charged under Miloš's direction, riding behind the Bosnians. They passed the dead who already littered the field, injured horses thrashing in agony, and wounded men dragging themselves to the rear.

The Turkish horse archers maintained good discipline, staying in a group, riding close enough to shower Tvrtko's men with a hail of Ottoman arrows, then retreating to safety and reorganizing before charging again.

Miloš repositioned his shield. Danilo and the others followed his example, holding them where they could protect their faces and necks from the projectiles hurled by their enemy. The Turkish horse archers were armored but only with leather and helmet. Few of their horses wore the thick trappers the Serb horses did, and that would leave them vulnerable to lance and saber.

The Serbs urged their horses into gallops and raced to close the distance to their enemy. Danilo kept to Ivan's side, and as they reached the Turks, Danilo picked out his first target and speared him with his lance. He tugged his lance free and felled a second man, then a third before his lance caught and disappeared to the ground with his fallen enemy. He took out his sword and continued the work of slashing and stabbing at the enemy.

Battle was taxing work. Danilo's fingers were tender and his arms sore from firing so many arrows, and soon all his muscles felt the strain. But he had fought hard battles before and pressed on. He was defending his people, his city, and, in a way, Maja. If the Turks overran the army and made it all the way to Sivi Gora, he doubted she would be spared.

Danilo stopped a Turkish scimitar aimed at his face and drove the Turk back with his spathion. Another came at him, and he sliced his blade into the man's exposed neck. The man's blood mingled with Danilo's sweat. The burning sun oppressed his skin, and a cloud of upturned dust choked his throat.

Resistance from the Turkish horse archers finally collapsed, and the remnant of the enemy retreated back to the more solid lines of Ottoman soldiers. Miloš looked as if he would give chase.

"We should be cautious," Ivan said. "They like to feign retreat and lead their enemy into ambushes." Ivan and Danilo had spent two years in Edirne as hostages for Konstantin's good behavior as vassal. They knew more about Turkish tactics than most.

Miloš nodded. "We'll keep our eyes open. But they look like they're really fleeing. If we don't destroy them now, they'll rearm, and we'll have to fight them again."

Ivan nodded his consent, and they gave chase. The Turks were curving back to their main line.

"We can cut them off!" Miloš shouted.

The way ahead looked clear. The grassy field was open, as yet untainted by battle. A straight ride would catch the enemy before they found safety in their lines. They galloped at top speed, and Danilo judged the distance between the Serbs, the horse archers, and the other Ottoman forces. It looked like the Serbs would intercept the other group while they were still isolated from their comrades.

The tall grasses suddenly parted to reveal an open pit. Stakes jutted from the bottom, but there wasn't time to stop. Miloš, Danilo, Ivan, and a score of others hurled into the pit. The drop was sudden and ended with a sickening sucking sound, then the cry of injured horses, the grunts of injured men, and the slam and slap of armored bodies colliding with each other.

Danilo managed to stay in the saddle at first. Then another Serb, unable to stop, plowed into him and knocked him off. He was lucky. He landed on freshly turned dirt. His destrier and Ivan's had landed on sharp spikes and now writhed in panic.

More men and horses fell into the pit, pushing Danilo up against Ivan's injured horse and then smashing him into the far side of the pit. Danilo clawed his way free of horse and man and fought to find something solid to put his feet on. He finally balanced. The lip of the pit was taller than his head, but if he made a foothold for himself in the side of the pit, he thought he'd be able to reach the level ground still covered in grass.

But before he escaped, he had to find his cousin.

"Ivan!"

The mass of horse and human shifted again, knocking the breath from him. Fear gnawed at him as he tried to fill his lungs. The pit was full of men and horses, dropped weapons, and sharp palisades. Anyone who fell to the ground under the dense collection of desperate men and animals was likely to be impaled or crushed.

"Ivan!" he yelled once he had caught his breath again.

The Serbs in the back of the group must have had enough warning to swerve or pull up, so new victims no longer crashed into the pit.

The respite was brief, for soon the first Turkish arrows struck.

Danilo didn't know where his shield was. He found Korab dying. He took a moment to try to calm his warhorse, but the most merciful thing he could do for his favorite destrier was end his suffering. He made the necessary cut with his dagger and told himself he could mourn later.

Miloš was nearby, trying to regain his feet amid a pulsing mass of panic.

Danilo helped pull him up. "Are you hurt?"

Miloš held a hand to his side, and blood covered his fingers, but he shook his head. "It's not deep. Nothing to fret over."

Danilo didn't believe that, but he trusted that the wound could wait. Danilo found his quiver first, then his bow. The string had snapped. He kept a spare in the bottom of his quiver, but he didn't dig it out at once. First, he would search for his župan. Ivan's destrier still thrashed. He checked the palisade impaled in the stallion's chest. Stribog was doomed, so Danilo took out his dagger again to end the horse's misery. The poor beast. Danilo remembered the day Ivan bought it. The two of them had purchased it and three others, Korab among them, from a Hungarian horse breeder, and then Ivan had given Danilo first choice. *I'm happy with any of them, Danilo. Pick your favorite, and its yours.* Danilo had to find his cousin.

An arrow zipped past Danilo's ear. Another thumped into a nearby soldier's chest, a tall man from Sivi Gora. He had two children, and his wife had been friendly with Tatjana. In the mess of fallen men and panicked horses, Danilo waded carefully, not wanting to step on anyone still alive. Something shoved him forward, smashing him into the side of the pit. His body ached from the strike. Horse hooves from another injured warhorse that wouldn't survive the day. Danilo would have ended its pain, both because he hated to see horses suffer and because that would prevent the animal from striking him again, but a pair of Turkish arrows took care of it for him.

Little was visible beyond the edge of the pit. A few Serb horsemen rallied together. He hoped they would drive the Turkish archers back because the men in the pit were vulnerable—half were injured, most had lost helmets or shields, and few had bows. Some still had lances or swords, but with nowhere to maneuver and the enemy up above them, those weapons were useless.

The end of a boot stuck out from under a dead horse. Danilo knew that boot. He knelt and tried to push the horse off, but the animal was heavy, and Danilo couldn't budge it. He pushed his feet against the edge of the pit and shoved with all his might. His heels dug into the freshly overturned dirt, and his shoulders wrenched against the still-warm horseflesh, but the animal stayed put.

A few Turkish raiders appeared on foot, shooting down into the trapped Serbs. Danilo grabbed out his arrows and reached into the bottom of his quiver for the new string. Precious moments slipped past as he strung his bow and nocked his first arrow. He shot three of the Turks before the rest drew back.

Danilo went back to the horse that covered Ivan. He went to the other side of the slain animal and found a hand. He took it, and to his relief, Ivan's hand gripped back. His cousin's hold was weak, but there was life there. Danilo put his other hand around Ivan's forearm and tugged while he pushed against the dead horse with his foot.

Slowly, gradually, he could see more of Ivan's arm, then his shoulder, and finally his head. Two trickles of blood streamed from his nose and mouth. They hadn't been there before they'd ridden into the pit.

"Behind you!" Ivan croaked.

Danilo turned and had to duck away to miss the Turkish arrow that had been aimed at him. A long moment passed as Danilo drew another arrow and nocked it to the bowstring, then released it. He took down two archers before they were driven away.

Ivan had managed to free his torso from the horse. Only his legs were still covered.

Danilo knelt to help him again. Far too often, he'd seen similar bleeding patterns among the wounded, and it often indicated approaching death. "Just rest. I don't want you making it worse."

"It's not bad." Ivan wiped the sleeve of his tunic across his face and noticed the blood. "I smashed my nose and bit my tongue. Knocked my head, too, but nothing is broken." He pushed himself to his feet.

Danilo retrieved another arrow and kept it handy. The two of them studied the situation, but they could still see very little beyond the border of the pit.

"Will you boost me up?" Ivan asked.

"Yes. But best do it over there." Danilo pointed to the opposite bank, where they'd first plowed into the pit. He didn't want to push Ivan into the hands of Turkish archers.

They made their way, gathering what men they could. Far too many were dead or grievously injured. The sharp stakes had taken their toll, as had enemy arrows. They were only ten strong when they reached the edge.

Ivan withdrew his sword and motioned for Danilo to give him a leg up.

Danilo hesitated. "Let me go first. We don't know what's up there, and you were smashed beneath that horse for a long time."

Ivan shook his head. "I'm well enough."

It was Ivan's custom to lead, so Danilo didn't outright discourage him. "Together, then."

Ivan nodded, and some of the other men pushed them up. The edge of the pit had crumbled as it had taken in men and horses. It crumbled further as Danilo and Ivan scrambled to their feet at the top.

The area around them was calm, for the moment. In the distance, a haze of dust hung over the main battle, where Christian and Muslim battled fiercely.

"Let's get all the men and salvage what horses we can." Ivan met Danilo's eyes for a moment before continuing his scan of the battlefield. "We'll hold here and make sure no one turns Tvrtko's flank."

Iskandar slashed his scimitar across the stomach of the Bosnian knight ahead of him and watched the man fall to the ground. Iskandar was on foot now, after losing his horse. Behind him, Bayezid fought, surrounded by his most loyal and most skilled bodyguards and advisers.

The fighting had begun early, and it hadn't slackened as the scalding sun had climbed and then fallen from its zenith. The dead covered the ground, but thus far, neither side had gained an edge. Iskandar had hoped to cross blades with the men of Sivi Gora, but thus far, he had seen only strangers.

"Iskandar."

He looked to the voice, one of Bayezid's runners. "Yes?"

"Fall back. To Bayezid."

Iskandar nodded. The only enemy close enough for him to engage at the moment were wounded or dead. He stuck his scimitar into the neck of one, speeding him on his way to death. Men on both sides were weary. Wars might endure for generations, but the physical burden of combat was such that few battles lasted as long as this one had. He suspected both sides were blooded, but neither would have the stamina to overrun the other, not now.

Bayezid dismounted as Iskandar approached.

"Peace be unto you, mighty son of a mighty sultan." Iskandar lowered his head in respect.

Bayezid took the greeting in stride and removed his helmet. "I think it will end for today."

"Should we pursue?"

"No. They'll pull back, but I don't see any panic. They could organize well enough to resist, should we pursue, but my men are weary. We'll wait. And finish them another day."

Iskandar remembered his last battle and how he had underestimated the enemy. His men had been routed and destroyed when they'd separated themselves from the main army to pillage a local village. Bayezid was wise to avoid Iskandar's mistake. The Serbs weren't beaten . . . yet. They might withdraw, but they wouldn't flee.

Bayezid scanned the battlefield, focusing on the enemy. "You told me there were divisions among them. I expect you to do what you can to exploit them. Succeed and you will be rewarded. Fail and that battle is ours to lose."

Iskandar nodded. He spoke Slavonic well enough to communicate, and he had practice at blending in. He would have to change from his blood-stained robes and Turkish armor, and he would have to make sure he wasn't recognized. But despite the difficulty of infiltrating the Serb camp and finding his sources, he was determined. He would work until the doom of the Serbs was fixed.

Chapter Twenty-Seven
The Face That Defied Goliath

Maja climbed down the scaffolding as quickly as she could, hoping to distract her brother before he got himself into trouble. "Luka, I need your help."

Luka continued to glare at Petar with hands balled into fists. Should her brother come to blows with the stonecutter, Maja had no illusions about who would win.

"That's treasonous talk." Luka spat the words at Petar.

Petar shook his head. "No, it's practical talk. The župan isn't invincible, and the Ottomans are a growing power. If things go poorly, it would be wise to look to Hungary. They're Christian, at least."

"We can't trust the Hungarian half believers." Luka seemed to hold something back, perhaps a remark about Bokori and his spy.

"Maybe not, but they're better than the Turks." Petar folded his arms across his chest. "I'm not suggesting Sivi Gora surrender to anyone. But subservience to Hungary would be better than slavery to the Turks."

Maja put a hand on Luka's shoulder, hoping to keep him from arguing further.

He spoke anyway. "I saw the župan and Danilo after Pločnik. They beat the Turks then. They'll beat them again."

Petar's expression showed condescension. "I hope you're right. Because if everyone dies, we might not be paid for our work."

Footsteps drew Maja's attention beyond Petar as Dama Helena, Christophoros, and Philippos entered the narthex. The stonecutter turned, too, and his face became the color of the red underpaint used beneath gold tesserae.

Dama Helena glanced at Petar but kept her face neutral. The same couldn't be said of Philippos, whose glower suggested the lad took Petar's lack of faith as a personal insult.

"I assure you that all contracts will be honored, regardless of the battle's outcome," Dama Helena said.

Petar nodded. "Thank you, my lady. If you'll excuse me, I need to see to the carvings on the west windows."

Dama Helena dismissed him with a nod, then turned her attention to Maja as Petar slunk out of sight. "I came to see your progress."

Maja swallowed back her surprise that the župan's wife had taken an interest in her work. Or perhaps it wasn't so much an interest in art as it was an interest in her husband's cousin and the woman Danilo planned to court. Or was that thought presumptuous? He had certainly kissed her back at their last farewell, but she'd been the one to initiate that blissful moment. She gestured to the half-finished mosaic above them. "That's what I've started."

Dama Helena's expression softened as she studied the images. "May I take a closer look?"

"Of course, my lady. Do you wish to climb the scaffolding?"

Dama Helena nodded. Maja climbed first, and when Dama Helena began her climb, Luka stood at the foot of the structure to lend support if she slipped.

Maja brushed aside a few gray marble tesserae that matched Goliath's tunic and reached to help Dama Helena to her feet. The župan's wife studied the image of David gravely, then reached her hands toward David's face.

"The likeness is unmistakable." Dama Helena turned to Maja with tears in her eyes and spoke with a soft tone. "Did you intend to make him like Ivan?"

Maja nodded, worried that she had done wrong. "It is often done that way, with a church patron. Danilo suggested David fighting Goliath."

"You captured him perfectly." The tears spilled onto Dama Helena's cheeks. "He's just as I remember him from when we first knew each other, before he was župan, still part boy, part man."

"You love him deeply."

"Yes." Dama Helena swallowed. "And I'm worried about him. He didn't say it in so many words, but when he said goodbye, he didn't think he was coming back."

Maja remembered what Danilo had said of Župan Ivan's dream, but she held her tongue.

Dama Helena stared at David again. "He has a stubborn look, doesn't he? As if he doesn't care how big the foe is or what happens to him. He's confident he's in the right, and nothing else matters, not even his death." Dama Helena turned to Maja. "How did you do it?"

"Just a piece at a time." Maja clasped her hands behind her back. "I suppose Danilo helped. He often speaks of your husband. Their friendship is admirable."

"Yes." Dama Helena looked at the mosaic again. "I watched them ride from the palace together. Danilo's mother was with me. She said they looked just like their fathers when they rode off to Maritsa." Dama Helena swallowed hard. "But neither of their fathers returned from Maritsa. They died there together. Slain by the Turks."

Despite the afternoon warmth coming into the narthex, a shiver needled through Maja's spine. Would history repeat itself? What would she do if Danilo didn't come back? She'd already lost her parents. She didn't want to lose Danilo too. She'd finally risked her heart, and worry that it would now be broken cut into her as sharply as a chisel.

"I'm going to go after him," Dama Helena said.

"What? To war?"

"I'm not a warrior, but I am a healer." She stared at David again. "I've seen war before, and it frightens me, yet the thought of losing Ivan when I might have been able to help him frightens me even more."

"But who will govern Sivi Gora if you leave?"

"Danilo's mother. She's watched her father, her brother, and two nephews become župans. She knows what to do."

"What of Sofija?"

"Again, Danilo's mother will step in as well as Sofija's nursemaid." Dama Helena looked about as if uncertain how to climb off the scaffolding. "I'll gather supplies and a few men and leave at first light."

Maja watched as Dama Helena climbed down, then looked back to the half-finished mosaic. Men of stone. At the moment, she cared far more about men of flesh.

"May I come?" Maja blurted.

Dama Helena raised an eyebrow. Christophoros and Philippos didn't react, but Luka frowned.

"Please." Maja nibbled on her lip for an instant. "I'm not scared of blood. I could help."

Dama Helena nodded. "Meet me at the palace at dawn."

Chapter Twenty-Eight
A Last Supper

The fighting had ended for the day. Danilo and the others gathered the wounded and helped them from the field. They left the dead. There were too many to bury quickly, and the survivors would need to save their strength because the battle was not yet over.

Back in camp, Danilo stopped his cousin. "How bad are your injuries?"

Ivan grunted. "If we were home, I'd skip training for the next week. But we're not home. I'll be ready to fight again tomorrow."

"You had better show me."

Ivan nodded. "After I get the numbers from Goran."

They didn't have to wait long. Goran approached, his face smeared with dust and blood. "You can tell Knez Lazar that two hundred of us will be able to fight tomorrow."

Two hundred. They'd had four hundred men and mercenaries that morning.

Ivan's face pinched in pain. "Of those missing, how many are wounded, and how many are dead or dying?"

"I don't have the final count, lord, but more are wounded than dead. The heaviest losses were among the horsemen."

That wasn't surprising. Danilo had experienced the horror of being trapped in that pit, had found more than one friend who was now a corpse.

Ivan nodded. "I'll visit the wounded before I report to Knez Lazar."

Danilo cleared his throat to remind Ivan of his previous commitment.

"And I'll visit the wounded as soon as I've let Danilo examine *my* injuries." Ivan's voice held no enthusiasm. He pulled at the spaulder covering his left shoulder, winced, and then let Danilo and Goran help him remove the rest of his armor and tunic. Large bruises covered his arms and his torso.

"Perhaps you should rest tomorrow, lord." Goran shook out Ivan's tunic, then handed it back to the župan.

"I'll be fine." Ivan pulled his tunic on. He didn't wince again, but Danilo suspected that was only because his jaw was clenched so tightly.

With their contingent cut in half, they would need every man available, especially a warrior and leader like Ivan. But if Ivan entered the battle already wounded, it made it all the more likely that his dreams of death would prove true.

"Ivan, I think Goran is right," Danilo said.

"I'll be ready, Danilo. We'll fight side by side tomorrow, and we'll send the sultan back to Anatolia. But by all means, assign tonight's watch to someone other than me." Ivan gave Danilo a small smile. Danilo never assigned the župan to guard duty; he had other responsibilities.

Then Ivan's gaze shifted.

Danilo turned to see what had caught Ivan's eye. One of Konstantin's men approached, and it looked as though he had been mauled by the day's battle.

"Miladin? Are you all right?" Ivan asked.

Miladin's face was drawn, his skin was filthy, and his shoulders were slumped. A bandage covered his forearm, and he walked with a limp. He cleared his throat before speaking. "Župan Konstantin has been injured." Miladin's eyes went to Ivan, then to Danilo. "I thought someone should tell the two of you. If you can spare the time, I think you ought to come."

Dread engulfed Danilo and chilled him. After a battle like the one they'd faced, both camps, from Rivak and from Sivi Gora, had wounded to tend, armor to repair, and exhausted men and animals to see to. Miladin wouldn't have come if it weren't serious.

Ivan turned to Goran. "See to the wounded as best you can. Have Father Dmitar help."

"He's with them now, lord." Goran, too, seemed to sense the urgency behind Miladin's visit. "We'll see that they're cared for."

Ivan nodded, and then he and Danilo followed Miladin.

"What happened?" Danilo asked.

"Do you remember Arslan, the envoy the sultan sent soon after Maritsa?" Miladin asked.

"Yes," Danilo said. Arslan had first come to Rivak as Murad's emissary when Danilo and Ivan were boys. He had traveled to Rivak regularly for a decade, had even joined members of the Rivak garrison once when brigands had threatened some of the villages. Then Murad had learned that Konstantin wished to ally with Knez Lazar, and as punishment, Arslan had been replaced with an alternate envoy, a man Konstantin loathed.

"They faced each other today. Konstantin hesitated. Arslan didn't."

Danilo could almost see it. Konstantin not wanting to strike a man he had fought with and respected, a man who had almost been a friend.

"And Kostya?" Ivan asked.

Miladin shook his head. "We got him out, but Kuzman didn't make it, nor did Bojan. Arslan, too, was slain, so perhaps that means your brother is avenged."

Danilo had seen many friends die that day, but the men from Rivak were an especially bitter loss. Bojan had been the one who had trained him in horsemanship after his father died. Kuzman had helped him string his first bow. They were part of his memories from as far back as he could remember, and losing them was like losing a part of himself. Knowing that the man who had injured Konstantin was dead didn't lessen the grief.

"What of Kostya's injuries?" Ivan asked.

Miladin hesitated. "Father Vlatko thinks that if he can avoid a fever, he might live. But he's lost an eye, one foot is crushed, and the gash in his forearm went to the bone."

"Is Father Vlatko tending him?" Ivan asked.

"Yes, as is Župan Nikola's physician." They reached the camp, and Miladin led them into Konstantin's tent.

Konstantin lay on a pallet. A bandage covered the left side of his face, leaving only the right side visible, and the skin there looked waxen. Another bandage covered his right forearm. Father Vlatko knelt nearby, and a man Danilo didn't recognize, no doubt the physician, was wrapping what remained of Konstantin's right foot.

Danilo had been injured before. He carried scars. But Konstantin's injuries . . . They would change his life, however long that was to be. Worry clawed at Danilo's stomach, multiplied because all over the camp, other men were finding the same thing: men they cared about suffering grievous injuries that might still take their lives.

Danilo knelt on one side of the pallet, beside the priest. "How is he?"

Father Vlatko frowned. "I am sure he suffers, but he has been largely silent."

Ivan had knelt on the opposite side of the bed. He took his brother's uninjured hand in his own. "Kostya?"

Konstantin's single gray eye opened and took in his visitors. "I heard Sivi Gora was ambushed. I was afraid for you."

Ivan nodded. "Danilo and I are well enough. We'll fight hard tomorrow, too, and send the sultan back where he belongs. We'll keep our freedom, by the sword."

Konstantin's lips turned slightly as Ivan repeated the rallying cry Kostya had given them at the Battle of Pločnik. They'd won their freedom there, and here, at Kosovo, they would do all they could to defend it.

Danilo swallowed against a sudden emotion that choked him. That day, Konstantin had been so strong, so dynamic and courageous. Now he seemed so weak and helpless. "Kostya, what can I do to help?"

Konstantin's eye closed. "Just look out for each other. I'm sorry I won't be able to fight beside you tomorrow."

Danilo inhaled deeply, trying to gather hope. Men often survived wounds only to die from infection. Danilo prayed Konstantin would be an exception. They stayed a while longer, until Konstantin told Ivan to see to his men and the war council.

Outside the tent, the sun was sinking lower and lower on the horizon. One day of battle had devastated their forces. Danilo doubted the Turks would withdraw, so they would face the same challenge the next day, only without their full forces. Nearby, Miladin and the physician conversed with Župan Nikola. Ivan moved to join them.

Danilo considered doing the same, but they had little time to spare before the war council. "I've another friend who was wounded today, not so seriously as Kostya, but Miloš might be too stubborn to seek help. I'll check on him and meet you at Knez Lazar's tent."

Ivan nodded. "I hope he is well."

So did Danilo. Miloš had said his wound wasn't deep when they were in the pit, but it had bled enough to soak through clothes and armor. Danilo walked through the various camps, where men slept or ate or repaired their armor as best they could. Sometimes, the wounded cried or whimpered; sometimes, the survivors laughed or prayed or swore. After living through that day, Danilo suspected all would be changed in some way. Hardened or broken, pushed to fear or pushed past all comprehension of horror.

Danilo found Miloš, but he didn't go to him right away. Miloš spoke with Vuk, and the angry words were audible, even from a distance.

"You galloped right into their trap!" Vuk yelled. "They're not stupid, and they're not cowards! You have to think before you pursue! We've talked about their tactics over and over again. You should have known better! And now our reserve force is halved and our main force exhausted. You should have been turning their flank! Instead, you led our warriors into a pit of death." Vuk stalked away.

Danilo wished he hadn't heard the reprimand. He thought of withdrawing, but Miloš had seen him, so it was too late for that.

Miloš met his eyes, then spoke in a soft voice. "He's right. I made a mistake, and we're all more vulnerable because of it."

Danilo remembered Ivan's warning and call for caution, remembered the headlong rush into the trap. Yet despite that, they had prevented the Turks from hooking around the left of the line. That was something. And that seemed to have been all anyone managed that day. "Did Vuk make no mistakes today? I hear they held, but they didn't push the Turks back. His men may not have fallen on palisades, but they were decimated almost as much as we were."

Miloš grunted.

"How is that cut?"

Miloš gazed absently at his side. "Bandaged and no longer bleeding. It won't keep me from fighting again when I'm needed. You?"

"Nothing worse than a few bruises."

"And your young župan?"

"He is bruised, severely, I suspect, but claims he is still capable of fighting."

Miloš crossed his arms. "I should have listened to him. He's young, but he knows how to fight the Turks."

They all knew how to fight the Turks. Their enemy was a menace that wouldn't go away, that kept rising even after defeat, always stronger and larger than they were before. Danilo wasn't sure how long they could keep up. There were only so many Serb warriors. In contrast, it seemed as if the Turks had an endless supply of levies they could call up, ghazis they could recruit, and subjected people they could conscript into their ranks.

"My other cousin is not so well." Danilo folded his arms. "He wasn't at death's door, but . . . well, you've seen how fever can change that. He's lost an eye and part of a foot. Possibly the use of his right arm."

Miloš frowned. "I am sorry. I will pray for Župan Konstantin."

Ivan and Župan Nikola walked toward them. Župan Nikola had a bandage around his arm and a fresh scab along his right cheek. His men, like

Konstantin's, had fought beside Knez Lazar's forces. If his appearance was any clue, they, too, had faced a sharp, determined foe.

Miloš nodded at the others but left before they arrived. "I'll be on my way. I have something to see to before we break bread."

Danilo stared after him as he strode to the edge of camp. Was Knez Lazar's son-by-marriage hesitant to meet the two župans, or was he simply in a hurry to complete another task before the war council assembled?

A weariness hung about Ivan and Župan Nikola.

"How went the battle for you?" Danilo asked the older župan.

"We didn't fall into a pit. But I lost a lot of good men today. And I fear I am in danger of losing my neighbor."

Ivan frowned. "Kostya will get better."

Župan Nikola didn't argue, but nor did he agree. "Župan Konstantin and I are not the only ones who were bled today. I hear Miloš ignored Župan Ivan's warning, and Sivi Gora's men were decimated."

"It wasn't like that," Ivan said. "I urged caution, but the pit was hidden. None of us could see it until we rode into it."

"Well, we can hope he'll be more careful tomorrow." Župan Nikola crossed his arms.

"Vuk already berated him for it. He doesn't need to hear it more than once." Miloš might have made a mistake, but Danilo knew there hadn't been any malice behind it. Who among them hadn't made an error in judgment from time to time? Miloš's had cost their side dearly, but it had cost him, too, in more than the wound at his side. "He lost a lot of men today too."

Župan Nikola had the decency not to press the matter further. Župan Dragomir joined them, and they went into Knez Lazar's tent for the war council. The group was smaller than it had been the night before. Those missing were either dead or wounded so badly that they couldn't rise to their feet. Of those present at the curved table, half wore bandages of some kind.

They recounted the events of the battle, hoping to learn something that would help them survive the coming day. The center, Knez Lazar's group, had faced the sultan and his janissaries. Tvrtko's men had fought a group commanded by Bayezid, and Vuk's men had squared off against the sultan's other son, Yakub. Names of known generals and viziers were mentioned and discussed, as were all the different contingents of Turks: archers, akinci, sipahis, and ghazis. Danilo tried to concentrate, but the battle had left him weary, and though the information was useful, it didn't much change his ultimate task for the morrow: meet the enemy and slay them.

Miloš wasn't at Knez Lazar's side, as was custom. He wasn't anywhere near the prince. Instead, he was seated at the end of a table near the tent entrance. Had he come in late? Or had he been banished from his place of honor?

Ivan followed Danilo's gaze. "Vuk's doing."

"We can't let petty rivalries divide us. We have an army to beat tomorrow." Frustration burned in Danilo's chest. "Given the same orders, Vuk very well might have made the same mistake."

Ivan didn't have a chance to respond before Knez Lazar called out to him. "Župan Ivan, how many horsemen from Sivi Gora will be ready to fight tomorrow?"

"Eighty, my knez. Eighty-five perhaps, depending on how the night fares for those who are wounded. And about six score footmen, mostly archers, but also some pikemen."

"Take command of your brother's men as well and serve in the center with me."

"Yes, lord."

Knez Lazar continued around the table, making a few other adjustments to the next day's disposition. Then his eyes fell on Miloš. He held up a goblet of gold. "Come forward, Miloš."

Miloš obeyed, limping slightly. He must have turned an ankle in the pit.

Knez Lazar handed the goblet to Miloš, who accepted it, but confusion turned the knez's mouth and lined his eyes. "It grieves me, Miloš, to hear that you have been unfaithful to your lord."

"Never, my knez. It grieves me to hear that my honor has been called into question." He glanced for a moment at Vuk, then squared his shoulders, still holding the goblet, as if in a toast. "Tomorrow, you will see. Tomorrow, you will all see whether I am loyal or disloyal to my lord. Tomorrow, there will be no question as to where I stand." Miloš placed the goblet on the table, turned, and strode from the tent.

Whispers hissed around the tent, and a frown crept across Knez Lazar's lips.

Danilo turned to Ivan. "He doesn't deserve that." He pushed the stool he sat on back from the table. "I'm going after him."

Ivan took his wrist. "Go, but be discreet. Save a friend, but don't make any enemies."

Danilo nodded and left. Outside, the dark of the night had grown complete, and the moon had not yet risen. Danilo knew where Miloš camped and went in that direction. But Miloš wasn't at his tent, wasn't at the church of silk and brocade, wasn't among the nearby pickets. Danilo couldn't find his slandered friend anywhere.

Chapter Twenty-Nine
Turning to the Enemy

Danilo gazed into the blackness that covered the Serb camp. He had volunteered to take the fourth watch of the night, standing alert in case the Turks tried a night raid, as they had at Maritsa when his father and uncle had been slain. He was exhausted, but he was unwounded, and the same couldn't be said for many of Sivi Gora's warriors. They'd lost nearly half to death or wounds, and the Turks hadn't withdrawn, so the battle would continue another day. The fighting had strained his body nearly to the breaking point, and it had played even greater havoc with his heart. He dreaded to think of what the coming day might bring.

The cry of a dying man filled his ears. Both sides had taken their wounded from the battlefield, but for some, there was nothing they could do other than bring them back to die among friends. Most of the damage to their bodies couldn't be undone, so the priests were busy administering last rites and offering comfort for their souls. Danilo briefly closed his eyes to say a prayer that Konstantin wouldn't be among those wounded who died before daybreak.

Interspersed with the sounds of the wounded were shrill chirps of squires sharpening swords, the steady beat of smithies repairing armor, and the thud of attendants hammering out dents in helmets and spaulders.

Danilo turned when he heard footsteps behind him. "Ivan? Shouldn't you be resting?"

"I couldn't sleep. And I know your eyes will pick up movement long before mine, but perhaps my ears can be of service. Or I'll stand watch, and you can return to your slumber."

When he'd been woken, Danilo could have easily rolled over and slept again, but for now, there was something comforting in being with his friend. They'd endured battle together, exile together, and heartache together. They'd been close since they were old enough to drag pull toys across the bailey in Rivakgrad. And if this was the last morning he could be with his cousin, Danilo didn't want to sleep through it. "I don't think I could fall back asleep."

"You fought hard. You should be tired."

"You also fought hard. Is there nothing I can do to ease your burden, Ivan?"

Ivan began to shake his head, then paused. Danilo could barely see the movement in the dark. "Take care of my family and my people for me, if I'm unable to do it myself."

"You know I'll do anything you ask."

"I know." Ivan met his eyes. "I've been blessed to have you in my life. You would have made a good župan, you know."

"Fortunately, I was born to the daughter of a župan rather than to the son of a župan."

"Was it fortunate?"

Danilo nodded. "I've never envied you your burden. Nor Kostya his."

"Kostya." Ivan sighed. "I worry for him. Three wounds like that . . . Any one of them could cause a fever. It almost makes me wish Helena were here to tend to him. But Župan Nikola's physician is doing all he can, and Kostya is strong, and I wouldn't really want Helena here, not so close to so large an enemy."

She had almost disappeared into an Ottoman camp before. It was far better that she was safe in Sivi Gora for this battle. "She has proved herself an asset to you and to your župa. I am glad she is by your side."

Ivan crossed his arms and nodded. "Now you just need someone at your side. Maja."

"That is my hope." If he survived the coming battle, Danilo would court her. He admired her resilience, felt more confident when she was near. But the road to that destination lay through Kosovo Polje, the field of blackbirds. Right now, it was more a field of corpses, so many he wondered how the ground could ever receive them all. If the earth were hungry for death, surely the previous day's fighting should have satiated it. But the Turks were still there, so another battle would be fought.

He and Ivan were silent for a time. Danilo tried not to think of Ivan's dream, but he couldn't help it. The world was a better place with his leader, his cousin, his best friend. He knew Ivan's weaknesses as well as he knew his own, but that didn't make his devotion any less. He prayed that whatever the coming dawn brought, at day's end, the two of them would stand together again.

The sky shifted from black to indigo to charcoal. Some men and horses stirred, but most slept on. Then he caught movement, and his eyes fell upon a horse and rider.

"Who is that?" Ivan squinted into the darkness.

Danilo couldn't see the rider well, but he recognized the horse. "Ždralin. It must be Miloš."

"Why is he riding from camp so early?"

Danilo didn't have an answer. It wasn't the direction he would expect Miloš to ride, but perhaps he had a message for the sentries. Regardless of the reason, Danilo knew Miloš, trusted him completely. Even after the drama of the night before, he didn't doubt Miloš's loyalty and devotion to the Serb cause. Yet a feeling of unease grew larger and larger as Miloš continued away from the Serbian camp and past the line of Christian sentries.

As he rode through the shallow river and drew nearer the enemy, Miloš took his lance and shifted it so the point was directed backward. A sign of betrayal and desertion.

Danilo couldn't believe it. "His lance is backward."

"What? Are you sure?"

Danilo blinked and squinted, making sure he saw correctly. "Yes. It's Miloš. And he's riding to the Turks."

"He knows all our plans. If he talks, the battle is lost." Ivan swallowed. "You have to shoot him."

Danilo drew his bow and wedged it between his feet to string it. But with an arrow in his hand, he paused. Miloš kept riding, not looking back. His path was straight and unmoving. Danilo could hit him, but he held the arrow rather than nocking it.

Ivan put a hand on his shoulder. "Danilo, if he's a traitor, he must be killed before he defects. I'd shoot him if I could, but I didn't bring my bow, and you're the better shot."

Danilo nocked his arrow and pulled back on the string, but he couldn't bring himself to aim at his friend.

"Danilo, now! Before it's too late!" Ivan's voice made it an order.

A Turkish sentry motioned to Miloš, and Miloš raised his hand in friendship. In other circumstances, the sentry would likely have shot an approaching Serb, but the backward lance had granted Miloš entry to the enemy camp. They were too far away for Danilo to hear their words, but they seemed to be conversing. Miloš rode right to the man and then dismounted and led his stallion forward.

Ivan ripped the bow from Danilo's grasp. He drew back the arrow and swore. "He's out of range now." He let the bow and arrow fall to the ground. "Why didn't you shoot?"

Danilo swallowed, trying to work some moisture into his mouth to overpower the shock he felt. He had never disobeyed Ivan before, but Ivan had asked the impossible. "He was my friend."

"Well, your *friend* has doomed us all." Ivan turned and stalked away.

CHAPTER THIRTY

MILOŠ'S KNIFE

ISKANDAR WOKE TO SOMEONE CALLING his name outside the tent he shared with nine other men. He groaned. The first light of day showed at the seams of his tent, but it was still early, and he'd been injured in battle the day before. It wasn't much, just a bruised leg and a cut forearm, but he had also visited a few enemy campfires the night before, hearing of the rift between Miloš and Lazar and doing all he could to fan the spark of discord into an inferno of despair. Weariness clung to him the same way it had when he'd been forced to work from dawn till dusk for his Venetian slave master. He forced himself to his feet, wincing a little at the pain from his wounds.

He saw the reason for his disturbed sleep at once. Miloš Obilić stood a few paces behind the messenger, one hand holding the reins to his stallion. Iskandar looked from Miloš to the messenger. "Did you capture him?"

"No, effendi. He says he has a message for you."

Iskandar walked forward. "You have a message for me?"

Miloš nodded. "You once said if I betrayed Knez Lazar, your sultan would reward me."

"Yes."

"I have a gift for your sultan. I know the key to beating the Serbs, but I will tell only Sultan Murad. And then I will want payment—my life and coin."

When Iskandar had gone to Kruševac, he had never thought to win help from Miloš. He had been content to stir up dissension and doubt. Iskandar tempered the thrill of success with a modicum of caution. "You were not willing to help before."

"I have changed my mind. My own people have failed to show me the honor I have earned, and I no longer believe that the Serbs can win."

A smile of satisfaction spread across Iskandar's face. He would have been content to ruin Miloš's reputation and sow distrust that would make it more difficult for the Serbs to cooperate in battle. To have instead succeeded in drawing Miloš to the Ottoman cause was nearly as satisfying as the thought of finding Maja again. "I will arrange it."

Iskandar led the way, and Miloš followed on foot, leading his stallion. No one wished to wake the sultan, so they waited outside his tent until the proper time for an audience. Miloš stood tall and silent, looking to the west or nuzzling his horse. Anticipation drove away Iskandar's fatigue. Winning a traitor of this magnitude for the sultan was a coup he had never hoped to achieve. What might it mean in terms of title and land grants? If he survived the battle, Iskandar's future would be bright. He would have the resources to track down Maja, and she would have no choice but to be impressed with his riches and prestige.

Eventually, a messenger left the sultan's chambers. "The sultan will see you now."

Iskandar followed Miloš into the sultan's lush tent, eagerness willing Miloš to move more quickly. Iskandar had seen the sultan before but only from a distance. Having an ally in the sultan's son was a triumph, but having the sultan himself show honor and gratitude for bringing him a turncoat, that would be much more satisfying and much more rewarding.

Sultan Murad stood tall, dignified, in an emerald robe with a scarlet sash and dolman, not yet dressed for battle. Several servants attended him, as did his vizier and other advisers. The sultan was about the same height as Miloš, but his turban made him look taller, and Iskandar thought he saw fear in Miloš's eyes.

"You may kiss the sultan's foot," one of the attendants said.

Sultan Murad brought his right foot forward, revealing his soft shoe.

Miloš knelt and began to prostrate himself before the sultan. He brought his hands back—Iskandar assumed as part of his obeisance—and then Miloš lunged forward, pulling the sultan to the ground. Miloš's dagger flashed twice, and then the Serb was on his feet again, running from the tent.

"Stop him!" Iskandar shouted. He turned to the fallen sultan, but Murad's attendants had gathered around him, blocking Iskandar's view. Iskandar drew his scimitar and gave chase to the Serb. Anger burned through him. Miloš had lied! He was no turncoat. He was an assassin.

Outside, commotion swirled round the tent as servants ran to the sultan and warriors tried to stop the Serb's escape. Miloš crossed blades with a sipahi thrice before slaying him. Then a janissary lunged at him, forcing his blade into Miloš's arm. Miloš cried out and struck back, skewering the man with his spathion.

Miloš whistled, and his stallion trotted to him. Miloš got one foot in the stirrup, and then Iskandar struck. He shoved his blade into Miloš's back, forcing it through the layers of chain-mail and leather. Miloš fell, taking Iskandar's sword with him to the ground.

Iskandar grabbed a dagger, but there was no need for it. Miloš groaned a few times, but his movements grew weaker and weaker as his lifeblood spilled onto the grass. He met Iskandar's eyes briefly before turning his gaze to the brightening sky. His face grew pale, almost luminous. And then the fallen warrior breathed his last.

Iskandar turned him over and pried his sword loose. He wiped the worst of the gore off on Miloš's clothing, then turned his attention to the sultan's tent.

He had failed the sultan, bringing in a viper who claimed to be a worm. Part of him wanted to run and hide, to hope his role in leading the assassin to the sultan would be forgotten in the rush to tend to Murad's wounds and prepare for another day of battle. Punishment for aiding the assassin, even unwittingly, could cost Iskandar his life, but he didn't run. He needed to know if the sultan's wounds were mortal. If they were, then Iskandar still had a chance. He hadn't forgotten Bayezid's wish to become sultan upon his father's death, nor had he forgotten the promised reward if he helped Bayezid achieve his goal.

The inside of the tent had calmed since Iskandar had left. A group of servants attended to the sultan, who lay on the ground. Someone had brought a pillow for his head, and a slave held a bandage over a gash running across the sultan's belly. Blood showed through a cloth wrapped around Murad's throat. The sultan's pallor told the story without equivocation: He was dying. His viziers consulted among themselves with long faces and worried mouths.

"I wish Bayezid to succeed me," Sultan Murad whispered.

"Bayezid? Are you sure, Your Eminence?" Çandarlızade Ali Pasha, the grand vizier, asked.

"Yes." The reply was labored, strained almost out of existence.

Iskandar had heard what he needed to hear. He left the dying sultan and ran through the early-morning light to Bayezid's tent, on the right wing of the encampment. Bayezid's guards stopped him when he arrived. He was out of breath from the journey, and it took him a while to get the words out. "I must . . . speak . . . with Bayezid . . . It's vital."

One of the guards raised an eyebrow, but he jerked his chin at the other guard, who went inside the tent. Soon Bayezid himself emerged.

Iskandar knelt on the ground. "Great One, I bring urgent news. Your father has been stabbed by a Serb assassin. I do not think he will survive. He has named you his successor, but some of the viziers question his choice. If you wish to secure the throne, you must go to your father's tent at once."

"Bring me a horse," Bayezid commanded one of his men. "And one for this man. Iskandar, you will find my brother. Tell Yakub nothing, and bring him to me in my father's tent."

Iskandar nodded. He took the reins of the horse when it was brought, then mounted and galloped to the other side of the encampment. Men were waking and preparing themselves and their animals. A few nursed small cooking fires. Others stretched weary muscles or sharpened weapons. Some prostrated themselves in prayer.

Yakub would recognize Iskandar from the time before Iskandar was sold into slavery. But Iskandar wasn't sure that Yakub would trust him. Former friends were hated with such a loathing that it made the disdain for constant enemies seem mild.

"I bring a message from the sultan," Iskandar said when he arrived. "Yakub is to come to his father's tent."

One of the guards glared at him. "Now? We're preparing for combat. The Serbs may be destined to be our slaves, but they'll fight hard today."

"It's urgent. Let Eyne Bĕg Subaşi oversee the preparations. Yakub must come at once."

In the end, Yakub came. Iskandar rode with him, though they didn't speak. When they arrived, Miloš's body still lay outside the tent, uncovered, undisturbed, other than by the flies. His stallion stood beside him, as if keeping watch over his master's body.

"What happened?" Yakub asked.

"He pretended to join our side. I slew him."

Yakub stared at the body a moment, then went to his father's tent. The guards outside were expecting him, and they let him pass. Iskandar followed.

"My father!" Yakub fell to his knees before Sultan Murad's listless body. The sultan still breathed, but his eyes did not open, and each breath was labored. He showed no sign that he'd heard Yakub's voice. Yakub reached for his father's hand and took it, but the sultan didn't react.

Bayezid stood tall, issuing orders to the viziers and generals. "You will leave me now." He looked at Iskandar and motioned him forward. As the others left and as Yakub felt his father's face, Iskandar strode toward his new master. Bayezid handed him a bow string. "My great-grandfather Osman told his son it was unwise to share power."

Iskandar looked at the bowstring, then back at Bayezid. Osman's son, Orhan, had ruled well, and his brother had served as his loyal and skilled vizier. But Iskandar couldn't see Bayezid and Yakub sharing power. Rivalry had long ago poisoned their relationship.

"Royal blood is not to be spilled. But an empire can have only one sultan. Show me your loyalty, Iskandar, and you will be rewarded."

Iskandar knew what Bayezid asked, and he didn't hesitate. The tent was empty now, save for Bayezid, Iskandar, Yakub kneeling over his dying father, and a few slaves. Yakub stood as Iskandar passed, but he ignored Iskandar and spoke to his brother.

"You have proclaimed yourself sultan?"

Bayezid straightened to his full height. "No. Our father proclaimed me his successor, in front of all his viziers." Bayezid nodded to Iskandar, who had taken up position behind Yakub.

Iskandar threw the cord around Yakub's neck, tightened it, and held. Yakub choked, clawing at Iskandar and struggling for breath. In his desperation, he nearly escaped. But Iskandar held until the son of the sultan ceased his struggles.

Sultan Bayezid, now free of rivals, left the tent to go to war.

Chapter Thirty-One
A Good Morning to Die

When his watch ended, Danilo sought out Knez Lazar to report what he had seen of Miloš.

"Yes," Knez Lazar said. "Your župan informed me."

"I'm sorry. I hesitated too long when I was ordered to shoot him." Ivan had given him so few orders. His cousin had made requests, asked for specific actions, and given advice. But rarely had Ivan ordered him, as was his right as župan. Ivan ordered him only when it was vital. As Danilo gazed around the camp and realized how many men's lives hung in the balance, he felt sick.

If he hadn't seen it with his own eyes, he wouldn't have believed Miloš capable of treason. But he had seen it. The signs had been unmistakable—Miloš had ridden toward the enemy with the sign of intended defection clear for all to see. Danilo should have sent an arrow into him regardless of the hardships they'd shared, regardless of the admiration Danilo had gained for the man over the last six years. Danilo had thought with his heart instead of with his head, and he'd failed his people.

Knez Lazar placed a hand on Danilo's arm. "When loyalty for one friend conflicts with loyalty to another, it is difficult to choose."

Danilo knew how he ought to have acted. He owed loyalty to his family first, to his župan second, and then to his best friend.

That meant Ivan every single time.

There was the higher loyalty—loyalty to God—but even that loyalty shouldn't have made him choose Miloš. "I disobeyed my župan, and my people are in greater danger because of it."

"In your position, I also would have hesitated." Knez Lazar gazed on the enemy camp. "I loved Miloš. It is hard to believe he would turn on us. But Miloš is gone. Perhaps I was too hard on him last night. I wanted to give him a chance to pledge his loyalty for all to hear. To squash the rumors that kept surfacing. He chose another path."

The night before, Danilo had thought Knez Lazar too harsh with his son-by-marriage, but the dishonorable charge had proved true. Miloš was a traitor, and that knowledge wounded Danilo more deeply than a Turkish arrow could.

"His defection will hurt us but a little."

Danilo looked at Knez Lazar in surprise. "Oh?"

"The Turks fought against us yesterday. They saw our forces and dispositions. Miloš can only confirm what they already know. And sometimes, the anger that comes from being betrayed can add cohesion to an army. We'll fight sharper for his treason."

Vuk approached, and Danilo excused himself. He couldn't forget Vuk's words from the night before. If anyone had pushed Miloš over the edge, it was the husband of his wife's sister.

"Is the rumor true?" Vuk's words carried to Danilo's ears as he walked away. "Has Miloš really defected? I thought him foolish, but I never thought him a traitor."

That was the universal reaction around camp. No one had expected Miloš to betray them. But the men had little time to dwell on it. There was a battle to prepare for. It was a wonder the Turks weren't already upon them.

Danilo returned to the Sivi Gora encampment to ready himself. He tightened the leather straps over his lamellar corselet and replenished his quiver. He prepared Dazhbog for battle, though the stallion was more palfrey than warhorse, and then he could put off no longer what he knew he had to do. He and Ivan had fought so rarely that they had little experience apologizing to each other. But given what the day might hold for them, Danilo didn't want to risk leaving reconciliation until it was too late.

"Danilo, can you help me?" Goran called to him. He stood before his courser, trying to calm the animal as it pulled away. "I didn't notice yesterday, but his knee's been gored. He won't hold still long enough for me to look at it."

Danilo took the horse by the halter. "Easy, boy. We're trying to help." He repeated the words over and over as he ran a gentle hand along the horse's forehead. "Is it deep?" he asked Goran.

"Shallow but wide. The hair's gone, and it probably stings. I'll put some oil on it and bandage it. I'd use another horse, but the other options are worse than this one."

Danilo understood. He would have preferred riding into battle on a destrier or a courser rather than a palfrey, but Korab was gone. Dazhbog was uninjured, he'd remained obedient through several skirmishes that spring, and he was large for a palfrey, but he was no warhorse. Such situations were common throughout Sivi Gora's section of the camp. War was always costly and spared neither man nor innocent animal.

Had Miloš led them into the palisades on purpose? Had he meant to kill man and beast with such brutality? Or had he only decided on treason after Vuk's reprimand?

"There. That should protect the wound." Goran stood and took the reins. "I hope we can last another day."

"They have to be tired too."

"Yes. But there are more of them than there are of us."

Danilo watched his friend walk away. Goran wasn't one to put things in a positive light, but nor was he one to wallow in sorrow. He saw situations in terms of work to be done, his mind always full of figures about available resources and potential loss. He'd served Ivan since Ivan had become župan and served Ivan's grandfather before that. Goran had smoothed the way on countless campaigns with his foresight and thorough knowledge of what an army needed for success. He was competent with the lance or the sword, but Danilo worried about him. He was a thinker first and a warrior second. Could a man like that survive the wrath of Murad's army? And what of Adamu, sharpening his sword a few paces away? His arm was bandaged where an arrow had pierced him the day before. He was normally good with the sword and with the mace, but his dominant side was now injured. How would his wound affect his chance of surviving the day? And what of Adamu's younger brother, Marjan, the youngest man in Sivi Gora's fighting contingent? He seemed unwounded as he fastened a new shaft to the head of his lance, but his eyes were different today. Older, more sober, less innocent.

Then there was Ivan, the best swordsman Danilo had ever seen, competent as well with a lance, mace, or battle-ax, and, until recently, with a bow or crossbow. He'd been bruised the day before, and that would give his opponents an edge. It might be only a small edge, but combined with exhaustion and a premonition of death, what might the enemy achieve against him?

"Danilo?" He recognized the voice and turned to find his župan. Ivan was ready for combat, clothed in a thick tunic covered by a layer of mail and a corselet of leather lamellar. "I'm sorry about this morning."

Danilo opened his mouth to reply, but Ivan held up a hand. "The thing I've always admired most in you is your loyalty. And the way you think things through instead of reacting in an instant. You've always balanced me when I've been too reckless." Ivan glanced away. The stubborn set of his cousin's lips was more familiar to Danilo than his own reflection. "I shouldn't have asked you to shoot someone you care about. It went against all that's good in you. You lost a friend this morning when Miloš went over to the Turks. I just want you to know that you haven't lost me. For my part, I will always be your friend, and I hope you'll forgive me."

Danilo walked to his cousin and put a hand on his shoulder. "There's no need for forgiveness. You ordered what was best for Sivi Gora. That's your duty, your burden. You've carried it well, Ivan, and I know it's been heavy."

Ivan returned the gesture, then pulled him into an embrace. "We'd better get ready. The Turks won't dawdle much longer."

They walked to their horses. Danilo wished his destrier had survived to carry him into battle again. "We'll be in the center?"

"Yes. Just like Pločnik."

Pločnik had been a hard battle, but they had smashed the Ottoman Army. "I hope today will bring a similar outcome."

Ivan tightened the saddle strap on his horse, a courser whose rider had been killed the day before, and tested the bridle. "I remember thinking Pločnik was hard at the time, as much as I could bear. But I'd take another Pločnik over that pit any day."

A trumpet blared the call to assemble. Danilo and Ivan mounted their horses and joined with the other men from Sivi Gora. So many were gone in comparison to the day before. They joined with the men from Rivak, and Konstantin's group, too, was significantly smaller. It wasn't just the diminished size of the force—specific faces were missing, including their župan.

They assembled in the center-left of the line, between Knez Lazar's own men and Župan Nikola's. That meant their battle would be against the sultan and his elite janissaries.

Danilo sought out Miladin as he adjusted his helmet and his gauntlets. "How is Kostya?"

Miladin frowned. "No worse. No better."

"He's not feverish?"

"Not when I left him." Miladin's expression softened. "And he's recovered from serious wounds before. When next I see him, I hope to tell him we've won another victory." Miladin had seen victory before, at Pločnik, but he'd also seen the devastating defeat at Maritsa, and fought in numerous campaigns for the sultan. If he could still see victory, then surely it remained within their reach.

Despite his injuries from the day before, Ivan sat tall in his saddle. Danilo watched him test his sword, then looked at the men who remained from Sivi Gora and from Rivak. Not all of them would survive the day. On the one hand, who better to go into battle with than men he trusted, men he had trained with for years, whose expressions he could read at a glance and whose courage he knew was sure? But with men like that, every casualty would be personal, every death a tragedy.

At risk was more than his body or his freedom. At risk was also his heart.

Chapter Thirty-Two
Desperate Ventures

Maja had learned a great deal about horsemanship from Danilo, and that education was coming in handy as she rode toward Kosovo. Dama Helena had helped by giving Maja a wide-skirted undertunic to make riding less awkward, for she wanted no wagons. They expected to stay on the road, but should plans change, they didn't want their baggage mired in the mud or unable to follow them over rocky ground.

The group had left at dawn, with fourteen riders and a dozen pack mules. Maja looked behind her as Sivi Gora disappeared from view. It felt like home to her. She'd found purpose there and friendship. Her father's work had meant that she had moved every few years when she was a child, and that pattern had held true after his death. She had always felt like she was still settling in, like she was constantly an outsider. She'd dwelt in Sivi Gora less than two moons, but already, she loved its tidy streets, its strong walls, its orderly population, and its magnificent church.

"Will the city be safe?" Luka asked. He had insisted on coming and rode with a bow on his left side and a mace on his right. Maja doubted he could use either effectively, but she supposed that from a distance, he would look like another of the soldiers, and that would discourage small groups of brigands from attacking them. If a large group of brigands attacked them, Luka's weapons were unlikely to change their fate. "Most of the garrison followed Župan Ivan. Now Dama Helena's guard is riding out as well."

Ten soldiers accompanied them, and the groom Ivan was training to be a spy, Philippos. "I don't think ten or eleven fewer men will make much of a difference," Maja said. "The walls would be difficult to breach should someone attack, and the soldiers who remain know who to trust and who to turn away if they try to enter the city. Besides, Dama Zorica is a capable leader."

Or at least everyone said she was. Maja had yet to hold a conversation with Danilo's mother, and even the thought of coming under her scrutiny left Maja nervous. If she didn't make a good impression, what would that do to her chances of a relationship with Danilo?

Threats more serious than parental disapproval hampered her future with Danilo though. Župan Ivan led a great force, and he had many allies, but Sultan Murad led an enormous force, and he had many vassals.

If they kept a good pace, Dama Helena thought they could make it to Kosovo in four days' time. They weren't sure what they'd find there, and Maja wasn't sure she wanted to ride so close to the Ottoman Army. Even in defeat, they would hold danger for her. Dama Helena knew that but said that if the battle had not yet taken place, they would find the Serb camp and be safe there. If the battle had already taken place, they would meet messengers carrying news before they reached the battleground, and they could adjust their plans accordingly.

Dama Helena slowed her horse until Maja was even with her. "What would Danilo say if he knew I was leading you from the safety of Sivi Gora?"

"Perhaps he would be glad to see me."

Dama Helena smiled. "Yes. But worried for you as well."

Maja studied Dama Helena for a moment, then dared speak to her as if she were not a župan's wife but a friend. "What will your husband say?"

"Ivan won't approve, but he will understand. He's done the same. We never would have met had he and Danilo not ridden off to find Konstantin's army when they were returning from campaign."

"What happened?"

"There was a battle, and he almost died. He was captured, and I was asked to heal him as we were in need of a hostage to hold for ransom."

"Did you love him at once?" Maja asked. That was how it had been for her the moment Danilo had spoken to her and cut her free of Iskandar's bonds. Her feelings for him had changed, deepened, but that initial meeting had marked her heart.

Dama Helena smiled. "He was an enemy soldier with a fierce reputation. I was frightened by him. Then frustrated by how stubborn he could be. But animosity turned to respect, then friendship, then love, and that love grew. Ivan was not my first husband, but he is the only man I have loved, and he is the only man who has made me feel truly cherished. I don't want to face the rest of my life without him. Beyond that, Sivi Gora has been his dream. He deserves to see it prosper and grow."

Maja turned in her saddle again to look back at the city, but Sivi Gora had long ago passed out of sight. A hint of movement caught her eye, almost hidden among the trees. She blinked, and it disappeared. She strained, looking for something out of the ordinary.

"Do you see something?" Dama Helena asked.

"I think someone might be following us."

Chapter Thirty-Three

A Field of Blood

Danilo pulled his lance from a dying Turkish sipahi. All morning, they'd been fighting a desperate struggle between two determined foes.

Another sipahi rode toward him, scimitar swinging. Danilo stuck him in the chest and watched the man choke for a moment before swaying with the lance when Danilo jerked it to the left. The man tumbled free of the weapon and fell to the earth. From the corner of his eye, Danilo saw Ivan swing his sword into an enemy neck, completely decapitating his opponent. Ivan was covered in blood and dust, and Danilo supposed he looked just as filthy.

About half the men from Sivi Gora and Rivak now fought on foot, as the toll of battle had injured horses as well as men. The Turks they fought were mostly sipahi horsemen and janissary foot soldiers. The janissaries were the sultan's elite men, soldiers who had no occupation other than war. They had begun the battle with clean white hats that clung to the crowns of their heads and then flapped over the back of their necks. None of the hats looked white now. Like Ivan's face, they were coated in the grime of battle.

Danilo speared a janissary running toward him in a group, but he couldn't fight off the man's three comrades, who attacked him at the same time. One hamstrung Danilo's stallion, and the horse collapsed beneath him. Danilo struggled to pull his feet free of the stirrups and his weapons free of the saddle, reins, and trapper. He met one enemy with his lance and another with his sword. But when the third came toward him, Danilo knew he wouldn't be able to deflect the man's scimitar.

"No!" The Slavonic shout carried over the constant clash of steel and occasional boom of cannon. Ivan, still mounted, struck the remaining janissaries with his lance, ending that threat, though more Turks approached as the others fell.

"How many horses have you gone through since yesterday?" Ivan asked.

"Three." They'd been good horses too. Korab, Dazhbog, and another whose rider had been wounded earlier in the day's battle. Thinking of their needless loss fueled a fury that was only spent after Danilo had battled and slain the next ten foes.

The ground was thick with mud. But they fought some distance from the river, so it wasn't swampland, and no rain had fallen recently, so it wasn't runoff. Blood had been spilled so thickly that it ran like a flood over the plains of Kosovo. The field of blackbirds was known for its red poppies that bloomed in late spring. Now the field was coated in a different sort of red.

Danilo fought on, desperate to prevent the Turks from killing him or his comrades. He dueled with one Turk, then another, and though he defeated each enemy, they succeeded in drawing him farther from his friends. And while he fought the enemy on foot, groups of janissaries struck those Serbs still on horse, working in groups to overwhelm the scattered horsemen. Everyone from Sivi Gora knew an isolated horseman was vulnerable. But knowing the best tactics was one thing. Maintaining them after hours under oppressive heat and persistent losses was another.

Ivan became their next target. Danilo was surprised they hadn't attacked the župan before. There was something about his upright posture and precise slashes with a sword that proclaimed without words that he was a leader and a great danger to them. But Ivan also commanded a love from his men that meant he was usually surrounded by others who wished to fight at his side. Until now.

Ten paces lay between Danilo and his cousin. Danilo ran, desperate to reach him in time. One of the janissaries crippled Ivan's horse, and Ivan jumped onto a second foe, stabbing him with his sword. He pulled his sword free and parried another Turk, and by then, Danilo and Adamu had arrived to fight off the other four attackers.

When the janissaries were dead, the three of them glanced around. Ivan's horse thrashed on the ground, joining a hundred others too wounded to walk. And all the men, wounded or slain. The magnitude of casualties was staggering, so Danilo pushed it from his mind. He would mourn later.

A thick cloud of dust hung in the air, so Danilo couldn't see how the battle progressed on either wing. For the moment, the space around them was clear.

Danilo examined the beautiful bay stallion. It was well-trained and fearless, but the animal would never recover. Danilo put the courser out of its misery.

They had been fighting near Župan Nikola's men, and the župan approached them in the lull of battle. He took out a water bladder and passed it around.

His breathing came in heavy gasps. "This isn't working. We're killing them faster than they're killing us, but there are more of them. Here, on the field, but also back in their own lands. If we win, but lose half our men, how will we fight back when they send the next army?"

That was the problem with the Turks—there was always another army.

"We need to learn from the Greeks," Ivan said. "Find a pretender to the throne and stir up trouble."

Danilo grabbed his bow and quiver from his fallen horse and shot a few janissaries as they approached. "Sultan Murad consolidated power a long time ago. I doubt anyone could pose a challenge to him."

Župan Nikola rubbed a hand across his face, smearing blood from another cut. "The sultan will be on the field, or near it, surrounded by his own elite guard. But what if we cut through and challenged him directly? If we defeat him, then any new sultan would be vulnerable. He would have to secure his throne before he could mount another campaign. And if that man was defeated at Kosovo, perhaps he would turn his eyes elsewhere. We know the Ottomans have enemies in Anatolia. I fought against them when I was his vassal, as did Župan Konstantin and many others. The right mix of incentive and suggestions to his enemies in Asia could cause all sorts of trouble for a new sultan."

"It sounds like a shadow war." Ivan took his helmet off briefly to wipe away the sweat and blood.

"Shadow or steel . . . whatever it takes to keep us free." Župan Nikola grabbed a discarded shield from the ground and shook off the worst of the gore splattered across the front. "I want to consult Knez Lazar."

Župan Nikola spoke wisdom. It was a hard truth, but that didn't make it any less real.

Danilo looked at Ivan. Finding Sultan Murad and facing the royal bodyguard sounded dangerous. Danilo worried for himself, but more than that, he worried for his friends, especially the one who had dreamed of his own demise night after night.

Ivan met Župan Nikola's gaze, then Danilo's. "It's bold. It's risky. But the payoff could be worthwhile. Attack the head and hope the wings fail. If Knez Lazar wishes it, I will join you."

Ivan retrieved bandages and another dagger from his saddlebags, and then they gathered men from Sivi Gora and Rivak and joined Župan Nikola. They fought their way to their knez. Then, while Župan Nikola spoke with Knez Lazar, Danilo fought against the vanguard of Turkish janissaries. Ivan and Goran fought to his left, standing shoulder to shoulder with him. Two men from Rivak fought on his right. Together their shields formed a row of protection, with their swords dashing above the barrier in systematic destruction.

The men they fought were not so different from themselves. They might have families praying they would return. They no doubt feared death and loved their comrades, had hopes and dreams and foibles and virtues. But they threatened his people—the people he had chosen not simply because of his birthplace and not solely because of his blood. He had chosen the Serb cause because he believed in freedom. He would show no mercy to anyone who tried to take that freedom away, so he performed each slash and thrust, each block and counterthrust with an unceasing relentlessness.

Župan Nikola joined them, leading some of his men-at-arms to hold back the few Turks still fighting in their area. "Come. I've found horses for us."

They pulled back to the horses. The animals weren't destriers or even coursers, but they would be swifter than fighting on foot. Danilo was surprised to see Knez Lazar's son holding the reins to half of them. Their task was a risky one—he wouldn't have thought the knez would send his son. In addition to Danilo, Ivan, Župan Nikola, and Knez Lazar's son, eight other Serb nobles stood ready. He knew most of the men by sight, if not by name. Three were Vuk's men. The rest were Knez Lazar's. Twelve men in total. It wasn't much, but they couldn't afford more. If they stuck together as a group, they would fight well, but this was the type of mission warriors didn't return from.

A pair of squires brought an injured Ottoman soldier forward.

Župan Nikola pointed his sword at the man's throat until the blade rested lightly on the skin. "Danilo, you speak their language, yes? Ask him where the sultan will fight."

Danilo translated.

The captured soldier looked along the bloodstained blade of the župan's spathion. His eyes flashed with defiance.

Župan Nikola twisted his lips to the side. He wasn't a harsh man, but he was fierce with his enemies. "Tell him this: He can talk, or he can be run through." Župan Nikola relaxed his blade a bit. "He has the chance to send a dozen of Knez Lazar's best men on a mission we are unlikely to return from. Chances are, we'll be dead long before we catch sight of the sultan. He can tell us the truth and be released when the battle is over. Or he can lie, and we'll see that he suffers a very slow, very excruciating death."

The prisoner's face grew hard as Danilo changed the words from Slavonic to Turkish.

The man spat on the ground.

Župan Nikola motioned to the squires, and they dragged the man away, taking little regard for the wretched state of his leg, mauled by a lance, a sword, or a mace.

The next prisoner they interrogated broke at the sight of Župan Nikola's sword. "I haven't seen the sultan today, but he'll be in the rear, where he can see the battle, surrounded by janissaries. If not there, his tent is in the center of camp. The most ornate, marked by a white banner with gold lettering."

Danilo repeated the man's words so everyone would know the information. He hoped they would all find the sultan together, but he had seen the janissaries in action and knew what they were capable of. If those surrounding the sultan were thick, they were bound to whittle down Danilo's small group.

The next prisoner said largely the same thing.

After they had interrogated the third man, they adjusted their saddles and bridles. Danilo's horse wore a Turkish saddle and had probably belonged to a sipahi. The animal was smaller than he preferred but responsive. Better a small trained horse than a large one unused to battle. Horses were easily frightened by warfare. Perhaps they were wiser than the men who rode them.

Knez Lazar's son took command. "We stay together, knee to knee as we break through the line. We'll find the sultan and strike him dead."

Iskandar fought as part of Sultan Bayezid's guard. He wasn't in the first line of warriors, so he had only the occasional Bosnian to deal with. The Christians had fought well that morning, forcing the right wing of the Ottoman Army back, but now Sultan Bayezid's men were holding steady.

"Come!" Sultan Bayezid shouted across the field. "Organize the line here." He waved his sword to the right. "We can push them back."

Iskandar stood with the rest of Sultan Bayezid's force, united in their efforts to hold together and drive the enemy before them. They growled and charged and pushed the weakened enemy back a few paces at a time. It wasn't easy work. The Bosnians were fine enough warriors. But they were outnumbered, and each charge commanded by Sultan Bayezid reduced their forces even further.

Time and time again, Iskandar and those fighting alongside him crashed into their Christian opponents, and with each attack, the Christians seemed less able to hold. Sultan Bayezid had saved the right wing of the Ottoman Army.

The viziers may have questioned it, but Sultan Murad had made the correct choice in his successor. Here was a sultan who could lead his people from victory to victory. Sultan Bayezid was hard—he had no sentimental weaknesses or quibbles. He could be ruthless when needed, as evidenced by his execution of his brother. He would sacrifice what was necessary to make the sultanate united—and invincible. Most of the Ottoman Army would still be unaware that Sultan Murad had died and Sultan Bayezid had come into power. But Iskandar knew, and pride in his role in Sultan Bayezid's rise made it easy for Iskandar to battle on, seeking victory for his people and honor for himself.

The Bosnians didn't break, not right away. But the slow process had started. Iskandar saw fear in the eyes of the next man he slew, then despair in the eyes of the man after that. Physically, the Bosnians weren't broken yet. But mentally, they were finished. It was only a matter of time until the line caved and Sultan Bayezid led his wing to flank the end of the Christian line. Then they would sweep the Serbs from the field and conquer them completely.

Chapter Thirty-Four
The Hunt for the Sultan

Danilo's group had lost all their horses and two of their men. Ivan's thigh had been slashed with a scimitar, and a janissary had left a shallow cut across Danilo's forearm. Knez Lazar's son bled from a shoulder wound, and one of Vuk's men was missing an eye. They were all bandaged, and all continued the fight, but each time they overcame a group of Ottomans, their respite seemed but a moment before the next challenge came into view.

Župan Nikola stopped and stooped over a body as they passed through the detritus of an earlier skirmish. Župan Nikola turned the body over, and Danilo sucked in his breath. Župan Dragomir. He'd survived the Battle of Maritsa because he'd been recovering from a hunting accident, but he'd lost his two sons the day Danilo's father and uncle had been slain. He had been Rivak's closest ally for decades, and he had helped them win their freedom at Pločnik after years of plotting and preparing.

Župan Nikola made the sign of the cross, then reached out a hand and closed the old župan's eyes. "Goodbye, my dear friend."

Danilo thought he recognized a nearby body. He hesitated, but curiosity compelled him to turn it over. Stojan, Dragomir's second grandson. His eldest grandson, Decimir, had died six years ago as a vassal fighting Murad's wars, not long after his wife, Danilo's cousin Lidija, had died in childbirth. One grandson dead fighting for the Turks, one dead fighting against them, and one still at home to inherit whatever measure of freedom or bondage was decided at Kosovo.

Ivan's expression showed a deep sorrow when he saw the župan's body. "He always seemed invincible. Even as his wrinkles grew and his hair grayed."

Danilo rose to his feet to help Lazar's son fight off a new group of foot soldiers, five Turks in thick leather armor. Ivan and Nikola soon joined them.

Danilo slew one carrying a pike, while Ivan and Lazar's son held off men with javelins. Nikola skewered one with an ax, while Danilo blocked a swing from the last one's scimitar, then slashed his spathion across the man's stomach.

"Where is the sultan hiding?" Frustration colored Župan Nikola's voice.

Over the last hour, they'd been weaving in and out of the battle lines, searching for and attacking groups of the most formidable janissaries, hoping to come across the sultan's guard, or at least that of his vizier. But they couldn't do that forever, not when they were so outnumbered. They battled their way to higher ground in hopes of a better view and an edge over their enemy.

Ivan limped closer. "Can you see anything, Danilo?"

Corpses carpeted the field as far as he could see, which was no great distance, given the dust cloaking the sky. He squinted. "It's hard to tell. Maybe . . . Those could be janissaries to our left." It looked as though the Bosnian forces were being driven back.

"Pushing against Tvrtko's forces?"

"Yes."

"I suggest we go there," Ivan said. "If we find the sultan, we'll accomplish our goal. If we don't, we can help break their rally."

The others agreed. Their group of ten was small, but they were disciplined and skilled, and the massive charges of the initial engagement had long ago broken down into scattered pockets of fighting. They would test their skill against small groups of the enemy, not a massive line, at least initially. Perhaps they could gather survivors and form a large enough group of Christians to halt the Ottoman advance.

They rushed around one group of undisciplined Turks—they were rabble, not royal guards—and broke through the center of another.

One of Lazar's knights tripped over a wounded Turk, and a cry of alarm escaped his lips. The man on the ground wasn't as far gone as supposed. He leaped upon the Serb warrior and slashed with his dagger. Ivan and Danilo were upon him immediately, and Ivan's sword finished the Turk off. But Lazar's man breathed his last, and now they were down to nine men.

One of Vuk's men fell next, his body shattered by a Turkish javelin. Not long after, a Turkish war hammer brought down another of their group.

"Should we keep going?" Lazar's son asked. "If we knew where he was, I would press on. But the field is large, and we are only seven strong. We could search all day, and meanwhile attrition racks our ranks just as surely as it does the foe." He looked to Župan Nikola, the most experienced of those still alive.

Their plight seemed hopeless. How could they expect to find a single man amid an enemy so vast? They could barely see beyond the next group of skirmishers, so thick was the air with dust. Finding the sultan seemed impossible, but the ranks of soldiers from their župas were so decimated that returning to command them would offer little edge to the Serbs.

Župan Nikola set his jaw. "I think the only way is forward."

The dust cleared for a moment, and Danilo caught sight of the Ottoman camp. After all their duels and skirmishes, they'd finally pushed their way through the bulk of the Ottoman Army and were approaching the rear of the enemy lines.

Danilo pointed. "Perhaps if we find his tent, someone there can be forced to tell us where he fights." Danilo looked for a white banner with gold lettering, but the thick air made it difficult to see beyond the initial tents, and the sultan's would be in the center.

A dozen sipahis circled toward them over a carpet of fresh corpses. Danilo moved to Ivan's side, where they could cooperate with their shields and swords. One of Lazar's men joined them on Ivan's right. From their horses, the sipahis would have tremendous power behind their blows, but the uneven ground slowed them.

"Ah!" The cry drew Danilo's eyes around to one of Vuk's men, now collapsed on the ground with an arrow through his throat.

Danilo drew his bow and aimed a shaft at the source of the barrage, a group of archers a score strong just emerging from behind the tents. He shifted his aim to the horseman nearest Ivan and struck a sipahi. The man fell under the thundering hooves of his comrade's horses, and the group of riders were forced to adjust their tightly coordinated stride.

Events moved with a swiftness that Danilo could scarcely follow. Lazar's son lifted his shield to block another barrage of Turkish arrows, the shafts fired from so close that they would likely pierce armor.

Danilo shot another of the archers, scattering a portion of the group. But most continued their barrage. Župan Nikola arched and twisted, an arrow in his back.

Danilo rushed to help the man who had once saved his entire family. Arrows could cause immediate death, but often, they didn't. Danilo and Ivan had both survived arrow wounds before. But this wound was different. The sharp barb had cut into vital flesh, and the sucking sound of the wound indicated it would only grow worse. Danilo found Župan Nikola's eyes and saw the knowledge there.

"Better to . . . die . . . free . . ." Župan Nikola whispered.

" . . . than to live a slave," Danilo finished for him.

Župan Nikola gave a small nod, and two heartbeats later, his head slumped to the side. He wasn't dead yet, but death was coming for him.

Mere paces away, the sipahis' scimitars crashed into Ivan's and the other Serbs' spathions. Danilo sprang to his feet to help. Ivan blocked the first sipahi's sword and the second's. Danilo drew his spathion to hamstring one of the horses as it sprinted past.

He turned to block the downward blow of a mace and saw a lance pierce Ivan's shoulder, pluck him from the ground, and carry him back a pace before Ivan fell, the spear still in his shoulder.

Danilo swung so hard at the last sipahi that his sword carried cleanly through the man's armor. Then he spun toward his cousin, hacking through a dismounted sipahi to reach him. "Ivan!"

His cousin's face was pale underneath the coating of splattered blood and dust. His eyes were only half open, as if he were struggling to stay conscious.

Danilo shot at an approaching Turkish archer but didn't aim at the others when they backed off. He had only three arrows left. The man who had fought beside Ivan cradled an injured arm, but he still stood, as did Knez Lazar's son and the last of Vuk's men.

Ivan's mouth moved.

"Shh. Don't try to talk." Danilo examined the spear that had spitted his cousin like a wild fowl, just beneath the spaulder. The sipahis were past, so Danilo set his weapons down long enough to cut the shaft out and wrap it. The wound needed better care. Danilo had seen broken bone amid the chewed-up mass of flesh.

Ivan tried to grab him with his good hand. The movement was without strength; little Sofija had a stronger grip. "I'm sorry . . . dragged you . . . into this."

"It was a good plan. Hang on, and I'll get you out of here, just like we've done time after time."

"This . . . bigger . . . other scrapes." Each word seemed a battle.

Danilo could guess what Ivan was saying. This was bigger, worse than the scrapes Danilo had helped with when they'd been younger. But that didn't mean he wouldn't do his best to get his cousin off the field and to safety. "You'll see Sivi Gora again."

Ivan drew in his breath as if to answer, but a shudder of pain shook him before he spoke.

Danilo looked to Lazar's son. The sipahis had circled back around and would trap them between the archers if they didn't move.

"We can't stay here," Danilo said.

Vuk's man checked another of their fallen comrades. "He's dead."

Danilo pulled Ivan's good arm over his shoulder and hoisted him to his feet. The sharp inhalation and trembling told him he'd made Ivan's pain worse, but he didn't have another choice. They needed horses and more bandages. Wine would be helpful as well. Danilo clung to his sword with his free hand and followed Vuk's man away from the sipahis.

He didn't understand why the sipahis weren't riding them down. Their group had blooded them on their first pass, but now the Serbs were weaker. What was holding them up? Surely mercy wasn't behind their delay.

They moved beyond the tents before Danilo understood. The sipahis had waited until the small group of rebels were surrounded on three sides: not just by sipahis or yaya archers but by janissaries too. The group of fifty warriors in battle-stained white hats marched to a stop ten paces in front of them, cutting off their retreat.

Knez Lazar's son dropped his sword. "We surrender."

Danilo forced himself not to glare. Surrender? The man should have asked the others first. Sivi Gora might ransom Ivan and Danilo, but at what cost? If Sivi Gora emptied her treasury, there would be nothing with which to finish the church, nothing to pay the mercenaries. With most of the garrison lying dead on the field, how would the town stand up to the Turks should they venture that far west? The payment of ransom might beggar Sivi Gora, and the beggared city would be an easy target for the Ottomans or the Hungarians.

Yet despite the instinct that told Danilo to keep fighting, he obeyed and let his sword fall to the ground. Perhaps Lazar's son was right. Sivi Gora would be better off with a living župan, even if their leader's body and their treasury were crippled. Where there was life, there was hope. Fighting on, in contrast, meant certain death.

But surrender was still bitter.

The sipahis closed in, as did the archers. Of the Serb's group of twelve, only five remained, most wounded, Ivan unconscious. Then the janissaries came, and with them, Danilo's worst fear.

Iskandar.

Chapter Thirty-Five
A Spy Among the Poplars

Maja winced as she and Luka drew water for their horses. They would press on until dark, but the horses needed rest. Maja's sore legs needed rest too. For a moment, she thought it might have been better to stay in Sivi Gora, but she quickly dismissed that idea. If there were anything she could do for Danilo—or for those he loved—she wished to help.

"Who do you think is following us? Vadas again?" Luka asked.

"Perhaps." Maja filled the bucket and set it on the ground near the stream. "I have an idea."

When they returned to camp and Maja explained her plan, Dama Helena seemed skeptical. "What if something goes wrong? He's dangerous. He might be murderous."

"What could he gain by killing me? I expect he'll want to *speak* with me. Or perhaps not—maybe he'll keep his distance. But it's worth a try, isn't it? We can ride the horses a bit harder to make up for the lost time."

Dama Helena didn't answer at once. Instead, she peered among the trees as if hoping to see Vadas. "I'll go. Danilo would never forgive me if something happened to you. I can't be responsible for your coming to harm, not after what happened with Tatjana."

"He said it wasn't your fault."

"It broke him, Maja. You don't know how hard it hit him because you've been the key to bringing him out of the dark cloud that was smothering him. I can't let him suffer like that again."

"You lead Sivi Gora in your husband's absence. It's not proper for you to wander without protection, nor would anyone watching us believe your guards would allow you to do something so reckless. We can't send one of the men because they might be too great a threat. It has to be me."

Dama Helena frowned, but after a few moments, she nodded her acceptance. "Philippos, get going. You, too, Luka, Christophoros." Dama Helena went to her saddlebag and came back with a small dagger. She handed it to Maja. "Just in case."

Maja tucked it into the belt cinching her tunic at her waist. She took a deep breath, then walked back the way they had come, in the center of the road, where anyone could clearly see she was alone and vulnerable. Her heart hammered loudly in her chest, but not because of the steady pace she forced her feet to follow. When she'd said she didn't think Vadas would hurt her, she had believed it. But alone, with nothing but a soft breeze and the pounding of her heart, she wasn't so sure, and her footsteps faltered. She was a witness to the letter that could destroy his master. Would he kill over that? What was the death of one insignificant artisan to someone like Vadas? Why else would he follow the group if not to silence them?

The breeze had felt pleasant most of the day. Now it chilled her. She forced herself to keep good posture, trying to picture what she must look like to whoever was following them. She preferred to look confident, like one of the warrior saints she might put in a mosaic. If something did go wrong, she wanted her last walk to be one of pleasure from the sun's warmth and appreciation of the lush fields on either side of the road. There were trees, too, tall billowing ash, spindly poplars, and cascading willows. If she ever did a mosaic of Adam and Eve, she would put willows and poplars in the Garden of Eden. If she could have changed the current view the way she could change a half-finished panel, she would have added more trees so Luka and the others would have an easier time staying hidden.

She walked a half mile before leaving the road's center. Anyone following the group would have seen she was alone by now, but he was unlikely to approach her if she could still be seen by Dama Helena and the remaining nine soldiers. Maja meandered through the trees, pretending to study the branches. For a moment, she thought not of the danger but of what color of glass she could best use to portray the leaves of an oak tree. Normally, she didn't go into detail with vegetation—she saved the emphasis in any piece for the humans—but in a private home rather than a church, a tree of tesserae could be stunning. In the palace of Sivi Gora, there was a long wall on the north side of the court with a covered portico. A mosaic would be beautiful there.

The snap of a twig pulled her from her daydreams. She turned around in a whir and took a step back. "Petar?" What was Petar doing here?

"Maja. It's nice to see you. Although I'm surprised to find you wandering alone. One would think that with your past, you'd be more careful."

"Why aren't you finishing the carvings around the west windows?"

Petar gestured about him at the empty trees and fields. "Perhaps I am sorry I was left behind when everyone else went to Kosovo."

"You're not a warrior." She'd heard him scoff at warriors on more than one occasion. "Why would you follow the army?"

"You're not a warrior either." Petar stepped closer, and Maja instinctively stepped back. She hadn't found Petar threatening before, but his current manner bordered on insolence.

"Dama Helena is a healer. I plan to help her, if I am needed."

"Dama Helena goes to Kosovo?"

Maja decided not to answer. Perhaps she had already said too much. She turned toward the road. "It's time for me to go back."

"Stay." Petar closed the distance between them. "I insist."

"You insist? Why?" She had seen the stones he carved and the muscles that lined his arms. Petar could stop her if he wished. But she didn't understand what he wanted from her. He took another step toward her, and the movement made her gasp. Her memory flashed to the night she had found someone riffling through her wooden chest. Just a shadow, really, but with large muscles matching those of a stonecutter. And the way the shadow had moved . . . She fingered the lingering bruise on her head.

Petar followed her movement. "I thought you didn't remember that night."

"Why did you break into my home?" What could he possibly have been looking for?

Christophoros appeared before Petar answered. He had an arrow nocked in his bow, and his sheathed spathion was plainly visible. Luka appeared next and came to stand beside Maja, his sword drawn, though Maja doubted he could beat Petar if it came to that. Philippos appeared last, and his arrival seemed to somewhat unnerve Petar.

"I think it best if you come with us." Christophoros jerked his head toward the road.

Petar cooperated, at least until they returned to the main party. Then he refused to speak, would give no explanation of why he'd come or what he intended, no confirmation or rejection that he'd been the one to strike Maja down when she'd found him in her home.

Dama Helena stood with regal posture as she questioned him, but she stopped one of the guards when he suggested forcing Petar to speak. "No. We'll not torture him. Bring him with us. We've already lost too much time."

Chapter Thirty-Six
Bayezid's Wrath

Danilo knelt before a group of Ottoman tents. Knez Lazar's son knelt on his left. To his right, Ivan, barely conscious, slumped forward so he was almost bent in half. Danilo wanted to examine the wound again, give it another layer of wrapping, see if it had stopped bleeding, but his hands were bound behind him.

"How bad is your wound?" Lazar's son asked one of his father's knights.

"Not mortal. But that might not matter."

From where they were held, Danilo couldn't see anything beyond the canvas tents. The battle might have been won or lost, but he couldn't tell. The Turks hadn't panicked yet, so the future didn't bode well for Danilo's side.

"I've a dagger in my boot," Danilo whispered. The way his hands were tied, he couldn't get to it. He'd tried to grab Ivan's, but his was missing. He'd probably used it during the battle and been unable to retrieve it.

"If those janissaries will take their eyes off me for more than a heartbeat, I'll grab it." Lazar's son kept all emotion from his face, except determination.

Iskandar walked over again. Danilo tensed. When they'd first been captured, Iskandar had struck him across the face with the flat of his sword. Blood still trickled from the broken skin. No other person on earth could inspire the dread Iskandar did in Danilo, for no one else hated him with such passion.

"Bayezid broke the Bosnians." Iskandar stood before them, gloating. "They scattered. Vuk Branković might have turned the tide, but he seemed to know the battle was lost, so he withdrew. Your army is destroyed, and your lands will be ours."

Danilo met Iskandar's smirk with a glare. The Turk was exaggerating. The Bosnians might have been pushed back, but defeat must not have been complete, or Vuk couldn't have managed an orderly withdrawal. And the battle must have bled the Turks, or they would have crushed Vuk as well as the Bosnians rather than letting a third of the Serbian hosts escape. The battle would likely result in a stalemate, at least for a while. Murad could call up more levies and replace the men he had lost, but it wouldn't be immediate. The Serbs would have time to prepare for siege. The question was whether Danilo would live to fight the next battle.

Iskandar folded his arms across his chest. "Bring them," he ordered a group of janissaries.

One of them tugged Danilo to his feet and pushed him forward.

Another kicked Ivan in the side. "Should we finish off this one?"

"He can pay a large ransom." Danilo met the janissary's eyes and pleaded for mercy.

The man hauled Ivan to his feet. Ivan groaned and opened his eyes a crack as the janissary pushed him toward Iskandar. Ivan stumbled forward only a few steps before collapsing to the ground again.

Iskandar drew his sword and marched toward Ivan with a sneer of satisfaction on his face. Danilo stepped in front of Ivan. "Kill me if you wish. But you've been to Sivi Gora. You know how prosperous we are. If you slay Ivan, you'll throw away a fortune."

Iskandar paused. "There is one thing in Sivi Gora that I want above all else. Help me get Maja, and I'll spare your župan. If Sultan Bayezid permits it."

"Sultan Bayezid?" What did Iskandar mean? Danilo had seen the sultan's sons while he and Ivan had been hostages in the Ottoman capital. He had always thought Bayezid would succeed Murad, but he wouldn't take the title until his father's death.

Iskandar's eyes narrowed with disbelief. "You didn't know?"

"Know what?"

Iskandar didn't answer. "Bring them, even the dying one." He strode before the janissaries and their captives and didn't stop until he reached a body just outside a large tent marked with a white banner and imperial gold lettering.

Iskandar kicked the body over, and Danilo gasped.

Miloš.

"Do you always execute defectors?" Knez Lazar's son asked. "You'll discourage anyone from joining you if you treat them like that."

Iskandar nudged Miloš's body with the tip of his boot. "Miloš was no defector. He was an assassin. But his work will do his cause little good. Sultan Bayezid is everything his father was and more."

Miloš had killed Sultan Murad. He'd been right the night before, when he'd promised that on the morrow, everyone would see where he stood. His loyalty to Knez Lazar had never wavered, had been strong enough to take him on a mission that offered no hope of escape. He had sacrificed himself for those who slandered him.

Danilo didn't know whether to rejoice or sob. Miloš, his friend, wasn't a traitor after all. But Miloš, his friend, was dead, as were a hundred others Danilo knew and thousands of others he had made common cause with. Miloš had given up his life. But the battle still hadn't been won.

Danilo glanced at Ivan, slumped to the ground again, and thought of Konstantin, weak and vulnerable from his wounds. Would his cousins, too, perish before the day was over?

Ottoman soldiers brought more prisoners. Danilo recognized most of them; they were all nobles. Squires and men-at-arms with no outward signs of wealth would have been slaughtered, not captured. Then a pair of men escorted Knez Lazar himself to the ground before the sultan's tent. Danilo's heart sank. The Christians had suffered a catastrophic loss. It was like Maritsa all over again, only worse because now Danilo was old enough to understand, and now he had more to lose.

Danilo recognized the prisoner forced to kneel beside him. Viktor. "So Iskandar spoke truth," Danilo whispered. "The line broke, and the battle is lost."

Viktor shook his head. "The line faltered and retreated. It didn't collapse. Most of the survivors withdrew to safety. I just . . . Some of us were separated from the main line. The Turks don't have the strength to pursue, not in force. Some will be tempted by the promise of plunder, but most are just as exhausted as we are. The battle was a draw."

Ivan had always said that anything less than an overwhelming victory against their enemies would leave the Serbs more susceptible. If both sides appeared evenly matched, the Turks would be tempted to try their luck and attack again. And they had an endless supply of new men to fight for them. The same couldn't be said of the Serbs. In a war of attrition, the Turks would win every time.

Bayezid appeared. The new sultan, flush from the battle, hadn't changed much since Danilo had last seen him three years ago. He was in his mid-thirties, of sufficient age to have reached his full physical prowess but not old enough for the years to humble him.

He spoke his orders with an unquestionable authority. "Strip them of their armor."

Several nobles had already been stripped down to undertunics and hose. Danilo didn't resist as the janissaries took his iron helmet and lamellar corselet, chain-mail hauberk and chausses, wrist guards, bracer, spaulders, and coif. His weapons had long ago been confiscated, but Danilo was lucky. No one took his boots.

He maintained his calm while the men stole his armor, but he barely restrained the rage when a particularly rough janissary pillaged Ivan's body. He deposited the stripped župan back into the dirt like the discarded chaff of harvest. The man had pulled the bandage loose, and Ivan's shoulder bled again.

"I am a merciful man," Bayezid said. "I will spare the young. Those not yet twenty will be my slaves. But justice must also be paid." The sultan strode to stand before Knez Lazar. "A mighty sultan was killed this morning. He will have a worthy adversary to keep him company in the afterlife." He pointed to two of the janissaries. "Bring Lazar forward."

Knez Lazar looked older now. The janissaries had taken his fine tunic and armor, and he was coated in a layer of battle grime. But he still looked majestic, and if he felt any fear, it didn't show.

Bayezid motioned to one of his men, who took out his sword and held it overhead, ready to strike off Lazar's head.

"Please, slay me first so that I will not have to witness the end of my knez," one of the nobles cried.

Bayezid nodded, and the man was brought forward and thrust onto his knees. One of the Ottoman soldiers raised his scimitar and let it fall, slicing the man's head from his torso.

"Me as well," Lazar's son said. "I do not wish to see my father slain."

Knez Lazar showed emotion then—regret and sorrow.

"He's only a boy," Danilo said. "He should be spared." Lazar's son was older than twenty but not by much. He could pass as younger.

Knez Lazar's son turned to Danilo. "I'm not afraid to die."

"I never said you were, but your people will need you. Think of your mother, the princess."

"Stefan and Vuk still live. They didn't come to Kosovo. Like my father, I will forsake this earthly kingdom."

Bayezid spoke in an undertone to his viziers, and Lazar's son was brought forward and executed. Then the knez himself was beheaded.

Bayezid wasn't content with the knez and his son. He singled out another of the nobles and then that man, too, was executed.

"Great One, the Serbs are wealthy. But you will receive no ransom for them if they are dead." Bayezid's vizier approached the sultan in an attitude of humility, perhaps frightened that the blood lust could easily turn from a defeated enemy to a too-bold servant.

"Today, I prefer blood to money. I'll take their lands at my leisure, without bickering over a ransom." Bayezid nudged his most recent victim until the corpse fell to the ground. "I will ride to the north, the south, the east, and the west. I will defeat all Christendom, and then I will water my horse in Rome from the altar at St. Peter's."

The slaughter continued as the sun sank and the shadows of the tents lengthened, casting a darkness on both prisoners and executioners. Danilo wondered if perhaps Knez Lazar's son had been wiser than Danilo, requesting a quick end before he was forced to witness the flower of Serbian nobility systematically murdered.

Finally, Bayezid stood before Danilo.

Danilo raised his eyes to the sultan and found his voice. "Sultan, please slay me before you slay my župan." He couldn't bear to witness the death of his best friend, especially not today, when he'd said farewell to so many others. Ivan hadn't moved since the janissaries had taken his armor, but Danilo knew he lived because he could hear the wheezing as his body fought for air.

The new sultan's face remained hard at the plea. "I remember the two of you. Iskandar?"

Danilo's heart sank. If Bayezid recognized them, a fate worse than beheading might be pronounced, especially if Iskandar were involved.

Iskandar drew up behind Bayezid. "Yes, my sultan."

"I believe I once ordered these men impaled and their bodies displayed outside the gates of Edirne."

"Yes, my sultan."

"I leave them to you. Have your revenge—impale them, flay them, crucify them. Or take their wealth through ransom. The choice is yours."

In those few phrases, Danilo and Ivan were at once spared and condemned.

Danilo remembered Iskandar's taunts three years ago on the fields of Kırkpınar, when Ivan and Danilo had been doomed to impalement. Danilo didn't doubt Iskandar would relish the opportunity to skewer their bodies on long wooden poles. And this time, Danilo didn't think the two of them would escape.

A beheading would have been easier.

Bayezid moved on to his next victims. Iskandar loomed over Danilo, a smile growing on his face. His eyes moved from Danilo to Ivan and back again several times until Danilo looked away. Dread grew in his stomach, for himself and for his cousin.

Iskandar shifted, and his shadow fell across Ivan. "Bring your župan," Iskandar ordered.

With his hands still tied behind his back, Danilo wasn't sure how he was supposed to carry Ivan. He glanced at the executed prisoners, glad he would soon have a different view, but he also envied them. Impalement sounded far worse than a beheading, and he had a feeling Iskandar would add an extra measure of misery before the death.

Danilo bent toward his cousin. "Ivan?"

No response.

Danilo tried to grab his cousin's hand, but a janissary yanked him to his feet before he could so much as touch Ivan. The man pushed Danilo forward and followed, dragging Ivan behind him. Danilo winced to see Ivan carted around like a slaughtered animal, but at least the man held Ivan's torso, so it was his feet, not his head that dragged.

They were brought to a tent. The soldier dumped Ivan on the ground and stood guard at the entrance.

Iskandar paced. He held all the power, and he wouldn't be afraid to use it. Danilo and Ivan were absolutely helpless.

"For years, I wasn't sure which one of you I hated more," Iskandar said. "You, who upset all my hard work in Rivak, then humiliated me before Bayezid, then stole the woman I loved when she was within my grasp. Or your župan, who slew my father and foiled my siege on a rich Greek kastron. I hated both of you for selling me into slavery. But when I saw you again, when you robbed me of Maja again, that's when I knew I hated you more."

Iskandar kicked Ivan, drawing out a gasp of pain. "I don't suppose he'll survive. If he does, he'll be crippled. And since I won't allow you both to live, he'll also be without his cousin, without his closest adviser, without his most important ambassador. Bereft of health and friends, he'll no longer be a threat. He can return to Sivi Gora and die in his beloved city, knowing that he failed. I expect he'll die soon, but perhaps he'll surprise me and last out the summer. Even if he survives, he's finished. What better revenge can I have than depriving him of his health and his closest friend?"

Several questions burned in Danilo's mind. Primary among them was how Iskandar intended to kill him. Impalement or something slightly more merciful? And had Iskandar really described his feelings for Maja as *love*? The ghazi had assaulted her and tried to enslave her. That wasn't love. Iskandar couldn't know anything about Maja beyond her appearance. He wouldn't appreciate her passion for art, her ability to see the best in others, or the resilience that had carried her through heartache and trial without destroying her goodness or her hope.

Danilo's death would be yet another trial for Maja, and it filled him with sorrow. He would never see her again. But she was safe in Sivi Gora, and that was some comfort. Their garrison had been ravaged at Kosovo, but they had left enough men behind to defend the city and its inhabitants. Iskandar could torture and execute Danilo and Ivan, but his reach would end there.

"You want to save him?" Iskandar gestured to Ivan.

Danilo stared at his captor. He didn't answer. He didn't have to. Iskandar knew there was little Danilo wouldn't sacrifice if it could somehow save Ivan.

"Cooperate, and I will give you bandages and herbs for your župan."

Wariness mixed with desperation and curiosity. "What cooperation do you require?"

"I told you there is one thing in Sivi Gora I want above all else. Maja."

Danilo nearly choked on his rage. He bit it down, thinking through his response before he answered. Iskandar wouldn't know the depth of Danilo's feelings for Maja, and that could work to his advantage. "Maja? The blonde woman you captured as we traveled from Hungary?"

"The same."

"You want me to get her for you?"

"I do."

"How?"

"You and your župan will come with me and my men. I'll release you to return to Sivi Gora. If you bring back Maja and a reasonable ransom for a wealthy župan, I will set Ivan free. If you disappear, I'll kill him. Be assured it will be a slow, painful death as atonement for all the wrongs you and he have heaped upon me."

"And what becomes of the woman? Suppose she does not wish to stay with you."

"She will be wife to a powerful ally of the sultan. She'll have no reason for complaint."

Danilo could think of numerous reasons for complaint, but he didn't voice them. "And what manner of death am I to expect?" Iskandar had, after all, said he wouldn't let Danilo live.

"That depends entirely upon how well you cooperate."

Iskandar was forcing Danilo to choose between his best friend and the woman he loved. If the former raider had known the full truth, he would have relished his moment even more.

Danilo couldn't hand Maja over to Iskandar. He wouldn't betray her like that, no matter the consequences. But nor could he reject a chance to save his cousin.

Danilo doubted he could save himself, but maybe along the journey, he could find a way to save Ivan and Maja. Danilo might not be able to avoid his death, but he might, by playing along, at least delay it. And so he would lie to gain more time. And perhaps with time would come opportunity. He swallowed back his fear and answered. "Then let us go to Sivi Gora."

Chapter Thirty-Seven
An Ispán's Revenge

Maja and the others rode until the sun sank beneath the horizon, then in the dying light of day, they erected two tents and hobbled their animals. They made no fires because they preferred that no one see their camp from a distance. Their supper was a cold meal of bread and cheese. In a few days, it would be boukellaton, but for the night, Maja savored the tangy goat cheese and the crusty edge of the bread baked early that morning.

Christophoros tied Petar to a tree. Maja wasn't sure what to think of Petar. What motive did he have to stalk the župan's family? She had seen his wages, and she knew the wages of other stonecutters on previous projects. He was paid better than average for his skill level. Arcadius could be difficult to work with, but that wasn't Župan Ivan's fault, unless Petar blamed him for hiring the man. If Petar had nothing to hide, why didn't he talk? And if he did have something to hide, what was it?

Maja retired for the night, sharing a tent with Dama Helena. She would have never presumed to share a tent with the wife of the župan, but they were traveling light. There wasn't room on their pack animals to carry the luxury or privacy Dama Helena's station ought to have entitled her to.

Only a single candle cast its glow about the tent, leaving everything dim, but enough light shone to reflect off the necklace Dama Helena held in her hand. An oval pendant rather than a cross.

"Does your necklace carry memory?" It was simpler than the jewelry Maja had seen Dama Helena wear before, but something in the woman's expression suggested the pendant held sentimental value.

Dama Helena smiled softly. "I gave it to Ivan once. Then he returned it." She cradled the necklace in her palm, running a finger over the image of a saint. "It reminds me of him."

Maja's fingers went to the brooch Danilo had given her. Dama Helena noticed the movement and smiled.

"I've been meaning to thank you," Maja said, "for the role you had in this gift."

"And I've been meaning to apologize. I didn't want Danilo to have to marry a Bulgarian child, but nor did I wish us to be without an ally when we might lose everything without them." Dama Helena sighed. "I like Ekaterina. She's not right for Danilo . . . but I worry that Župan Dragomir's grandson won't be right for her."

"Why not?" Maja was desperate for Ekaterina to be betrothed to someone else.

Dama Helena tucked her pendant beneath her tunic. "If Danilo married her, he would treat her like a child until she was a woman. If a lad of seventeen or eighteen—I forget how old he is—marries her, he might treat her like a bride, and she's not ready for that. But I do not know Župan Dragomir's grandson, so perhaps I judge him unfairly."

Maja pulled her knees up and leaned into them. "So much of a woman's life depends on her husband."

Dama Helena smiled sadly. "Yes. I have experienced both extremes. A husband I hated and feared and a husband I love more than I thought possible. And you, I hope, will soon know the wonder of marriage to a good man who is completely devoted to you."

There was nothing Maja wanted more than a future with Danilo. She hoped he was unharmed. Had the battle begun? Had it ended?

The clash of steel and a series of shouts made it seem as if a battle had commenced outside their tent. Philippos burst through the canvas flap with a sword drawn. He kept his back to them, facing the opening so he could attack anyone who tried to enter. "My lady, we're under attack."

"From whom?" Dama Helena gripped a dagger in one hand. Maja followed her example.

"Vadas and Bokori. Petar was working with them."

A tall man in armor barged into the tent. He dwarfed young Philippos, but the groom didn't back down. He rushed the warrior, slicing downward with his blade. The other man blocked it, then riposted with such force that it sent Philippos stumbling backward a few steps.

Maja grabbed a small chest and hurled it at their attacker. It crashed into him, throwing off his next stab, which had been aimed at Philippos. She reached for another trunk, but it was too big for her to throw. She threw the lid back, hoping to find something more suitable inside.

Two more men plowed into the tent. Where were all the guards from Sivi Gora? And where was Luka?

Philippos wouldn't be able to fight off all three of the enemy, but he stood his ground, remaining between the attackers and Dama Helena.

"Stop." Dama Helena stepped forward. "Don't hurt him. We yield."

Philippos frowned as he lowered his weapon.

"Drop it," the tall armored man said.

Philippos's lips pinched in frustration as he released his weapon, and it thumped to the ground, much like Maja's hope.

"Who are you?" Dama Helena asked. She had to be frightened—Maja was terrified—but she hid it well.

One of the other men stepped into the light, and Maja recognized the scar on his face. Vadas.

The first who had entered the tent bowed slightly. "Ispán Janos Bokori."

"And what do you seek, Ispán Bokori?"

"I seek to stare with my own eyes on the woman who would dare blackmail me."

"That requires eyes, not swords."

Bokori strode closer to Dama Helena. Maja and Philippos both drew nearer to protect her, but Dama Helena lifted her chin in defiance.

"Tell me." Bokori stared down at Dama Helena. "What is important enough to draw out a župan's wife with only ten men and two boys to protect her?"

"I travel as a healer, not as a župan's wife, and if you have injured any of my men, you will allow me to tend to them at once."

"You and your party are my prisoners and will remain so until the threat you pose to me is resolved. But I am a reasonable man. I will not confine you to your tent while wounded men need your care." Bokori turned and held open the tent flap.

Helena strode outside, and Maja didn't hesitate to follow. She needed to see Luka.

Her brother knelt on the ground with his hands on the back of his neck. A bruise swelled his left temple, and blood trickled from his swollen and split lip. He and seven of the other guards, most of them wounded, were surrounded by twenty Hungarian soldiers. Another of Sivi Gora's guards, Christophoros, lay on the ground, bleeding from a wound in his thigh. The ninth lay beside Christophoros, his eyes closed, the left side of his head covered in blood. The last guard was missing.

"Where is Dalibor?" Dama Helena asked.

"Dead, my lady." Philippos clenched his jaw and turned away.

Dama Helena cast a cold glare at Bokori. "You've attacked me and slain one of my guards. You had better have a good explanation for your crimes."

"Your men struck down nine of mine."

"As they had every right to. You attacked us without provocation." Dama Helena knelt beside Christophoros. "Philippos, I'll need the kit Maja threw across the tent. Along with water, wine, and clean bandages."

"I'll get it," Maja said, wondering what she had thrown. Herbs? Needles and thread?

"No, Maja. You will stay where I can see you so that I know you aren't being mistreated." Dama Helena examined Christophoros's wound, then the other guard's. "These Hungarian men are not to be trusted." Bokori looked like he was about to speak, but Dama Helena cut him off. "I'll need a fire so I can better see. We didn't light one before, for fear of attracting bandits, but I believe our circumstances have changed."

Bokori looked to Vadas, who merely shrugged. Neither of them stopped Philippos when he went to fetch Dama Helena's supplies.

Luka started work on a fire and glared when Petar began helping. "Traitor. You were supposed to be working for Župan Ivan."

Petar scoffed. "Župan Ivan hired me to cut stone in his church, and I have done so. Ispán Bokori hired me to provide information. That, too, I have done, though it grew harder after Hensel died."

Luka's disgust was visible even before the flames caught and illuminated the clearing.

Dama Helena began her work, and before long, Christophoros had a line of silk stitches in his thigh and a clean bandage over it. Then she placed stitches in the skin of the other severely wounded guard's face, from his eyebrow to a spot above his ear. The other injuries were less severe, though Maja assumed Dama Helena would treat them next.

"Where does a župan's wife learn to repair torn skin?" Bokori asked.

"Can a župan's wife not also be a healer?"

"Will you help my men?" Bokori asked. "Several of them are wounded so severely that I fear for their lives."

Maja expected Dama Helena to agree, but instead, Dama Helena said, "No, I don't suppose I will. You've shown hostility to Sivi Gora, and I suspect you intend to hold me and my companions hostage. I have no incentive to restore any of your soldiers to health."

"Have a heart. They need help, and none of us have the skill. One is my nephew. Please, my lady."

Dama Helena didn't answer immediately. She stared at the fire, drawing out the suspense. "You hire a stonecutter to spy on us, attack without provocation, and slay a guard who leaves behind a wife, five children, and an elderly mother. I've more motivation to poison your men than heal them. Besides, I have limited supplies. I may need them for my own people, if they have met the Turks in battle."

Maja was stunned. Dama Helena's words went against everything she knew of the župan's wife. She had always offered her healing services to anyone—friend or foe, rich or poor. She must have found Bokori's acts beyond heinous to deny him care. Or she was bluffing.

Dama Helena began examining the other guards. Most needed only bandages.

"Perhaps my attack was rash." Bokori clasped his hands behind his back as Dama Helena examined the bruise on Luka's temple.

"Why *did* you attack?" Dama Helena asked. "To capture us? Murder us?"

Bokori lowered his voice. "I did not leave Hungary with the intention to attack, only with the hope of purchasing back a certain item and ensuring silence. But when I learned that you were without the city walls, it seemed foolish to pay for something that could easily be taken by force."

"You ought not to have deviated from your original plan, Ispán Bokori." Dama Helena washed and bandaged a shallow cut in one of her guards' arms. "Slaying or abducting me won't solve your problem. I carry no documents with me, nor am I the only witness to what you wish to remain secret. If you kill me, news of your past *will* reach your király. I won't tell you from where, but know that Sivi Gora is not the only place that holds the key to your undoing. If you wish us to keep your secret, you ought to negotiate with us, not attack us."

Bokori's men had brought their wounded to lie near the fire. One of them whimpered in pain. The sound was so pitiful that Maja nearly went to him. She couldn't heal him, but she could at least offer a drink of water or a hand of comfort.

Bokori glanced from the man back to Dama Helena. "I underestimated you."

"You're not the first."

"On my word of honor, we will leave you in peace, if you will tend to my nephew's wounds."

"For how long will you leave us in peace?"

"As long as my király allows it."

Dama Helena glanced up from the bandage she was tying and gave Bokori a hard stare. "Your király, who considers you his loyal supporter. Your király, who would be so disappointed to learn that his confidence in you has been misplaced. Király Sigismund lusts after Serb lands. If it is up to him, our reprieve might not last through harvest."

The wounded man sobbed.

"Are you so heartless?" Anger leaked into Bokori's voice.

"No. I am not heartless, but I am acquainted with hard sacrifices. I would sacrifice every single one of your men if it would help my people."

"I will leave you in peace until the end of my days. I swear it."

Dama Helena nodded. "I'll need more water. And more bandages."

Maja forced back a yawn. Dawn would soon come, and already, the sky was changing from hematite black to cobalt blue. Her knees were sore from kneeling in the dirt, and the skin of her hands was worn from the frequent abrasion of the bandages. She couldn't imagine how exhausted Dama Helena must be. She'd worked all through the night on Serb and Hungarian wounded.

"Perhaps this can be a lesson to you, Ispán Bokori. It is far better to make friends than to make enemies." Dama Helena finished checking the last man. "Especially where no ill will is directed against you."

"You are friends with our enemy Tvrtko."

"And we all have a common enemy in the Ottomans."

"That is why you travel." Bokori gestured to the wine, the bandages, the silk thread. "To heal?"

"Yes. I've seen some of the destruction an Ottoman Army can cause. And I've heard of more. Ispán Bokori, now that you have sworn to leave Sivi Gora in peace until the end of your days, am I correct to assume you will take your men and return to Hungary?"

"Yes, after I allow them to sleep."

"We have not that luxury." Dama Helena met Maja's eyes for a moment. "We cannot delay our mission."

"Perhaps a sign of friendship between my lands and yours would be in order," Bokori said.

"We had no quarrel with you, until you attacked us. You would have been wise to ask for friendship earlier."

Bokori swallowed. "You are bold, for a woman."

A hint of a smile caressed her lips. "I have learned from my husband. Župan Ivan will not be bought or intimidated. But you can have no stronger ally, and he will always hate the Turks more than he distrusts our neighbors to the north."

"And if your husband does not survive the battle at Kosovo?"

"Then I will be regent, and I will not fail to teach my daughter who slew both her father and her grandfather."

"Yes, you have a daughter, and I assume she will have a generous dowry. I have a son. He is almost thirteen. A marriage alliance, perhaps?"

"You would have your son marry a schismatic?" Dama Helena shook her head. "It is not our custom to betroth our children before they are at least seven years of age. Nor without the permission of her father." Dama Helena ended it there, but Maja didn't doubt she found the prospect repulsive. The Hungarians followed the Latin rite, and Bokori's attack had resulted in Dalibor's death. Bokori would have to do more than bargain with their freedom in exchange for medical care if he wanted to earn their trust.

"I fear Király Sigismund will find Serbia a rather tempting target should Kosovo leave Knez Lazar weakened," Bokori said.

"He would attack his sworn vassal?"

Bokori glanced at Maja. She stood to leave, but Dama Helena held out a hand to stop her. "You may speak in my friend's presence."

Maja sat back down.

"He is young, hotheaded, and ambitious." Bokori glanced at the dying embers of the fire. "That is why I did not initially give him my support. But he has consolidated his power now, and I think he will hold it. He has his strengths as well as his weaknesses. Enough strengths that I will continue to support him."

"And what if he turns his eyes on Sivi Gora? Surely you will not retract your promise."

"I will tell him that under compulsion, Sivi Gora would become a thorn in his side. Complete destruction might be possible, but that would be a waste. Better to seek trade agreements and let them throw their wealth and their warriors against the Ottomans."

"And if your király does not agree?"

"I'll explain how difficult it would be to seize Sivi Gora, given its terrain and extensive fortifications. He'll see things my way. Especially if there are mutually beneficial arrangements made. Your lands are prosperous. We'll both benefit more from trade than from war, wouldn't you agree?"

"I'm glad we have finally come to an understanding." Dama Helena folded the remaining bandages.

"If you'll excuse me. I need to speak with my men." Bokori stood and walked to where Petar and Vadas spoke.

Maja glanced at Dama Helena. "My lady, do you believe him?"

Dama Helena bit her bottom lip. "I believe that for now, he intends to keep his promise. Time and circumstances may make his resolution fade."

"Why did you wish me to stay?" Maja wasn't qualified to advise on matters of state, and she was discovering that they were far more complicated than the layers of mortar under a mosaic.

"To help me remember everything he says. It's been a long night, and I am weary. And I wished to ensure you are unharmed." Dama Helena glanced at Philippos and Luka, sleeping not far from them. "I feared for them. Especially Philippos. He would have died defending me if I hadn't stopped him. And I would have had to sacrifice the lad if it were a choice between him and the rest of Sivi Gora." Dama Helena sighed. "I wouldn't trade away my marriage, but there are times when I wish Ivan were a carpenter or a miner rather than a župan. At the moment, I just want him to still be alive."

Maja folded her arms, wondering how things would play out on the fields of Kosovo—or how they had played out, if the battle had begun. Hungary, for the moment, was held in check, but Ispán Bokori would not live forever. Nor, she feared, would he keep his resolution until the end of his days. Király Sigismund would find Sivi Gora too tempting, especially if battle with the Turks left them weak. Bokori needed more than a memory of Dama Helena's defiance, more than a bargain for healing when the men were long ago recovered, more than the threat of blackmail as his letter grew older and his standing with Sigismund grew stronger with time and experience.

"Is Ekaterina as fond of you as you are of her?" Maja asked.

Dama Helena smiled. "I believe she is. Certainly, she is very fond of Sofija."

"Boyar Kalin wishes his daughter to escape an Ottoman harem, and he wishes her marriage to bring Vidin an ally. An ispán's son is more prestigious than a župan's cousin. Hungary is farther away from the Turks than even Sivi

Gora. And Kalin fears the Hungarians, so who better to make an alliance with? Ekaterina is young. So is Ispán Bokori's son. He would be unable to take a bride for at least two years, according to church law. Two years more for Ekaterina to grow into less of a little girl. And if those years were spent in Sivi Gora, where she would be safe from the Turks and happy in the župan's court, then we could expect her to be an ally to Sivi Gora as well as Vidin in the home of her future father-by-marriage."

Dama Helena was quiet for a moment, nodding. "An arrangement like that would be better for her father, better for Ekaterina, better for Danilo, better for you, and better for Sivi Gora. And I expect Ekaterina to grow into a lovely, wise woman. An asset for Hungary should Bokori recognize a golden opportunity when it is offered to him."

Maja felt a burden lift from her shoulders. What would it be like to know Danilo was completely free to pursue her, without any secrets, without the risk of losing a vital alliance? "I must confess to an ulterior motive. I would like to see Ekaterina happy, but more than that, I would like to see her betrothed to someone other than Danilo."

Dama Helena took Maja's hand and grasped it. "As would I. We need to leave soon, but first, I will make the suggestion to Ispán Bokori, and then we will continue on our way. I hope Sivi Gora's army will not need my talents, but in a battle against the Turks, I am almost certain that someone will."

Chapter Thirty-Eight
Iskandar's Schemes

Danilo watched Ivan's body bounce around on the back of the pack mule. The župan was slung over the animal like a piece of baggage. Danilo had cleaned the wounds with wine and bandaged them securely, but he wasn't sure how much Ivan could take in his weakened state.

Danilo had asked to hold Ivan in front of him—more work for Danilo but a journey of less jostling for his cousin. Iskandar had refused. It would be far too easy for Danilo to gallop off if he held Ivan. Iskandar knew Danilo wouldn't escape without his cousin. As long as Ivan lived, Danilo would stay, and so Iskandar kept them apart.

The sun reached its zenith before they stopped to rest. Danilo dismounted, even with his hands bound in front of him, and went to check on his cousin. One of Iskandar's men had set him in the shade of an oak tree. Danilo checked the bandages on Ivan's shoulder and thigh. The wounds hadn't bled through yet, so he left them. Danilo wasn't sure he'd get any cooperation—Ivan hadn't been responsive all night, nor that morning—but he tried to pour some of the contents of a waterskin down his cousin's throat.

Ivan gulped, then sputtered. Slowly, his eyes opened, and he glanced at Danilo, then at their surroundings. "What happened?" His voice was weak and raspy.

"Miloš killed Murad. Bayezid is sultan now, and he executed Knez Lazar. Do you remember that?"

"I had hoped it was a nightmare instead of a memory."

Danilo thought of Miloš lying in the dust. He hoped someone had buried him and all the others by now. So many bodies, enough to fill a hundred cemeteries. And so many of the slain dear to him.

"I've heard different things about the battle." Danilo helped Ivan take another sip of water. "I think they won, but it was costly for them too. Bayezid returned to Edirne to consolidate power. We'll have a bit of breathing room, if we can escape. Iskandar has us."

A line of pain had marred Ivan's face since before he had opened his eyes. The line deepened. "I'm surprised he didn't kill us."

"He expects a ransom."

Ivan grimaced. "I dread to think what he'll ask. I'm not sure I'll last that long anyway. I can't move my arm. I don't feel any movement, just pain."

"Helena will fix it."

"There are some things even Helena cannot fix. Dragomir and Nikola are gone, aren't they?"

Danilo nodded.

"I was so hoping that was a dream." Ivan's voice cracked. "And Rivak? Was Kostya evacuated?"

"I don't know." He prayed someone had helped Konstantin make it to safety after the battle, prayed no marauding ghazi had slain his older cousin or the other men wounded in battle. Even if Konstantin had escaped, everything would be harder. His garrison had been devastated, his body permanently damaged. Konstantin had only just won back what their fathers lost at Maritsa. Now, with Kosovo, everything was again changed.

Danilo watched Iskandar's men share out their food. They didn't offer any to the prisoners.

Ivan coughed. "Danilo, are you injured?"

"Nothing of note."

"Good. Because right now, I'm useless. But that could be to your advantage. Iskandar doesn't think you'll leave without me. But if you have a chance to escape, I want you to take it."

"I'm not leaving without you."

"Iskandar doesn't intend to let me live. When they took me off the mule, they said it wouldn't take much poison to finish me off. Iskandar might accept a ransom for me, but if he releases me, he'll make sure I'm headed for the grave."

Danilo watched Iskandar and his twenty men relax in the sunshine. He shouldn't have been surprised that Iskandar planned to kill them both, but he had almost believed Iskandar would let a crippled Ivan return home. "He doesn't intend for me to live either. I'll be given a more merciful form of death if I behave myself."

"Were you going to tell me that he plans to kill you?"

Danilo shrugged. "You haven't been awake to tell. Besides, would you tell, were our positions reversed?"

"Probably not. What else are you not telling me?"

Danilo glanced at the Ottoman soldiers, making sure none were close enough to overhear. He didn't think any of them other than Iskandar spoke Slavonic, but he didn't want to risk it. "He wants Maja. I'm to go to Sivi Gora and bring back Maja and a ransom. He said that when I return, he will free you, marry Maja, and slay me."

"Then the solution is obvious. If the right opportunity comes along, you escape. Without me. That's an order. If no opportunity comes, then you tell Iskandar you'll cooperate. Go to Sivi Gora, find Maja, and marry her. Then you both stay safely in the city, where Iskandar can't touch you."

"But what about you?"

"He's not going to release me anyway, not without poison in me." Ivan's face suddenly calmed. "Do you suppose he has it already? Here?"

"The poison? He must." Danilo didn't think Iskandar had used it yet, but he would have brought what he needed to complete his plan.

"I have an idea."

Iskandar watched the župan of Sivi Gora fall off his horse. Iskandar reined in his stallion and waited for one of his soldiers to investigate. After their rest, Ivan had said he was well enough to ride normally. Iskandar glanced at the sun. The wounded župan had managed an hour.

He turned to check Danilo. He rode with his hands bound, and his horse had a lead rope rather than reins. Iskandar wasn't overly worried about Danilo bolting, not when it would mean leaving his cousin behind. Even if he tried, the twenty men Sultan Bayezid had given Iskandar would finish him off before he made it ten paces. Danilo and Ivan had escaped from him before, but Ivan hadn't had a mangled shoulder and an injured thigh then. Iskandar's main concern, for the moment, was keeping Ivan alive. Dead, he was worth little in the way of ransom. Nor could he be used as leverage against Danilo, and Iskandar wanted Danilo to bring Maja to him. That was far less risky than Iskandar searching for her himself within the walls of Sivi Gora.

One of his soldiers, Sanduk, pulled Ivan to his feet. He seemed to be conscious, at least, but the way he lurched toward the horse for support suggested he was struggling to keep his footing.

They had only horses and mules, so Ivan had to either ride, and probably fall off again and again, or be carted like a sack across the back of a horse. Neither option was conducive to keeping the prisoner alive. Danilo had offered to ride with his cousin, holding him in the saddle, but Iskandar preferred to keep them apart. Even with both injured and beaten, Iskandar wouldn't underestimate them.

One of the men he had sent ahead as a scout appeared in the distance.

Iskandar turned to Sanduk. "Get him back up. Tie him to the cantle." He wasn't sure that would really keep Ivan in the saddle, but it might work. "I'm riding ahead a bit. Catch up to me."

He spurred his horse and galloped to the scout, slowing as he approached. "What did you see?"

"No dangers. There's a small village, about a half hour's ride away. No defenses to speak of. I almost took it myself but didn't want to act without your permission."

"Does it have anything worthwhile?"

"Fresh food."

Iskandar chuckled to himself. The scout's excessive girth suggested food was a common thought. Yet all the men would enjoy freshly slaughtered meat. "If it's as small and vulnerable as you say, we'll take what we can from it."

But when the group reached the village, it was abandoned. The homes were tidy and well kept, and some of the hearths were still warm. It had been only recently abandoned.

"Did they see you and run off?"

The scout frowned. "I saw them. Perhaps they saw me."

"And left with all their livestock?" Iskandar had been looking forward to something better than the campaign food they'd been eating since they'd left Edirne. They could track the villagers down, but he wasn't sure it was worth it. He glanced at Ivan apparently unconscious in the saddle. He had limited time if he wanted to draw a ransom from the dying župan. "See if there's anything worthwhile. Burn the rest."

Iskandar kept a close eye on Danilo as the flames lapped at the thatch roofs and spread to the walls. The half-breed's face was hard, angry, as if he thought such a pitiful village were worth saving.

"Unhappy?" Iskandar asked.

"The people who live here worked hard for what they have."

Iskandar couldn't contain his mirth. "We intend to take it from them."

"You seem to be destroying it, not taking it."

"We're taking what's of worth." Iskandar gestured to a few pots, tools, and cloaks.

"Why burn what you can't take?"

"Because it will make my men happy. Sultan Bayezid was generous to loan them to me, but they'll only stay with me if I lead them to plunder and wealth. That's how it works."

Danilo glared at the fire. "You burn their homes, and they freeze when winter comes. You burn their crops, and they starve. That's how it works. What do you gain from it?"

"An easier conquest when the time comes. Sultan Bayezid has enemies in Edirne to take care of, but he'll subjugate all of Serbia soon enough. Even Sivi Gora." Iskandar didn't think Sultan Bayezid would make it to Sivi Gora in the next year or two. It was too far to the west. But eventually, if his enemies in the east were quiet, Iskandar didn't doubt the sultan would expand his reach past Sivi Gora, all the way to the Adriatic. Perhaps beyond. There were few things Iskandar would rather see than the fulfillment of Sultan Bayezid's prophecy to take Rome and turn the holiest buildings in Christendom into stables for his stallions. The only thing Iskandar wanted more was Maja in his bed.

One of the men brought a cart from a barn and held a torch to it.

"Wait," Iskandar called. "Bring that here."

The man obeyed.

"I'm not so heartless after all, Danilo." Iskandar gestured to the cart. "I think your cousin would prefer that for his transport, don't you?"

One of the men yoked two of the pack horses to the cart and transferred their burdens and Ivan into the back of it. The rest of the day went smoothly. One of the soldiers even shot a rabbit, so they would have warm food for their evening meal.

Danilo glowered as they rode, but there was nothing he could do. Iskandar had him and his cousin completely within his power. It was a fitting revenge for the men who had sold him into slavery.

When they stopped for the night, Iskandar frowned as he watched Danilo help his cousin from the cart and change his bandages. Their devotion to each other was ridiculous. Iskandar might perform a task like that for a sultan but not for a mere župan, especially not one who was nearly dead.

He had allowed them to speak together when they'd stopped to rest midday, but he didn't like the hope they seemed to glean from each other.

Hope, after all, could become a weapon. And he would allow his prisoners no weapons.

With one of the stolen pots from the village, they were to have rabbit soup for dinner. He thought of making Danilo skin and mince the hare, but he didn't trust his prisoner with a knife. Yet there were other tasks he could give his captive. For Danilo's final days, Iskandar wanted him to feel the burden of slavery the way Iskandar had felt it.

"Danilo, fill the pot with water. Sanduk, keep an eye on him."

When Danilo came back, Iskandar had him build a fire, then brush every horse in the camp, set up all the tents, gather extra firewood, and dig a latrine. By then the soup was ready to eat. The soldier acting as cook had added cabbage, carrots, and kohlrabi to the hare. A sweet type of seasoning, too, but Iskandar couldn't place it. Divided among the twenty of them, their portions weren't generous, but the soup made the hardtack more edible.

He glanced at Danilo sitting by Ivan, who looked to be asleep. Someone had given them hard, twice-baked pieces of barley loaf but nothing warm. Iskandar wouldn't have given them even that, but he supposed he could work Danilo harder if he had something to eat, and he didn't want Ivan to die before Iskandar had Maja and the župan's ransom.

Iskandar finished his share of the soup and drained his waterskin, but he was still thirsty. He ordered Danilo to refill his skin at the nearby stream, but the dryness in his throat remained. Probably from burning the village. So much smoke, and the wind had directed it toward him several times. Iskandar drank more. Others, too, made Danilo refill their waterskins, and Iskandar took some satisfaction in seeing his enemy turned to a common slave, forced to carry water rather than rest.

As it grew dark, the flames of the fire seemed too bright for Iskandar's eyes, and his head hurt. It had been a long day, as had the days that preceded it. Sultan Bayezid's victory and the coming rewards would make all Iskandar's efforts worthwhile, but for now, he needed sleep.

"Sanduk, make sure the prisoners are secured and set the watch." Iskandar went to his tent to sleep off the growing headache.

Chapter Thirty-Nine
Shades of Night

Danilo kept a close eye on the Ottoman troops as Iskandar and several of the others retired to bed. Sanduk held his head as if in pain and neglected to set a watch.

Ivan slept. When they'd taken him off the wagon, Danilo had seen him just long enough to feel the burning heat of his forehead and to accept the small knife and pouch of dried nightshade berries Ivan had found among the supplies next to him in the wagon. Thirty berries total. Enough to send Ivan into hallucinations, convulsions, and then death after his ransom was paid. Danilo had slipped them all into the rabbit soup while adding wood to the fire, but he wasn't sure how potent they would be when divided among twenty soldiers. He was no expert when it came to poisons.

He removed the small knife from where he'd hidden it within the bandages around Ivan's thigh. He hoped the Ottomans would all be dead by morning, but it was far more likely that they'd simply feel ill. The effects would likely be uneven. Some might suffer only a dry throat. Others might be delirious for a day or two. He wasn't sure how large his opportunity for escape was, but he suspected it was narrow.

He cut through the ropes binding his wrists and ankles, then did the same with Ivan's. He let his cousin sleep, for the moment.

Danilo crept noiselessly through the grass, away from the light of the campfire. Most of the soldiers had disappeared into tents. He contemplated sneaking inside and killing them, but he didn't know how strong the poison would be. He didn't want to risk being overpowered or have someone raise an alarm. He couldn't fight off all twenty of them, even if they each had headaches.

He circled around camp to where the horses were hobbled and cut apart the bindings on their legs. If the Ottomans went in pursuit of their escaped prisoners, they would first have to find their horses. He kept four and saddled two of them, then urged the others away.

While he worked, he heard one soldier moan and another mutter gibberish, as if drunk or dreaming. The three men around the fire looked to be sleeping. Danilo didn't want to press his luck, so he took the horses around the outside of camp, away from the firelight.

When he was twenty paces from Ivan, a shadow stepped in front of him. The man mumbled something, then drew his scimitar and lunged at Danilo. Danilo dodged to the side, and the Ottoman blade bit into the horse instead. Danilo brought the small knife around and thrust it into the man's side, then grabbed the man's waist and mouth to hold him and keep him from yelling. The man bit Danilo's palm, but Danilo didn't let go. Escape was his only hope of surviving. He twisted the knife, trying to make the damage worse so the man would die more swiftly. Already they'd made too much noise. In normal circumstances, a watchman would have sounded the alarm by now, but these weren't normal circumstances. Danilo yanked the knife out and slit the man's throat.

The soldier dropped to the ground. Danilo wiped the blade clean on the man's robes and examined the horse. The dim light made it hard to see how deep the sword had pierced the coat, but he thought the saddle had stopped the worst of it.

He took the man's scimitar, dagger, and leather cuirass, then led the horses the rest of the way to his cousin.

He knelt and grabbed Ivan's good shoulder. "Ivan?" he whispered.

It took a few more shakes and prods to get Ivan to respond. "Danilo?"

"Come on. Get on this horse."

Danilo pulled Ivan from the ground and pushed him onto the back of the animal. "Hold on until we're a little farther from camp." Ivan gripped the reins with his good hand and seemed to sag in the saddle. He was getting worse.

When they were far enough from the Ottomans, Danilo climbed on behind his cousin and urged the horse into a trot. It wasn't long before his cousin's body relaxed in sleep. Danilo could feel the burning fever through their clothing. Sivi Gora was at least three days away. Would his cousin still be alive when they arrived?

Danilo rode until he could barely keep his eyes open. Blackness cloaked the sky completely; dawn was still distant. He laid Ivan down, then unsaddled the horses and tied them to a tree, where they could pick at the grass. Then he slept.

He woke with the sun. His first thought was that he should have delayed their escape long enough to steal some of the food, but they'd been lucky to get away at all. Pilfering might have resulted in discovery. He knew that in his head, but it was hard to convince his stomach. They had not even a waterskin. He'd have to keep a lookout for streams or wells.

Danilo saddled a new horse. Not the one he'd ridden the night before, nor the one with a cut, though the animal's injury was minor. Today, he would switch animals every hour or so. Changing that often would take time, especially if Ivan remained feverish and weak, but the frequent changes would give him the most he could get from the animals, and he needed much from them. They had to outrun any pursuing Turks and reach Sivi Gora before Ivan's wound took him.

"Ivan?"

His cousin sighed as Danilo pulled him to his feet and forced him onto one of the horses.

"You'd go faster without me," Ivan said as Danilo climbed on behind him.

"If you're suggesting I leave you behind, then I think you're delirious."

"That doesn't mean I'm wrong."

"I might need you to dig through Turkish baggage and find poison again. Best keep you with me."

"He didn't hide it very well." Ivan's voice was barely a whisper.

"Hang on a few days more. Then you'll be home. Helena will heal your wounds, and the new mercenaries you've been planning to hire will be here by summer's end. You'll have work to do, making Sivi Gora a fortress the Turks will break themselves upon if they ever attempt to take it."

"Do you know what happened to our army?"

"No." They might all be dead. Or Sivi Gora's men might be a day ahead of Danilo and Ivan, returning home with news of the battle. Or perhaps the survivors were behind their župan, the healthy trying to help the injured. "They know the way home. You have good officers. They'll bring as many back as they can."

"I should have evacuated the wounded after the first day."

"We couldn't have spared healthy men to carry the wounded. The Turks may have broken part of the line, but I don't think they were strong enough to ravage our base camp." Danilo prayed that was true, for Sivi Gora's wounded and for Rivak's wounded. "Bayezid returned to Edirne. He'll have brought most of his men with him rather than releasing them for pillage."

They rode and switched mounts often and found a spring midday. Danilo watered the horses and helped Ivan drink and rest. The fever seemed stronger, and Ivan's shoulder wound was beginning to smell. Danilo wished he'd found wine to steal, but many of the Turks followed the Muslim prohibition on alcohol. The wine he'd used on Ivan's wounds at Kosovo had been taken from a fallen Christian.

At nightfall, Ivan took a turn for the worse. He wouldn't drink and didn't seem to understand anything Danilo said. He winced when Danilo helped him on and off the horses, and his skin was pale. Danilo forced the horses to keep a harder pace longer than he should have. He would exhaust their mounts if he wasn't careful, but he feared what would happen if he didn't get Ivan back to his wife soon.

"Slap him," Iskandar ordered. A full day had passed since their poisoned soup, and one of the men was still having nightshade-induced hallucinations. The poison had killed one, and Danilo had killed another, but most had recovered by midday, and they'd been tracking the prisoners ever since.

Iskandar cursed the man who had put Ivan and the poison on the same cart. Ivan had seemed unconscious, but that must have been what happened. The berries had disappeared, and the symptoms matched, in hindsight anyway.

No one had seen Danilo and Ivan leave, other than perhaps the man who was dead. One of the soldiers had claimed to witness a dragon riding across the nearby field, and another had said he saw the ghost of Sultan Murad. Only nightshade illusions, Iskandar was sure, but it had taken hours to convince the men of that. Most of them resented the fact that Iskandar had carried poison without telling them.

"This was a campsite. Recent." Sanduk knelt on the ground near a patch of short grass—perhaps clipped by the four horses Danilo had stolen? "There's blood here."

"You think it was two men?"

"I'm almost certain of it. Two men, at least that many horses."

It had taken Iskandar's men hours to round up their horses. Four had been missing. The men whose trail they had found could be anyone. But he had a feeling it was the men he sought. If Ivan was riding, he wouldn't be able to ride hard, not with the wounds he had. More likely, they were riding double, and that would make them easy to catch.

"Good work. We'll follow them." Iskandar would pursue them to the gates of Sivi Gora, if needed. But he didn't think he would have to go that far. He was only half a day behind them, and he and his men would make speed their ally. They had several days to catch up, and that was more than they needed.

Chapter Forty
Remnants of an Army

A rider, a Bosnian by the looks of his clothing, slowed long enough to tell Maja's group that the battle was over, Sultan Murad was dead, and the Christians had won.

"And the army from Sivi Gora? Do you have news of them?" Dama Helena asked.

"No." The rider nodded his goodbye, then rode off again.

They were content with their good news for an entire afternoon. Then they were met by a different group, one that included several wounded men. "Yes, Sultan Murad is dead. But so is Knez Lazar. No, we didn't win. Both sides were devastated. Kosovo is covered with corpses."

Dama Helena's face grew pale. "And Sivi Gora, what became of their army?"

The man shook his head. "The first day, they were hit hard. Pulled into a trap and ambushed. Cut in half. I don't know what happened to them the second day."

They moved with added urgency after that. Dama Helena looked devastated as they made camp for the night and prepared to rest. Maja was certain her face mirrored her friend's. Had Danilo been among those ambushed? Was he alive? Wounded? What would she do if he were dead?

She didn't sleep well that night. Nor, she suspected, did Dama Helena.

The next day at noon, they ran into the remnant of Sivi Gora's army. Four hundred men had marched out. Perhaps one hundred remained, and most of them appeared injured.

"Goran?" Dama Helena rode to one of the men near the front of the group. A bloodstained bandage covered one eye and most of his forehead, and he rode one-handed. His right arm lay in a sling. "Where's Ivan?"

Goran frowned in sorrow. "I'm sorry, my lady. Knez Lazar called him away for a special task. He and Danilo went, and I never saw them return. I don't think they survived."

"Did you see their bodies?"

"No, my lady. We would have searched, but finding one body among so many would have taken days, and the Turks were upon us. To stay would have halved our numbers yet again. I did not think your husband would have approved. He would have wanted us to return and defend the city."

Dama Helena didn't speak for several long moments. Maja could barely breathe as grief threatened to crush her. "Yes," Dama Helena said. "You were wise to take the army to safety. Are there any who need my care?"

Goran glanced at the men. "Many. About a half mile back, there's a water mill. It would give the men shelter, those who need it. And there's plenty of fresh water."

Dama Helena nodded. "We'll go there."

Orders spread throughout the ranks, and the men returned to the mill. Dama Helena went with them, as did the rest of the group. Maja couldn't move. One of the soldiers waited, planning to bring up the rear, and she reluctantly urged her horse to follow the group.

"Maja?"

She turned to Luka, trying to hold back tears. "Yes?"

"He can't be dead. Who could get close enough to slay him? He'd shoot them with an arrow before they were within ten paces. Danilo is too strong to fall in battle."

She knew enough of battle to know better, and so did he. She inhaled deeply but didn't speak.

"He's just a little behind is all." Luka rode closer to her. "Maybe he lost his horse. It will take longer for him to come, but he'll make his way back to you. I'm sure of it."

"Look at the army. Sivi Gora will be filled with mourning wives and sweethearts." Hers was but one broken heart, like a single tessera in a mosaic full of grief, pain, and darkness. But being one of many didn't make the agony any less sharp.

She should be comforting Dama Helena. She'd lost her husband, and her husband's best friend, men she had known far longer than Maja had known Danilo. Maja couldn't let her grief consume her. There would be time to mourn, but that time would come later. For now, there was an army to heal.

They reached the mill, and Maja worked long into the night, fetching water and wine, cutting bandages, looking for violet and malache for those with fevers, wormwood and hyssop for those who were cold, yarrow to slow bleeding, and mandragora for pain. She didn't remember falling asleep, but she woke as the first hint of dawn changed the sky from black stone to violet glass.

Goran and Dama Helena stood nearby, Goran shaking his head. "It's not safe for you to continue on to Kosovo."

"I have to know for sure." Dama Helena's voice betrayed her exhaustion and her grief.

"My lady, Bayezid took most of his army back to Edirne, but there are still numerous ghazis. I doubt they'll come this far west, but Kosovo won't be safe for weeks. You're needed in Sivi Gora. The people will mourn with you, and then they will follow you. It's not my place to command you, but were your husband here, he would tell you not to risk it."

"But what if he's alive? What if he needs me?"

"I will go back, if you wish, and search for his body."

"You're absolutely certain it's just a body?" Dama Helena looked so broken. Maja rose to her feet and went to offer her friend comfort. Dama Helena took her hand and held it tightly.

Goran nodded. "If you could see the field, you would understand why I have no hope. But I would like to see his body returned to his city. I can take a few men. We'll have to be cautious, but a few of us might be able to avoid the ghazis."

"You're wounded," Dama Helena adjusted his sling as she spoke. "I can't send you. You ought to return to the city. Your wife and children will be glad to see that you've returned."

"I'll go." Philippos had been asleep only moments ago, but his now-alert eyes seemed to understand exactly what he was volunteering for.

Dama Helena nodded her consent.

"I'll go too," Luka said.

Maja inhaled sharply. She wasn't surprised that her brother had volunteered, but the thought of Luka going into danger made her tremble. What if he didn't come back?

Dama Helena glanced at Maja, then at her brother. "I think your sister needs you."

"I think Danilo would comfort her more than I could, and I'm not ready to assume he's dead." Luka walked outside before either of the women could reply.

Goran frowned. "I admire his faith. I wish I shared it, but in this case, I believe he is wrong. I'm sorry." He looked first at Dama Helena, then at Maja. "I think the most we can hope for is to find their bodies. With your permission, I'll seek four unwounded men willing to go back and search." He glanced at Maja. "Warriors, not mosaicists. Men, not boys."

Dama Helena hesitated. "Yes, that would be better. I'm sorry, Philippos."

Philippos frowned but nodded. "I will stay at your side, then, my lady."

Goran left, as did Philippos, leaving the women with those whose wounds were most severe.

Part of Maja wanted to go with them, to find out for certain if Danilo was really gone. Part of her was terrified of finding him dead. Far better, wasn't it, to keep the memory of the last time she'd seen him in her heart, to think of his kiss and his embrace, to remember him whole and seemingly invincible? Her arms ached to wrap themselves around his muscled body, her lips longed to caress his mouth, and her head craved a moment resting against his chest.

"I don't know how I'll do it," Dama Helena whispered. "I'm not strong enough." As she spoke, tears ran down her cheeks. "Sivi Gora will be full of people mourning their husbands, their sons, their brothers. The other widows will look to me. If I am overcome with grief, they will feel their own sorrow all the greater. I know I have to be strong, but I'm not ready yet."

"They may yet live." Maja spoke the words, but she didn't believe them. If they were alive, surely they would have caught up to their army.

"He didn't think he was coming back, and he was right."

"But he thought Danilo would live." Župan Ivan's dream had haunted Maja. She had hoped it wasn't true but had assumed that any variance would be that both men survived, not that both were slain.

Dama Helena squeezed Maja's hand. "He would have wished Danilo's survival, even above his own. I'm so sorry, Maja. Danilo was fond of you, and he was a good man. You would have been happy together."

"I'm not ready to give up hope. Not yet." The hurt inside Maja's chest threatened to overwhelm her; it would suffocate her if she couldn't hold on to some small shred of promise.

Goran returned. "Dama Helena, I've gathered the volunteers. They wish to leave at once."

"Let me speak to them first."

"I'll bring them. Then perhaps it will be time for the rest of us to return home." Goran's face was drawn, weary, and saddened. "Sivi Gora needs a leader, my lady. Especially now."

Maja watched the emotions play across Dama Helena's face. Leaving would be admitting that no one else was coming. Not Župan Ivan. Not Danilo. Not any of the other hundreds who were missing.

Philippos entered the mill, two soldiers right behind him. "Stragglers, my lady."

"Adamu?" Dama Helena walked to the injured soldier. "Let me see those wounds." Bandages wrapped his left thigh and both arms.

Maja brought a bucket of water closer to the men. She had worked with Dama Helena often enough now to know what to do. First, they would wash with water, then with wine. All dirt and clothing would be removed from the wound. Stitches would come next, if needed. Then a bandage or a layer of oil for protection.

"How did you fall behind?" Dama Helena asked as she examined the gash in his thigh.

"I was knocked unconscious the second day of battle. My brother found me." He nodded to the other soldier. "We walked the first day, then we found a horse—like us, a refugee from the battle."

"Any news of Ivan or Danilo?" Dama Helena asked.

"Knez Lazar called them. They went with Lazar's son and Župan Nikola. I didn't see them after that."

"Župan Nikola was slain," the other soldier said. "As was Lazar's son. I saw their bodies. Knez Lazar and his son were both beheaded, as were most of the prisoners. Župan Ivan wasn't among them. I would have recognized my župan, even without a head."

Goran cleared his throat loudly. "Perhaps such details are not for Dama Helena's ears."

"How would you know him? By his armor?" Dama Helena ignored Goran's suggestion and walked closer, the light of hope shining in her eyes just as it was igniting in Maja's heart.

The soldier looked at Goran briefly, then back at Dama Helena. "His tunics, my lady. I know he's supporting Matthias's widow. Her work is very fine, very elaborate, and distinctly Greek. The bodies were stripped of their armor, but most were still clothed. I checked the shoulders and abdomens of those without clothes."

"You know his scars?" Dama Helena asked.

"I've seen him at the bathhouse often enough."

"And Danilo?" Maja asked.

The soldier shifted his gaze to Maja. "I would expect Danilo to be right beside him if they perished. I am also familiar with Danilo's scars. I would have recognized either body when I searched after the battle. By now, who knows, especially in the heat."

"That is enough, Marjan." Goran scowled. "I confess, my lady, that the ghazis are not the only reason I don't wish you to go to Kosovo. I know you are familiar with the wounds of war, but some sights are best left unseen."

Maja had one more question. "If they went with Knez Lazar's son and with Župan Nikola but weren't killed with either of them, does that mean they still live?"

Marjan glanced at Adamu, then back at Maja. "Kosovo is a large field, and thousands of bodies are heaped upon it. I didn't search everywhere, just where I knew men from Sivi Gora had fought. It's possible they went elsewhere. They might have survived or been taken prisoner. But I would have expected to see them by now if they still lived."

Hope alternated with despair as the volunteers set out to search for the župan's body. Maybe Župan Ivan and Danilo were both dead. Or maybe, against all odds, they were still alive, somewhere. Maja mourned for them—even if they lived, they had lost so much. A defeat at Kosovo, even if it had hurt the enemy as much as it had hurt them, would leave their lands under a constant threat. Sivi Gora, the beautiful city that had come to feel like home, would be changed regardless of what had happened.

Another set of stragglers arrived that afternoon. They hadn't seen Danilo or Župan Ivan, neither alive nor as corpses, so Maja's hope remained small and fragile, like a thin tessera of glass not yet protected in mortar. In the battle and its aftermath, the army had lost many of its baggage wagons and even more of the horses meant to pull them, so Goran sent a rider ahead to Sivi Gora to request that carts and animals be brought back to the mill, and Dama Helena sorted which of the wounded should leave at once and which would benefit from a day or two of rest before their next journey. Then Goran took the bulk of the army home. No one thought the Turks would press this far west, not at first, but they carried limited supplies, and after surviving a battle so enormous, they were eager to return to Sivi Gora. A dozen wounded remained at the mill, as did a group large enough to care for them: Dama Helena, Maja, Luka, Philippos, the young soldier Marjan, and those in Dama Helena's guard who were still uninjured.

Maja helped change bandages and gave the injured their food. And her mind constantly turned to Kosovo and what fate Danilo had met there.

CHAPTER FORTY-ONE
THE OLD MILL

DAWN WAS APPROACHING, THEIR THIRD since escaping Iskandar's men. Danilo mounted the horse. He'd already hoisted Ivan up. "Come on, Ivan. Hang on a while longer."

His cousin didn't answer. Danilo hadn't expected him to. His body was limp and hot. Danilo doubted Ivan heard any of the words he spoke, but he kept speaking, kept hoping that something he said would penetrate his cousin's delirium. They had made poor time. On his own, with a fresh horse, Danilo might have been able to reach Sivi Gora that night, but riding double, with an injury, on weary horses . . . he suspected Sivi Gora was still two days away. He wasn't sure what would be harder on his cousin's broken body—a hard ride and a quicker return or an easier pace and a later arrival.

Ivan shuddered. Danilo kept hold of him, hoping the movement didn't signal a sudden worsening of his condition. "Think of Sofija. You're going to get better and see her grow into a stunning beauty, just like her mother. A daughter like that will need a father to sort through all the suitors she'll have." Ivan was a good father, but his work was far from finished.

"And your wife will be desperate to have you back. Imagine holding Helena in your arms again. You caused quite a scandal with the servants, you know. They say their mistress's bedroom has silk all the way from Constantinople, just like her, and the finest carved wood in the entire palace. Yet the bed is never used because she always sleeps in her husband's chambers, even on holy days." Danilo thought he felt a bit of movement. A response? "I intend to follow your example, should Maja marry me. So you'd best recover. I want you at my marriage."

Danilo rambled on all morning, discussing plans for the mine, the market, the church, the palace. He chattered about Konstantin and his family, about Sofija, and about future children that might be born to both of them. He spoke on and on, hoping the familiar voice would somehow tie his cousin's soul in his body a little longer.

When Danilo stopped at a stream to switch horses, the sun was at its zenith. He had the distinct impression that he was being watched, but after scanning the area, he couldn't see anyone. He drank quickly from the stream and did his best to get some water into Ivan.

A twig snapped, and Danilo spun around and drew his stolen scimitar.

"Danilo?" Philippos ran through the bushes, a grin on his face. "We feared you dead." Then he saw Ivan, and his face froze. "Is he . . . ? Is he alive?"

"Barely. What are you doing out here?"

"Keeping watch. Dama Helena is at the water mill." He gestured back the way he'd come. "Two hundred paces back."

Danilo didn't know what business Helena had at a water mill so far from the safety of Sivi Gora, but he couldn't have been happier for her presence. If anyone could save Ivan, she could.

"Climb on the horse. I'll hand him up to you," Danilo told Philippos.

Another watchman spotted them as they drew near and called news of the župan's arrival. Helena, then Maja rushed from the mill. A gasp of surprise and joy escaped Helena, and she held a hand over her mouth to cover the sobs as she went to her husband and Philippos. Danilo smiled at Maja and wrapped an arm around her waist when she ran to him. She was beautiful, and the tears gathered on her lashes suggested she was as delighted to see him as he was to see her, despite his filthy condition. He took her face gently in his hands and kissed her forehead in front of everyone. But there wasn't time for any greater show of affection.

Two of Helena's guards carried Ivan into the mill and the others followed. Helena undid the bandages and gasped. Danilo knelt on the other side of Ivan. "I know it's bad. Can you save him?"

She swallowed. "I'm not sure." She felt her husband's fever and checked his pulse. "I hope to save his life. But the way these muscles are cut—I don't know that they'll ever heal completely."

"He said he couldn't move his arm, could only feel pain."

Helena nodded and washed her hands in a nearby bowl of water. "Will you take his tunic off?"

Danilo complied.

"Is there anything else, other than the wound in his leg?"

"Bruises and scrapes. Iskandar and a few others kicked him, but I don't think they broke any bones."

"And you. Are you injured?"

"No." He was sore from riding so hard, small cuts laced his hands, a long scab had formed over the cut on his forearm, and bruises lined his body from the battle and his time as prisoner, but there was nothing that wouldn't heal on its own.

Helena met his eyes for a brief moment. "Thank you for bringing him back."

"I would have followed him into hell to bring him back to you. You know that."

"Yes." Helena bent over the wound, removing a thread from the bandage that had stuck to the injury.

"I washed it with wine, but that was the night of the battle. I haven't had wine since."

"You did fine." Helena touched something, and Ivan groaned, and his arm moved. "I'll have to cut some of the infection away. Will you hold him still?"

Danilo held his cousin's arm at the elbow and the collar bone. Maja came into view behind Helena, threading a needle with silk thread. His first thought on seeing her had been how beautiful she looked, but now he noticed the dark skin under her eyes and the weariness in her posture, as if she, too, had been through a battle of some kind.

Helena finished cleaning and started slicing. Ivan tried to move under Danilo's hands.

"Hold still, Ivan." She finished her cuts, then wiped at the wound again with a wine-soaked rag. "When was he last lucid?"

"Two days ago. That morning was the last he spoke. I've thought he might have heard me a time or two since then, but he hasn't replied."

Helena took the wine-dampened thread from Maja. "How much malache do we have? I'll need it to try to bring his fever down."

"Just a cupful from what we boiled last night," Maja said. "I'll get more. I found some not far from here yesterday, within the line the sentries patrol."

"Take someone with you." Helena began her stitches. Ivan's arm twitched under Danilo's hold, and he shifted his grip to keep it still. Helena glanced at him. "Sorry, I'd tell you to escort her, but I need your help here."

"I'll go." Luka had a dagger strapped to his side. He looked confident and competent, but he was still a boy.

"Take Zlatan too." Helena motioned to one of her guards. He wasn't free of injury, but that seemed true for everyone in the mill, other than perhaps the women and the boys.

Maja nodded, and she, her brother, and their escort slipped outside to look for the cooling herb.

"Where did the mill's owners go?" Until Philippos had appeared, Danilo had seen neither settlement nor traveler on his journey, but they were in open country. Wandering might not be safe.

"We've not seen them. Since we arrived, we've not seen anyone except the bits of the army coming back. The main group headed on to Sivi Gora yesterday."

"How many are left?"

Helena's face fell. "Four score who can fight again, if needed, though most are injured. Another score that I expect to recover, but not for another moon at least. And a score that I expect will remain crippled for the rest of their lives." Helena finished Ivan's shoulder. "Hold him up so I can bandage it properly. Goran said you went off to help Knez Lazar and never returned."

"We were trying to slay Murad. We made it almost to his tent before we were overwhelmed."

"You killed the sultan? We heard news of his death."

"No." Danilo swallowed back the bitterness as he followed Helena to Ivan's thigh and held his cousin's leg while she cleaned it. "We didn't kill Sultan Murad. Miloš did, but none of us knew he succeeded. We didn't even know his plan." Danilo felt a catch in his throat and cleared it. Miloš was but one of a hundred friends he had lost. "Bayezid won't be any less dangerous than his father, but he'll need time to consolidate his power. Perhaps that will give us some breathing room."

"Ivan?" Helena's voice made Danilo turn. His cousin's eyes were open.

Helena moved closer to Ivan's head, where he could see her. She brushed the hair off his forehead and cradled his face in her hand.

"Helena . . ." Ivan's voice was raspy and quiet. "Glad to . . . have a chance . . . to say goodbye."

"This isn't goodbye. You have to get better," Helena said. "I'll never forgive you if you die before your time."

"That's not fair." He exhaled with effort. Pain made him haggard, and weakness from his wound made it seem as if a slight breeze could sweep him away.

"You are a man of honor, and you have made me a promise and not yet fulfilled it."

A look of surprise crossed the župan's face. "What promise?"

"You promised me another child. If you wish to remain a man of your word, you will have to recover." Helena took the hand on his uninjured side and kissed it. "My work on your leg will hurt. Danilo is trying to hold you still, but he is weary. Don't make it difficult for him."

There had been a time when Danilo had resented Helena's influence over her husband. She was foreign, and she'd once broken Ivan's heart so completely that Danilo had feared his cousin would never recover. Ivan had always looked to Danilo before, ever since they'd been children, and theirs was a relationship built on a lifetime of shared experiences. The resentment had long ago softened, especially since Helena's advice usually matched Danilo's. Today, there was no resentment. Only gratitude. They both wanted to save the same person, but now Helena could do it better than Danilo could.

"I told you he wasn't dead."

Maja didn't reply to Luka's comment. She didn't need too. She had doubted for a time, and she was thrilled to be proven wrong.

Zlatan walked ahead of them. Maja wasn't sure if he'd heard. Probably not, because a bandage covered one of his ears.

"I can't believe he kissed you in front of everyone."

Maja felt warmth flood her face. Danilo was alive, and he hadn't hesitated to show everyone that he cared for her. He would have to marry her now, or live with the knowledge that he'd ruined her reputation. She didn't completely understand why he loved her, but knowledge that he did thrilled her. As soon as there was time, she would pull him aside and, in a private moment, give him a more substantial kiss.

"Are you going to answer me, Maja?"

"You haven't asked any questions yet."

Luka shook his head. "Are you going to marry him?"

"He hasn't proposed."

"But if he does?"

Maja stepped closer to the stream, where she'd seen the malache the day before. "If he asks, I will say yes."

Luka grinned. "Good. I'd like to have Danilo for a brother."

"He hasn't asked me yet." Maja watched her brother for a moment. The last few days had brought them more sorrow than relief, but Danilo and Župan Ivan's return—how could they not feel joy over it, even while mourning the loss of so many others? "Do you remember where the wormwood was? We're almost out."

"I remember. I'll fetch some and leave you alone with your daydreams." He chuckled and headed over to a burr, where they'd found herbs the day before.

Maja used a knife to dig at the bottom of the malache, trying to get as much of the roots as she could. She wanted Župan Ivan to live. Sivi Gora owed its goodness, in part, to its leader. Beyond that, she cared for Danilo and Dama Helena, and they both loved him. There wasn't much she wouldn't sacrifice to bring them the joy that would come with Župan Ivan's recovery.

The župan had looked so fragile, so different from the day she'd challenged him with a spear, when Danilo had been wounded by brigands. And Danilo . . . Bruises lined what skin she could see, his clothes were filthy, and he looked exhausted. His burdens—a battle, grief, and the struggle to keep his best friend alive—had been heavy since they'd parted that morning in Sivi Gora.

The nearby bushes rustled. Maja looked behind her. Horror stole her breath and made her blood freeze. She dropped the malache and took a step back, terrified. Iskandar stood before her, with two Ottoman archers on either side of him, arrows nocked on their bows.

"Don't scream," Iskandar said softly. "Because if you do, your brother will run to you, and I'll have my men strike him down the way they struck down your guard and several Serb sentries."

Maja took another step back.

"Stay where you are," Iskandar ordered. "I've come to rescue you. Your people have forced you into poverty, into having to work for your keep. I am honored of the sultan, and you will be my beloved wife. You'll want for nothing."

"I wasn't in need of rescuing, not until you arrived."

Iskandar exhaled in a huff. "You will be mine. Allah has ordained it. Why else would He lead me to you three times? Come. The sooner we arrive in Edirne, the sooner I can show you what an excellent husband I will be."

Maja shook her head. "I'm not going anywhere with you."

Iskandar scowled, and the expression made his face match the ugliness of his soul. "I'll make a bargain with you. Come with me, and I'll ride off and not touch your brother or any of those waiting in the mill. Resist, and I'll kill them all."

"But the mill is full of wounded men! Have you no decency?"

"The choice is yours, Maja. I'll be content with you, if you cooperate. Or you can struggle and bring death to all your friends. Don't think you'll escape. I have eighteen men at my command, and we've already whittled down the Serb forces."

She'd felt sick to her stomach the moment she'd seen Iskandar, but now that feeling was worse. She didn't have a choice, not really. Iskandar would have her either way. Perhaps, if she were lucky, she could run, and the archers would shoot her and kill her. She would prefer death to marrying Iskandar. But she believed him when he said he would kill the others if she struggled. Was a doomed attempt at escape worth all their lives? How many of the wounded had families back home? She couldn't sacrifice Danilo, not even to save her own life. Nor did she wish Iskandar to rob Dama Helena and Župan Ivan of their miraculous reunion.

Beyond that, she had vowed to keep Luka safe. If she resisted, he would be killed. If she left, Danilo would take care of him like a brother. "If you promise to leave them unharmed, I will cooperate."

Iskandar smiled. "I promise that *I will not touch them*." He strode forward and took her wrist, gripping it tightly enough that she'd have trouble getting away. He led her through the forest, past Zlatan's body. Maja looked back, hoping to see her brother, but all she saw was the clump of malache she'd dug up. She hoped someone would find it soon. If her sacrifice didn't save Župan Ivan, it would be partially in vain.

"You will ride with me." Iskandar released her when they reached the clearing where most of his men waited. He held the horse, expecting her to mount.

Maja looked back again, hoping that somehow, someone would come to her aid. The group in the mill was larger than Iskandar's, but most were wounded, and if Iskandar had killed all the sentries . . . that would leave only six who could fight. Seven, if she counted Luka. That was the thought that propelled her to mount. Luka wasn't a warrior. He thought he was, but he wasn't ready for battle, and she didn't want him killed in a reckless attempt to save her.

Iskandar climbed on behind her and held her snug against his chest. He inhaled deeply, nose and mouth next to her hair. "Now, at last, you are mine," he whispered.

Maja felt her skin crawl.

Iskandar turned to his men and gave them orders. Maja expected them to all ride east, toward Edirne. Iskandar turned their horse that way, but the others rode toward the mill.

"What's going on? You promised to spare the others."

Iskandar laughed. "No. I promised that *I* would not touch them, and I shan't. There's no need for my involvement. Destroying everyone at the mill is more a job for a butcher than for a trusted retainer of the greatest sultan to ever live. My men can handle it. Besides, I have better things to do. I've been waiting almost three years for you."

Maja swung her elbow into his ribs and tried to jump off the horse. He grabbed her before she could get a leg free. "You lied! You let me believe they'd be safe!"

"They deserve death. All of them. I'll recount their crimes to you as we ride."

"I'll never marry you. Not after this."

"Willing or unwilling, I will have you." He chuckled again, a deep sound that was more threat than mirth. "Wife, concubine, or slave, you will be mine." He pulled her closer to him, as if reminding her that he was stronger and more powerful.

She didn't need the reminder. She already knew.

Chapter Forty-Two
A Storm of Arrows

The scene before Danilo was just as Ivan had described in his dream. Helena, leaning over his body, weeping. But Ivan wasn't dead; he was only sleeping. Or perhaps he was unconscious after the latest blood loss.

"I shouldn't cry." Helena wiped at her cheeks. "I thought he was dead, and I'm so relieved that he's not, but that shoulder will never fully recover. That's his sword arm. And I'm so tired. I've been stitching and washing all night long instead of sleeping. And when I thought I had lost him . . ."

Danilo touched her hand briefly. "You deserve to let the emotions out." He stood to give her a few moments alone, or as alone as she could be surrounded by the other wounded. Danilo would go find Maja. Perhaps she needed help with the herbs. Even if she didn't, he wanted to hold her in his arms again.

Luka burst into the mill before Danilo reached the door. "Iskandar's here, and he's got Maja!"

Despair enveloped him, and for a moment, Danilo couldn't move. Iskandar had tracked him. Danilo had led the man right to her. He didn't linger on the guilt. He ran through the room, collecting a hauberk here, a shield there, a bow from one wounded man, and quivers from two others. "Are there any swords?"

"In the corner." Helena stood and helped Marjan and another soldier arm themselves. "I'm sorry. We set multiple sentries. I thought it was safe to gather the herbs."

"It's my fault. I should have known he would track us."

"How many do you wish to take?"

Danilo glanced at the wounded. He couldn't leave them unprotected. "Just the two should be enough." He wasn't sure it really would be, but there was no better option.

He went to the door, planning to saddle the horses, but the moment he opened it, five Turkish arrows sailed into the wooden frame. One plowed into his ribs, knocking him backward.

"Danilo!" Helena was next to him in a moment. She examined the wound, and he winced.

"They must be close for it to have gone through the mail." He tried to breathe in through his nose and out through his mouth, because the pain made it hard to think clearly.

Philippos forced the door shut. Arrows swooshed through the window. They hadn't hit anyone else, yet, but if the shooters changed their aim, it was possible.

"Move the wounded," Danilo told Luka, who was standing over him with wide eyes, watching Helena cut the arrow out.

Luka nodded, then worked with Philippos to move the wounded men where they couldn't be hit. The other soldiers aimed through the windows at their attackers.

"There were twenty-one of them." Danilo tried to speak clearly, but pain blurred some of the words. "I killed one when we escaped. There might be as many as twenty against us." Maybe a few less, if any had been killed by the nightshade.

"Hold still." Helena stood and went to grab wine, needle, and thread.

"There's not time to stitch it up. Just bandage it."

"If you want to drive off the Turks *and* save Maja, you'll need this repaired, at least as much as I can repair it with thread. The mail kept if from going deeper than muscle, but it needs more than a bandage."

Danilo grimaced as the wine seared his wounded flesh, then he bit his lip to keep silent while Helena stuck the needle into the tender skin. He wanted to chase after Iskandar and save Maja, but Helena had a good point. He couldn't save Maja if he bled to death first.

As Helena finished, the first fire arrow hit. Helena slapped the flames out with a corselet of leather. But then three more flew through the windows. Luka smothered one, crying out as his fingers were singed. Danilo and Marjan took care of the others.

"Give me a bow." Danilo held his hand out, and one of the soldiers gave up his. Danilo would have preferred his own bow, but it was lost somewhere on the plains of Kosovo. He nocked an arrow and aimed at the first Turk he spotted. He wouldn't normally watch it hit, but this time, he did to evaluate the bow's aim. True enough. He shot the next arrow and the next.

Luka knelt beside him at the window. Danilo eyed him. "Don't waste any arrows. Only shoot if you're sure you'll hit."

Luka nodded. "Will you save her?"

"Yes." Danilo shot another of the Turks. "Or I will die trying."

One of the fire arrows had hit the roof, beyond where they could reach, and the ceiling above them smoldered. Which would be worse for the wounded? Burning to death or being shot by Turkish arrows?

"How many of your patients can walk by themselves?" Danilo spoke loudly so Helena could hear over the noise of the fire and the Turkish shouts.

"About half. Seven would have to be carried."

Philippos pulled the string of his bow back to his right cheek and released it. Danilo saw it strike down one of the Turks.

"Where would we take them?" Philippos asked as he pulled another arrow from his quiver. "The river is to our backs, and there's little cover outside, just a few trees and bushes."

"But outside's not on fire." Luka took a shot and missed. He swore. "What will he do with her?"

Danilo had a good idea of what Iskandar would do to Maja, but he didn't want to think about that, not now. He had to win this skirmish first. Those in the mill needed somewhere safe to rest, or they needed all the Turks killed. He and the others had lessened the numbers, but enough remained to be lethal.

"Helena?" Danilo said.

"Yes?"

"I'm going to take the boys and create a distraction. Once they start chasing us, get the wounded out."

"Don't do anything reckless. They're only boys."

Boys who would burn to death if they did nothing. Already, the smell of smoke filled the mill, and Danilo's throat felt dry. "Philippos. Luka. Follow me."

That would leave seven wounded to be carried by four soldiers and Helena, and six wounded to escape themselves. They would have to move quickly, but they couldn't flee until he distracted the enemy, so there was little time to plan.

Danilo kicked open the mill's door. Smoke masked the mill's outline, so the Turks didn't seem to notice. "Run to that set of trees there. On my signal. Ready?"

Luka nodded and set his face. Philippos bit his lips and gripped his bow so hard his knuckles turned white.

"Go." The three of them sprinted for the group of trees, the only shelter to speak of within sight of the mill. Several of the Turks saw them and shouted. Danilo loosed a few arrows, taking down two of them.

Once they reached the trees, they gasped for breath. The wound in Danilo's side burned even worse than his lungs, but he did his best to ignore it. "You two stay here," Danilo said. "If the others head for those bushes back there"—Danilo pointed—"shoot at any of the Turks who approach. They'll have to come around if they want to make the shot, and they'll have poor cover."

"And you?" Luka asked.

"I'm going closer. There can't be more than twenty of them, and I know we've hit at least half." The odds weren't in his favor, but failure here would mean the death of his župan, among others, and a life of misery for the woman he loved.

Danilo had six arrows left. After that, he would need to confront the enemy at close quarters with his borrowed sword. He wasn't even sure who the sword belonged to. He hoped the blade hadn't been dulled too much at Kosovo.

He ran first for a clump of bushes. He paused there, watching those in the mill carry out the first group of wounded. He loosed two arrows at Turks trying to get closer and hit them both. Next, he ran to an empty hen coop, sheltering behind its wooden wall as he shot another enemy soldier. He couldn't see the door of the mill anymore, so he had to assume the evacuation was continuing as planned. The roof was engulfed in flames, hastening the urgency of their eviction, but also masking the movements of those trying to escape.

He ducked lower when a pair of Ottomans loosed arrows at him. Someone from the house hit one of them. Danilo took out the other. One of the wounded Turks crawled away from the mill. Danilo let him go, not wanting to waste one of his last two arrows.

The Turks were harder to see now. There were fewer of them, and perhaps they were hiding. Luka and Philippos could cover this side of the mill. Danilo needed to move to the other side to ensure that none of the Turks got to the wounded by coming at them from behind.

He kept an arrow nocked in his bow as he rushed first to a tree, then to the burning hull of the mill. He saw none of the enemy. Where were they? They couldn't all be dead, not yet. Around the corner of the building, he saw a group of four Turks sneaking closer to the back of the mill, where they could attack the wounded. He ran for them, slaying two with the last of his arrows. Then he discarded his bow and drew his sword for the remaining two.

The first slashed at him with his curved scimitar. Danilo blocked the sword and shoved the man back, then parried the next strike before sticking the man in the gut. The sword's blade was dull, so he had trouble yanking it from the body as the second Turk aimed his bow.

Danilo jerked the dying man in front of him to catch the arrow when it released. The other Turk seemed to know Danilo had no more arrows, so he stepped back, keeping his distance and pulling out another arrow. Danilo held the body a little longer, even though it made the wound in his side burn. He had no other shield, and the enemy was close enough that a decent shot would put the arrow through his mail. He would have to drop the body and run at the last man, but he didn't see how he could run fast enough to avoid death.

An arrow whistled through the air and plowed into the last Ottoman soldier. Danilo looked in the direction the arrow had come from. Luka stood there, breathing hard as he gripped his bow.

"I thought I told you and Philippos to watch the other end of the mill."

"We didn't see anyone, and I thought you might need help." Luka glanced at the man he'd shot. The boy was right; Danilo had needed help. "And I think you're the only one who can save Maja."

Danilo glanced around. Maybe they'd shot the last of Iskandar's men. He let the body he'd been holding drop to the ground and used his foot to help draw out his sword. "If I'm going to save your sister, I need a better sword, a fresh quiver, a fast horse, and a prisoner."

During the fighting, the Turks had killed one of the wounded as he was leaving the mill, and one of Helena's guards when he stopped the evacuation long enough to shoot back. Danilo and the others found eighteen Ottoman soldiers. Most were dead. But three were alive and lucid enough for questioning. The first two said the same things when Danilo questioned them, each in turn, each where the others could not hear: Iskandar had ridden off alone with Maja and had told the men to meet him back at their camp when they had finished off everyone inside the mill.

"He said there was a beautiful woman inside," the third prisoner said. "We could have her if we wished. Everyone else was to die." The prisoner glanced at Helena, who sat next to her husband.

"Where is your camp?" Danilo asked.

"About three miles to the east. There's a copse of trees to the north of the road. A hill beyond that. We're camped on the other side of the hill."

His words matched what the others had told him, and Danilo was in a hurry. How long had the attack on the mill lasted? The intensity of the danger had stretched out the time, though he was sure it had been less than an hour. But what could Iskandar do to Maja in an hour's time?

Luka found Danilo a dagger to go with his replacement sword. Philippos gathered arrows from nearly spent quivers until Danilo had a full set. He also had a bow, helmet, and hauberk. It was time to chase Iskandar.

"I wish I could go with you," Ivan mumbled.

"Just get better. I'll bring Maja back soon."

"Will you let me come?" Luka pleaded with his eyes.

"You can't ride as fast as I can. And it's just him."

Luka nodded, but reluctance showed in his eyes and in his frown. The boy wanted to be a hero. One of these days, Danilo would teach him the skills he craved. But that would have to wait.

"Take my horse," Helena said. "Calliope is more rested than any of the others."

Danilo nodded. He'd selected Helena's horse himself, a mare with a rare combination of speed and endurance, because Ivan had wanted his wife to have a horse that could outride any brigands should she ever be attacked while out delivering an infant. Danilo mounted Calliope, then spurred the mare into a gallop toward his most bitter enemy and toward his beloved.

Chapter Forty-Three
The Ghazi Camp

Maja ran as soon as Iskandar let her off the horse. Her shoes were mere canvas, so she felt every rock she ran over, but she didn't stop, not until Iskandar caught her ten paces from where she'd started.

"Where do you think you can go?" He gripped her upper arms tightly enough to bruise. "I have a horse. I'll catch you."

Yes, he would most likely catch her, but any chance of escape, even a chance of delay—that was worth pursuing.

He pulled her along toward the cluster of tents. "I don't think you understand what I am offering. I will be your husband. I am favored of the sultan and will soon have a timar of my own to draw revenue from. Do you know how many women would gladly change places with you?"

"Then let them change places with me."

He scowled, and his fingers dug even harder into her skin. "I will give you some advice. You are mine now. If you are obedient, I will be kind. If you resist, I will tame you into submission."

Something in her stomach seemed to flip, as if she were about to vomit. She knew what would happen in his tent, knew it was inevitable. Should she cooperate, accept her fate, choose the easier path? Or fight, knowing she would lose in the end? She didn't ponder her options long. This was the man who had ordered those she loved most slaughtered, not once but twice. He planned to take her by force, and he would help the sultan enslave her people. He had ripped her dreams away when they had been so near her grasp—her hope of a future with Danilo, her vision for the mosaics in the church, the sense of home and peace she'd found in Sivi Gora.

There could never be anything but hatred in her heart for Iskandar.

"Danilo will save me." It was a foolish statement. Danilo was probably dead. But what if he weren't? He had saved her from Iskandar twice before. Perhaps Danilo could save her again.

"Danilo and the others are dead by now."

"No, they aren't." She didn't believe it until she spoke it, but as she did, a sliver of hope grew inside her, and she grasped it with desperation. "They have the mill to protect them. Your men can't shoot through walls. Danilo will shoot them all, one by one. There are more arrows than ghazis. Then he will rescue me."

Iskandar huffed. "Even if he survives, why would he come after you?"

"Because I love him."

"You love the Turkish half-breed?" Iskandar seemed surprised, then angry. "And does he love you?"

"Yes." Danilo hadn't spoken the words. There had never been time, but she knew in her heart that her feelings were reciprocated.

"Are you sure? Because in Kosovo, we agreed to a trade. Ivan's life in exchange for ransom—and for you. Why would he trade away the woman he loves?"

Maja's throat felt tight. Was Iskandar telling the truth? Would Danilo sell her into misery in order to save Župan Ivan? She didn't know. What would she do if Iskandar made her choose between Luka and Danilo? She would postpone the decision as long as she could and hope a better choice presented itself. That had to be what Danilo had done. "He didn't trade me, did he?"

"The results are the same." Iskandar's face twisted with malice. "Now I almost hope he survives, to live with the knowledge that I stole his beloved from him. Taking you will injure him in a way no arrow or sword ever could."

Maja wished she had kept quiet. Iskandar's lust for her would mix with his hatred for Danilo, and she would suffer the more for it. She jerked her arm, trying to break free, but she couldn't get out of his grasp. "You may be stronger than I, but you will never possess my heart or my soul."

Iskandar pulled her body tight against his. "I don't need your heart or your soul. Just your body. And I will possess that." One of his hands held the back of her head as he forced his mouth over hers. She tried to pull away, but he was too strong. His rough mouth forced her lips apart, and no matter how hard she tried, she couldn't turn her head enough to escape. Terror filled her. She tried to get her hands free, tried to push away. In the end, she used her teeth.

Iskandar drew back, startled. Blood formed on his lip where she'd bitten him. He slapped her, so hard that she fell to the ground. Her cheek throbbed, and tears filled her eyes. She had thought she had a few more moments of safety—they were still several paces from the tent. But the volatile mix of anger and lust in his eyes told her he would take her there, in the dirt, and that he would ravage her completely, painfully, and with no mercy.

Maja gripped a loose stone, one about the size of her fist. Iskandar tackled her, trying to pin her to the ground. She smashed the rock into the side of his head, and he floundered. She hit him again, then scrambled out from under him and ran.

Iskandar was between her and the horse, and though he swayed as he pushed himself from the ground, she wasn't sure she could make it past him. She ran for a copse of trees and pulled herself up into one, climbing until she hoped she was out of sight. She held a fist to her mouth, trying to quiet her breathing. Her tunic was torn about the neck, her cheek stung from his strike, and she knew far worse was to come if he caught her again.

If he caught her again . . . When he caught her again. She couldn't hope to hide for long. But maybe, just maybe, Iskandar would walk past the tree now holding her, and she could climb down and steal the horse. She wasn't sure it would work, but she would try. And if that plan failed, she would try another. No matter how hopeless, she would always try for escape.

Danilo turned off the road, riding hard for the Ottoman camp. He prayed he would find Maja there, that he would arrive before Iskandar hurt her. But that hope felt flimsy. Iskandar had been searching for Maja since Pločnik. His obsession had consumed him and become more important to him than his sultan or his people. Why would he wait?

Danilo expected to find Maja with a violated body and a broken spirit. As much as he wished he could, he didn't think he could save her from the full horror of the day. But he could at least save her from a lifetime as Iskandar's slave. He would deliver out a just punishment to Iskandar and pray Maja would prove resilient enough to survive the nightmare Iskandar had inflicted on her.

He slowed when he saw the tents. Which one was Iskandar's? Danilo had set them all up that night in Iskandar's camp, but he hadn't seen which men had gone into which tents, and now their positions were shifted. Should he shout and hope Maja could answer? Or would he be foolish to give up the advantage of surprise?

An arrow hissed through the air, narrowly missing his head. He dismounted and used Calliope as a shield. Iskandar stood beside a tree, another arrow nocked in his bow. Danilo grabbed his own bow, but Iskandar moved behind the tree before Danilo could nock and release.

Danilo would have to get closer.

"Where is she?" Danilo hoped Maja wasn't bleeding in a tent somewhere.

"I loved her first. She's mine." Iskandar shot the horse's shoulder.

The mare bucked in panic, but Danilo was able to calm her. He turned the horse around and pulled the arrow from the mare's muscles before moving closer to his enemy. "You may be familiar with desire and lust, but you know nothing of love. Real love involves kindness and self-sacrifice, and it admires more than the flesh. It doesn't frighten or take by force."

Danilo had nearly reached the tree. He slipped his bow over the pommel and drew his spathion. He slapped the horse forward and lunged at Iskandar.

Iskandar was prepared with his scimitar. He met Danilo's blow, and the blades tangled for a moment before they came apart again.

Danilo parried Iskandar's next strike, a hard blow that made the steel of their weapons ring. The arrow wound in Danilo's side flared in pain, and he stepped back as Iskandar attacked with a force strengthened by rage and ambition.

The two had fought before. Danilo would have won then had Iskandar not had help. Danilo couldn't fail today. Maja's fate depended on him.

He still hadn't seen her. She could be dead or injured or hiding. He prayed she still lived. He struck hard at Iskandar, making him step back, but then Iskandar lashed out, kicking Danilo right where he'd been wounded. The pain was so sharp it stole his breath. Iskandar struck again, hitting past the hilt of Danilo's sword and slicing into the skin of his hand.

Danilo kept his grip on his sword, barely, and retreated a few steps as he tried to catch his breath and determine how deep the cut was. He switched the blade from his right to his left hand, blessing his cousin for insisting they spar with their left hands every few days, even though both were stronger with their right.

Iskandar pressed the attack, seeming to sense he now had the advantage. He struck, and Danilo parried. Iskandar riposted, and Danilo blocked. Each strike forced Danilo back a step, and unless something changed, Iskandar would continue to control the duel.

Danilo flexed his injured hand. Everything bent the way it was supposed to, with an added dose of pain. But he needed his better hand. He switched the blade back into his right hand and struck Iskandar hard, three times in a row, with enough force to drive Iskandar back to the trunk of an ash tree.

Iskandar sneered, then charged, striking downward with force. The blood from Danilo's hand made the hilt of his sword slippery, and he lost his grip. The spathion echoed against a rock as it fell to the earth. Iskandar stepped in quickly to ensure Danilo couldn't pick it up. Danilo drew a dagger instead. The inferior weapon was better than nothing, but fear that he might not defeat Iskandar suddenly felt real.

Iskandar charged him.

Maja appeared from the trees, holding a long branch, and ran at Iskandar as if she would pummel him with the wooden limb.

Danilo knew the moment Iskandar spotted her, but it happened too fast for him to shout a warning. Iskandar stepped back, and as Maja tried to hit him, he grabbed her from behind and held his sword across her neck.

A strangled cry escaped her lips. Iskandar had not been kind to her since her abduction. One side of her face was red and swollen, and her tunic was torn. Rage filled Danilo, but he dared not step closer. Iskandar's blade would shed her blood before Danilo could close the distance.

"You say you love her," Danilo said. "Yet you threaten her."

"If she won't be mine, then she won't be yours." Iskandar set his mouth, looking from Danilo to Maja and back again. "All this time, I have wanted to hurt you. Make you suffer. But maybe I was aiming at the wrong person. If I want to really punish you, she's the one I should target."

Danilo took a panicked step forward.

"Don't move." Iskandar pulled his sword in and Maja inhaled sharply, pulling back into Iskandar. A line of blood appeared on her neck.

Danilo held out his hands, though he didn't think the motions that calmed a horse would work for the ghazi. "What do you want, Iskandar?"

"I want her. I want you and your cousin dead. And I want wealth and the ear of the sultan."

"Which do you want most?" Danilo studied Maja again. If Iskandar had already satiated his obsession, perhaps he would let her go. "Maja or my death?"

"I'll have both." Iskandar eyed Maja's profile. "But I'll have your death first."

"Let her go, and I'll set down my dagger. If you release her, I'll let you kill me. Ivan will pay something for my body. A start to your wealth."

Iskandar huffed. "I'm to trust your word?"

Danilo didn't want to negotiate with Iskandar, but he saw no other choice. "If you let her ride off, I'll not lift a finger against you. It will be like slaying a lamb."

Iskandar nodded, which Danilo took for agreement.

"Lower your sword, and I'll set my dagger down." As he spoke, Danilo changed his grip on his dagger, so it hung ready to drop to the ground.

Iskandar lowered his blade from Maja's neck to his side, though he didn't yet release her.

Danilo dropped his dagger. "Now let her go, and I'll step where I can't reach my blade."

"Step away from your weapon first."

When Danilo was five paces from his dagger, Iskandar shoved Maja away. She ran toward Danilo.

"Don't run to me, Maja. Run to the horse. Ride for the mill. They'll protect you. We slew all his soldiers, so the only danger you have to fear is Iskandar chasing you from behind. But you can make it. It's not far, and Calliope is swift." The horse was also injured, but Iskandar's horse was fifty paces away, by the tents, and Danilo would do what he could to make sure Maja had a head start. He had kept his eyes on Iskandar as he spoke, but he glanced at Maja, giving her a nod of encouragement.

"You can't mean it," she whispered.

"I gave my word."

"But he broke his word to me when he attacked the mill, and I need you."

Iskandar held his bow in one hand and an arrow in the other. He hadn't nocked the arrow yet, but that would come soon enough.

"Hurry, Maja. There's not much time." Regardless of what Danilo wanted, Iskandar was close enough that he was unlikely to miss. Danilo would dodge to slow Iskandar down, and a single arrow might not finish him off, but he expected Iskandar to win their duel, and then Iskandar would chase her, and Iskandar was undoubtedly the better rider. Maja needed to ride at once.

Tears streaked Maja's cheeks, but she mounted and looked back at him.

"Go," he urged. Danilo was going to die, but instead of fear, he felt calm. He had saved Ivan from Iskandar and delivered him to Helena. He had saved Maja from Iskandar, and Calliope would carry her back to her brother. On the eve of Kosovo, Danilo had wanted life with a desperation that felt painful. But now death held less of a sting. He'd done what he could for his friends, and his soul, safely in the hands of his Redeemer, would be well no matter what happened to his body. Was that how his father had felt before marching to Maritsa? And how Knez Lazar had felt before the battle against Sultan Murad? What happened to their mortal bodies mattered, of that there was no question. But of far more importance was what happened to their immortal souls.

Iskandar watched, seeming amused at the pain he had caused. But then his expression changed. He nocked his arrow, and as he drew back the string of his bow, an arrow slammed into the Turk's chest.

Iskandar's shot went wild. Danilo looked to Maja, sitting atop Calliope, nocking a second arrow into the bow Danilo had left on the pommel. She pulled back the string and shot Iskandar a second time, and he fell to the ground.

Danilo retrieved his dagger and stepped toward his enemy. Maja dismounted and ran to Danilo, holding the bow and another arrow in one hand. Together, they looked on the fallen Iskandar.

Arrows pierced his chest and his stomach. The ghazi's eyes blinked once, then twice. His lips pulled into a defiant scowl. Then he winced and coughed and winced again. "You promised," he whispered.

"No," Maja said. "Danilo promised. And he didn't lift a finger against you. But I made no such concession. One arrow for my mother. And one for my father. Now they are avenged."

The distinctive sucking sound of a pierced lung grew stronger for a few of Iskandar's breaths, then it weakened, then it stopped.

Maja turned toward Danilo and drew him into an embrace. Her body shook with the aftermath of so much fear, so much danger, and Danilo held her tightly.

"You saved my life," he whispered.

"How could I do otherwise?" Her hands moved across his back. "But I was so afraid it wouldn't work. I couldn't draw the bow all the way back. But he was close, and he wasn't wearing armor."

Danilo smiled down at her and ran his hand along the uninjured side of her face. "You are remarkable, Maja Dinić."

"Right now, I'm a trembling mess. If you let go of me, I might crumple to the ground."

"Then I will hold you up for as long as you need me to." He pressed his lips onto her forehead and held her.

This nightmare was over. His side burned in pain, and his injured hand throbbed, but he didn't want to let go. He gently fingered her neck where Iskandar's blade had drawn blood, but the bleeding had stopped.

She took his injured hand gently in hers, then used the sash from around her waist to bandage it. "I should get you back to the mill for stitches."

"It might not need stitches. But you're right, we should get back. Everyone will be worried." He wanted to return to the mill, but he also knew they would have little privacy once there.

She kept hold of his hand. "Danilo, would you really have died for me?"

"Yes."

"Why?" She stared at him with those intensely blue eyes.

"Because I love you."

They already stood near each other, but she stepped even closer, placing one hand on his chest and slipping the fingers of her other hand around the muscles of his upper arm. She glanced from his mouth to his eyes and then back again. He wrapped an arm around her waist and leaned in to meet her perfect lips.

He was gentle at first, slowly memorizing the curve of her mouth, tasting her skin, breathing her in. But the longer he kissed her, the more urgent his need for her became. Her response teased him and invited him and captured him until he was completely at her mercy.

"Maja," he whispered. "Will you marry me?"

"Of course I will." Her voice was breathless as she smiled up at him. "Once rescued, and you never left my mind. Twice rescued, and you never left my heart. Thrice rescued, and I pray you will never leave my side."

He kissed her again. And then a third kiss and a fourth. But he knew they had to get back to the others, and his hand ached, as did the stitches in his side.

"We really should go back now," he whispered as she leaned her head on his chest. "Your brother was terrified for you."

Maja nodded. "You will marry me soon?"

"As soon as the priest will allow it."

Maja smiled, and together they fetched both horses, Helena's and Iskandar's.

"Will you be able to ride?" Danilo asked. "I can see he bruised your face, and there's the cut on your neck. But did he . . . ? Are you all right?" He wanted her for his bride regardless of what Iskandar had or hadn't done to her, but he wondered if she, too, had wounds for Helena to clean and stitch.

Maja frowned. "He tried. I hit him with a rock and hid in the trees. He would have found me, eventually, if it hadn't been for you."

Danilo mounted Iskandar's horse, wanting the injured mare to have a lighter load. "I would have married you anyway, but I'm glad I was here in time."

She glanced at Calliope, then back at Danilo. "Would you mind if I rode with you? I feel safe in your arms . . . And after everything, it would be nice to be held."

Danilo reached a hand out and helped her settle into the saddle in front of him. He would gladly hold her on the ride to the mill, on the way back to Sivi Gora, and after that, every night, until the end of their days.

Epilogue

1390

When the soft light of coming dawn peeked through the window, Danilo ran his fingers through Maja's golden hair. They'd been married a year, and the pleasure of waking up next to her every morning still hadn't faded. Maybe it never would.

"Good morning," she mumbled into her pillow.

He slipped his arms around her and pulled her next to him. "I thought you'd sleep longer this morning." She'd woken with a nightmare earlier that night. She still had them, sometimes, even with Iskandar dead. They had grown less frequent over the past year, though, and she calmed quickly when he lit a candle and held her. Still, she usually slept in after an ordeal like that.

"Some things are difficult to sleep through." She guided his hand to her swollen abdomen and held it where he could feel the soft spasm that came at roughly regular intervals. "I think our baby has the hiccups."

Danilo chuckled and pressed a soft kiss into the back of her neck. "I am sorry the baby is already disturbing your sleep, but I am delighted that we will soon become parents."

Delight wasn't the only emotion he felt as Maja's time drew near. He'd lost a wife in childbirth before. Worry that he might lose Maja, too, never left for long, and she knew him well enough to know his fears.

She turned toward him and placed a hand on his cheek, gently running her fingers along his skin. "I'm going to be fine. And so is the baby."

"Of course you are." He kissed her, hoping the words he'd said were true, though he wouldn't be convinced until he saw it with his own eyes. Helena said the baby would come soon, but whether *soon* meant "hours" or "days" or "weeks" . . . that was something no one could predict with precision.

They dressed and ate, and then Danilo headed to the palace. Until recently, he had walked Maja to the church most days, but her changing body meant climbing and balancing on the scaffolds could wait until later. Instead, sketches and drawings of a dozen ideas for each of the remaining panels covered her writing table in their home.

Marjan stood watch at the palace gate when Danilo arrived. "The group from Rivak rode in last night."

Joy brought a smile to Danilo's face. He and Maja had visited Rivak shortly after their wedding, but he hadn't seen Konstantin or his family since then. Konstantin and Suzana had hoped to visit Sivi Gora sometime this summer, but back then, everything had still seemed so uncertain. "How late was their arrival?"

"After dark, but I wasn't on duty then."

Danilo nodded. He went to the hall and found a sizable group at the tables for the morning meal. His mother saw him first, and her smile drew the attention of Konstantin and Suzana sitting across the table from her. Konstantin turned and stood. His face was changed now, with a long scar across the left side, running from his eyebrow to his beard. The eyelid sagged, covering all but a slit of pink flesh where the eye had once been. He balanced well on his damaged foot—far better than Danilo remembered from when he had last seen him only a few moons after the battle at Kosovo.

Danilo closed the distance and embraced his older cousin. "I am very pleased to see you both."

Suzana gave him a warm smile. In her arms, she cradled Ivan and Helena's infant son, born two moons ago. "We could hardly stay away, not when there's a new nephew to meet and another baby expected soon. How is Maja? I assume the baby has not yet come?"

"Maja is well. Eager for the little one to join us."

"I'm eager to meet the little one as well." Suzana kissed baby Đurad's head. "I almost forget how small they are. Danica seems enormous now in comparison to her cousin."

Danilo scanned the room until he found Danica playing with Sofija. "She's grown." When he'd seen the little girl at harvest time, she'd been a baby with only a few wisps of hair. Now she chased her cousin Sofija and squealed with delight when Ekaterina's dog licked her hand.

Suzana's smile grew wistful. "Yes, she seems to be growing up faster than the boys did."

Konstantin chuckled. “I know that look, Suzana. Surely you’re not ready for another baby already?”

Suzana gave a little shrug. “For now, I can snuggle with baby Đurad, and soon, I’ll be able to snuggle with Danilo and Maja’s baby, but Sivi Gora is too far for regular visits, and this will be Danica’s second winter.”

Konstantin brushed his hand along his wife’s shoulder. “One of these days, you’re going to stop wanting kisses from a face as ugly as this.”

Suzana handed baby Đurad to Danilo’s mother. Then she stood on her tiptoes to kiss Konstantin’s scar. “Nonsense. Your scars aren’t ugly. They’re a reminder of how blessed I am that you came home to me again. I’ll leave you to catch up with Danilo while I make sure our youngest eats something.”

Konstantin’s smile was bittersweet as Suzana and Danilo’s mother went to help Danica. He sat at the table and eased his damaged foot from the floor. “In some ways, it feels like little has changed since we went to Bosnia in search of allies last spring. Then, we expected Sultan Murad to strike. Now we expect the same from Sultan Bayezid, only we have fewer options for allies. Fewer options for leaders too. It’s a blow I’m not sure we can recover from: Knez Lazar dead, his lands pledged as vassals to the sultan.”

Danilo joined his cousin at the table. “I don’t suppose Knez Lazar’s widow could fight the Turks and the Hungarians at the same time.” Kruševac, facing attack from Hungary, had made peace with Bayezid. Dama Milica had sent not only tribute to the sultan but also her youngest daughter to serve as his wife. Her two remaining sons, not yet men, would be required to visit the sultan’s court yearly as part of their vassalage.

“No.” Konstantin sighed. “If the Hungarians would ally with us instead of attacking us, we might have a chance. Had they been at Kosovo . . . if they had been on our side . . . perhaps things would have been different. Sivi Gora is blessed to have escaped attention from both Sultan Bayezid and Király Sigismund.”

Danilo well knew that. Ivan too. Sigismund of Hungary, perhaps on the suggestion of his ispán, Bokori, showed no interest in conquering or raiding Sivi Gora. He remained content with trade. The other threat, the sultan, seemed to have forgotten about the little župa ruled by a man Bayezid had once ordered executed. “How will Rivak fare?”

Konstantin shook his head. “That remains to be seen. Vuk stands between Rivak and Bayezid. I will continue to ally with him. I know he wasn’t fair to Miloš, but he’s the most powerful man in Serbia now. Rivak is weaker after Kosovo. We lost far too many from our garrison, and we lost firm allies with the deaths of Župan Dragomir and Župan Nikola. But for as long as I am able, I will do all I can for my people."

Danilo leaned on the table. "You have been a good župan to them."

"I have done my best." He gestured to his face. "Except the time I hesitated to kill an Ottoman emissary I once considered a friend."

"I think that means you have done all you can for your people, save for becoming as ruthless as the enemy you have shielded them from."

Konstantin's expression softened. "Perhaps. After Maritsa, it took fifteen years to win our freedom back at Pločnik. Freedom felt fragile even then. After Kosovo, it feels even frailer, but that doesn't lessen my hunger for it."

"If Bayezid attacks again, you and your family will always be welcome in Sivi Gora."

"Ivan said much the same thing. For now, I'm grateful for what we have, even if it feels fleeting. And grateful that I have more time with my family. When I went to Kosovo, when I was lying on the field, blinded by blood, unable to stand or use my arm . . . I wasn't sure I'd ever see them again."

Danilo, too, had feared he would not return from Kosovo. So many hadn't. He remembered one of his last conversations with Miloš, when the knight had said he could imagine Danilo and Maja being happy together after the battle. That dream, at least, had come true. "I pray daily to thank the Lord for sparing me, sparing Ivan, sparing you. No matter what comes next, I am grateful for more time with family, grateful for the chance to marry Maja."

"Pavle is eager to see Maja's mosaics," Konstantin said.

"She will be pleased to show them to him." Danilo told Konstantin about Maja's work in the church, then more general news. "Overall, it's been a quiet summer in Sivi Gora. And I am glad for that. I don't know how many summers like the last one our people can survive."

"You'll soon be a father. That hardly makes it a quiet summer."

He smiled. "I suppose not, and I will be quite content if I am needed more at home than on campaign for the remainder of my days."

His cousin studied him. "You seem happier now. No longer wandering."

"No. Sivi Gora is my home. There are a great many reasons for worry, a great many reasons for sorrow, but with Maja, I am reminded daily of how beautiful life can be. Fragile, too, but that's all the more reason to love deeply while we can."

Nearby laughter drew his attention to the young man sitting next to Ekaterina, someone Danilo recognized but only because he'd known the lad's older brothers. "Has Župan Dragomir's grandson come to court?"

Konstantin followed Danilo's gaze. "Župan Dragomir escorted me when it was time to meet my bride. I thought I would return the favor for Župan Todor."

Župan Todor. Since before Danilo's birth, it had been Župan Dragomir leading those lands. That loss, and so many others, still sneaked up on him at times, bringing grief and a reminder of his duty to defend Serbia against all threats.

"Are they betrothed?" Danilo asked.

Konstantin shook his head. "Your mother and Helena made it quite clear that Ekaterina will have a choice. Whether to marry a Serbian župan, whose lands lie in the sultan's path, or the heir of a Hungarian ispán, who follows the Latin rite rather than the Greek."

"I am glad she will have a choice and that I am no longer one of those possibilities."

Konstantin smiled. "As am I."

Pavle found Ekaterina's dog and held the animal still for Danica and Sofija. But Danilo had yet to see Konstantin's heir.

"Where's Marko?" Danilo asked.

"He and Ivan went to the archery fields. No doubt he'll drag you out there soon. Ivan said he's using a full-weight bow now."

Danilo nodded. Ivan's body wasn't the same as it had been before his wounds at Kosovo, but sheer will, a great deal of work, and a wife wise in the workings of the body had resulted in more progress than any of them had hoped for upon their return to Sivi Gora the summer before. "He does better with a crossbow than the bow. His sword work is coming along well. He managed to beat Philippos last week."

"How skilled is Philippos?"

"He's quick. Technically sound. But still young. I expect he'll be a threat in a few years when he's grown a little taller and gained his full strength. How has your arm healed?"

Konstantin flexed his left hand. "It's not quite the same. And with my damaged foot, I don't move as fast as I should. I'll plan accordingly for any battles to come."

Danilo hoped there would be no more battles to come, but he knew better. In time, another enemy would arise, or old enemies would again attack.

Ivan and Marko entered the hall. Neither was armed, so they must have left the bows elsewhere.

Ivan joined Konstantin and Danilo. "Good morning, Danilo. Have you been here long?"

"No. I haven't even said hello to the children yet."

Ivan glanced at Sofija, Danica, and Pavle. "I imagine there's time for that, but Luka just came by the palace."

"Was he looking for me?" Danilo asked.

Ivan shook his head. "He was looking for Helena. Maja sent him for the midwife." Ivan grinned. "It seems your wait to become a father is almost over."

Maja stood next to the window and nestled her son in her arms. The babe had been born yesterday with the last light of day, healthy and plump, with his father's hair and his mother's eyes, although Helena had said the eye color might change. "That's the palace, over there, where I expect you'll spend much of your time as you grow. That's the church, where you will worship God and where your mother and uncle have done their best to make the walls tell stories. And that is the župan's mighty wall that will keep Sivi Gora safe so it can always be a marvelous place to live, just as it is now."

Baby Miloš didn't look at any of the landmarks she pointed out. He was too busy sleeping.

The door to the bedchamber opened, and Danilo came inside with a tray of food. "I leave for a few moments to bring you breakfast, and you get out of bed? I thought you were supposed to rest." He put the tray on a table and came up behind her, wrapping his arms around her and the baby and kissing the back of her neck. Even after a year, even when she was exhausted, his touch still brought a pleasant heat to her skin.

"How are you this morning?" he asked.

"I am still weary, but I am also happy." Maja had always found pleasure in the beauty of the earth and fulfillment through her art. But in the year since she'd married Danilo, she'd come to know joy more fully than ever before. He was like the mortar of a mosaic, holding together all the pieces of her soul. And he was also the sunshine, enhancing her strengths with his warmth and light.

Danilo arranged the pillows of the bed and then took the baby from her. "You ought to eat before he's hungry again. Helena will be here to check on you soon."

Maja climbed back into bed and bit into a ripe pear. Danilo watched the baby, then watched her. "You're acting as though you've never seen me eat before," she said after she swallowed.

His face grew solemn for a moment. "I was worried. But you're so strong. I needn't have been concerned."

She'd known he feared losing her the way he'd lost his first wife, but she hadn't known how to ease his worry. To feel so much love from a man as wonderful as Danilo . . . sometimes it still left her a little breathless.

He bent and gently kissed her forehead. "And little Miloš is healthy and strong. I couldn't be happier or prouder of both of you."

"I love you."

"And I adore you." He slipped into the bed next to her, one arm around her shoulders, the other arm holding their baby.

She leaned into him and sighed with contentment. She had Danilo, and she also had a son, and though her love for little Miloš was different, it already felt deeper and richer than she'd imagined possible.

A knock sounded on the door, and one of the servants let Helena in.

"Good morning." Helena's smile was warm, full of joy for Maja, Danilo, and Miloš.

Maja answered all Helena's questions about residual pains and Miloš's eating habits and cooperated for the examination.

"You're healing well," Helena said as she wiped her hands clean. "But try to take it easy for a few days, at least."

"After he was born, I wanted to sleep for a week straight. But now all I want to do is study each of his fingers and watch his little nose. And I want to finish my mosaic." She needed only another fortnight, perhaps, to complete it. Over the past year, working with Arcadius had grown easier. The old master had ceased questioning Maja's skill the moment she'd finished her mosaic of David, and as Luka felt less resentment on his sister's behalf, his attitude toward the Greek master had changed. Luka had shifted into a willing student, and Arcadius had seemed to find satisfaction in teaching and training him. But if Maja shirked her work for too long, she suspected Arcadius would again question the wisdom of a female mosaicist.

"The mosaic can wait." Danilo shifted the baby as Miloš wiggled in his sleep.

"But it's nearly completed."

"Luka finished the lions' faces. They were fierce enough to frighten Sofija." Danilo shook his head. "Danilo and the lion's den. You'll have to change the face and the hands. Daniel was a Hebrew, not a Turk."

"You can't change it." Helena reached for the baby. "It's Ivan's favorite mosaic in the whole church."

Maja smiled. She didn't want to change the mosaic. And she was proud of Luka. His passion was more with bow than chisel lately, but he had completed the work they had begun together. Their father would be proud.

Helena sat on the edge of the bed and unwrapped Miloš enough to examine his remaining umbilical cord. Then she wrapped him again, kissed his forehead, and returned him to his father. "Maja, are you feeling up to visitors?" Helena asked.

"Who?"

"My mother, for one." Danilo played with his son's hand, getting the tiny fingers to grip his thumb. "She's eager to meet her grandson. Ivan is also eager to meet him. Suzana and Konstantin too. And Luka wants to see him again."

She had expected Dama Zorica to come soon. Having either župan come when she was still so fresh from the birth was more intimidating, but she nodded her consent. She didn't think anyone could love Danilo more than she did, but the friendship between Danilo and Ivan went back to before she was born, and there was a power in that relationship that she'd come to respect. Both men were better for it. Nor would she deny Župan Konstantin or Dama Suzana the chance to meet Danilo's son.

When Helena opened the door, Sofija ran into the room first.

"Another baby?" She slowed as she drew near Danilo and gazed in awe at her new cousin.

Ivan came next, carrying his own son. The župan's crippled arm had gained enough strength to hold the small infant, who cooed softly as he caught sight of his mother. Danilo had told her Ivan's swordplay with his left hand was progressing well enough that Danilo expected to be beaten soundly by his cousin sometime before winter set in.

Ivan handed baby Đurad to Helena and bent over Danilo to gaze at Maja's newborn son. He reached out with his good hand, touching the plump cheeks and the dark hair. "He's perfect. And they'll be the best of friends. Just like their fathers and their grandfathers."

Maja scooted back into the pillows and leaned into Danilo, watching as her son was accepted into the family with an enthusiasm that warmed her soul. There were dark times in her past, dull and discouraging like a tessera of black slate. But here in Sivi Gora, the kinship and love she had found was like a tessera gilded in gold. If her father was right and life was like a mosaic, then Maja's was going to be beautiful.

AUTHOR'S NOTES AND ACKNOWLEDGMENTS

The Battle of Kosovo is history, but it is wrapped in layer upon layer of legend. The battle plays a large role in Serbian history and culture, though many elements are still debated or remain a mystery. I hope you have enjoyed my fictional version. I did my best to incorporate as many events from the various accounts—historical and legendary—as I could while telling a compelling narrative.

Some details about the Battle of Kosovo are undisputed: Knez Lazar (or Tsar Lazar) and Sultan Murad both died, and both sides of the battle suffered heavy losses. Bayezid emerged as the new sultan after having his brother Yakub killed. Time would remember the Battle of Kosovo as a loss for the Serbs, but some of the earliest references to the battle from Christian sources report the war as a Christian victory on account of Sultan Murad's death. Most historians now look at the battle as a draw, but the Ottomans had the population and resources to recover more quickly than the Serbs. With defeats at Maritsa and Kosovo, the medieval Serb warrior class was decimated and would not recover.

Other details about the Battle of Kosovo and the history surrounding it are less clear-cut. Sources differ on whether the battle lasted one, two, or three days. Solid scholarship lends weight to the theory that the battle was only one day, but there are no accounts written by eyewitnesses to the events. Konstantin Mihailovic, a janissary a century later and the first writer to name Murad's assassin, claims the battle lasted three days. Given all that is said to have occurred during the battle, I decided to portray it as a two-day event. The physically demanding nature of medieval combat limited how much could realistically take place in a single day, and though much of the lore surrounding the battle is likely based in storytelling rather than in historical fact, that lore has played such an enormous role in historical perceptions of the battle for centuries that I felt it was important to include it.

As mentioned, legends, ballads, and epic poetry surround the Battle of Kosovo. Various accounts, many of them likely to have been created after the battle, during a time of intense rivalry between the various surviving Serb nobles houses, tell stories of Miloš Obilić, Vuk Branković, and the disputes between their wives. Other sources detail Lazar's dream and his choice between a heavenly kingdom or an earthly one. In some tellings of the battle, Miloš is credited with the assassination of Sultan Murad after being slandered before the other Serb nobles. (As an aside, the name of Miloš's horse, Ždralin, also comes from legend.) In other versions of the battle, a group of twelve Serb noblemen set out to seek the sultan. I wanted to include each of these elements in my story, but readers are advised that this novel is historical *fiction*, not historical *fact*. I have tried to be true to what is known about the battle, what is surmised about the battle, and what has become part of the battle's legend. I hope there is a grain of truth in each piece of the Kosovo puzzle that I have included, but much about what really happened simply isn't known with any level of certainty.

Tvrtko and Sigismund, like Lazar and Murad, come from history. As depicted in this novel, Tvrtko was at war with Hungary and seeking to expand into Dalmatia. By most accounts, he did not personally fight at Kosovo but sent a large contingent under his general, Vlatko Vuković. Sigismund of Hungary remained a threat to the Serbs throughout the period of this novel's setting and attacked Lazar's lands after the defeat at Kosovo. As mentioned in the epilogue, Lazar's widow and his teenage heir decided that an agreement with the Ottomans was preferable to an agreement with the Hungarians, even when it meant Lazar's youngest daughter would be married to Sultan Bayezid and both surviving sons would be required to visit Bayezid's court yearly to renew their vassalage. Both Tvrtko and Sigismund have histories that include inheriting power at a young age, then having challengers arise and launch attempts to take the throne. The letter prominently featured in the plot of this book is fictional, but the marriage scheme to cut Sigismund out of his promised inheritance is from history.

Most of the Bulgarian characters who appear on page are fictional: Emanuil Asen, Boyar Kalin, and Ekaterina. The situation in Bulgaria, however, is from history. The Bulgar lands had been divided in two, with a Stratsimir the Tsar of Vidin and a Shishman the Tsar of Târnovo. In addition to internal divisions, they faced threats from Hungary and other neighbors as well as subjugation by the Ottomans. At Kosovo, Bulgarian soldiers fought on both sides of the battle. While the marriage alliance suggested by Emanuil in this book is fictional, it felt very plausible to me, given the situation in Bulgaria and the plethora of similar marriage alliances throughout the Balkans.

I began writing this story in the summer of 2017 while I was waiting for feedback about the novel now titled *Beyond the Crescent Sky.* I had already done extensive research on the time period, and I had already fallen in love with many of the characters, so the first draft flew its way quickly into existence. Then the entire series was put on hold for several years. It's been a dream come true to release it now. Thank you to all the readers who took this journey to medieval Serbia with me.

I also wish to thank my test readers: Mandy Biesinger, Ron Machado, Kathi Oram Peterson, and Bev Walkling. Thank you also goes to the incredible team at Shadow Mountain: Samantha Millburn, Chris Schoebinger, Heidi Gordon, Amy Parker, Callie Hansen, Halle Ballingham, Rachael Ward, Haley Haskins, Bri Cornell, Lehi Quiroz, Tasha Bradford, Troy Butcher, and many others whose talents and hard work have made this book possible.

If you enjoyed this book, I would be very grateful for your review on websites where books are sold or discussed or your recommendation to other readers in person or via social media.

DISCUSSION QUESTIONS

1. Danilo is torn when asked to marry for the good of his people despite loving someone else. If you were given the same choice, what process would you go through to reach your decision? How would you choose to respond?
2. Discuss this quote from Maja: "Life was like a great mosaic and each experience a tessera of glass or marble, limestone or ceramic. Some experiences were vibrant, others pale. Some were luminous, others dull. Some were light, others dark, but they all fit together to form a whole. Each was needful in its own way. Each had greater meaning and beauty only when complete." Do you feel a life needs opposite emotions (good and bad, happy and sad) to be complete?
3. In the story, Danilo quotes Ivan's frequent question, "Is it better to do what is wise or what is right?" As a general rule, do you agree or disagree with Ivan? When it comes to something more specific, such as marriage alliances or battlefield tactics, does your opinion change?
4. Discuss this quote from Maja and compare it to life: "A mosaic is made up of hundreds of shattered pieces of rock and glass. Somehow, it's still beautiful." Think of events in your past that were hard at the time—perhaps experiences that left you feeling broken. Can you look back and see any beauty that resulted from them, either directly or indirectly, or in how those events shaped you as a person?
5. How do Luka's relationships with Maja, Danilo, and Arcadius change throughout the course of the novel? What elements of those relationships remain constant?
6. How did your opinion of Miloš Obilić shift and change over the course of the book? Or did it stay the same throughout? Do you agree or disagree

with the decision he made and the action he took on the second morning of the battle?

7. Did you ever feel any empathy for Iskandar? During which parts of the story? If your feelings changed, why?
8. Maja assists Helena in dealing with a Hungarian spy while Danilo, Ivan, and many others from Sivi Gora are away. How would you have handled the situation with Vadas? Were there alternative responses that Helena could have used that you think would have turned out better?
9. Maja says: "It seems we have to immortalize hardships either in song or in art. Perhaps to remind us that they can be overcome." Are there pieces of art depicting moments of hardship that have touched you? Pieces of music? Novels? Name them and explain why they resonate with you.
10. Did your opinion of Helena change throughout the course of the novel? Did you feel more anger or empathy for her when she confronted Danilo about his arranged marriage? If some members of your book club have also read *Beyond the Crescent Sky*, book two in The Balkan Legends series, did that seem to affect their opinions at all?
11. In the immediate aftermath of the 1389 Battle of Kosovo, most saw the battle as a draw, though some of the earliest Christian references to the event considered it a victory due to the sultan's death. Yet as the Ottoman Empire took over the Balkans, more and more people saw it as a defeat of the Christian forces, and that perception remained strong for centuries. Newer historians tend to conclude that though both sides suffered tremendous losses at Kosovo, the battle was a draw, but the Ottoman forces recovered more quickly. Kosovo, paired with the earlier battle of Maritsa, devastated the Serb warrior class. Those facts affected centuries of history—and still affect the region today. Prior to reading this novel, did you have any knowledge about the Battle of Kosovo or about the centuries-long Ottoman rule in the Balkans? If so, did this story change your perception at all?
12. Are there other characters in The Balkan Legends cast who you would like to see in future books? Who and why?

Enjoy this bonus chapter from the series prequel, which takes place in 1371, eighteen years before the events portrayed in *Against a Crescent Storm*.

AFTER THE CRESCENT STRIKE

THE BALKAN LEGENDS

Chapter One
The Campaign

The Maritsa River Valley, 1371

The river murmured past in the distant darkness, its swollen waters flowing from Christian lands into territories the Turks now claimed. Over the past generation, the Ottoman sultan had expanded his realm at the expense of the Serb, Greek, and Bulgarian inhabitants. Miladin hadn't been there when the great city of Adrianople had fallen to Sultan Murad, but now, several years later, he had followed his kral and his župan on a campaign to take back the city on the crossroads between east and west. Men had battled for Adrianople since Roman times, but for most of the past thousand years, the city had belonged to Christians, and Miladin, like the rest of the army, was eager to make that true once again.

A glance at the stars told him that the second watch of the night—his assignment—neared its end. He expected Bojan to relieve him soon. Rest would be welcome after sentry duty several nights in a row. Beyond that, passage two days ago through the village of his birth had left his emotions raw and made sleep elusive. Seeing the homes and fields again after a ten-year absence, seeing *her* again . . . Maybe tonight his thoughts would calm enough for real rest.

Something snapped in the brush, and Miladin's hand gripped the hilt of the spathion strapped to his side. "Who is it?"

"You're one of Župan Miroslav's men, are you not? With the Rivak garrison?" The voice was unfamiliar, but as the man stepped closer, Miladin recognized the face in the moonlight.

"Yes, lord." Miladin straightened as he spoke. Radomir wasn't a župan, but on this campaign, he led the contingent from Rivak's closest ally.

Radomir motioned toward the camp. "The kral assigned Župan Miroslav a scouting mission. You'll leave before dawn, so my men will take over sentry duty here. The discussions were long, so it's likely no one other than Miroslav and Darras knows, but you had best get some rest."

Miladin needed sleep, but he hesitated. Župan Miroslav wouldn't usually track down sentries himself, especially when planning reconnaissance for the kral, but Miladin would have expected the messenger to be from Rivak. Perhaps with another option available, Župan Miroslav had been practical enough to spare his men an interruption to their sleep. Yet Radomir's status, brother to a župan, made him an unlikely choice for sentry duty.

"You will stand watch, lord?" Miladin asked.

Radomir tsked. "Not for long. My men will relieve me as soon as they put on their armor. They were not planning to stand watch, but all of us serve at the kral's pleasure, even when he changes his mind long after nightfall. You may go."

"Yes, lord." Miladin hid a yawn, barely, and headed toward camp.

One of the other garrison members joined him as a low-burning campfire came into view. "Any wagers on where our scouting assignment will take us?" Grigorii asked.

"We'll probably be asked to find the next campsite. It's hard to hide this many men." The assembled army was enormous. Rivak's contingent camped on the southernmost portion of the sprawling group of Serb warriors. Miladin preferred the edge of the encampment, for the most part, because it wasn't as crowded, but sentry duty night after night took a toll.

Grigorii rubbed his hawkish nose. "If the Turks see us now, we'll still be able to take Adrianople long before the sultan can bring his devils back from Anatolia."

Miladin nodded. That was why they had campaigned this summer—Sultan Murad was elsewhere, trying to expand Ottoman lands in the east. And Kral Vukašin was wise enough to recognize an opportunity to drive out the remaining invaders while they were weak. The timing was perfect, and though they expected the Adrianople garrison to put up a good fight, the call of reconquest promised glory before harvest time.

"Maybe we can take the roundabout way while scouting." Grigorii smirked. "I daresay you wouldn't mind passing through that village again."

"What village?" Miladin scratched at his beard and tried to keep his voice casual.

"The one with the blacksmith who did such a poor job on my destrier's shoes. You could scarcely take your eyes off his daughter, the one with chestnut hair."

In Miladin's mind, he and Magdalena were young again, carefree and laughing, the sunlight turning her hair auburn. "The woman is not his daughter; she is his wife."

Grigorii's mouth pulled in distaste. "He looked a great deal older than her."

"He is, by thirty years." Miladin could hear the resentment in his own voice. After all the years and all the conversations with Rivakgrad's priest, Miladin had thought he'd buried most of his pain. It had all come back, raw and potent, when he saw the village again. "At one time, I thought we might marry, but her father considered a widower with an established trade a more practical choice than a lad of seventeen with nothing more than fallow, overgrown fields for an inheritance. I left the village so I would stop seeing them. Ended up in Rivak."

Grigorii frowned. "The father should have been more patient. The blacksmith's house looked like a pigsty compared to your home in the grad. And our army will soon retake Adrianople. That's no small accomplishment."

Miladin shook his head. "Magdalena's father never cared about anything beyond the village border, unless it was a feast day at my uncle's villa. Anyway, it's too late for that. But it's not too late to stop the Turks."

While the two helped themselves to bowls of stew at one of the campfires, Miladin changed the subject away from Magdalena. He didn't want to feel that pain anymore, didn't want thoughts of what might have been to disturb another night's sleep. "I wonder if Župan Dragomir is sorry to miss the campaign. I heard rumors . . . I'm surprised he sent his brother with his army."

"What rumors?" Grigorii asked as they sat by the fire.

"That Dragomir and Radomir had a falling-out."

Grigorii chewed slowly, thinking. "Dragomir could have put one of his sons in charge if he didn't trust his brother. Whatever it was, they must have reconciled. Not so surprising. The bond between siblings is strong."

Miladin wouldn't know about the bond between siblings. His entire family, save he and his mother, had died of plague before he'd seen his second winter.

Grigorii continued, the firelight revealing softness in his brown eyes. "I argued with my sister often enough growing up, but that doesn't mean I wouldn't sell my soul for her, if needed, though I imagine that will not be necessary." Grigorii glanced at one of the tents. Viktor would be sleeping inside. He and Grigorii's sister planned to marry when the campaign ended and the men returned home. "Anyway, a župan can't very well lead his men to war if he's broken his leg. Did you see the fall?"

Miladin shook his head. He'd been on the hunt with the župans because for the past five years, Miladin's primary role in the garrison had been to act as bodyguard to Župan Miroslav's heir. "I was with Konstantin up ahead of the rest of them. Saw Župan Dragomir after it happened. The man looked gray." Both župan and mount had broken legs in the collision with a panicked packhorse. The župan was expected to recover; one of his men had given the courser a mercy killing.

Grigorii raised an eyebrow. "I heard Konstantin was not happy to be left behind."

Miladin let out a humorless laugh. "No." He'd spent a lot of time with the župan's oldest son, but he'd never before seen Konstantin so disappointed and frustrated. "I think there is little he would not have given if it meant he could come."

"I admire his spirit, but I understand the župan's reasons. Seventeen winters is almost old enough to go into battle . . . almost."

Miladin nodded. As Konstantin had pointed out, plenty of boys younger than him would accompany the army. But they would act as grooms and messengers, cooks and servants, not as men-at-arms. And none of them were expected to inherit a župa one day.

"And after everything else . . ." Grigorii didn't finish his thought. He didn't need to. Unlike the plague that had struck when Miladin was a toddler, the camp fever that had swept through the grad just last year was hard to forget. It had taken Grigorii's wife and both his children, taken the župan's wife and one of his daughters, rendered Konstantin's young brother weak and sickly, and left entire quarters of the grad abandoned. Little wonder that Župan Miroslav was reluctant to risk his older son in battle now.

Grigorii had no one back in Rivak waiting for him other than his sister. Nor did anyone wait for Miladin other than his aging mother and perhaps the lad he'd hired to help her while Miladin was away. But a journey to retake Adrianople offered their people a redemption of sorts. Victory might not remove the sting of loneliness, but maybe it would restore their hope.

Cries and shouts pulled Miladin from his slumber, dragging him from the calm of repose to the stench of smoke and the sounds of panic. A dull headache of exhaustion fogged his mind. Had fire broken out in the camp?

"We're under attack!" The dark of night prevented Miladin from seeing the other men in the tent, but he recognized Viktor's voice.

Someone rushed outside, parting the canvas to reveal raging flames against the black sky. In a moment, dreams of reconquest crumbled into the raw fear of imminent disaster.

Miladin grabbed his spathion and his mail hauberk, but he couldn't delay long enough to put on his armor. He had barely enough light to find his boots and scarcely enough time to pull them over his ankles. If the camp was under attack, they needed to find and defend their župan.

He followed Grigorii from the tent and caught his breath at the sight. The tents of Dragomir's men were all alight, and in the flickering glow of flaming canvas, men with turbaned heads rode past on swift horses, stabbing the Serbs as they emerged from their burning tents.

The thunder of hooves drew Miladin's attention, and he dove away as a Turk with a lance rode directly at him. Miladin rolled past a fiery tent, dodging a second Turk on horseback. He held on to his sword, but his mail had slipped from his grasp. He stayed near the ground, harder to reach, as a dozen horsemen rode past, then stood to confront the Turkish foot soldiers who followed in their wake. He inhaled deeply and took up a defensive stance, preparing for the onslaught.

One Turk swung his curved scimitar at Miladin, who blocked it with his own blade, then shoved the man back and hewed toward him, the swing ending in the man's ribs. As the first man fell, two more came forward. Miladin adjusted his grip on the spathion. He longed for a shield, a helmet—anything to help in a battle against an overwhelming enemy.

He traded blows with both men, slicing into one and ducking away from the other. Sweat trickled along his neck and under his arms. Panicked cries filled the air and smoke choked his throat. Around him, more and more enemy troops swirled through the small numbers of Serb warriors, attacking and overwhelming. Death seemed certain, but Miladin would evade it as long as he could. A strong repulse here, even if it was doomed, could buy more time for the rest of the army.

One of the Turks grinned with pleasure and thrust his blade toward Miladin's neck. Miladin blocked the blow and held the man's blade in a bind for several long moments. His muscles strained as they tried to overpower each other. One of the wounded men rushed back into position for another attack. Miladin twisted away from one opponent, blocked the wounded man's scimitar, kicked with desperation, and swung his blade into the enemy's side. The Turks, both wounded now, pulled back, but more and more converged. He couldn't fight them all.

Three paces away, Viktor fought off a pair of Turks. Miladin ran to him and engaged one of the men. The swordsman's movements were sloppy but powerful. The man was a beast: strong, with little intelligence showing in his eyes. Miladin slew him at the same time Viktor slew the other.

"We should rally to Župan Miroslav," Miladin shouted over the ever-growing sound of battle. That was their duty, and they'd be better able to meet the attack if they stood with other members of the garrison. In ones or twos, they'd quickly be picked off.

Miladin turned to where the župan's tent had been and thought he saw the glint of flame reflecting on Darras's helmet. Darras was the župan's kinsman and most trusted man—he would be next to the župan when disaster threatened.

Viktor nodded, but at least a score of Turks stood between them and their župan.

A tall Ottoman warrior shouted, ran at Miladin, and swung his war hammer at Miladin's head. Miladin ducked, then sliced his sword up under the enemy's shield, piercing skin and bringing the man to his knees. But another enemy was upon Miladin in an instant, this one with a spear that had a longer reach than Miladin's sword. Miladin retreated a pace and twisted away from another man attacking with a javelin. He and Viktor had been split apart, and now each was surrounded.

Viktor cried out, and Miladin turned to see him fall to the ground. The shaft of a javelin stuck from his chest, and an Ottoman horseman rode past in triumph. The man turned his horse toward Miladin and kicked the mount forward. Miladin gasped for air. The fighting had winded him, and the pinch of grief seemed to make a full breath impossible. Regardless, Miladin gripped his spathion in both hands and raised it to meet the scimitar the man had drawn.

The blow, coming from the top of a horse, knocked the blade from Miladin's hand. The foot soldiers immediately closed in. Miladin grabbed the only thing he could reach—an abandoned helmet—and swung it into the nearest man's face. When the man raised his hand in reaction, Miladin stole his spear and used it to skewer one of the other Turks.

Miladin wouldn't survive if he stayed where he was. Too many enemy footmen surrounded him, and the only other Serbs within sight were on the ground, dead or dying.

The horseman turned around for another charge. Miladin pulled the spear free of its recent victim and aimed for the warrior atop the bay warhorse. He hit the man's shoulder, and the rider reeled, barely staying mounted. Miladin grabbed at the horseman's leg, and when the wounded Turk somehow managed to stay in the saddle, Miladin pulled harder, using the enemy as leverage to pull himself up onto the horse behind him. From there, he pummeled his fist into the man's wound. When the enemy jerked in pain, losing his grip, Miladin dumped him from the saddle.

The horse trotted away from the swordsmen and past the burning remnants of a dozen tents, moving the wrong direction. The reins had fallen away, so using pressure from his legs, Miladin slowed the horse in Dragomir's camp and dismounted, grabbing the reins and looking for a spathion, a lance, a shield, anything to help him fight his way back to his župan. The flames surrounding him cast uneven bursts of light and shadow. The fires lit the ground enough for a search, but weapons remained elusive, likely in the tents, and the tents still burned. He turned over five fallen Serbs, all of them merophs called from their fields for the campaign rather than members of a garrison. All had died without retrieving their armor, helmets, or polearms.

An arrow plowed into the ground nearby. Miladin couldn't see who had shot it, but he quickly climbed back on his captured horse. There were other bodies he could search for weapons, but he didn't want to duel with a Turkish archer.

The archer, however, wasn't finished. An arrow plowed into his mount's hindquarter, and when the horse reared up in pain, another arrow pierced the animal's belly. A third arrow cut into the sleeve of Miladin's tunic, slashing into his skin with sharp pain. The horse screamed in panic and fell, bringing Miladin to the ground with a thump that knocked the wind from his chest and left his body bruised. The wounded horse, now riderless, struggled to its feet and fled.

As Miladin fought to fill his lungs, a dozen Turks stepped toward him, coordinating their efforts the way the župans had coordinated their last hunt. Miladin searched the ground for anything he could use as a weapon, but even after turning over two more corpses, the best he could find was a tent stake.

The Turks moved forward, and Miladin ran. He couldn't fight off a dozen men with only a tent stake, couldn't pass through them to rally with his župan, couldn't catch the injured horse that had already disappeared in the darkness. The only thing he could do was flee, and the only open path led toward the Maritsa River.

Each stride brought pain to his battered body, and the slash on his arm burned. The alternative was death, so he kept moving. He could swim, but he'd seen the surging waves of the river, with the currents swollen to a flood. It was doubtful anyone could survive those waters in the daylight. The darkness would make them even more dangerous.

Burning tents made a swath of blazing pillars as far as Miladin could see. Disaster had struck the Serbian army with a sudden, powerful, unstoppable force. So many dead. So many wounded. So many enemies still riding through with deadly speed. More cries met his ears, coming from the water. The calls were desperate, of men struggling for their lives against an unrelenting current. The river's flow and the layout of the camp meant the waters were pulling men from the more central part of the army to the south, past Miladin. This was no raid meant to probe the edges of the Serbian encampment. This was a massive strike reaching toward the heart of the camp, maybe all the way to the kral.

Miladin's strides slowed as the river came closer, but the pursuing enemy gave him no quarter. He could face their javelins and scimitars, or he could take his chances in the flood. He wore no armor, nothing to pull him to the bottom of the stream, so with a prayer on his lips and desperation spurring his feet, he ran into the Maritsa.

ENJOY ALL THE BOOKS IN

THE BALKAN LEGENDS SERIES

Photo by VaLynn Woolley

About the Author

A. L. Sowards is the author of multiple historical fiction novels, with settings spanning the globe from the fourteenth to twentieth centuries. Her stories have been named *Foreword* INDIES finalists, earned an Editor's Choice selection from the Historical Novel Society, and won a Readers' Favorite gold medal along with other awards.

Sowards grew up in Washington State, spent a few decades in Utah, and now resides in Alaska with her husband, three children, and ever-growing library. She enjoys hiking and swimming, usually manages to keep up with the laundry, and loves it when someone else cooks dinner.

Sowards enjoys connecting with readers and can be found online at ALSowards.com or on Facebook, Goodreads, and Instagram. Readers can sign up for her newsletter at ALSowards.com/newsletter to receive author updates and a free electronic copy of The Balkan Legends prequel novella.

Against a Crescent Storm is also available in audio and ebook.